DEAD DOLLS DON'T TALK

They didn't have a body, but all the evidence proves to the jury that Harry L. Cotton murdered Bonnie Deering on her husband's yacht. Doc Hart is so sure, he even persuades the one holdout on the jury to change her vote. After the trial is over, Hart picks up a young lady outside the courthouse and allows himself to be seduced by her, only to find himself in bed with Cotton's wife. That's when he realizes a mistake has been made. Because though Peggy Cotton has no intention of helping her cheating husband escape the death penalty, she has seen Bonnie alive and well. Hart leaves the room but when he returns he finds Peggy murdered. That's when Hart learns just what it feels like to be an innocent man accused of a crime he didn't commit—with almost no time at all to find the living Bonnie to prove otherwise!

HUNT THE KILLER

Framed by someone named *Senor Peso*, Charlie White has been sitting in Raiford Prison for the past four years, waiting to see who would be there for him when he got out—his faithful wife Beth, or his Cuban mistress Zo. If Beth is there, he promises himself to go straight. If Zo, well, he'd deal with that when it happened. And, of course, it is Zo who shows up, with a fast car, a bottle of rum and a rented cabin. Later that evening, he finds the letter from Beth, asking him to come to her. But before he can leave, someone crashes their little love nest, smashing him over the head—and shooting Zo! Before Charlie can get used to freedom, he is on the lam, framed for the murder of Zo, with no where else to go but back to the arms of Beth. But who would want to kill Zo? And where— and who—is *Senor Peso?*

TOO HOT TO HOLD

If only Lew Dix hadn't picked Linda Lou to carry the payoff money, none of this would be happening and the cab driver would still be alive. It starts when Linda Lou takes the plane from Chicago to New York as planned. It's raining when she gets there and she's already plenty nervous with this pretty package in her hands. She manages to get a taxi but she stuffs the package between the seat cushions just to be extra careful. How is she to know that the big man who opens the cab door with his hand in his pocket isn't carrying a gun, ready to blast her and grab the money? But all Jim Brady wants is a cab. When he opens the door, Linda bolts, leaving the package behind—and setting off a series of events that begins with murder and ends with worse.

DAY KEENE BIBLIOGRAPHY

This is Murder, Mr. Herbert and Other Stories (1948)
Framed in Guilt [aka Evidence Most Blind] (1949)
Farewell to Passion [aka The Passion Murders] (1951)
Love Me—and Die [as by Keene, collaboration with Gil Brewer] (1951)
My Flesh is Sweet (1951)
To Kiss, or Kill (1951)
About Doctor Ferrel (1952)
Home is the Sailor (1952)
Hunt the Killer (1952)
If the Coffin Fits (1952)
Naked Fury (1952)
Wake Up to Murder (1952)
Mrs. Homicide (1953)
Strange Witness (1953)
The Big Kiss-Off (1954)
Death House Doll (1954)
His Father's Wife (1954)
Homicidal Lady (1954)
Joy House (1954)
Notorious (1954)
Sleep With the Devil [aka Sin With the Devil] (1954)
There Was a Crooked Man (1954; revised 1963)
The Dangling Carrot (1955)
Who Has Wilma Lathrop? (1955)
Bring Him Back Dead (1956; revised 1963)
Flight by Night (1956)
Murder on the Side (1956)
Passage to Samoa (1958)
Dead Dolls Don't Talk (1959)
Dead in Bed (1959)*

Moran's Woman (1959)
So Dead My Lovely (1959)
Take a Step to Murder (1959)
Too Black for Heaven (1959)
Too Hot to Hold (1959)
The Brimstone Bed (1960)
Chautauqua [with Dwight Vincent] (1960)
Miami 59 (1960)
Payola (1960)*
World Without Women [with Leonard Pruyn] (1960)
Seed of Doubt (1961)
Bye, Bye Bunting (1963)
L.A. 46 [aka City of Angels] (1964)
Carnival of Death (1965)
Chicago 11 (1966)
Acapulco G.P.O. (1967)
Guns Along the Brazos (1967)
Live Again, Love Again (1970)
*Johnny Aloha series

As Lewis Dixon
Wild Girl [reprinted 1969 as by Keene] (1952)

As William Richards
Dead Man's Tide [reprinted 1958 as It's a Sin to Kill as by Keene] (1953)

As Daniel White
Southern Daughter [reprinted 1967 as by Keene] (1954)

DEAD DOLLS DON'T TALK

. . . .

HUNT THE KILLER

. . . .

TOO HOT TO HOLD

BY DAY KEENE

Introduction by David Laurence Wilson

STARK HOUSE

Stark House Press • Eureka California

DEAD DOLLS DON'T TALK / HUNT THE KILLER/ TOO HOT
TO HOLD

Published by Stark House Press
1315 H Street
Eureka, CA 95501
griffinskye3@sbcglobal.net
www.starkhousepress.com

ISBN: 1-933586-33-8
ISBN-13: 978-1-933586-33-5

Cover design and layout by Mark Shepard, www.shepgraphics.com
Proofreading by Rick Ollerman

PUBLISHER'S NOTE

First Stark House Press Edition: August 2011

Day Keene: The Pro's Pro

by David Laurence Wilson

Day Keene was one of the big three, The Triumvirate. In the nineteen fifties, along the Florida Gulf Coast, it was Keene, Harry Whittington, and Gil Brewer who formed the Great Trio of postwar American crime fiction.

In another line of work, if they had all played guitars, they could have been Eric Clapton, Jeff Beck and Jimmy Page. If they were private eye writers they could have been Hammett, Chandler and Ross MacDonald.

Honest readers could disagree as to which of the three was the most proficient and entertaining. All of them were engaging storytellers with their own quirks, settings and subjects.

Unlike those other combos, Keene, Whittington and Brewer were all in the same place—St. Petersburg, Florida—at the same time—the nineteen fifties—and the three of them were friends, socially and professionally. They had parties and attended book signings together. They gave one another gifts. They were the kinds of friends who might show up unannounced; a little bit of a nuisance, perhaps, if they pulled you away from your own writing, but friends.

They were almost a conspiracy. They wrote about sex and crime, corruption and violence. It was a high level of problem solving including the greatest problem of all: how to stay alive. Sometimes their books were awkward or unattractive but they all kept going, one plot after another, millions of words. Three big producers with over 300 novels between them, nearly all of them paperback originals.

Not one of them had a Holmes or a Poirot in their closets. They wrote the crime novel *their* way.

Between them, they wrote 39 titles for Fawcett's respected, well-paying Gold Medal line of paperbacks, almost an American equivalent of the French Serie Noire series published by Gallimard. That meant they wrote around 270 novels for nearly every other publisher in North America. They were riding on an ocean of plots and hard-boiled attitude. They hit all the markets.

Whittington acknowledged Keene when he spoke before a Florida writer's group: "Day Keene said it best: You could sell those editors easily. All you had to do was hack off a foot of your intestines, stuff it, bleeding and still quivering, into a manila envelope—with return postage of course—and the editors would unfailingly buy."

The trio was a mismatched set. They proved that you don't have to be saints or philosophers to take up the craft of writing. They became paperback writers, perhaps, because there was no other place they fit. Two of them were alcoholics.

Keene looked like an actor, almost courtly, with a mustache and bow tie and he'd smell of cigarettes and sometimes his eyes were red, from the drinking. He fashioned himself as a performer. Sometimes it seemed like he was taking on the role of a writer, as if he'd declared himself to be a writer and he simply had the will to do it.

Brewer looked like a beatnik. He painted—he'd done an oil of Lady Godiva for his stepson—and he went drinking with Jack Kerouac, listened to jazz and owned his own theremin.

Harry had been a letter carrier and liked to listen to musicals while he worked, and he was almost always working. Harry was friendly but he was also preoccupied, like he wanted to get back to his typewriter, like part of him had been left behind on the page. He'd give you the shirt off his back if he could just get back to typing.

"Write until you are ready to collapse," Whittington advised. "Then write some more."

They were all percussionists on the typewriter.

Whittington had not written for posterity but in the eighties it was posterity—and a consistent volume of effort that rescued him. Harry had dropped out of the business but was back to writing for Fawcett when Black Lizard began reprinting his crime novels. After years of financial struggle, between retirement benefits and writing "Ashley Carter" historical romances, Harry was making the best money of his life.

Brewer's career faded away as his drinking and his attempts to get back into shape consumed his attention. He was doing odd jobs—writing movie tie-ins and erotica, a nonconformist who was still hoping to publish his greatest books, to push the boundaries of the printed page. He died in 1983 at the age of sixty, twenty years before a new generation discovered his work.

Keene was the oldest and most successful among them. He had published his first stories nearly twenty years before the younger men, who were actually closer to the age of his son, the writer Al James. He had lived or travelled all over North America and had already been an actor and a successful writer of radio dramas. Over the long run, Keene, the mentor, sustained his writing career more successfully than Whittington or Brewer.

Keene was skilled in settings, with a familiarity of locales. He was as convincing as a man giving directions on the corner of Sex and Jeopardy. It was almost like listening to your neighbor. He'd give you a high-speed chase right up to the threshold of your own front door.

Today a seedy patina of age hangs over Keene's novels and short stories. They are like yellowed, curled up postcards or prints in a dusty window, evocative of the photos of Walker Evans or Robert Frank, fading characters from another time and ethos.

His women could be mercenary and unfaithful, altogether deserving of the difficulties they've earned, but by today's standards, the violence against them in Keene's novels can become oppressive. Many of them are quaintly attired employees in the sex industry of fifty or sixty years ago.

In a recent review of Keene's *Take a Step to Murder* (1959), the contemporary mystery writer Bill Crider tiptoed around some of the details of Keene's plotting: "It's not a good plan," Crider wrote, "...in fact the sexual nature of it is likely to be highly distasteful to modern readers." In his novels Keene is often to be found on the far side of political correctness. It isn't what you'd call sexism, exactly... it's more like a completely different view of the world.

Keene could write a bad book but he couldn't write an inept book. He was more controlled and also more manipulative than either Whittington or Brewer. He was a master of pace and misdirection.

He would play with the timeframe of his stories, breaking the fourth wall with a prescient aside to readers, a "had I but known," or a warning to watch the next bit of action particularly closely.

Keene wrote fast and he pushed his readers to read quickly, to move on to the next thrill. Don't look too closely. Guilt—in all its lovely forms—could be better savored later.

He was a whiz at logistics. Keene assembled details like the precision of a spider web. Sometimes he'd label his chapters by location and time of day, like the directions in a screenplay. He could maintain a crisp, coherent narrative despite all kinds of jumps from character to character, from place to place. He offered plausibility, even in his most garish stories.

Like the artist Stuart Davis or writer John Dos Passos, Keene used elements of the life around him: headlines, signs and notes. He pasted them into his stories like a scrapbook.

He was a transitional writer, a bridge between the careful, optimistic constructions of a Judson Philips or Erle Stanley Gardner and the troubled, brooding, sometimes undisciplined narratives of Whittington, Brewer, Jim Thompson, David Goodis or Charles Williams. Keene was a plotter. He didn't share the first person intensity, the Freudian stream of consciousness and fury of his successors. Keene's scenes were staged instead of screamed. Noir Lite. Passions subdued. It was a kind of discipline that demanded realism instead of nightmares.

Describing Keene as a transitional writer gives him license to have tried different approaches in his fiction. It also gave him a wider spread of hits and misses. Keene was more of a pro and more of a hack, more of a commercial writer than his fellows, and he proved it by writing successfully in many forms. If he had a disappointment it was that he never had a bestseller. Keene was the first, a success and an example for the younger writers, sometimes a counselor and raconteur.

You'd get the impression that Keene gave good value for money. He met his deadlines and pulled in readers but he was not going to bleed all over his manuscripts, not going to live or die at the whim of an editor. He took a more practical view of his craft. As a pulp writer he'd made a good living. Writing was entertainment. Show business. He wouldn't have called it an art.

□ □ □

Keene was born in 1904 in Chicago. He wrote plays, radio shows, short stories, novels and screenplays. He died in Los Angeles in 1969 from lung cancer.

After the posthumous publication of *Live Again, Love Again,* in 1970, Keene's reputation went into eclipse. He became a forgotten man, his legacy waiting nearly forty years for a reappraisal.

Whittington's and Brewer's correspondence and journals are preserved at the American Heritage Center at the University of Wyoming campus. Keene has no archive. When Keene died, in 1969, there were no curators for his legacy.

Nobody, it seems, had thought to interview Day Keene, a fellow who wrote for the entertainment of his readers. It was like there was a plan to erase his presence. After his death in 1969 his widow threw out his letters, scripts and copies of manuscripts. Even then it was a small fortune discarded. A former agent first thought of publishing a collection of letters before he threw out "pounds" of correspondence with Day Keene.

After the death of Keene's son, his daughter-in-law cleared out a barn filled with letters and manuscripts. It would be nice to have a little weight, a few ounces, a few boxes, of those pages. A California bookseller wound up with a box of Keene's carbons but there was no way to trace the source of this stash. The manuscripts had all been sold and published and there was little but the smudges to distinguish them from Keene's printed stories. It was a dead end. There just wasn't much out there.

In the second edition of *Twentieth Century Crime and Mystery Writers*

(St. Martin's, 1985), Keene has one of its shortest biographical sketches in the encyclopedia: "American. Married. Wrote radio soap operas in 1930s and 1940s. Lived in Chicago, Florida, and California. Died c. 1969." The entry didn't have the birth and death dates for one of the century's most popular writers, a gentleman who was not even included in the encyclopedia's first edition.

If Keene was gone from the newsstands, from contemporary words, it was impossible for collectors of paperbacks and pulps to avoid him. There was a lot of Keene in the used book stores.

Today, more than forty years after his death, Keene's reputation is on the rise. Both Stark House and Hard Case Crime have produced reprints of some of Keene's best novels. Though he only wrote two stories for *Black Mask*, "Sauce for the Gander" (May 1943) was among the stories featured in *The Black Lizard Big Book of Black Mask Stories* (2010). As this Stark House volume goes to press a publisher is trying to reprint the bulk of Keene's pulp stories. Still, Keene's life remains a cipher. At this distance his life and career have become both legendary and generic, and not in a bad way. To be generic is not shameful, after all, when one is among those who have created a genre.

Day Keene wrote 51 novels, two linear feet of pulp, a monument in ink. That's 8,390 pages and I read them all, back to back, a tough odyssey and near-overdose, the cruelest thing a reader can do to any author. Do you think they ran together, *Joy House* and *Carnival of Death*, *Take a Step to Murder*, *Homicidal Lady*, *Mrs. Homicide*, *So Dead My Lovely*, *Murder on the Side* and *Death House Doll*? Well, they did.

□ □ □

There is no record of Keene's early years. He was not given to autobiographical writing and his family history is meager. His father is said to have been a paving contractor.

In fact, there was no "Day Keene," not until the Chicago writer was in his later thirties. He was born Gunard Hjertstedt, son of a Swedish father and Irish mother, Catherine Daisy Keeney. Hjertstedt left school early, at the age of seventeen, to become a Shakespearian actor. His early career as a performer has been variously described as repertory theater, vaudeville and Chautauqua. His son, Albert James Hjertstedt, was born in Chicago on February 28, 1924. According to the younger Hjertstedt, his father met and wed his mother while they were performing on the Chautauqua circuit.

These are the years that were effectively scrubbed from our understanding of Hjertstedt. There are traces of these years in the novel *Chautauqua*, written in collaboration with Dwight Babcock. This was one of Hjertstedt/Keene's finest efforts, his longest and most expansive novel and a good payoff, too, since it was filmed as the Elvis Presley vehicle, THE TROUBLE WITH GIRLS.

Hjertstedt was running his own troupe when it failed at the end of the 'twenties. At that point the legend is that Hjertstedt flipped a coin to decide whether to pursue a career in writing or acting. Writing won, so Hjertstedt stayed in New York while his former collaborator and roommate, Melvyn Douglas, began a successful career in motion pictures.

Hjerstedt's first writing took the form of plays, like the three act drama Sardonic Gods, finished in 1929. He also sold his first short story to *Detective Fiction Weekly*. References credit him with five stories for the magazine: "Pure and Simple" (October 31, 1931), "I Hadda Hunch" (November 21, 1931), "Excuse My Crust" (December 5, 1931), "Mr. Beaver, D.W." (January 30, 1932) and "Murder Mountain" (April 16, 1932). He also sold one story to the pulp *West*.

The December issue of *Detective Fiction Weekly* also featured a letter from Hjertstedt, explaining how a real life holdup was the springboard for his third story, "Pardon My Crust":

"Dear Editor:

"Here's a story with a story.

"To be brief, the last check which you so kindly initialed – or rather the cash value thereof – is at this moment reposing in the pockets of several gentry of the underworld.

"I cashed it rather late of an afternoon, and then I spent the evening with a friend uptown. I started homeward at about one in the morning. Started is correct, for I did not reach it until quite some hours, and happenings, later.

"It has always been my practice, when in New York, to live in the Greenwich Village section. For some twelve years, off and on, I have prowled its confines from dusk to dawn, absolutely unmolested. It being a habit of mine to walk at night, perhaps it is not exaggeration for me to say I know most of its windings and character better by lamplight than sunlight.... Emerging owl-like at one or two in the morning, I have strolled my way through most of the sections of the world noted for their viciousness and depravity, in search of both air and material.... Those murderously, or thievishly inclined have either passed me by as poor pickings or have looked upon me with commiseration as 'just one of those writers' and have forborne to exercise their proclivities. Not so upon the occasion of which I write.

"Now I have often written 'the moonlight glinted on the steel barrel of an automatic,' but this was my first dubious opportunity to witness it at first hand. Needless to say I complied with their request. The writer who first wrote 'the muzzle of the gun at his head looked as big as a tunnel,' was modest in his description. He should have said, 'as big as the doors of the Graf Zeppelin's hangar.'"

Then Hjertstedt went ahead and wrote a story about a crime fiction writer who gets knocked out and robbed: "Barefooted, and dust smeared, he looked like anything but the well paid writer of detective tales his name on a half dozen magazine covers purported him to be." Not lacking in confidence, Hjertstedt's character was both debonaire and vengeful.

Soon he returned to Chicago, where he would begin writing radio serials. The now divorced writer moved in with his mother. The key to riches was not in refinement but volume, so he wrote for "Little Orphan Annie," "Stella Dallas," "Just Plain Bill," "Jack Armstrong," "Betty and Bob," "Behind the Camera Lines," "First Nighter" and "Backstage Wife."

□ □ □

It's easy to see how the name Day Keene could be derived from Hjertsted's mother's name, Catherine Daisy Keeney. The evolution of this riddle-man, from Hjertstedt to Day Keene may have been a little more complicated than it appears, however.

During this nineteen forties Keene became one of the handful of pulp writers who was prolific and successful enough to live well. Usually his stories were featured on the covers. As late as 1949 Popular Publications had three Keene stories scheduled for the September issue of their *New Detective* pulp. The featured story, "Three Graves Have I" was published with the Keene name. "Who Dies Last?" was assigned the name "John Corbett", a second pseudonym that Hjertstedt had been using since 1942.

John Corbett is just an asterisk of a name but it gives Keene at least another fifteen stories to his credit. Corbett wrote for *Detective Tales, New Detective* and *Dime Detective*. He used colloquial speech and dialect that could be distracting, just like Keene. Corbett wrote no series characters, never appeared on a table of contents that didn't also feature Keene and unlike Keene, he only wrote for Popular Publications.

For the third story in *New Detective* Keene suggested the name "Donald King." "The Kid I Killed Last Night" became the only credit ever recorded for this Mr. King. To backtrack, however, Hjertstedt had picked up one lonely credit in 1935, when his story, "The Case of the Bearded Bride," appeared in *Clues Detective Stories* magazine. It is unlikely that this was an old story, waiting three years for publication. The market was too hungry for that. According to Scott Meredith, who had agented for Keene, at the height of the demand for fiction Popular Publications purchased 4,000 stories in a single year.

It appeared Hjertstedt was once again writing for the pulps, perhaps signaling an interruption in his work for the Chicago radio shows. But just the one story? Unlikely. There was the chance that Hjertstedt had written more but only the "Bearded Bride" found favor with an editor. It was even more likely that somewhere along the way an editor, perhaps the editor at Spicy Publications, suggested to Hjertstedt that he use another name for his stories. A name that couldn't be pronounced didn't make for good cover material.

He may have come up with "Don King," a short, hard and regal, American-sounding name. If this were true we could add seven more stories from 1935 and 1936 to Hjertstedt's total. These stories offered the titillating titles "Guts and the Girl," "Hell Hole of Horror," "Murder in Boots," "Speed Demon," "The Devil Takes His Dead" and "White Meat." "Million Dollar Dame" was the featured story in the April 1935 issue of *Spicy Detective*. All of these stories were flanked by *Spicy*'s star performer, the hypochondriac, tongue-in-cheek writer Robert Leslie Bellem.

These pulps went as far under the table as a pulp could go without disappearing completely. Usually they featured racy illustrations and the casual fondling of barely clothed women during tales of intrigue and adventure. One of these implausible stories, "Hell Hole of Horror," begins with a circus romance gone bad, and Hjertstedt/Keene often used a circus or carnival setting. It wouldn't have taken him long to write these stories, along with "The Bearded Bride" for *Clues*, maybe just a week or two. They certainly read a lot more like Day Keene than Bellem.

But why "Don King"? Unless he became a fight promoter, this Don King has never been heard from since. "Don King" sounded a lot like "Day Keene" but this explanation, like the connection between Donald King in 1949 and this "Don King," only sounds reasonable in reverse. Was there a context for "Don King"? That we don't know.

This is a case of extrapolation of real life through fiction. Otherwise, with Day Keene, we are going to be limited to the bios of dust jackets. Though there is nothing in the "Don King" stories to rule them out, to suggest that these were not written by Hjertstedt, a cautious man would want one more clue, a repetition of plot, a name or some kind of anagram in the story. Maybe, somewhere, that kind of clue is out there. If there is it didn't show up by our deadline.

After this presumed respite, Hjertstedt created a new radio serial for Proctor and Gamble, *Kitty Keene, Incorporated*, which ran daily for three and a half years, 1937-1941, measured out in eleven minute dramatic sequences. Kitty is a former Follies dancer, "a beautiful woman of the world" who owns and operates her own private detective agency. Much of the drama is of the domestic variety, as Kitty's husband, daughter and son-in-law take on major roles and Kitty becomes a grandmother. Only four of those broadcasts exist today.

Maybe it's simple enough to consider that this was a process without pattern, and these were simply the last steps before Hjertstedt became the celebrated fiction writer, Day Keene. Day Keene ... The name alone was one of Hjertstedt's best fictions. Whatever the circumstances, Day Keene was a name that would sell.

□ □ □

Hjertstedt first visited Florida for six months in 1938, with his second wife, Irene, while he continued to commute to Chicago for his work on the radio serials. During the next two years the Hjertstedts lived in Mexico, they purchased a home in Los Angeles and lived in Oregon. In 1940 the couple returned to the Gulf Coast and adopted a Chow dog. By 1940 Hjertstedt was signing his checks "Day Keene." He had legally changed his name.

At the age of 37, Keene said he was settled for good. He wrote a column for the St. Petersburg Times: "As I sit... overlooking the placid blue waters of an arm of Boca Ciega bay in which a stately white heron stalks a dinner, his for the taking, the thought crosses my mind, 'Where have I been all these years?'"

With his wife Irene, Keene set up a fiction factory. Keene, a four-fingered typist, chain-smoked as he wrote while Irene typed the finished copy. Sometimes they would argue about the stories. It seemed to be a method that worked.

At his best, Keene was a fine gentleman, but between his drinking and the hand held hearing aid Irene used to compensate for hearing loss, they appeared an odd, eccentric couple. They were also quite formal. Not everyone was comfortable in their company.

For the next six years Keene would average more than twenty short stories and novelette sales a year, most of them to Popular Publications. In ten years Keene published over 200 short stories. Every other week his name was featured on a magazine cover.

One of the first of them was "Murder Is My Sponsor", a crime story about a radio writer in in *Detective Tales* (April, 1942). It offers a few reasons why Hjertstedt might have left the radio shows: "He had sold Flannigan... the idea of a radio serial for the soap chip trade built around a woman of the world—a woman detective of experience and a burning desire to help young girls of no experience, a woman crusading against the one hundred and one snares and pitfalls into which O'Hara, himself, as a reporter had seen young girls fall. The show's Crossley rating and the fan letters during the first three years had proven that there was a need for such a show. Then the Client, the Agency, and the Networks stepped in. Dope was a naughty word. You mustn't use it on the air. Sex, unless it was swaddled in the maudlin meanderings of a half-baked Mother Someone, was taboo. Vice simply didn't exist. You mustn't step on these toes. You mustn't step on those."

Later, using the pseudonym Daniel White for the novel *Southern Daughter* (1954), Keene returned to a Chicago radio show setting. His character sighs:

"I'm beginning to think I'm just oe of the almost boys, a good reliable hack who can take an unbelieveably bad script and a mediocre cast and sell a fantastic amount of whatever the sponsor who hires me is hawking."

"That's why you drink so much?"

"I imagine it is."

Even without an obvious track record, Keene was getting good press. The *St. Petersburg Times* of May 4, 1941, announced: "When not engaged in planting palm trees around his attractive Don CeSar home, author Day Keene contributes literary copy to hair-raising detective and crime periodicals. Three sold in one week recently were 'The Lady From Hellas,' 'Yankee Doodle Dandy,' and 'Pay Off or Die.' They'll be published soon...."

Keene could write the breezy, wise guy stuff, stories where the patter is just as important as the plot and some of the lines are good enough for greeting cards.

From "The Murder Frame," Thrilling Detective, 1941:

"I couldn't afford to take chances. For all I knew she might be a she wolf in lamb's panties."

"Just how will you have your killer, miss? Broiled plain or smothered with mushrooms."

"She opened her purse and laid a flat sheaf of bills on the table, all of them fifties... I looked at the picture of Grant. I hadn't seen old Ulysses' beard in a long time. I found myself liking the dame."

Keene could also do weird, as he proved in "If The Coffin Fits," from *Dime Mystery Magazine*, March 1945: "The day, for October, had been warm. Shortly after sundown a cold wind crossed the border, sweeping south. Now sighing mournfully through the pines, now battering at the bare branches of the trees in the Hudson River Valley, it reached New York on the stroke of midnight.

"Slate-eyed, his face a dead-white, the corpse-like man clinging to the stone wall of the building just below Phil Morton's Times Square penthouse laboratory was one of the first to feel the wind's fury. Twenty-eight floors above the street, intent on murder, the man clung with desperate toes and fingers to the indentations in the stone as the wind attempted to pluck him from the building and hurl him into space."

At least five of Keene's shorter works would later be reworked as novels. The first person Hollywood story "Mary the Sixth for Murder!," in *Detective Tales* (May 1948) became *Love Me and Die (1951)*, expanded to novel length with Gil Brewer's assistance. "Blonde Trouble in Nightmare City" (*Detective Tales*, August, 1948) became *If the Coffin Fits* (1952). "They Call It Murder, Honey Chile," (*Detective Tales*, February 1950), became the novel *Notorious* (1954).

Keene's first book length publication, *This is Murder, Mr. Herbert and Other Stories* (Avon, 1948) was a collection of four pulp reprints including "With Blood in His Eye" (*Detective Tales*, November, 1945), which became *Mrs. Homicide* (1953) and "If a Body Meet a Body" (*Detective Tales*, June 1946), rewritten as *Home is the Sailor* (1952).

Two of Keene's pulp characters, Tom Doyle, the Chicago Private Eye, and Herman Stone, sometimes known as "Herman the Great," would reappear in book length fiction. Others, like Matt Mercer, the one-armed detective, "Silent Smith," casino-owner and "Dean of Broadway" and "Doc Egg," a pharmacist and former prizefighter, were retired with Keene's last pulp sales.

□ □ □

One of Keene's favorite activities was fishing. It made sense that rivers, oceans and seas were frequent settings in his novels. In *Home is the Sailor* Keene's hero is Swede Larson, a sailor with money saved and a dream of settling on land. *Passage to Samoa* (1958) is an outright nautical adventure.

Sailors and fishermen were among Keene's favorite characters. Whittington, Brewer and Talmage Powell, Keene's closest writer-friend, all joined him on his fishing trips. Sixty years ago, if the wrong boat had gone down it might have forever changed popular American fiction.

□ □ □

I got to know Albert James Hjertstedt a little bit, in 1985, when one late night, 3 a.m., he put a letter for someone else in an envelope with my address. Al was proud of his father though there was acute discomfort in their relationship. Like his father, Al had changed his name and written his own novels as "Al James." *Blind Lust*, *Potent Stuff*, *Weak and Wicked* and *Sex Bomb* were four of the eight novels James published in 1961. In his later years he left fiction for technical writing.

He wrote me: "My Dad always said that you made new friends by going to strange bars and sending letters to the wrong addresses. So be it! I'm glad we met this way."

James had settled in Franklin, North Carolina, where he echoed his father: "Somehow we wandered from the big cities up to these backwaters of civilization. This is truly God's country. From my porch I look out into the Smokeys all day. I suppose it's escapism. But I did my fifteen years in Los Angeles and loved every damned minute of it. That was then and this is now...

"I got into the trade by the back door. Dad's agent had a secretary who was moonlighting by selling short stuff, mostly pseudo-trues to *Battle Cry, Male,* and the like. She needed copy and asked Dad to do some. He didn't have time and handed me the letter and said: 'Put up or shut up.' I did, I sold my second story and haven't worked for another man in thirty years.

"Dad was a writer's writer. He helped a lot of young writers get started... Never was a man more generous of his time. All of us miss him but what better success can a man have than that. In truth that is Dad's 'best seller.'"

□ □ □

For fifty years Talmage Powell exchanged weekly letters with writer and musician Charles Boeckman of Corpus Christi, author of 1953's little-known classic *Honky Tonk Girl* for Falcon Books. Many of these letters related to Powell's friend Keene. Powell had taken Boeckman to two meetings of the local writer's group in a glassed-in den at Keene's home in Passe-a-Grille, a "Florida room."

Two weeks later Boeckman returned home to Texas and wrote "Ybor City" for *Manhunt* magazine. Keene wrote to Boeckman: "You lousy Texan. You come to Florida, drink our beer, spend time in our home, then steal a setting from under our noses and write a damn good story."

Powell's letters told of Keene's alcoholic pranks, routines that became both funnier and more extravagant in the retelling. Here's a few of them, relayed by Boeckman: "Day was a binge drinker. On one of his binges he woke up in a hotel with no idea of where he was or how he got there. He had spent all his money. He called the desk and asked that a typewriter be sent to his room. He dashed off a story and airmailed it to his agent. He had such a big name that anything he wrote quickly sold. His agent airmailed him a check so he could bail himself out of the hotel." (Readers of Stark House's first collection of Keene novels, with *My Flesh is Sweet* (1951) may recall this same story dressed in fiction.)

"Irene was determined to put a lid on Day's drinking. He made an arrangement with his liquor store to deliver a bottle of his favorite brand early in the morning. While everyone was still in bed the liquor store would bury the bottle in one of his flower beds. Later, Irene told Talmage that she was so proud of Day because he was spending more time in their flower beds."

"Powell often wrote about going fishing with Day. One time they were headed home after a fishing trip. On their way home Day pulled the boat into a small coastal town and went ashore to check his mail box. He told Talmage that he kept a mail box in the town and had instructed his agent to send any checks of less than $400 to that address. He said that was his drinking money and he didn't want his wife to find out about it. Sometime later Irene bragged to Talmage that Day never wrote anything that paid less than $400."

There were also sadder moments in this regimen.

In his 1985 letter Al James confided: "The flip side of the glamour and the character he made of himself was the drinking. This was a bad scene. The whole family spent a lot of years worrying about him when he didn't show on time."

Harry Whittington recalled Keene passing out into a plate of lasagna.

Keene's agent, Don MacCampbell, called him "a wonderful human being." In his own memoir, *Don't Step On It—It May Be a Writer*, MacCampbell wrote: "Day was a rough and lovable Swedish-American who could down more liquor than any two men I have ever known."

He introduced Keene to Jacques David, a French veteran of both the first and second world wars who had translated many of Keene's novels for the Serie Noire books. Over dinner Keene drank rum until his voice became an "undecipherable mumble."

The Frenchman told MacCampbell: "Alcohol is the scourge of writers and this includes your writer Day Keene."

That was the legend of Day Keene. Somebody else can do the job of psychoanalyzing him.

There was the great, reckless writing from the first page of *Joy House*: "I sat a moment, wracked with nausea, not yet sober, no longer drunk. I was, I decided, in a skid row mission. The small chapel smelled of unwashed male bodies, cheap whiskey and dreams that had been dead so long they had turned rancid.

"I sat with my face in my hands, trying not to think, trying not to hear the glory shouter on the platform beating the drum. I looked at him through my fingers. He was a pot-bellied little man with silver watch chain across his pot and the wet eyes of a pregnant goldfish.

"'Death, my friends, is an illusion.'"

And on the other side, a notice from the police blotter of the St. Petersburg Times:

"Driver Bound Over To Traffic Court: On December 27, 1941, Day Keene of Pass-a-Grille, after pleading nolo contendre before Magistrate

Joe E. Carpenter yesterday, was bound over to County Court under $25 bond charged with driving while under the influence of liquor. Keene was arrested on Welch causeway by the state highway patrol."

In the end, Keene didn't leave us any life lessons or advice, he only left us his prose.

□ □ □

In the nineteen fifties the new form of mass entertainment was the paperback original. As good as the magazines had been, the paperbacks were a step up. They were better paying, there was more freedom and the top writers could still sell almost everything they wrote.

After one hardback from Morrow, *Framed in Guilt* (1949), Keene would write 47 paperback novels, including digests with the pseudonyms Lewis Dixon, William Richards, and Daniel White.

Three of Keene's most moody novels were published by Lion Books: *My Flesh is Sweet*, *Joy House* (1954) and *Sleep with the Devil* (1954). The original title of *Joy House* was *House of Evil*, one of those curious choices of title that does it's best to throw away whatever benefit it might have from suspense. (*So the house is evil? Who would have guessed?*) Luckily, *Joy Street* (1951), by Cuthbert Clifton, had been a hit for Lion so Keene's manuscript became *Joy House*, one of the best reads in the noir genre. If Keene has a masterpiece, this is it.

His later novels included *World Without Women* (1960), one of the strangest novels in the Gold Medal line, a mixture of crime, science fiction and brutal sex that reads like Ed Wood but was written by Keene and a younger conspirator, Leonard Pruyn.

The paperback boom had nearly exhausted itself by 1960 and the industry was being crowded by television. Keene returned to hardbacks and began writing what he hoped would be mainstream novels slanted towards a female audience. Others were for a casual reader who didn't necessarily want to read Day Keene but had a hankering to read something about Acapulco, Miami, or a story about artificial insemination. Keene wrote two of the latter.

In *Seed of Doubt* (1961), published by Simon and Schuster, Keene created one of the most self-empowered women characters in pulp.

Anyone who enjoys Keene should try his later, non-category fiction. Here his endings are not so neat, leaving the reader wishing he could spend another scene or two with these characters, just like the stars of a radio serial.

□ □ □

Keene had to try for the money in the motion picture business. He moved to California and the valley side of Hollywood, a brisk walk from the Revue Studio, where Talmage Powell was working on Alfred Hitchcock's television show. Often Powell met with the Keenes for dinner.

Keene had moderate success in selling his stories for film. Keene's first sale was in 1951, when a story was purchased for "Studio One in Hollywood," produced as "Mighty Like a Rogue." He was most successful in France. *Strange Witness* (1953) sold twice to France, as KEEP TALKING, BABY, in 1961, and, thirty years later, for the television movie BILLY (1991).

After his move to L.A., Keene's credits were modest. In 1959 he sold a story to producer Roy Huggins for the series *Colt .45* and he began writing with former pulp writer Dwight Babcock, another contributor to *Colt .45*. The two began collaborating on the screenplay that would become CHAUTAUQUA.

Later that year they sold two original screenplays for the *Hawaiian Eye* series. "Three Tickets to Lanai," directed by Robert Altman from a Keene story and screenplay, was the story of a badger scheme turned to murder. It begins when stuntman Carey Loftin, uncredited as the embezzler J. Harrison Rennie, is thrown from a fishing boat.

In "The Kamehameha Cloak" a scuba diver comes across an underwater cavern and an ancestral winged cape. Later his wife summons private eye Robert Conrad, claiming that her husband is being "prayed to death." A younger wife, an impetuous daughter, and two songs lip synced by Connie Stevens and Poncie Ponce make up the rest of this story.

Keene also sold two episodes to the series *Burke's Law*. The cast for "Who Killed the Paper Dragon?" included stripper Tura Satana and "Who Killed Cythia Royale?" guest-starred Frankie Avalon.

The high point of Keene's experience in film occurred in France, when director Rene Clement adapted *Joy House*, in 1964. Charles Williams, another writer with Gold Medal credentials, worked on the script.

▢ ▢ ▢

For the uninitiated, and for anyone who lacks the first and only editions of these fifty year old novels, this volume is a fine introduction to Day Keene, offering stories set in the author's three favorite settings, Southern California, Florida and the big cities, Chicago and New York. *Hunt the Killer* was one of six novels published in 1952, *Dead Dolls Don't Talk* and *Too Hot to Hold*, two of seven novels published in 1959.

According to his agent Donald MacCampbell, who handled the sales for as many as half of the writers of paperback originals, "Day Keene

... knew how to put his hero in bed with a blonde corpse and get him out of trouble on the last page." If this is true, then *Dead Dolls Don't Talk* is the quintessential Keene novel, since it offers multiple stiffs and nautical settings in Southern California and Mexico.

Here Keene is at his hard-boiled best: "He eyed his conquest with fresh respect as he staggered after her down the deck." And about a dozen paragraphs later: "...for one of the few times in his life Cotton felt mildly ashamed of himself. When they'd first come aboard the cabin it looked like something out of a color advertisement in Yachting. Now it looked like two apes had wrestled in it. Half of the chairs were overturned. The drape over the portal he'd just closed was hanging by a scrap of cloth. The floor was littered with empty bottles and greasy looking french fried potatoes and two extremely well-gnawed steak bones."

Charter Boat captain Charlie White is the title character in this second selection, *Hunt the Killer*, and Charlie too, is not an innocent. He has smuggled, he's been convicted, and after four years of incarceration he is on his way out of the Florida State Prison.

There's a murder, and an execution, and only Charlie and the reader know that this time he is innocent. *Hunt the Killer* becomes a great extended chase throughout Florida, from swamps and islands to Palmetto City, Keene's alias for St. Petersburg. Wisdom comes from Swede, a convict in the death house who has kept White out of a failed prison break. Swede says: "A guy hauls in the fish he baits for and at the depth at which he fishes."

In *Too Hot to Hold* Keene returns to Chicago and New York with a great sense of the familiar. A coincidental connection between two characters throws a system for Mafia payoffs out of joint. Now a whole group of innocents are in jeopardy from two low-key, collegiate killers who are waiting to make your acquaintance. International gangsterism comes up against a middle class worker with a stressed and sordid home life. Who wins?

Welcome to the world of Day Keene. It's a thrilling world to visit. God help you if you should ever get stuck here.

Downieville, CA
April 2011

DEAD DOLLS DON'T TALK

BY DAY KEENE

JANUARY 2, 1958
8:23 P.M.

There was no boy and girl business about it. Both of them knew what they were doing. It was a thoroughly adult and sordid affair involving proven lewd and licentious conduct, resulting, so the State alleged, in murder.

The man's name was Harry L. Cotton. He had been a professional aerial crop duster. He was big. He was young. He had a way with women.

It began as a New Year's Eve pickup at the bar of one of the better known night clubs on the Sunset Strip in Los Angeles. Now, some forty-eight hours later, Cotton felt fine. He'd never felt better. For long minutes after full consciousness returned, he continued to lie with his eyes closed, enjoying being drunk, savoring the past two days and nights. He was on a wing-ding this time, a dilly. Only one thing troubled him. The last thing he remembered was the proprietor of the motel in Santa Monica shaking his fist in Cotton's face and telling him to take his business and the red-haired little tramp with him some other place or he would phone the police.

This, after Bonnie'd given the man fifty dollars to pay for the mattress they'd burned.

Now he seemed to be in a boat, a small boat. Cotton could hear the rhythmic churn of the screw.

He opened his eyes and looked up. It was night but the moon was full. And wherever he was, Bonnie was still with him. He was lying with his head in her lap. Except for her wind-blown hair and the fact that, instead of a white evening gown and a mink cape, she was wearing a smart hand-knit dress and a yellow polo coat, she looked much the same as she'd looked on the bar stool next to his at Ciro's. More important, she was still wearing the diamond necklace and earrings and bracelet that had attracted him to her in the first place. The Cotton luck was holding. He'd picked a live one this time.

"Do we happen to be in a boat?" he asked her.

The girl was alcoholically hurt. "I knew you didn't believe me when I told you." She added, thickly, "But you'll see."

"See what?"

"That my husband does have a yacht."

"You're kidding."

"Cross my heart."

She tried but had trouble due to the over ample flesh under the hand-knit dress.

She's a bitch but she's cute, Cotton thought. He lifted his head from the warm comfort of her lap. More, she wasn't kidding. Not only were they in a twenty-foot speedboat manned by a foreign-looking seaman, they seemed to be headed through the Santa Monica channel toward the lights of a good-sized yacht standing a mile or more off shore.

Cotton didn't feel quite as well as he had. Making love to a married woman in her home or in a hotel room was one thing. A yacht was something else. Few yachts had doors or windows.

Bonnie guessed what he was thinking. "Don't tell me you're chicken?"

Put that way, Cotton shrugged. He'd handled other husbands. If he had to he could handle John R. Deering.

Bonnie searched the seat for a bottle and drank from the neck of it. "To us."

"I'll drink to that," Cotton said.

The yacht was as large and luxurious as it had appeared to be from a distance. The captain looked Spanish.

A heavy sea was running so Bonnie's coat and dress were soaked with salt water before the captain and the steward managed to get her up the landing ladder. Despite her flow of chorus girl vituperation both men remained properly obsequious since she was the owner's wife.

It was "Sí, señora," this and "Sí, señora," that.

Neither man seemed surprised to see them and Cotton imagined that his playmate had used the yacht for similar rendezvous in the past. If Bonnie wanted to impress him she'd succeeded. He eyed his conquest with fresh respect as he staggered after her down the deck. It seemed that if a tart married money, this kind of money, it lifted her up beyond the pale imposed on ordinary mortals.

The interior of the cabin was beautiful. It might have been a swank suite in a luxury hotel.

As Bonnie closed the door behind them she asked, "Like it, Harry?"

"Yes," Cotton said. "Very much."

He walked around the suite touching this object and that. When he turned again Bonnie had dropped her wet coat on the floor and was peeling her equally as wet dress over her flame-red hair. Her scanties and bra followed until all she wore were her diamonds.

"Ugh. Nasty stuff, water," she shuddered.

Cotton's suit was wet, too. He took off his coat and shirt and skivvies as he watched her stagger into the bathroom for a towel. Even after knowing her intimately for two days she still excited him. If there was anything prettier than a nude woman he'd never seen it. Especially if the woman was a Bonnie Deering.

She realized he was looking at her and stopped toweling. Her eyes were sullen as she reached for a robe. "What are you looking at?"

Cotton told her. "You."

The sullen look left her eyes as she closed the distance between them, trailing her robe behind her. Her voice was drunkenly grave. "You know why I like you?"

"Why?"

She thought a moment. "Because you're no good and neither am I," she said. "And our kind belong together."

She lifted her lips to be kissed. Then she insisted he towel her. When he finished she toweled him and one thing led to another. Between interludes they drank. Sometime during the evening they ate. The next thing Cotton knew it was morning.

It was cold in the cabin. The weather had become stormy through the night. The yacht rolled. As he'd done in the small boat, Cotton lay with his eyes closed but no longer enjoying the spree. This thing couldn't go on forever. He'd had it. He had to figure out some way to cash in and get out before Bonnie's husband caught up with his wife and shot both of them.

He opened his eyes and saw the oversized porthole across from the bed was open. He padded across the floor and looked out. The porthole opened directly on the water. The sea looked gray and angry. A stiff onshore wind was blowing.

He closed the porthole and walked back to the bed. Bonnie wasn't in it. He sat on the edge, shivering in the cold, waiting for her to come out of the bathroom. When she didn't, he opened the door and looked in.

Wherever she was, Bonnie wasn't in the bathroom. It seemed that during the drunken night just past, he or the girl had spilled some sticky substance on the carpet. It felt unpleasant on the soles of his bare feet.

For want of anything better to do he returned to the edge of the bed. He wished he knew the correct etiquette in a situation like this. Perhaps a man was supposed to ring the buzzer for the steward and announce: "Will you please inform Madame her lover is awake and craves her presence?"

As he sat looking around the cabin, for one of the few times in his life, Cotton felt mildly ashamed of himself. When they'd first come aboard, the cabin had looked like something out of a color advertisement in *Yachting.* Now it looked like two apes had wrestled in it. Half of the chairs were overturned. The drape over the portal he'd just closed was hanging by a scrap of cloth. The floor was littered with empty bottles and greasy looking French fried potatoes and two extremely well-gnawed steak bones.

He wondered where they came from, then remembered. That had been just before the fight. Bonnie had insisted that sex made her hungry and

God knew she had a right to eat. She'd demanded that he call the steward and have him fix two thick steaks.

He tried to recall the fight. Women. Just because he'd mentioned Jean, Bonnie had claimed he didn't love her. She'd even snatched up one of the steak knives and threatened to cut his heart out and he'd had to slap the knife out of her hand. As he recalled, he'd had to slap her quite a few times. As if Jean meant anything to him.

Still, that explained Bonnie's absence. In her drunken anger she'd probably moved to another stateroom or cabin, he supposed it was called on this kind of a boat. Now if he hoped to cash in he'd have to go through the whole thing again.

Cotton found his shirt and skivvies and slacks and put them on. But when he tried to put on his socks they stuck to the substance he'd walked in. He tried to brush it off and merely succeeded in transferring it to his fingers. It looked like clotted blood. It had the same cloying sweetness. He tried to remember either of them bleeding and couldn't. He hadn't slapped Bonnie that hard.

Then he saw the knit dress and Bonnie's filmy underthings. They were lying where she'd dropped them but they looked different. Cotton picked them up and wished he hadn't. The garments were sticky with blood. They looked as if someone had mopped the floor with them.

The exclamation was instinctive. "Oh, no."

In sudden panic he searched the floor for the steak knives. He could find one but not the other. Both Bonnie and the knife were gone. The only tangible evidence that she'd ever been in the cabin were the blood-sodden clothes on the floor and the diamond necklace and bracelet and earrings on the elaborate dressing table.

Cotton finished dressing with trembling fingers. It was a gag of some kind. It had to be. Finished dressing, he tried to open the door. It was held by a safety chain so would open only about eight inches. Cotton peered through the crack and saw a barefooted seaman swabbing the deck, incuriously looking at him.

Cotton worked the film and phlegm of fear from his mouth. "Would you please tell Mrs. Deering I'm awake and would like to see her?"

The seaman looked puzzled. "But, *señor*," he protested gently. "The *señora* has not yet come out on deck." His face brightened in understanding. "You will maybe find her in the—" He paused, his native politeness making him hesitant to use the word.

Cotton forced himself to say, "Oh. Yes. Of course." He closed the door and stood staring at the safety chain.

He wasn't thinking clearly. Bonnie couldn't have left the cabin with the door fastened on the inside by the chain.

Sudden unreasoning fear formed a hard lump in his stomach. He hadn't been *that* drunk. Or had he? After all, he'd been drinking for two days and three nights. And if nothing had happened to Bonnie, who had been bleeding on the floor? She couldn't have left the cabin, locked as it was and even if she could, no girl would just walk out and leave a fortune in diamonds behind her.

The hard lump in Cotton's stomach dissolved in a freshet of self-pity. He felt as if he were crying internally. This was it, the big one. It had caught up with him at last! There was only one thing he could do. That was to get off the yacht and put as much distance as he could between himself and the scene before the disappearance of the red-haired Mrs. Deering was discovered. And to do that he would need money.

Almost without thinking he swept the diamonds from the dressing table and dropped them into his side pocket. His hands were trembling so badly he had difficulty unfastening the chain. The seaman who'd been swabbing the deck was gone but the sailor who'd manned the small boat the night before was lounging on the rail near the landing ladder.

Cotton closed the door and made certain the spring lock was caught. Then he strode up the deck with an air of confidence he didn't feel and spoke as calmly as he could.

"I'm afraid I have to go ashore," he told the man. He expected a protest. There was none. "*Sí, señor,*" the seaman said and stepped aside to allow Cotton to precede him down the ladder.

Halfway down Cotton stopped and added as if it were an afterthought, "Oh, by the way."

"*Sí—?*"

Cotton took a deep breath and exhaled. "Before we push off you'd better tell the steward that Mrs. Deering doesn't want to be disturbed before noon."

The seaman acted as if he were bored. "It is her usual hour for arising, *señor.* Please to make yourself easy. The *señora* will not be disturbed."

JULY 2, 1958
8:14 A.M.

To out of town tourists still awed by having fitted their mortal feet into the footprints of the stars immortalized for posterity in concrete in the foyer of Grauman's Chinese Theatre, to those who were slightly bleary-eyed from trying to separate the stars from the sweet young things en route to their various jobs in stores and offices along the fabulous Sunset Strip, it was just another drugstore, well-stocked and staffed by young men and women who looked like they might have just stepped off a movie lot or a television set.

The chances were they had.

To the initiate it wasn't a drugstore. It was Hart's. Everyone in the know knew it. If you were sincere in your attempt to break into show business and you needed a temporary job until the studios recognized your talent, Doc Hart could always use another clerk or waitress or stock boy. If you'd broken through the barrier but casting was slow and you needed a few meals on credit, tell Doc. He'd even been known to dig up the rent, no strings attached.

Not that he ever lost a thing by trying to be a good guy. On the contrary, what had begun some years before as a hole in the wall with one clerk, a four-stool fountain, and prescription department so small that Hart had been hard put for room enough to wield a pestle, had become a glittering show place on a boulevard of show places.

Hart himself was a mild-mannered man in his early thirties with a ready smile that had a nice effect on women. At one time he'd hoped to be a doctor but lack of funds decided him to settle on being a pharmacist as the next best thing. He was glad now that he had. Before he opened his own store he'd never realized what an integral part of a community a druggist really is.

The morning was warm. The breakfast trade was normal. There was a lot of it. The benches in the booths and nearly all the stools at the fountain were filled with earnest young men with long hair and sweet young things done up in ponytails and vari-colored Capri pants.

The delayed summons for jury service came in the morning mail. Hart read it while sipping his second cup of coffee. In common with most busy business and professional men he considered phoning his lawyer and having Kelly try to get him off the hook. He really couldn't afford the time. Then, sighing, he laid the summons to one side and decided to accept his civic duty.

Gerta, the new fountain girl, was concerned. "You do something, Doc?" she asked him. "The law catch you speeding or something?"

The druggist was amused. "No. It's just a jury summons."

The girl was impressed. She'd also read the morning papers. "Gee. Maybe you'll get on the Cotton jury."

Hart was more amused. "I'm afraid that's not very likely," he told her. "Judging from past experience, I'll probably be sitting on some suit to determine whose avocado tree hangs how far over whose property line."

Gerta warmed his coffee. "Do you think he killed her?"

Hart had dismissed the subject from his mind and was immersed in the front page of *Daily Variety*. "Killed who?" he asked absently.

The waitress was patient. "Bonnie Deering. Do you think Cotton killed her?"

"I haven't any idea."

"You knew her?"

"Not personally. But she used to come in here once in a while."

"While she was still working the night clubs? Before she married Mr. Deering?"

"That's right."

"Was she as pretty as her picture?"

Hart tried to remember. "Y-yes. As I recall she was very pretty. Sort of a slob's Jayne Mansfield."

Gerta leaned one elbow on the counter. "Did you ever see her act?"

"Several times."

"Was it as raw as they say? Did she really take off everything?"

Hart lowered his voice to match the girl's. "No," he whispered hoarsely. "As I remember, she kept on one earring."

Gerta straightened and moved on up the counter to serve a boy and girl who'd just come in. Hart smiled as he watched her back. Gerta had a cute little backside. All of her was cute. Besides, she had a lot of talent. But God help any producer who tried to sign up the kid via the casting couch routine. When Gerta took off her clothes for a man there was going to be a ring on the third finger of her left hand.

He glanced at his watch, then motioned to Manny Coe. His head pharmacist joined him at the counter.

"What now, Doc?"

Hart showed him the jury summons. "It looks like I've been tagged again and the darn thing seems to have been held up in the mail. I'm supposed to report at ten o'clock this morning."

Coe was sympathetic. "Tough. You going to try to get off the hook?"

"I don't think so."

"Then I suppose that means I'd better call the agency and have them send out a couple of boys."

"I suppose you'd better."

Coe put a cigarette in his mouth and offered the package to his employer. "The hell of it is we haven't any way of knowing for how long you may be stuck."

Hart lit his first cigarette of the day and enjoyed it. "That's the hell of it," he agreed. "But if I'm not back in a couple of days you might try sending out a Saint Bernard with a keg of dry Martinis."

SEPTEMBER 1, 1958
11:36 P.M.

It had been quiet all afternoon and during the early evening. However, shortly after eleven o'clock, the muted tempo of the city quickened as the maze of freeways and clover leafs and over- and underpasses visible from the upper floors of the Temple of Justice filled with the cars of returning celebrants, eager to be home before the last hours of the day dedicated to labor ushered in a fall, indistinguishable from the summer except as a date in time.

Even this high there was no breeze and the late night air verging on morning lay hot and still and humid in the big, wood-paneled jury room and on the flushed, angry faces of the jurors.

Sitting on the wide sill of one of the high windows, watching the flow of traffic, Hart thought it was a wonder, with all the hundreds of thousands of dollars, millions of dollars, the State of California and the County of Los Angeles took in every year in taxes that they wouldn't spend a few dollars of it to air-condition their jury rooms.

So a man's life was involved. God knew Cotton had had a fair trial. It had gone on for almost two months. He'd done his civic duty. He'd listened to the evidence. He'd weighed it. He'd formed an opinion. He'd cast his vote. He wanted to go home. He wanted to get back to his store. Still, if young Mrs. Slagle continued to hold out, nobody knew how much longer this thing might go on. Eleven men could be just as stubborn as one woman.

Hart loosened the wilted collar of his shirt as he looked at the young matron. She was a pretty little thing, slight and intense and exquisitely formed. She was still, after all these weeks, mildly embarrassed by having to spend the greater part of the last two months in such close proximity to eleven strange men, the last five days of which had been spent in discussing intimate biological details in the life of a dead girl who'd been far beneath her, morally and socially. In fact, they literally lived in two different worlds.

Mrs. Slagle's normally sleek blonde hair was disordered. A lock of it had escaped its pin and was dangling over one eye. The huge black leather chair in which she was sitting was much too large for her. If she sat back her feet wouldn't reach the floor. If she kept her feet on the floor she had to sit on the very edge of the chair. Hart didn't have the slightest doubt that, despite the firm jut of her pretty little jaw, she was an excellent wife and mother. She looked lonely sitting by herself. It was a pity she was so stupid. If Hart wasn't so angry with her, he could have been sorry for the girl.

Old man Gilmore stopped riffling the deck of cards and called from the far end of the table, "How about a few hands of gin, Doc?"

Hart shook his head. "No, thanks. At least, not right now."

The thin quaver of the old man's voice was beginning to make his skin crawl. If old man Gilmore announced just once more that this was the first Labor Day in forty-seven years that he hadn't gone fishing off Rainbow Pier in Long Beach, he'd—Hart didn't know what he'd do. He could hardly tell the old man to shut up and he couldn't walk out. The heavy oak door was locked and would stay locked until midnight when a court attaché would unlock it to ask if they wanted to continue their deliberations or be escorted back to the hotel in which they'd been lodged as the guests of the County of Los Angeles for the past sixty-one days.

Hart patted the sweat from his face with his breast pocket handkerchief. Continue what deliberations?

They all knew the dead girl's name was Bonnie Deering, better known professionally as Bonnie Tempest. They knew that in life she'd been a flame-haired, sullen-eyed, smeared-mouthed night-club entertainer with an unlimited capacity for alcohol and the more earthy and erotic pleasures afforded the willing female by the more than willing male.

They all knew that three years before in Las Vegas, at the ripe age of twenty-five, she'd climaxed a stormy ten-year career of one-night stands and taking off her clothes, professionally and socially, by marrying the eminently respectable and fabulously wealthy John R. Deering of the Los Angeles investment counseling firm of the same name.

They knew from the testimony of impartial and unbiased witnesses that everyone who'd known her had said the marriage wouldn't last but that it had, at least for two years. Then, the secondary narcotic of the great washed masses wore off and Bonnie reverted to type. As with the reformed hoyden in the Salvation Army band, Bonnie had become tired of doing nothing but beat a damn drum and a nostalgic itch in her more private parts had won out over her marriage vows.

The State had alleged and proven a number of minor slips, including a butler, a chauffeur and a golf pro at the swank country club to which the John R. Deerings belonged. There had also been a police citation and a five-hundred-dollar fine for driving a motor vehicle while under the influence of intoxicants, plus one night of incarceration in the Lincoln Heights jail as a common drunk.

The pay-off had come on New Year's Eve when she met Cotton.

Hart mopped at his face again. Now, eight months later, after a seven week and two day trial and one hundred and eight hours of deliberation by the jury, he was firmly convinced that the State of California, in the Superior Court of the County of Los Angeles, the Honorable M. L. Manners presiding, had proven that one Mrs. John R. Deering, professionally known as Bonnie Tempest, had climaxed a three day alcoholic and sexual orgy beginning in Ciro's and progressing to various lesser clubs and hotel rooms to a cabin in her husband's palatial sea-going yacht, at the moment standing off Santa Monica in readiness for the Panamanian cruise, by meeting death in a manner unknown at the hands of one Harry L. Cotton.

This Hart believed. He believed it with every ounce of his intelligence. So did his fellow male members of the jury. Even the alternate believed it.

But not so young Mrs. Slagle. After one hundred and ten hours of having eleven angry men plead and argue and shout at her, the woman still insisted, despite all the legal precedent the prosecution had cited, that she could not and would not find anyone, Harry L. Cotton in particular, guilty of murder in any degree until the State of California in the County of Los Angeles produced Bonnie Tempest's body.

Hart tried to find some basis for the young matron's stand. He marshaled the known ingredients in the trial. Over the strenuous objections of the defense the State had succeeded in establishing the fact that Cotton's crop dusting service had been bankrupt for five years and that for that period he'd made the bulk of his living swindling women attracted by his good looks and vaunted ability as a stud. Cotton admitted climaxing their three day spree by going aboard the yacht with Bonnie. He admitted being intimate with her in the cabin. He also admitted vaguely remembering quarreling with her. But he couldn't account for the knit dress, plus her few intimate garments, plus a partial denture without which not even her husband had ever seen her, being found on the floor of the cabin, all saturated with blood of the same type as hers, an amount of blood estimated by a police pathologist ample enough to cause the death of the person losing it.

Nor could Cotton account for a pearl-handled steak knife the steward swore had been in the cabin the last time he'd seen Mrs. Deering.

Cotton's only defense was that he awakened alone in the cabin and seeing the blood and finding the porthole open and Bonnie missing he'd panicked and being without funds to finance a flight he'd snatched up the dead woman's jewels before persuading a member of the crew to put him ashore.

"I didn't kill her," he'd sworn on the stand. "I may have slapped her around a little but I didn't kill her. It had to be someone who came through that open porthole."

Hart was wryly amused. This in spite of the established fact that there'd been nothing under the porthole but thirty fathoms of water, a heavy sea running and the yacht standing a mile and a half off shore. Nor had anyone entered the cabin through the door. He'd covered that point by asking to see the transcript of the trial covering the crew's testimony. All of them swore no one had boarded the yacht between the time Bonnie and Cotton had come aboard the night before and the time the startled steward discovered the mess in the cabin. As a clincher, a seaman testified that Cotton had opened the door on the chain that morning. The steward then gave the information that it was the practice of Mrs. Deering to keep the door secured on the inside by the chain when she was entertaining a male guest.

Hart realized one of his fellow jurors, a big red-faced building contractor by the name of Kelly, had stopped pacing and was looking out the window.

"I wonder how the ball game came out?" he said.

Hart returned his handkerchief to his pocket. "Yes. So do I."

Kelly turned his head and gave Mrs. Slagle a sour look. "The last double header of the year. And me with two season tickets right back of first base."

"Tough," Hart sympathized with him.

"You know something?" old man Gilmore began without preamble. "This is the first Labor Day in forty-seven years that I haven't gone fishing off Rainbow Pier in Long Beach." His aged voice quavered on. "I mind one time back in nineteen twenty-four, or maybe it was twenty-three—"

To keep from listening to him Hart took a pad of prescription blanks embossed with his letterhead from his pocket and tried to calculate how much his two months of jury duty and the dead Bonnie Tempest had cost him. It was plenty.

And if young Mrs. Slagle continued to hold out, only God knew how much more Bonnie's now permanently cured nymphomania might cost him before judge Manners decided the jury was hopelessly deadlocked and declared it a mistrial.

On impulse, Hart got up from the window sill and sat beside Mrs. Slagle and talked earnestly for the next fifteen minutes. Gradually her firm little jaw ceased to jut and began to quiver. She was crying softly to herself and nodding agreement with what Hart was saying when Harp Igoe, the bailiff, unlocked the door of the jury room and asked if they were ready to call it a night and be escorted to their hotel.

Hart looked at the young woman a few seconds, then made a suggestion.

"Let's take one more ballot."

It was as simple as that. When the ballots were counted they were all agreed. Harry L. Cotton was guilty of murder in the first degree and his punishment set at death in the gas chamber.

The atmosphere changed immediately. The tenseness and feeling of strain in the large wood-paneled room were gone. It no longer seemed so hot. It was as if a cool breeze off the ocean had found its way inland and swept through the open windows. The jurymen laughed and pounded each other on the back, exchanged addresses and made plans that would never come to fruition, to get together again. Only Hart and Mrs. Slagle were subdued.

While they waited for the judge to be informed that they'd reached a verdict and for the prisoner to be brought into court, Kelly took Hart to one side.

"How did you do it, Doc?" he enthused. "How did you get her to change her mind? What kind of a line did you hand her?"

Hart wasn't proud of his method. The psychology he'd used smacked of dirty pool. He'd attacked her in her most vulnerable point.

"I just reminded her," he said quietly, "that tomorrow is the first day of school and that one of the most wonderful experiences a young mother can enjoy is seeing her children off for their first day of school." He shrugged. "She has a pair of twins who are supposed to start to school tomorrow. And I guess I convinced her that it was a shame that both she and the twins should be cheated out of one of the high points in their lives because of a little tramp like Bonnie Tempest."

Kelly chuckled. "I have three kids of my own and I see what you mean. That was hitting below the girdle. But why be so down in the mouth about it? A druggist is a very valuable member of a community. After being away from your store for two months, I should think you'd be glad to get out of here."

"I am, I am," Hart assured him. "But one thing bothers me."

"What's that?"

"After all, the State didn't produce a body. Strong as it was, the evidence and presumption of death was entirely circumstantial. What if Mrs. Slagle is right and we're wrong?"

SEPTEMBER 2, 1958
12:18 A.M.

It was cooler in the court, much cooler than it had been in the jury room.

He settled uncomfortably in his seat, wishing Mrs. Slagle would stop crying. Her tears made him feel like a heel.

He studied the scattered faces in the courtroom. At this late hour the majority of the spectators, the morbidly curious, the pornographic-minded, interested only in the physical excesses and erotic practices of the dead girl and not in the fact that a man was on trial for his life, were missing.

Most of those present were newspapermen and women. One exception was the dead girl's husband. Hart studied the financier's face. It was thin and pale and tended toward the aesthetic. He'd given his age as fifty-six. Hart wondered, considering the man's background, what he'd seen in the dead girl and knew as he wondered. Her pretty face and over-developed mammary glands had been contributing factors. But what Deering had really seen, what he was now seeing through his grief and what he would continue to see in retrospect had been a triangular flag, in Bonnie's case a red one.

He continued to study Deering. Considering the number the State had detailed, it must have been very embarrassing for such a man to sit through the trial just past and listen to his dead wife's sheets being laundered. Still, in a way, Deering was as much to blame for Bonnie's death as young Cotton. Any older man who married a young woman was a fool.

On the other hand, it happened every day, three hundred and sixty-five days a year. Then they came to him or their doctor or another druggist, crying.

"I can't go on like this, Doc. Why I used to be able to stay four times with a girl. I can't believe it's gone. You have to give me something."

The hell of it was, despite all the patent medicine advertisements concerning 'pep,' for men over forty there wasn't a thing in pharmacopoeia that any druggist or doctor could give them. The only known positive aphrodisiac was a young and pretty woman. And when a man could no longer dip into the fountain of youth he'd had it!

Hart looked from Deering to the captain of the Deering yacht. One of the truest of old saws was that no man could live unto himself alone. Everything he did affected somebody else. And in killing Bonnie, Cotton had done Captain Enrico Morales out of a job. After the death of his wife, Deering had been in no frame of mind for a long cruise, business or otherwise. Hart wondered where the yacht was now and if Morales was still in Deering's employ. A big swart man in his early thirties, handsome in a virile, Latin manner, Morales had sat, bored, through two or three days of the trial in addition to testifying as to Bonnie's and Cotton's condition when they'd come aboard the yacht and to the fact that with the chain hooked on the inside of the cabin door, there was no way that the wife of his employer could have left except through the fatal porthole. As Hart watched him the seaman yawned widely and Hart turned his attention to the dark-haired girl sitting alone in the rear of the room.

To the best of Hart's knowledge, the girl had attended every session of the trial. For a time he and the other jurors thought she might be a former admirer or victim of Cotton's whom either the defense or the prosecution intended to call to the stand. But neither side had. For the entire seven weeks the girl had merely sat and listened and watched.

Hart studied the prisoner's face as he sat beside the counsel appointed by the court. Cotton was good-looking in a rugged way but he had a weak mouth, the petulant mouth of a child who took but never gave. The long stay in a cell had faded his skin to a sickly yellow. His once expensive suit hung on his big-boned frame like a rag. His eyes were heavily shadowed and sunk deep into his skull. He looked sick and frightened. He probably was. Hart hoped his few days of alcoholic and sexual excesses with Bonnie had been worth what he was going to pay for them.

After the strain and tension of the trial and the long hours of deliberation, what followed was anti-climactical. Hart was glad when sentence had been pronounced and the judge had made his short speech of thanks to the jury and the clerk banged his gavel a few times and the whole thing was over.

Hart was hot and tired. He wanted a drink, a stiff one. He fended off the reporters with no comment and avoided Deering who was making his way toward the jury box with the obvious intention of thanking the members individually. He walked out into the corridor and down it to the bank of elevators.

The dark-haired girl he'd seen in court so many times had left the courtroom before he had and was waiting for an elevator. Hart studied her surreptitiously. She was prettier close up than from a distance. As they rode down in the elevator he took her in in detail. She was about five feet tall and weighed around one hundred pounds. Her summer suit was smart but inexpensive. So was the large shoulder bag she carried. Her face was small and oval and Hart imagined, under normal circumstances, rather elfin. Right now, from the way her lips quivered from time to time, she was laboring under an emotional strain but kept herself well in hand.

It was even hotter on the street level than it had been in the jury room. Hart took off his coat and hung it over his arm. He'd half expected Manny or Gerta to meet him. On the other hand, they had no way of knowing when the jury would break. Not that he needed them. He'd given the bailiff instructions to have his car brought from the garage where it was stored. He could see it in the parking lot now.

Three of his fellow jurymen trickled out but Hart stood where he was, looking out over the city, glad to be his own man again, free to come and go as he pleased.

The rush of late holiday traffic on the freeways had lessened to a normal flow and the city was mute again and would be until morning, if a metropolis could ever be mute.

More jurymen and court attachés and late-staying-up interested parties, John R. Deering among them, came out. The others, as if sensing his mood, passed Hart by but the financier came up to him and insisted on shaking his hand.

"I missed you upstairs when I thanked the others, Doctor," Deering said. "I know it wasn't an easy thing to do. But thank God we still have men of principle, men who believe in decency and justice."

Hart shook hands because there was no way out of it. But he was glad when Deering left it there and walked into the parking lot where a uniformed chauffeur was waiting beside a big, imported limousine.

The garage attendant had put down the top of the convertible, Hart was glad to see. The leather upholstery was comfortably cool. He started the motor and drove out of the lot.

The dark-haired girl hadn't gone very far. She was standing on the curb, with one white-gloved hand resting lightly on a Bus Stop sign. It had been years since Hart had ridden a bus, at least in the downtown section but to the best of his memory if there were any buses at this hour they ran very infrequently.

On impulse he stopped the car in front of the loading zone and said, "I don't want you to think I'm being forward, Miss. But I'm afraid the bus service isn't too good at this time of morning. And if you happen to be going out Hollywood way, I'll be very happy to give you a lift."

The girl regarded him soberly, "How deep into Hollywood?"

"Into and beyond," Hart told her. "All the way out to the Sunset Strip. I own a drugstore out there."

The girl continued to regard him. "I know. I had a soda in your place once. I was a secretary for Assorted Artists, a talent agency, about a mile beyond your store."

"That makes us practically relatives," Hart smiled. "I know Ben well. I play poker with him every Tuesday night. Do you live anywhere near the office?"

"I have an apartment about two blocks away."

"Then get in. I'll take you home."

As Hart leaned over to open the door a car horn beeped softly behind him and he saw that Deering's limousine had emerged from the parking lot and his car was blocking its entrance to the street. He pulled up a few feet and waved the other car around him. Deering nodded his thanks as he passed.

Hart opened the door for the girl. "He would have a horn like that. Beep beep."

The girl sat next to him and smoothed her skirt over her knees. "You're nice," she said, gravely. "I don't like him either. He reminds me of a boy cat I had once." She looked away. "A not quite complete boy cat."

Hart put his car into motion. "Yes. I know what you mean."

At this hour of the morning it was as easy to thread the maze of downtown streets to Sunset as it was to take the freeway. There was little traffic and once the big car was moving Hart felt cool for the first time in two months. The girl rode without speaking, her hands in her lap.

As he braked his car to give the right of way to a truck loaded with morning papers, he glanced sideways. The girl's skirt had slipped up exposing her silk-sheathed knees and a narrow ribbon of white thigh. Hart was amused by his own reaction. It seemed the trial hadn't dulled his libido. Or perhaps it was the two months of abstinence. After sitting through seven weeks of detailed testimony concerning the sexual peccadilloes of Bonnie Tempest and her various paramours, he was still a normal male.

As he drove on across the street he made conversation. "A nice night, isn't it?"

"Nice, but warm," the girl agreed. "I imagine you're glad to get out of that jury room, glad to be able to go home."

"I am. It got kind of sticky in there."

"I can imagine." She wet her lips with the tip of her tongue. She seemed to be trying to reach some decision. They rode several blocks in silence, then she said, "You're curious about me, aren't you?"

"Yes," Hart admitted, "I am."

The girl offered her hand after she took off one glove. "My name is Peggy."

Hart took his right hand off the wheel. "I'm Doc. Glad to know you, Peggy."

Her hand felt soft and small but unnaturally warm, even feverish. "You feel all right?" he asked her.

"I feel fine, just fine," she said. Then she added, "Now."

Hart refrained from questioning her any further.

She continued, quietly. "You're wondering, aren't you? I mean about why I went to the trial every day."

"We all wondered," Hart said. "In fact, we had a small pool as to whether the prosecution or the defense was going to put you on the stand."

The girl who said her name was Peggy looked at him for a long time. When she spoke her voice was quiet but vehement. "They didn't dare."

"Who didn't dare?"

"The defense."

Hart waited for her to continue. She didn't. They drove several more miles before she spoke again. Then, as the car sped past the huge N.B.C. building on the corner of Vine, she said, "He got just exactly what he had coming to him. And I'm glad."

Hart said, "I gather you don't like Cotton."

"You sat through the trial. Did you hear any reason why I should? Why any girl should?"

"No."

She repeated, "Just what he had coming to him. They have to execute him now, don't they?"

The vehemence bordering on hysteria in her voice made Hart feel uncomfortable. He almost wished he hadn't offered her a ride. "I'm afraid so," he said, quietly. "That is, unless his attorney appeals to the Supreme Court or comes up with sufficient new evidence to warrant a new trial."

"What sort of evidence?"

"Pretty strong evidence."

"Like what?"

"In Cotton's case I imagine it would have to be proof that Bonnie Tempest is alive."

"I see."

Hart enjoyed the wind on his face and the soft sucking sound of the tires and the low purr of the powerful motor. They were passing Hollywood High School now. He was glad they'd come as far as they had. He would, he decided, be glad to drop Peggy at her door and say good night. Normally she was probably very good company but right now some inner fire, some hate was consuming the girl. From what little she'd said and the vehemence with which she'd said it, he figured that Cotton had victimized her at some time.

Almost as if she could read his mind, Peggy put one of her hands in his. "Please don't be uncomfortable with me. From all I've heard about you, you're a swell guy, Doc. I want you to like me."

Hart was truthful. "I do."

"It's just that I've been under a strain."

Hart said, "I see," and was struck by the banality of the remark as he made it. He didn't see anything.

"You mean that?" she asked.

"Do I mean what?"

"That you like me?"

"Yes, of course."

"Well enough to date me?"

Hart considered his answer. "Yes," he said finally. He meant it.

"When?"

"You name it."

"How about tonight?"

"You mean tomorrow night?"

"No. Tonight. Now."

Hart tried to see her eyes in the dim light from the dash board. "You're joking."

The girl slowly moved her head from side to side. "No. Please don't ask me why but I don't want to be alone tonight. You won't be sorry, I promise."

The whole idea was absurd. Hart couldn't think of anything to say. All he could do was repeat, "You're joking."

"Believe me, I'm not," the girl said. "Look. All the way out from town you've been glancing at the bar signs trying to make up your mind whether it would be proper for you to suggest that we stop and have a drink."

Hart laughed. "That's right," he said.

"Now it's past two o'clock and all the bars are closed. So why not come up to my place and let me make some Martinis."

On impulse Hart swung his big car into the curb and stopped. "Look, honey—"

The girl met his eyes. "Yes—?"

Hart was frank with her. "It's probably none of my business," he said, "but unless they have an axe of some kind to grind, pretty girls like you don't invite men they've just met up to their apartments at eighteen after two in the morning. And I'm fresh out of grindstones. What's the gimmick?"

"No gimmick. I just don't want to be alone."

"Why not?"

"If you come to the apartment I'll tell you."

Hart sat with both hands on the wheel. "The word 'date' can have a lot of meanings."

"I—know."

It was the way she said it. It angered and excited Hart. He was still hot. He was tired. He felt put upon. Women were peculiar creatures. They seemed to think all they had to do to get their own way with a man, any man, was to wave their triangular flag as bait. And the fantastic truth of it was in ninety-nine cases out of a hundred they were right.

"Please," she said quietly.

Hart still hesitated. "Well, all right," he finally agreed. He was lying. He knew it. Having gone that far the affair surely wouldn't stop there. "But just for two Martinis."

She sat back with her hands in her lap. "We'll see."

Hart started to put his car into motion and stopped again as a police cruiser drew up beside him and an officer got out. "Just a minute, fellow," he said. Then he recognized Hart and called over his shoulder to his partner. "Hey, Joe. Come here. It's Doc home from the wars."

Both men were pleased to see Hart. The one who'd spoken first said, "Good for you, Doc. You gave it to Cotton but good. We got the flash over our radio a few minutes ago."

Hart was a little embarrassed by the presence of the girl in his car. He felt impelled to introduce her. "Nice seeing you boys again. This is Miss Peggy—"

"Jones," the girl supplied the name.

Both officers acknowledged the introduction but were more interested in and pleased with Cotton's conviction. As they gleefully informed Hart, because the State hadn't produced a *corpus delicti* the betting along the Strip had been eight to two that Cotton would not be convicted and both of them had bet a week's pay at the short odds. Both men patronized his drugstore and he liked them but he was glad when their car radio blared and they had to leave.

When they were gone he drove on more slowly. He wished the incident hadn't occurred. For all its veneer of sophistication the Strip was really a small village, a village of clacking tongues. By morning everyone from the porter in Bernie's Liquor Store to the maitre d' in A Little Bit of Sweden would know that Joe Feeney and Matt Hooper had stopped Doc Hart at two o'clock in the morning with a mysterious brown-haired girl in his car, a pretty girl who'd given the obviously phony name of Jones. This on his way home from jury duty, two months of it.

Peggy put her hand on his knee. "What are you thinking?"

Hart told her. "That for a hard-working druggist who minds his own business, I can get into the most peculiar situations."

"You're angry with me, aren't you?"

Hart continued to be truthful. "No. Not exactly angry. Hooked."

"Hooked?"

"Yes. Now I simply have to know who you are and what you want with me."

SEPTEMBER 2, 1958
3:01 A.M.

The apartment was about what Hart had expected, two rooms and a bath with a tiny kitchenette in one of the old remodeled mansions in the hills north of the boulevard and about a mile west of his store.

The best thing about it was the view. From where he stood in front of the living room windows he could see the lights of the city spread out for miles.

As he sipped his second drink Hart gave the girl her due. Peggy made good Martinis, albeit they were a trifle strong and she served them in Old-fashioned glasses.

The date, if it could be called that, was proceeding according to pattern. Peggy had made the usual announcement that she wanted to change into something cooler and more comfortable. However, instead of donning the usual filmy negligee, she'd put on a smart red shantung coolie coat that ended halfway down her thighs, creating the illusion that there was nothing but flesh and girl under the provocative garment.

"How's that?" she called from the kitchenette.

Hart moved from the sill to the couch. "Excellent," he called back. "After having been cooped up the way I have for the last two months these Martinis fit just fine."

He was wryly amused at himself. In a book or a movie, being a reputable businessman and a pillar of the community, in a few minutes he would put on his coat, thank Peggy for the drinks and make a stuffy departure. But that wasn't the way these things happened. He knew. He'd traveled this route before. And he had plenty of company. If all the reputable business and professional men on the Strip and in Beverly Hills in the wrong bed were to die on any given night there wouldn't be enough priests or preachers or rabbis in the greater Los Angeles area to pray them into their particular heaven. Having a few dollars and position in the community didn't make a man less male. If, for some reason of her own and he wondered what it could be, the brown-haired girl wanted him, she could have him. Hart wished he knew why she didn't want to be alone on this particular night. A cut and dried proposition, he sighed to himself.

The girl padded in from the kitchen bare-footed and set a sweating pitcher of fresh Martinis on a low coffee table before sitting down on the couch beside him.

She sat sideways on the couch and naturally the red coolie coat crept up her thighs until it almost reached the point of disclosure. Hart wiped his sweating palms on his trousers. He tried to think of something bright to say. He couldn't.

Her blue-gray eyes solemn, Peggy moved closer to him. "You're wondering, aren't you?"

"Wondering what?"

"If there's anything under this coat but me."

"Yes," Hart admitted, "I am."

She brushed his lips with hers. "There's not a damn thing," she assured him. Her voice was suddenly harsh as she pressed his hand into her lap to prove it. "So why don't we stop stalling and do what we both want to do?"

"Here?" Hart asked her.

"No. In the bedroom," she said.

The covers on the bed had been turned back, in anticipation, Hart presumed. For a long time there was no sound in the dimly lighted room but the hoarse, animal-like breathing and exclamations of the girl and the fevered spat of flesh on flesh. Even as he labored toward his goal, Hart was disgusted with himself. *Well, all right. But just for two Martinis.* And here he was back in the saddle, riding hell bent for Jericho. Any man, even a smart one, was putty in the hands of a pretty woman. It seemed that nature or God or whatever force had created him, had made the biological urge in man so strong that he was unable to help himself.

He was glad when the girl in his arms cried out one last time and lay still. Seconds later, he relaxed on his side of the bed, spent. He lay a long time without moving, then rolled on his side and rested his weight on his elbow.

"Satisfied?"

Her smeared lips were still sullen with passion. Her small, perfectly formed breasts still rose and fell with her efforts. She nodded like a little girl who'd been naughty. "Yes." She added needlessly, "I needed that."

Hart felt cool, really deliciously cool for the first time in two months. "That was obvious. So did I." He reached over the slight, spent body beside his and took two cigarettes from the bed table and lighted them. "But now that I've been raped, suppose you tell me why."

Peggy accepted the smoke he gave her. "Let's say I just wanted a man."

Hart puffed his cigarette. "Why me?"

She studied his face for a long moment. "Would you believe me if I told you you were the reason I went to court, that I've been sitting there every day for two months watching you and thinking how good it would be with you?"

"No," Hart said. "I would not." His years on the Strip had destroyed all his illusions. "For one thing, that wasn't all passion. At least half of it was spite." He put his fingers under her chin and lifted her face so he could see her eyes, "Who were you getting even with, honey?"

"You didn't like me?"

Hart gave her a light caress. "I adored you. But that still doesn't answer my question."

"Do I have to tell you?"

"I wish you would."

The girl lay silent a moment longer, then swung her bare feet to the floor and stood up, a trifle unsteady. "Excuse me a moment, first. I want a drink of water."

Hart watched her out of the room, mentally comparing the bobble of her round buttocks to Gerta's. It was sad but true. Stripped down to fundamentals, one woman was very much like another. When she returned she was even more unsteady and her breath reeked of gin.

"Are you certain you went for water?" he asked her.

She was honest with him. "No. More gin." She lay back on the bed and looked up at him, unsmiling. "If you want to again, you can."

"Just like that."

"Like that."

Hart resisted an impulse to slap her. "If you don't mind, I'll take a rain check. Now suppose you tell me what this is all about."

"You'll be angry with me."

"Probably."

"And with Harry."

Hart felt a drop of perspiration escape the pit of his arm and trickle down his side. But despite the fact that it was stifling hot in the small bedroom, the drop of perspiration was cold. He forced himself to ask, "Harry who?"

"Harry Cotton."

"No!"

"You asked me."

"You knew him well?"

The girl's lips twisted in a bitter smile. "I'm his wife, his legal wife. We were married in Waco, Texas, while he was still running the crop dusting company." The girl glared up at him defiantly. "Now go ahead and hit me."

Hart fought down an impulse to be sick. Cotton must have hurt the girl and hurt her badly to make her feel as she did, to condition her to do a thing like this. It was small wonder the defense counsel hadn't put her on the stand. "Why should I hit you?" he asked her.

She was bitter. "Harry would. It was all right for him to make love to every bag between here and Waco. He cheated on me right from the first week we were married. I know that now. And between bags he'd come back to me. And because he had such a guilty conscience, if a man admired me on the street he could hardly wait to get me home to hit me. Sometimes he beat me up so bad I couldn't even go to work." Her voice became thicker and shriller. "And he got just what he had coming Hear me?"

"I hear you," Hart said quietly.

At least one thing was clear. This was his night for getting thanked. In Peggy's grief-twisted mind, along with getting physically and sexually even with her condemned husband, she'd also been thanking him for his one-twelfth part in that same condemnation. He tried to be angry with her. He couldn't. There had been nothing personal about it. Given the opportunity, she would have 'thanked' any or all of his fellow members of the jury. There was no telling what hell Cotton had put her through to make her feel as she did.

"How old are you, honey?" he asked her.

"I'm twenty-one."

Her small face and upper body were beaded with small drops of perspiration. Hart used one corner of the wadded sheet to wipe her face. "That's not too old to cry," he said gently. "Why don't you quit trying to hold it in and wash him out of your system?"

Peggy moved her head from side to side on the pillow. "I've tried."

"He knew you were in court?"

"He couldn't help but see me. That's why I went every day."

She had trouble forming the words. Her voice was growing thicker momentarily. Hart wondered how much raw gin she'd drunk on top of the Martinis to screw up enough courage to do what she'd done. Even half drunk and just loved by a stranger, lying naked on a bed waiting to be loved again, she was still, in her way, a lady.

She misunderstood his admiring inspection and made a small gesture of resignation. "Well, I told you you could. If you want me again, take me."

Hart continued to be gentle with her. "Under the circumstances, if you don't mind, I'll make that a permanent rain check." He sat up on the edge of the bed and snuffed his cigarette. "And now that I've played my part in your revenge, tell me about you and Cotton."

"What about us?"

"You loved him a lot, didn't you?"

Peggy covered the lower part of her body with a sheet. "I thought he was Jesus L. Christ." The raw gin she'd gulped caught up with her and she giggled. "Get it? Jesus L. Christ. That's a good one."

Hart shook his head. "I'm afraid I'm not following you."

Peggy was pleased with Peggy as she explained, "Don't you see? I gave him the same sort of deal. I cruc—" She had trouble with the word and had to start over. "I crucified him, see? I crucified him by just sitting there in the back of the courtroom and keeping my little mouth shut."

The short hairs on the back of Hart's neck tingled. "What are you talking about, Peggy?"

The gin and her grief and the sexual relief after her months of pent-up hatred and self-imposed solitude washed at the base of her high wall of silence and undermined it. Her eyes filled with tears. "About Harry."

"What about him?"

"He didn't do it."

"He didn't do what?"

The girl looked at him through wet eyes, as if he was moronic. "Why, kill Bonnie Tempest," she explained. "He couldn't have. I know."

Hart's lips suddenly felt numb. It was an effort for him to speak. "How do you know?"

Peggy told him, "Because she isn't dead. I saw her myself in Ensenada less than four months ago."

"You're drunk."

Peggy bobbed her head in agreement. "That's right." She dried her eyes with the back of one hand. "I feel like I'm flying through space. But I wasn't drunk when I saw Bonnie. She had her red hair dyed black." She cupped her own meager breasts. "And she had these pulled in real tight to make her look flat where she isn't. She was using the name Señora Alveredo Montez and pretending she was a rich widow from some place in Venezuela."

The story was fantastic. It couldn't be true. Hart lit a cigarette and averted his head to keep from blowing smoke in the girl's face. "You mean you saw a girl who resembled Bonnie Tempest."

Peggy rolled her head on the pillow. "No. It was Bonnie Tempest. I know her. Assorted Artists handled her for a time. And she used to come into the office all the time and throw tantrums about what she claimed were lousy bookings until they got disgusted with her and tore up her contract."

Hart played along with the gag. At least he hoped it was a gag. "And just what were you doing in Ensenada?"

Instead of answering the question, Peggy sat up on the bed and brushing the sheet off her lap, announced belligerently, "I want another drink."

"You stay put," Hart told her. "I'll get it."

He found his shorts on the floor under her red coolie coat and put them on, then walked into the kitchenette and put a quarter of a glass of gin in an Old-fashioned glass and an equal amount of water.

When he returned to the bedroom Peggy was sitting on the edge of the bed with her head bent over, examining the perfection of her thighs. "I'm very pretty, aren't I?" she asked.

"Very," Hart assured her.

"As pretty as Bonnie Tempest?"

Hart sighed. "I'm certain I wouldn't know." He gave her the glass and watched her drink the mixture. "Now tell me what you were doing in Ensenada."

The girl's articulation was becoming thicker and thicker. "I went there with Mr. Sutton."

Hart was relieved. The statement was a breath of cool, fresh air blowing through the small room. That he didn't believe. That he knew was untrue. He knew Ben Sutton too well. Ensenada was a popular resort, some miles down the coast in Baja California. The Mexicans were a practical people. They didn't ask questions. They reasoned if a man was financially able to pay for a hotel room he was adult enough to know what he wanted to do in it and with whom he wanted to do it. For that reason it was popular with a good many Hollywood producers, casting directors, business and agency men. He'd even flown down a few times himself. But not Ben Sutton. The jovial head of Assorted Artists liked a few friendly drinks. He would rather play poker than eat. But Ben didn't chase. He didn't have to. He was married to one of the most beautiful girls in Hollywood and was very much in love with her and she with him.

"I don't believe you," Hart said flatly.

Sitting slumped as she was, Peggy's hair had fallen over her eyes. She parted it to look up at him. "I did so. But not the way you're thinking. Mr. Sutton had to fly down to see Grace Thomas about playing the lead in a Playhouse 90 production. His regular secretary had Asiatic flu so he took me along to make notes and type the contract."

She sounded like she was telling the truth. "I see," he said grimly. "And it was then that you saw this South American woman who looked like Bonnie Tempest."

Peggy lay back on the bed. "It didn't look like. It was Bonnie Tempest."

"You spoke to her?"

The girl on the bed grew coy. "What? And tip her off that I'd recognized her and let Harry off the hook?" She lifted her hand and waggled a finger at Hart. "Not by the hair on your chinny-chin-chin. He's going to the gas chamber. And I'm just the little girl who's going to send him there." She squirmed like an amorous little kitten and her slight body arced in a taut bow as the alcohol she'd consumed burned away the last of her inhibitions. "Now why don't you come back to bed and let's get even with Harry again."

Hart had never felt less amorous. He wished he knew how much of what she said was the truth and how much the product of an over-stimulated imagination. One way or another he had to know.

He said, "In a few minutes, perhaps," and left the room.

He knew Ben's office phone number but had to look up his home number in the directory. The phone rang for a long time. When Sutton answered, his voice was fogged with sleep.

"Yes—?"

"Doc Hart, here, Ben," Hart said. "I'm sorry to trouble you this time of morning, but this could be very important."

SEPTEMBER 2, 1958
3:59 A.M.

Sutton cleared his throat. "Not at all, Doc. Glad to be able to do something for you. Just what do you want?"

"Do you have a girl," Hart began. He corrected himself. "That is, did you have a girl working for you by the name of Peggy Jones?"

"That's right," Sutton said. "Until about two months ago. Then she suddenly quit without notice and I haven't seen her since. Why?"

Hart ignored the question. "Now tell me this, Ben. While she was in your employ, did you take her down to Ensenada on a business trip?"

"I did."

"Do you recall the occasion?"

"I do. I was trying to get Grace Thomas for a Playhouse 90 script and my regular secretary had the flu. Why? What's up, Doc?"

"I'm not positive, but I may be right in the middle of a very nasty situation. How long were you in Ensenada?"

"Two days and two nights, as I recall. Then I didn't close the deal because Grace wanted more money for the part than they were willing to pay."

Hart felt for his cigarettes and realized, wryly, that all he had on were his shorts. He was glad Sutton couldn't see as well as hear him. He'd never live it down.

"Think back, Ben," he said. "While you were in Ensenada with her, did Peggy say anything about having seen someone she knew?"

Sutton was silent a moment. "N-no. Not that I recall. If you know her you know she's a pretty little thing but very quiet and reserved. At least she was with me. She never had much to say, outside of business."

"You're positive?"

"I'm positive," Sutton said. He added, "But, wait just a moment, Doc."

"Yes—?"

"I do remember her coming back to the hotel that second afternoon with a rather smug sort of a cat and canary expression on her face. It was so out of character I commented on it."

"What did she say?"

"Nothing."

"Nothing?"

"Nothing. Just shrugged it off. But I remember now that she kept smiling all afternoon, you know, like she was *very* pleased about something."

"It could be she was," Hart said. "Well, thanks a lot, Ben."

He cradled the phone and returned to the bedroom. The brown-haired girl's abortive spurt of rekindled passion hadn't been as strong as the gin she'd drunk. She'd forgotten all about getting even with Harry again. The rumpled sheet was kicked down to the foot of the bed and she was lying on her back, eyes closed, small breasts rising and falling in cadence with the easy rhythm of her breathing.

Hart took a cigarette from the package on the bed table and studied the sleeping girl through the flame of his lighter. There were two things he could do. He could dress and walk out the door and forget he'd ever seen her. He could try to sober her up enough to talk. He decided on the latter course. It was the army game all over again. If position in a community gave a man certain privileges, it also imposed certain obligations. If Bonnie Tempest was alive he had to know. He wouldn't be able to live with himself knowing that he'd taken an active part in condemning an innocent man to death.

He dressed, still studying Peggy.

If he knew women, and he thought he did, by morning Peggy wouldn't talk. Nothing would make her talk. She'd only said as much as she had under the stimuli of drink and sex and pent-up emotion. By morning, hating Harry Cotton as she did, determined to be even with him, wanting him to die, she would deny everything she'd said.

Hart sighed and walked into the bathroom to put a towel to soak. As he waited for the fibers to absorb the cold water, he studied his face in the mirror over the basin. A pleasant-looking man of medium height stared back at him.

"Look, Doc," Hart told his reflection. "You re getting too old for this sort of jazz. It's about time you began to stick to your mortar and pestle."

He returned to the bedroom and raised the girl to a sitting position. First he held the cold towel to the back of neck, then wiped her face and chest with it.

"Peggy. Come on. Snap out of it."

The girl lay limp in his arms, breathing rhythmically. Hart tried slapping her lightly. It had no effect. He would have to try something more astringent. He searched the medicine chest in the bathroom for spirits of ammonia and then the kitchenette for the more common household variety, without success.

He stood a moment, undecided. Then he knew what he had to do. His store was less than a mile away. He could get what he needed there.

He found the girl's purse but her keys weren't in it. After a moment's hesitation, he set the lock on the door so he could get back in and closed the door gently behind him. In the condition she was in, Peggy wouldn't go anywhere during the few minutes he'd be gone.

The wind was still off the desert. The morning was warm with another hot day in prospect. He opened the door of his car, then stood a moment looking back at the building he'd just left. Peggy's apartment was the only one with a light. As far as he could tell no nosy insomniac getting up for a glass of water, to go to the bathroom or to brood on the state of the world, had seen him enter or leave. Hart hoped he could keep it that way, then smiled at himself. It was remarkable how proper and respectable a man could become immediately following the gratification of an appetite that a few moments before had impelled him to kick down doors.

There was no pedestrian traffic on the side street and little on the boulevard. Hart drove the distance in minutes. He sat a moment in his parked car in front of his store, admiring it. He had reason. Ignoring the substantial sum of money involved, the drugstore, three times as large as most, represented uncounted hours of hard work and worry, besides sacrificing, in his younger days, the normal goal of any normal young man, a wife and family. If any of the banal old sayings were true, the one about a man paying for what he got should stand as Number One in the Old Saw Parade. The hell of it was the saying applied to his misdeeds as well as his good ones.

He crossed the walk and unlocked the front door. The lights were on as a precaution against thieves, so all night every corner of the store's interior could be seen from the walk.

Air-conditioning made the interior a welcome relief from the outside heat. It smelled clean and fresh, of expensive perfumes and good food and good tobaccos laced together with the pungent, intangible medicinal odor of all drugstores. The porters and clean-up women had long since finished with their work. The wide aisles were spotless. The fronts and tops of the glass showcases gleamed. Hart was impatient with himself all over again. A man spent three-fourths of his life fighting for and surrounded by antisepsis. He made a fetish of it. Then, in the most personal matter possible, he made a fool of himself with a girl he'd known less than an hour, a girl he'd picked up at a bus stop.

"Then get in. I'll take you home," he'd told her.

He walked directly to the prescription counter and got what he thought he might need, including some bromides and a sedative to quiet Peggy's nerves and put her back to sleep after he'd talked to her.

He still didn't know what he intended to do, what he could do, if he decided Peggy was telling the truth, if she insisted she'd seen the woman supposedly dead. Just how did he impart the information to the State Attorney's office without revealing the manner in which he'd obtained it?

Despite the air conditioning it suddenly felt as hot in the store as it had in the jury room and in Peggy's small bedroom. Hart took a piece of tissue from the box on the work counter and blotted his damp face with it.

Even if Peggy's story was true, even if in her little twisted mind she was willing to let Harry Cotton go to his death for a crime he hadn't committed, he didn't see how either he or she could prove the truth of her statement. And without tangible proof, the State Attorney would do one of three things. He'd laugh him out of his office. He'd commit him for psychopathic observation. He'd order him locked up for the same lascivious conduct the State had proved against Bonnie and Cotton. True, he was a reputable businessman.

But the whole thing was a matter of semantics. No matter how sweet a rose smelled it usually had thorns, and stripped to fundamentals, if one wanted to be factual about it, a romantic vagabond could be called a frigging bum. It all depended on where you sat, whether you are being tried or you were sitting on the jury.

Hart made his decision. He would sober Peggy enough so she could talk. He would force her to repeat what she'd told him. Then if he decided she was telling the truth he would phone his lawyer and ask Kelly for advice. Kelly would know what to do. He would know how to pass the information along and institute an investigation that could lead to a new trial for Cotton without involving either Peggy or himself.

He was probably making more of a fool of himself by putting any credence in the girl's story. The odds were twelve to one against its being true. Bonnie had to be dead. Cotton had killed her for her diamonds and pushed her body through a porthole, reasoning that even if he was caught the State wouldn't be able to establish a corpus delicti.

Hart made sure he had everything he wanted and started down the aisle behind the wall counter and stopped, a sick, sinking feeling in the pit of his stomach as he discovered he wasn't alone in the store. Someone was hiding in one of the booths in the fountain section. He could see the distorted, crouched-over reflection in the front plate glass window. There was a revolver in a drawer back of the cigar counter. He got the gun and walked cautiously back the way he'd come and through the store room and the kitchen to come upon the intruder from behind. Ten feet from the booth he said quietly, "All right. Come out of there with your hands up."

There was no answer from the booth. Hart took three more cautious steps and felt foolish. The reflection he'd seen was Gerta's. Her short ponytail sticking up jauntily from the back of her head, which was resting on her arms on the table, the blonde girl was sleeping as peacefully as Peggy had been when he'd last seen her. On the table beside her, a few inches from her crooked elbow, was a three-layer chocolate cake, his favorite, across the top of which the pastry chef had written in white frosting an ornate:

WELCOME HOME DOC

Hart reconstructed the scene. Manny and Gerta and his other employees had planned a party for him as soon as they'd learned the jury had come in. They'd waited in the closed store for hours. While they were waiting he was engaged in horizontal calisthenics with a psychosomatic girl whose only interest in the exercise was to get even with a man who'd given her good reason to hate him. The others had finally gone home but Gerta had stayed on. He could almost hear her youthful voice saying, "Well, gee. Somebody has to wait. Somebody has to be here to tell Doc we're glad he's back."

Hart felt depressed. He'd let her down. He'd let all of them down. He started to put his hands on the girl's shoulder and thought better of the idea. The best thing he could do would be to conclude his business with Peggy as quickly as he could and return and escort Gerta home.

The short drive back to Peggy's apartment seemed endless. He hadn't realized until he was out on the walk that he still had the gun in his hand. Rather than unlock the store again he dropped the gun into his side coat pocket. Before he'd gone two blocks he wished he hadn't. The heavy gun sagged the light material of his summer-weight sports coat and caused the collar to pull down, rubbing his neck.

To add to his annoyance, during the few minutes he'd been gone, someone had maneuvered a late-model car into the parking space in front of Peggy's building and he had to drive up the hill and past the next intersection before he could find a place to park.

By the time he walked the long block back to the building his body was drenched with perspiration. He was tired and irritable. The shabby flight of stairs to the second floor seemed very steep. The door he'd left closed was ajar and swinging gently in the hot breeze that wafted up the stair well from time to time as if to remind the sleeping tenants that at one time, not too far in the past, the City of the Angels had been an arid desert.

Hart closed the door and locked it. After the air-conditioned vastness of his drugstore, the apartment had the feel of a hot box in a steam room. It smelled of stale cigarette smoke and gin and spent flesh. As he passed the door of the dimly lighted bedroom he looked in. Peggy was still lying motionless on her back but she'd thrown up one bare knee in a convulsive gesture of abandonment.

Hart worked the sour taste from his mouth and walked into the kitchenette where he arranged the medications on the sink. Then he measured a small quantity of spirits of ammonia into a glass, added water and carried the glass and a vial of pungent smelling-salts into the tiny room lighted only by the thin yellow shaft knifing through the crack of the partially open bathroom door.

"All right. Let's wake up, Peggy," he said.

One of the pillows had fallen to the floor beside the bed. Hart kicked it out of his way and set the glass on the bed table. Then holding the vial of salts in his right hand, he stooped to slip his left arm under the girl's shoulders. He sensed motion behind him as a dark shadow detached itself from the wall.

Hart thought, "The open door. Of course. It wasn't the wind."

Immediately alerted, but too late, he dropped the vial of smelling-salts and attempted to claw the gun from his pocket as he turned and only succeeded in deflecting the viciously swung blackjack from the back of his head to his right temple. There was no immediate pain. He only had a sensation of falling, a short fall terminated by an impact with yielding flesh. Then the small bedroom seemed to explode and take off in a blinding white flash with the speed of a guided missile being launched into space.

Hart lay for a long time after consciousness came back, attempting to orient himself. He'd returned to Peggy's apartment. He'd fixed a mixture of spirits of ammonia. He'd carried it into the bedroom. He'd stooped to lift her and someone had stepped away from the wall and sapped him twice, on his right temple and from the pain in the back of his head, at the base of his skull.

He forced himself to open his eyes. He was kneeling beside the bed in an attitude of prayer, his right cheek resting on Peggy's right thigh. The girl's eyes were open but she wasn't looking at him. He pushed himself to a sitting position and turned on the bright bed lamp.

Bonnie Tempest might still be alive. She might be dead, as the State had alleged and proven. But either way, the wife of the man condemned to die for killing her wasn't going to affirm or deny it. Hart knew just by looking at the girl, but confirmed what he knew by holding his cheek close to her mouth, then feeling for a nonexistent pulse under the small mound of lifeless flesh covering her heart.

As far as he could tell, there were no marks of violence on the slight body but the pillow on the floor and the girl's position were explained. Life was fragile. It didn't take much to extinguish it. The simple act of holding a pillow over the face of an intoxicated girl for a few minutes was sufficient. Peggy would never be hurt again. She'd stopped hating Harry Cotton. She was finished with getting even with him, finished with passion and gratitude, with giving and taking, with living.

Hart walked into the other room and picked up the pitcher of ice-cube-diluted Martinis, took a mouthful of the mixture, spat it out and went into the kitchenette and drank from the neck of the almost emptied bottle of gin. It helped some but not much. When he tried to set the bottle back on the sink it dropped from his trembling fingers and shattered on the floor.

He'd had it. This time he'd bought the big one. The first thing the medical examiner would determine would be that Peggy was dead. The second that shortly before her death, willing or forced, she'd been intimate with a man. No one would believe his fantastic story that the girl had been the aggressor, that she'd insisted on going to bed with him to get even with Harry Cotton, or that she'd sworn that Bonnie Tempest was still alive. It was the type of story the police would expect of a reasonably imaginative, successful businessman trying to pry himself out of a jam.

The police would reason he'd picked up the girl. He'd had her. Then because he wanted her again and she refused, or on the threat of a nasty scandal she'd demanded more money than he'd been willing to pay, or merely because they'd had a drunken struggle and he'd played a little too rough, what had begun as a casual bit of sex had ended in tragedy.

The police had half a dozen motives to choose from, none of them true but all of them plausible.

Avoiding glancing into the bedroom as he passed the door, Hart returned to the living room and stood a long time looking at the phone. He should call the police at once. He was afraid to call them.

Hart knew how Harry Cotton had felt in the cabin of the Deering yacht when he claimed to have awakened and found Bonnie gone. Every throbbing nerve in his body impelled him toward one course, erase every trace of his presence in the apartment and run. It didn't matter where as long as he got out of the place.

Instead, he picked up the phone and dialed 116 and asked to be connected with the Hollywood Precinct Station. When the desk sergeant answered his phone, Hart said what he had to say in a rush.

"This is John Hart calling from 5437 La Paloma Drive, Apartment 10. I want to report a murder."

SEPTEMBER 2, 1958
12:05 P.M.

In the private washroom off the State Attorney's office, Hart changed into the freshly pressed suit and clean linen Manny had been allowed to bring to the detective bureau to replace the suit and linen Hart had been wearing when he'd been taken into custody and which Inspector Garcia wanted sent to the laboratory.

Before putting on the clean shirt, Hart rinsed his face with cold water and wet and combed his hair.

"How do you feel?" Kelly asked him.

Hart looked into the mirror over the bowl and studied his lawyer's reflection. "Not too bad," he said, finally.

To his own surprise he didn't. During the early morning hours at Peggy's apartment, in the precinct station, during the longer hours of questioning at the detective bureau, repeating the same story time after time, he'd been so tired and frightened he had a hard time talking coherently. Now, for some reason, he felt more composed. He turned and leaned his buttocks against the bowl.

"What do you think, Bill?"

A tall man, thin to the point of emaciation, the lawyer lit one of the cigarettes he habitually chain-smoked and blew smoke through his nose. "About what?"

"Do they believe me?"

Kelly spoke, looking at Inspector Garcia. "That's hard to say, Doc. It's difficult to follow the ramifications of the official police mind. But just keep on telling the truth. So you were a fool. They can't hang you for that. If the State threw the book at every man who, at one time or another, has made a chump of himself over an attractive little piece of quail, three-fourths of the male population of California, including Inspector Garcia here, would be doing time."

Garcia gathered up the clothes Hart had taken off and gave them to a plain-clothes man standing by. "How true," the inspector sighed. "The trick is not to get caught." He inclined his head toward the door. "You know where to take these, Tom."

"Yes, sir," the officer said and left the room.

Hart put on the clean shirt and knotted a new Countess Mara tie. "What are you fellows going to do with me, Inspector?"

Garcia shrugged. "If it was up to me, I'd book you if only to keep you handy until the grand jury can convene and vote a true bill. Frankly, I don't know whether you killed the babe or not. But one thing is very certain."

"What?"

"Someone did. You sure you didn't see anyone in the apartment when you got back from your store?"

"I'm positive." Hart touched the back of his head with great care. "I merely sensed motion behind me."

"And you can't remember the make of car you saw in the parking space you'd vacated?"

"No."

"All right," Garcia said. "Let's go back in the office."

Hart used a soiled towel to flick a film of dust from the shoes Manny had brought him. "What do you think, Bill? I mean if they do book me, will I be admissable to bail?"

Kelly refused to commit himself. "That's hard to say. But I do know I would just as soon be in your spot as the one the State Attorney's in."

"I don't get you."

"Look, Doc," the lawyer said, wryly, "don't be so naive. How would you like it if you had just successfully prosecuted a man for murder, brilliantly, I might add, and then one of your jurors turned up with a fantastic yarn that on his way home from the verdict he picked up the condemned man's wife and that while they were being intimate, on three quarters of an hour's acquaintance, he insisted that said wife not only told him she was doing what she was doing to get even with her husband but she was also—what was the word she used?"

"Crucifying him."

"That's right. That she was nailing her husband to a cross by keeping her pretty mouth shut because she, herself, in person, had seen the woman he was supposed to have murdered alive and well four months after her supposed murder."

"I see what you mean," Hart said.

Kelly lit a fresh cigarette. "If by any chance what Peggy told you should hold up, he's finished both professionally and politically."

Inspector Garcia opened the door. "All right, Hart. Let's go."

Hart walked through the door into the office and sat in the chair Garcia indicated. A man about Hart's age, State Attorney Manson was fingering through a sheaf of papers on a clipboard. He glanced up as Hart sat down.

"What was the name you say the deceased said that Bonnie was using in Ensenada?"

"Señora Alveredo Montez."

Manson found the report he wanted. "That was the name I recalled." He sighed as he laid the clipboard on his desk. "And it may interest you to know, Mr. Hart, that this office contacted the Ensenada police some hours ago and they have just reported that, on the approximate date you gave, no such woman was registered in any of the hotels in Ensenada."

Hart couldn't think of anything to say so he didn't say anything.

Manson continued, "Please don't misunderstand me. This office is not trying to whitewash this case. It is as much our duty to protect the innocent as it is to prosecute the guilty. And to that end we will use every means available to us to ascertain if such a person exists."

"I'm certain you will," Hart said.

Manson picked up the clipboard again. "But supposing we admit the dead girl did see someone who resembled the late Mrs. Deering. In my opinion it was just a resemblance. You, yourself, sat in judgment on the evidence for seven weeks and yours was one of twelve opinions that Bonnie Tempest is dead, that the only way she could have gotten out of the cabin, outside of the fantastic assumption that Bonnie wriggled through that porthole herself and swam a mile and a half through a heavy sea to shore, was for Cotton to deliberately force her dead body through the porthole."

"That's right," Hart admitted.

"Now, as to you, Mr. Hart," Manson said, "I'm afraid you're going to be obliged to stand trial. I don't think the grand jury is going to believe your story." He paused a moment and studied Hart's face before continuing. "But I do. In your business you have to know drugs and their chemical reactions. In mine, I have to know men. You were born in this city. You've lived here all your life. In checking back we haven't been able to find anything more serious than a few minor traffic violations against you. You're a man of property and standing in your community, a civic leader, and while, being male myself, I can readily understand how you might stay with a young woman who attracted you, as you admit you did with this Miss Peggy Jones, nee Mrs. Harry Cotton, I can't believe you'd kill her."

"I didn't," Hart said. "After she'd told me what she did and I called Ben Sutton and went back to find her passed out—"

"I know," Manson stopped him. "We've been over the same ground fifty times. And if your story is true, and for the moment I'm assuming it is, during the time you were gone some party known only as X entered the door you left on the latch and brought about Mrs. Cotton's death by suffocation."

Kelly lit a fresh cigarette from the stub of the one he was smoking. "So where does that leave my client, Mr. State's Attorney?"

Manson studied the lawyer's face. "If I book him on any lesser charge than murder I suppose you have a writ in mind."

"Not in mind. Drawn up. And a judge ready to sign it."

"And if I book Hart on suspicion of murder?"

"You just said you didn't think he'd killed the girl."

"I don't."

Kelly offered him an out. "Then why don't you release him on his own recognizance as a reputable businessman? Or in my custody, if you prefer. I'll give you my word that if and when the grand jury does indict him, I will surrender him to this office as soon as we are notified."

Manson considered the matter a moment, then nodded. "In this instance, taking into account both your own and Hart's standing in the community, I'm going to do just that, counselor. Until such time as the grand jury does or does not vote a true bill, I'm going to parole Mr. Hart into your custody."

"Thank you, sir," Hart said. "I assure you I'm not going to leave town and run out on a half million dollar investment."

Manson said, dryly, "I'm taking that into consideration." He nodded at Garcia. "You may give Mr. Hart his personal possessions, Inspector."

Garcia took a brown manila envelope from his pocket and handed it to Hart. As he returned his watch to the proper place on his wrist and his fountain pen and wallet and keys and change to their proper pockets, Hart asked, "This means I'm free to go?"

"For now."

Hart stood up. "Now I wonder if I may make a rather unusual request."

"What?"

"Might I talk to Cotton? It doesn't have to be alone. Inspector Garcia can be with me."

"And just why do you want to talk to Cotton?"

"I don't know exactly. I guess I'm hoping he may be able to tell me something that will help me later, if I do have to stand trial."

"Such as?"

"If he knows anyone who might have had reason to follow Peggy and myself to her apartment, anyone who would have reason to kill her."

"For giving herself to you?"

"Or for some other reason."

Inspector Garcia protested, "Oh, come now. This whole thing is very irregular."

Manson shrugged. "Agreed. So let him talk to Cotton, Inspector. But you go with him."

Hart waited with Kelly in the corridor outside the office while Inspector Garcia made the necessary arrangements to have Cotton brought down from his cell and taken into one of the interrogation rooms.

"What do you think?" Hart asked Kelly. "Why isn't he booking me?"

Kelly shrugged. "You heard the man. Personally, I think that fantastic story Peggy told you has made him wonder if he has convicted an innocent man. And I think he hopes if a mistake has been made, you'll help him wash his dirty linen."

"How?"

"By getting yourself killed. Figure it out yourself. If Bonnie is miraculously alive and Peggy was killed because she knew it, the smart thing for the killer to do now is to kill you. Then Manson figures he'll nab him and everyone will be off the hook."

"Except me."

"Except you."

Inspector Garcia came out of the office. "They're bringing him down now."

Even after seeing him daily for seven weeks, Hart could hardly recognize the youth. Now he was condemned to die, his appearance had changed overnight. His big frame seemed to have shrunk. His eyes were already dead, buried in their hollow sockets. He walked like an old man.

"I recognize you," he said to Hart. "You were one of the jurors."

"That's right," Hart admitted.

Cotton opened his mouth as if to curse him and didn't have the strength. "Okay. So you found me guilty," he said, finally. "What kind of a weird kick are you getting by coming around to rub it in? Guilty in the first degree. That's the verdict the twelve of you decided on, isn't it?"

Hart asked, quietly, "Did you kill Bonnie, Harry? Off the record. Nothing can hurt you now."

Cotton was silent a long time. Then he said, "I don't know. I don't think so. No matter how drunk a guy got, it seems he'd remember a thing like that. If I hadn't taken those damn diamonds you wouldn't even have had a motive." He shook his head. "No. For all the good it does me now, I don't think I killed her."

"Your wife Peggy didn't think so either," Hart said. "In fact, last night she told me you couldn't have killed Bonnie."

Cotton laughed weakly. "I'll bet. I'll just bet. I saw her sitting there every day, enjoying every minute of it, gloating over me getting my lumps." He stopped laughing and both his eyes and his voice turned bleak. "Not that I blame the kid. I guess I gave her a pretty rough time."

Hart was deliberately brutal. "She's dead, Harry. Peggy was murdered last night. I think because she told me you couldn't be guilty. She told me that four months after you were supposed to have killed her, she saw Bonnie alive in Ensenada."

There was a plain deal table in the interrogation room. Cotton gripped the edge of it to steady himself. "Look, fellow. Don't kid about a thing like that."

"I wouldn't," Hart assured him.

"And Peggy is dead?"

"That's right."

Cotton fumbled for cigarettes he didn't have and Hart offered him his package. Cotton thumbed a cigarette into his mouth and accepted a light. "Poor kid," he said quietly. "There was only one thing the matter with her. She didn't have any sense. No matter how I treated her or how many other girls I had, she kept right on loving me. You say she's dead?"

"Yes."

"But before she died she said she'd seen Bonnie?"

"Yes."

"Then why didn't she come forward?" Cotton answered his own question. "Of course. She wanted me to die. That way she'd have me all to herself. Who killed her?"

Hart saw no point in confusing the issue by telling the condemned man he, himself, was under suspicion. He said, "The police don't know as yet. Do you know of anyone who had reason to dislike her?"

Cotton shook his head. "No one. She was a right kid all the way."

Inspector Garcia was anxious to terminate the interview. "If you're finished with him, Mr. Hart, I'll send him back upstairs."

"Just one more question," Hart said. "It wasn't brought out too clearly at the trial. Think back. Think carefully and then tell me this, Harry. Who picked up whom at Ciro's?"

"Bonnie picked me up," Cotton said promptly. He was frank about it. "Of course I didn't put up any struggle. I was on the make. I was looking for a babe. And I knew she was in the chips as soon as I saw all the ice she was wearing."

"And after she picked you up who kept the party going?"

"I'd say it was mutual." Cotton added, "But it was her idea to go to the yacht. I remember arguing with that old Joe in Santa Monica, the one who testified we rented a unit from him and burned a mattress. Then the next thing I knew we were off the Santa Monica pier in a speed boat. And I wasn't too happy about it but she inferred I was chicken, so I went along with the gag."

Hart considered the information. It could be the interview hadn't been a complete waste of time. He'd learned two things that the lawyer appointed by the court to defend Cotton hadn't brought out at the trial. Bonnie had made the first advances. It had been Bonnie's idea to go to the yacht. He caught at the glimmering of an idea that refused to solidify. "Now tell me this," he said. "How did she act during the time you were together?"

"You mean Bonnie?" Cotton rested his hips on the table. "That's funny."

"What's funny?"

"That you should ask me that. I've been thinking about it all morning.

And looking back I would say she was frightened."

"Frightened of you?"

"No."

"Of her husband?"

"No."

"Then who?"

Cotton shook his head. "I don't know. It was more like she was frightened of *something* than someone." He was silent a moment, then continued, "Yeah. That was it. Right from the very start, between drinks and parties, she was all the time going to the window and looking out. Acting wild and not always talking straight."

"What did she say?"

"I don't know. I didn't pay much attention to her at the time. I thought she was drunk."

Hart didn't say anything.

Garcia returned his hat to his head. His smile was cynical. "You should have thought up this gag during your trial, Cotton. Okay. Just tell me one thing. If you didn't kill her, who did? And how did you get her out of that cabin?"

Cotton protested, "But Mr. Hart, here, just said that Peggy swore she saw Bonnie alive in Ensenada."

"Forget it," Inspector Garcia said. "Forget it. If your wife saw anyone in Ensenada it was just some babe who resembled Bonnie. Now go ahead. Answer my question. If you didn't kill Bonnie, who did? And how did you get her out of the cabin?"

Cotton's cigarette was burning his fingers. He held it a moment longer, as if his searing flesh had already lost the power of feeling, then carefully placed the stub in the ash tray on the table. "I don't know," he said, quietly. "If I could tell you that I wouldn't be in the spot I am in."

SEPTEMBER 2, 1958
1:23 P.M.

Kelly was waiting in the corridor outside the door of the State's Attorney's office. "Did you get anything out of him, Doc?" he asked.

Hart shook his head. "Nothing concerning Peggy. However Cotton claims that Bonnie was deathly afraid of something or someone."

Inspector Garcia was amused. "Look, Mr. Hart. Use your head. If you were a girl married to umpteen million dollars and you were cheating on your husband, don't you think you might look out the window once in a while?"

"I probably would," Hart admitted.

The two uniformed turnkeys who'd brought Cotton down from his cell escorted him toward the elevator that serviced the cell blocks. As they passed the group standing in the corridor, Cotton held back, forcing the officers to stop. His face was contorted with anger as he faced Hart. "These boys tell me you were with Peggy when she died. They tell me you did it to her and then put a pillow over her face to keep her from telling on you."

"We didn't know he didn't know," one of the turnkeys explained to Inspector Garcia. "It's in all the morning papers."

"That's not so, Cotton," Hart said. "I was in her apartment, yes, but I didn't kill her."

"That's what you say," Cotton said. "And that's what comes of having money. I'm going to die for the murder of a dame they don't even know is dead. You kill a nice kid like Peggy and here you are walking around, palling with the cops, even coming in here asking me questions."

Before the guards could stop him he smashed his fist into Hart's mouth.

Garcia inclined his head toward the elevator. "Take him back upstairs."

The guards forced Cotton down the hall, struggling and cursing as he went.

"You see how it's going to be," the inspector said. "Even your best friends will tell you. If I were you I don't know but what I'd just as soon be sitting in a cell until I was either convicted or acquitted."

He entered the State's Attorney's office and closed the door behind him.

Kelly was concerned about Hart. "That was quite a wallop. You okay, Doc?"

Hart took his handkerchief away from his mouth. "Yes, I'm all right. He just cut my lip a little."

"We'd better go down in one of the service elevators and out the side way," Kelly said. "They've managed to keep them off the floor here but there's a mob of reporters and photographers on the main floor."

As he rode down in the elevator, successive waves of weariness swept over Hart. So much had happened it seemed almost incredible that only a little over twelve hours had passed since he'd persuaded young Mrs. Slagle to change her vote to guilty. He realized Kelly was talking to him.

"While you were talking to Cotton," the lawyer said, "I called Jim Masterson and told him to put two of his best men on the case. The police will follow up what they have but I don't imagine they'll do much digging. The way I see it, Manson thinks your story is a phony but he doesn't dare take a chance that you may be telling the truth."

Kelly lit another of his endless chain of cigarettes. "There's a lot more here than has boiled up so far. And our job is to ferret it out before the grand jury indicts you. How tired are you, Doc?"

"More numb than tired."

"I figured that." Kelly led the way out a side door and through the maze of cars in the official parking lot to a private parking lot almost a block distant. "So here's what I want you to do. I want you to drive out to Beverly Hills and talk to Deering."

"Talk to Deering?"

"Yes."

"Why me?"

"Because he'll talk more freely to you than he will to a private agency man. After all, you were one of the jurors who convicted the man charged with killing his wife. Find out all you can about his life with Bonnie. You know, how he came to marry her in the first place and how they got along before she went back to drinking. And by all means, follow up what Cotton said about her being afraid and ask him if he knows what she was afraid of."

Hart's lip was bleeding again. He pressed his handkerchief to it. "If you say so, I'll try. But I doubt if he'll even talk to me."

Manny had gone back to the store but Gerta saw them coming and slipped out from behind the wheel of Hart's big cream-colored convertible and walked a few steps to meet them. The girl didn't even try to smile.

"Did anyone follow you?" Kelly asked her.

Gerta shook her head. "No. At least I don't think so. After Manny gave the clean clothes to one of Inspector Garcia's men, he made a crack about us having to get right back to the store. Then we drove here and parked like you told us to and he took a taxi."

"Good," Kelly said. "Doc's in enough trouble without being pestered by reporters." He gave Gerta his own car keys and nodded at a blue sedan two cars down. "Now you and I are going to switch cars. I'll drive Doc's car back past the building as if I'm going to pick him up somewhere. If I know the newspaper boys they'll spot me and start tailing me. Meanwhile you scoot out the other way, with you, Gerta, doing the driving." He looked at Hart. "And you keep scrunched down until Gerta's sure you're not being followed."

It sounded slightly melodramatic to Hart. On the other hand he wasn't in any mood to fend off a horde of reporters asking questions, especially the type of questions they were bound to ask. "How's this affecting business?" he asked the girl.

She looked at the tip of her open-toed shoes. "Like crazy. The store has been swamped with locals and tourists all morning. They're crowding in in the hope of seeing you."

"Well, let's get going," Kelly said. "Call me after you've talked to Deering, Doc." He got into Hart's car. "Oh, yes. Just one more thing. And this could be very important. Jim Masterson said I should ask you if anyone saw you pick up Peggy or if you met anyone you knew on your way to her apartment."

Hart recalled the incident of the beeping horn. "Yes, they did."

"Who?"

"Mr. Deering and his chauffeur."

"You told Inspector Garcia this?"

"I did."

"Did anyone else see you pick her up?"

"Probably. There was quite a crowd coming out of the building. Then on the way to her place I stopped a minute to talk to Joe Feeny and Matt Hooper."

Kelly thought a minute. "I think we can scratch them. But while you are talking to Deering, if he will talk, find out all you can about his chauffeur."

The lawyer made a vee with his first and second fingers and drove out of the lot. Gerta opened the door of the blue sedan and slipped behind the wheel. "Where do you want me to drive you?" she asked Hart.

Hart sighed as he got in beside her. Judging from the way she was acting he'd hurt Gerta badly. Despite the fact that she was merely an employee, the girl had a crush on him. He'd seen it developing for months. Because he was a pretty good Joe in general, because he'd been good to her, along with all his employees, because he knew and was known by most of the celebrities of the show business world to which she wanted to belong, the girl had placed him on one of the high but very fragile pedestals peculiar to girls of her age.

There ought, Hart thought, to be some other way for a man to assuage his libido. Perhaps, some day, there would be. Perhaps some druggist, fooling around, would invent instant sex. It was an idea. A man could make a fortune if he could come up with something similar to instant coffee. Just put a teaspoonful into a cup and add hot water.

"I asked a question," Gerta said.

Hart lighted a cigarette. "Head out Wilshire or Sunset to Beverly Hills. I don't know the exact address. I'll have to stop at a phone booth on the way and look it up."

Neither of them spoke again until the girl had driven almost a mile. Then Hart tried to make his peace with her. "Look, Gerta—"

She continued to look straight ahead. "I'm sure you don't have to explain anything to me. It's none of my business how many girls you sleep with. I'm just a waitress in your drugstore. I have no interest whatsoever in your private life."

"Okay. If that's the way you want it," Hart said.

Gerta bit at her lower lip to keep it from quivering. "What's more, I know I don't mean a thing to you. You're nice to all your employees."

"I try to be."

"I'm just angry with myself."

"Why?"

Gerta turned wet eyes on him. "Because I almost made a fool of myself. I damn near died the two months you were cooped up on that jury. That's why I stayed in the store after everyone else went home last night. I was going to make you like me. You know how. I put on my best dress and made myself as pretty as I could so you would want me. I mean as a woman. Then you didn't even come. You were too busy playing stud with a girl you picked up at a bus stop."

Hart wondered if any man understood women. "But look, Gerta," he said, quietly.

"I know," she interrupted him. "How many times have you heard me say that when I gave myself to a man I was going to have a ring on my finger. But if you'd known anything at all about women, you'd have known that didn't apply to you. So it would have been wrong. Any time after the first week I came to work in the store you could have had me in the stock room, on the duck boards behind the fountain, on the corner of Hollywood and Vine, for that matter. I always wanted to be your girl. But did you ever make even one pass? No." She was crying harder now. "You didn't care how much I suffered. You always treated me like a goddam lady."

Hart sighed mentally. This was all he needed. On top of everything else a hysterical girl had to happen to him. "Look, honey," he said, gently. "Pull into the corner gas station and have them fill the tank while I use the phone directory. Then I'll take it from here."

Gerta swung the car into the station and braked in front of the pumps.

"Fill it up," Hart told the attendant, then sat a moment, undecided.

He knew from past experience there was only one way Gerta could be consoled. And he didn't want that to happen. Despite her outburst, Gerta only thought she was in love with him. In her immature mind she'd led up to her big moment, the big moment in any girl's life. She'd been all ready to lay her virginity on what she believed to be an altar of all-consuming love. Then the high priest hadn't even shown up. He'd been too busy getting euchred by another girl with her own sacrificial altar. In his mind's eye, he could still see Peggy's slight body lifted in passion.

"Now why don't you come back to bed and let's get even with Harry again."

Now she was dead and he was in trouble. He said the only thing he could think of to say. "I'm sorry, Gerta."

As he spoke, he put his hand on her arm and Gerta brushed it away. "Don't touch me."

"All right," Hart said. "I won't."

There was a directory dangling from a chain in the phone booth. Hart wrote Deering's address on the back of a prescription card and then, on impulse, he looked up Mrs. Slagle's number. He found that he would pass within a mile of her home on his way to see Deering. It might pay him to stop off and talk to her. It could be there had been some reason other than the absence of a corpus delicti that caused her to hold out as long as she had.

Gerta was still crying when he returned to the car and the youthful attendant was attempting to be gallant.

"This guy bothering you, Miss?" he asked. "Do you want me to call the cops?"

Gerta shook her head. "No."

The boy recognized Hart from his picture in the morning paper. "Hey! I thought you looked familiar," he said. "You're that guy Hart, aren't you? The one who stayed with and killed that girl last night." He picked up a tire iron. "How come you're not in jail? What are you doing running around with another young doll?"

Hart paid for the gas and slid in behind the wheel. He was no longer tired. He no longer felt numb. He was angry. He hadn't done a thing that ninety-nine out of a hundred men wouldn't have done. And now, after a lifetime of law-abiding respectability, everyone from the State's Attorney to a gasoline station attendant was ready to believe the worst of him.

"You'd better ask the police that," he said, as he put Kelly's car into gear.

"You know something, Mister," the youth called after him, "I just think I will."

Hart glanced in the rear vision mirror as he drove out of the station and merged with the traffic on the boulevard. The attendant meant what he said. He was already in the phone booth, dialing.

Gerta stopped crying and was smug. "If you'd have come back to the store last night, none of this would have happened."

Hart was short with her. "I know. You told me. You not only baked a cake. You were ready to light the candle."

Gerta blushed. "I know. I'm just being bitchy. I'm sorry. That guy made me so darn mad. From the way he looked at us you can tell he thinks you killed that girl."

"Don't you?"

Gerta shook her head so emphatically her short blonde ponytail whipped from side to side. "No, I do not. And no one could ever make me believe you did."

It was a small thing but it made Hart feel better. "Good," he said as he eased the car into motion. "If I have to stand trial I'll ask Kelly to get you to sit on the jury."

The Deering house was huge, a baronial affair of rough-hewn timber and cut field stone set well back from a winding street on a wooded hillside overlooking the city. The house was almost completely hidden by towering eucalyptus trees and a high stone wall topped by broken glass. There was an equally massive gate but it was open. Gerta was properly impressed as they drove down the leaf-covered driveway edged with flowering hibiscus and oleander bushes.

"Gee. Imagine living in a place like this and taking a chance of getting kicked out for fooling around with the hired hands."

"Imagine," Hart said, dryly.

He parked in the circular drive in front of the house. "Perhaps you'd better wait in the car."

Gerta got out on the other side. "Nothing doing." Then she grinned. "Mr. Deering might have a pretty maid."

Hart shrugged and rang the front door bell. He could hear the bell pealing inside but for a long time there was no movement behind the glass door. Then the chauffeur he'd seen driving the Deering limousine opened the door.

"Yes—?"

"My name is Hart, John Hart," Hart introduced himself. "Would you ask Mr. Deering if he'll see me for a few minutes?" When the butler-chauffeur looked dubious, he added, "Tell him I was one of the jurors on the Cotton trial."

"Oh, yes, of course," the chauffeur said. "Won't you and the young lady come in? I will inform Mr. Deering."

When he had gone, Gerta brushed up her hair with one hand and twisted her slim hips to one side in her Mid-western conception of how a member of the *haute monde* might stand. "He will inform Mr. Deering."

Hart wasn't amused. The cathedral-ceilinged living room was in keeping with the exterior of the house. It was at least forty feet wide and long enough to dwarf the concert grand piano at the far end. It was air-conditioned beyond the point of comfort.

It seemed Deering went in for masks and models as a hobby. There were half a dozen masks on the walls, most of them African primitives. Under them, standing around the room in individual glass cases, were twice that number of scaled models of famous sailing and power vessels and yachts, including the model of the Deering yacht the prosecution had used in court to demonstrate the impossibility of Bonnie Deering or anyone leaving the master cabin by any means except through the door or one of the portholes.

Gerta tried to repress a shudder and failed. "Ugh. This place gives me the creeps. Living here would be like living in a museum or in one of those—what's the name of those fancy stone places where they bury kings and rich people on top of the ground."

"Mausoleums."

"That's the word. No wonder Bonnie went out and had a time for herself now and then. Any girl would go nuts living in a place like this."

Hart turned as Deering came into the room.

"Good day, Mr. Hart," the financier smiled. "Is there something I can do for you?"

"I don't know," Hart said. "I suppose you've read the stories about me in the papers?"

Deering seemed more amused than shocked. "Yes, I have." He indicated an oversized divan. "But won't you and the young lady sit down?"

As he sat on the indicated sofa, Hart studied the broker's face. Seen close up, it wasn't as aesthetic as it appeared from a distance. Even if what Peggy had said the night before was true, if Deering reminded her of a cat she'd once had, a not quite complete boy cat, Deering hadn't lost all his interest in licking cream. He took a keen interest in Gerta's slim ankles and his eyes roved over her repeatedly.

Hart cleared his throat. "I believe you and your chauffeur saw Mrs. Cotton get into my car last night."

"Yes. And while I'd seen her every day while the trial was in progress, I must say I was surprised when I read her identity."

"So was I," Hart said, dryly. "Now let me ask you this. Did you happen to notice anyone else paying attention to us when she got into my car?"

Deering shook his head. "No, I did not."

"How about your chauffeur?"

Deering pushed one of the buttons on the desk next to his chair. "You may ask him yourself if you care to. And now while we're waiting for Mayer, let me ask you a question. Is it true, as reported in the papers, that shortly before Mrs. Cotton was killed she claimed to have seen my wife alive in Ensenada?"

"That's right. With her hair dyed black, posing as a wealthy South American widow."

Deering thought a moment. "Absurd. Bonnie is dead. Cotton killed her. You, yourself, were a member of the jury that convicted him."

"I realize that," Hart said. "But you see, I didn't kill Peggy. And I'm working on the theory that whoever did did so because she'd seen Bonnie."

"In other words, to close her mouth."

"Exactly."

Deering seemed to withdraw into himself, his friendliness much diminished. He repeated, "Absurd. Bonnie is dead. And I consider your coming here in very poor taste, Mr. Hart. What it really amounts to is that, in an effort to save your own neck, to invent a mysterious murderer with a purpose to his crime, you are insinuating that the State has convicted an innocent man, that for some reason, God only knows what, my deceased wife, Bonnie Deering, has perpetrated a hoax, that she lured Cotton to the yacht and then somehow, against all the known physical facts, she managed to get out of the cabin, leaving him to be charged with her murder."

"That's about it," Hart said.

Deering looked gravely at his well-cared for hands. Then he said, "I don't believe it."

Hart stood up. "You aren't alone. But may I ask you a very personal question? How did you and Bonnie get along?"

Deering said coldly, "I believe that came out at the trial. I was a fool to marry her. Except in rare instances, any older man is a fool to marry a young woman. You know it isn't a very pleasant experience for a man to sit in court and be forced to listen to the intimate biological details of his wife's amatory escapades with his butler, his chauffeur, the golf pro at his club and finally, the itinerant crop duster who killed her."

"No, I imagine it isn't," Hart said. "Well, sorry to have troubled you. But I wonder if you would tell me two more things before I leave."

"That depends," Deering said, thinly.

"Where is your yacht now?"

"Decommissioned in the yacht basin in Newport."

"You trust the crew?"

"Implicitly."

Hart glanced at the display of model rockets. "Now just one more thing. Do you know of any reason why, during her last spree with Cotton, Bonnie should have expressed a fear of someone or something?"

Deering was puzzled. "I don't recall that coming out at the trial."

"It didn't. Cotton told us this morning."

"I see," Deering said. "And the answer to your question is no. I can't imagine my late wife being afraid of anything unless it was losing her figure. Now, if you'll excuse me, Mayer will show you out." As the butler-chauffeur appeared in the doorway, he added, "and while you're showing them out, Mayer, Mr. Hart has a question for you. You remember seeing Mr. Hart and the young lady who was killed last night in front of the courthouse."

"Yes, sir. His car was blocking our way and I was obliged to touch my horn."

"I know that," Hart said. "What I want to know is did you notice anyone else paying any attention to us?"

The chauffeur shook his head. "I'm afraid not, sir. It had been a long and trying day for Mr. Deering and I really didn't pay much attention. I was concerned with getting him home as quickly as I could."

After the excessive air conditioning of the house, the heat of the sun felt good. Hart stood a moment enjoying the warmth on his back and shoulders before getting into Kelly's car. "What do you think?" he asked Gerta.

She was youthfully blunt. "I don't like them, either of them. Especially Mr. Deering. Could they have followed you to that girl's apartment last night?"

"They could have."

"And overheard her telling you that she'd seen Mrs. Deering in Ensenada?"

Hart thought a moment. "No. That was in the bedroom. After—" his face colored and he hastened to add, "well, afterward. But anyone standing outside the door could have heard me talking to Ben Sutton on the phone. And while I didn't tell him outright what Peggy had told me, I did ask him if he had taken her to Ensenada and if she'd said anything about seeing someone she knew."

Gerta spread her hands. "And there you are."

"Where?"

"Either Mr. Deering or his chauffeur killed that girl last night."

"Why?"

"To keep her from telling the police what she told you."

Hart protested. "But that doesn't make sense."

Gerta shrugged. "None of it does to us, including you making such a fool of yourself. Maybe Bonnie isn't dead, but for some reason Mr.

Deering wants everyone to believe she is. Was she insured?"

"Quite heavily."

"How heavily?"

"It was brought out at the trial that shortly after her marriage to Deering they took out a joint survival policy for a quarter of a million dollars."

Gerta whistled softly. "That's a lot of aspirin."

Hart was factual. "Not to people in Deering's bracket. It was also brought out that in addition to the survival policy his own life was insured for almost a million dollars."

Gerta pointed out, "But no one is trying to collect on that. Where was he on the night Cotton is supposed to have killed Bonnie?"

"Out of town. Out of the country, on business."

"Where?"

"In Mexico City."

"Did he prove it?"

"The prosecution was satisfied. And the defense didn't ask any questions."

"So what are you going to do now?"

Hart got behind the wheel of the car. It felt good just to sit down. He was so tired the taut fingers of fatigue were beginning to tune up an invisible orchestra in his head but he was too keyed up to rest. He had the odd sensation that he didn't dare to rest.

He felt impelled to run, almost as if he were running, sitting still.

So what *did* he do now?

He didn't want to go back to the store. He couldn't go to his apartment. Reporters were without doubt waiting in both places and he was in no mood or mental condition to cope with the type of questions they would ask.

"Just why did you go to her apartment, Doc?"

"How was she? Pretty good?"

"When did she tell you she was Cotton's wife, before or after you gave her the business?"

And more important:

"If you didn't kill her, who did?"

All right, Hart thought, I'll bite. Who had killed Peggy? Deering? His chauffeur? A prowler? And why? And if Peggy had been killed because she had seen Bonnie alive, why hadn't he, himself, been killed? Another blow of the sap would have done it.

As Gerta had just remarked, none of it made sense. Of course, he wasn't a detective. He was a registered pharmacist, a dispenser of pills and medicine, a compiler of chocolate sodas and banana splits, a salesman of lipsticks, skin lotions, perfumes, lollipops and tobaccos. He imagined the smart thing for him to do would be to lie low and let the private detective agency that Kelly had engaged ferret out what they could in their attempt to clear him. Against that line of reasoning, to Jim Masterson and his operatives this was just another assignment, a way to earn a day's pay. To him it could mean life or death. If he was indicted and brought to trial and failed to prove he hadn't killed Peggy, he could well join Harry Cotton in sweating out the months and weeks and days and finally hours until it was time to walk that short last mile to the lethal chamber.

Gerta was concerned. "What are you going to do?" she repeated.

Hart made up his mind. "I think I'll call Kelly," he said. "I'll have him check into the state of Deering's finances and whether or not he has tried to collect on Bonnie's life insurance. But as I know he'll try to stop us, I won't phone Kelly until we're down the coast a few miles."

"We?"

"Yes. If you want to come along for the ride."

"Where are we going?"

"Newport. I want to see that yacht again. I want to make a personal inspection of the cabin and find out for sure that there was no way Bonnie could have gotten out except by being pushed through a porthole."

"And if there is?"

"We'll drive down to Ensenada and have a look-see around there, see if we can locate the mysterious Señora Alveredo Montez whom Peggy swore was Bonnie with her red hair dyed black."

Gerta smoothed the skirt of her light summer dress over her lap. "That's fine with me. I've always wanted to see Ensenada." She nudged him. "But look at the porch as we go by. Both Mr. Deering and his chauffeur seem to be very interested in us." She closed the door of the car. "And they aren't looking at my legs."

Hart glanced at the open gallery of the mansion as he drove around the drive. Mr. Deering and "Mayer" had come out of the house and were watching them, the chauffeur slightly forward, with his right hand in the pocket of his sack coat, glancing back at his employer at intervals as if awaiting instructions.

"I don't think they like you," Gerta said.

A drop of sweat dripped from the cleft in Hart's chin and splattered on the wheel. "No," he agreed. "So it seems."

SEPTEMBER 3, 1958
1:28 A.M.

He was on or near the sea. There was a distant sound of rollers breaking on a beach and Hart could smell fish and salt air and the commingled sweet-sour smell of all boat basins and wharfs and piers; oakum and tar and new rope, wet wood and rusting metal, fresh paint and mildewed canvas and crude oil. For a moment his sleep-drugged mind refused to function. Then he remembered where he was.

It had been early evening by the time he and Gerta reached Newport, growing dark but still too light to prowl the Deering yacht unobserved. There'd been too many people around, returning fishermen from the day boats, other hopefuls signing up for bunks on the night boats leaving at 2 A.M. for San Clemente Island, the usual tourists always attracted by boats, still more fishermen of the commercial variety unloading their tuna and sardine catches at the fish packing plant on the far side of the narrow basin.

Checking into a motel until things quieted down had seemed a good idea. Now Hart wasn't so certain. The vertebrae in his neck seemed to have separated. He had a crick in his back. His left foot was asleep. His mouth felt like it was full of burnt feathers which must be the anchovies in the pizza pie he and Gerta had eaten for supper. He sat up in the chair in which he'd fallen asleep and looked across the room at the bed.

Neither the ceiling nor the bed lamp were lighted. The only illumination in the small room came from the evenly timed flashes of the red neon motel sign in front of the building. At regular intervals a red glow shined through the venetian blinds. When the sign flashed off it was dark. As far as he could tell, Gerta was no longer lying on the bed.

There was no reason why she should be. The blonde teen-ager had built up to her big moment and he'd let her down. In her desire to get even with Cotton, Peggy had fixed him but good. For the time being, he'd lost all interest in sex. He was only interested in his neck at the present time.

Hart felt through the dark for his shoes and put them on. Then he walked to the window and looked out. The motel was directly across a wide street from the elliptical basin of water and combination bar and grill in which he and Gerta had eaten. Ringed as it was by overhead floodlights on tall poles, the boat basin was as light or even lighter than it had been five hours before. There were just as many people. Loose little groups of men and a sprinkling of women, most of them carrying their own deep sea fishing rods and reels and tackle boxes, were clustered on the stringers in front of the broad sterns of the boats on which they had booked passage. Others were already going aboard to secure good places at the rails or buying additional tackle at the bait houses on the pier.

Across the basin, their bright work lights reflecting on the placid water and their power winches chugging noisily, a half dozen commercial fishing boats were either still unloading or filling their holds with ice. There was a constant coming and going of small boats and exchange of good-natured banter. Inside the combination bar and grill a lachrymose tenor, accompanied by a jukebox combo was extolling the pleasures and penalties of succumbing to a pair of lips sweeter than wine. As with the sea itself, the people who took their living or recreation from it were never still.

Hart hadn't meant to sleep so long. He was sorry he had. He felt refreshed physically but not mentally. He was depressed. This all went to prove something, perhaps the truth of the old saw that nothing was certain but death and taxes.

The heat persisted. It was so close in the little room that he found it difficult to breathe. Due to the absence of a shore wind, of any movement of air, it was as hot on the edge of the ocean as it had been in Beverly Hills.

He left the window and crossed to the bed. The pillow was depressed from Gerta's head but she was gone, no doubt across the street to drink a coke or a cup of coffee while she listened to the jukebox.

Hart walked on into the bathroom and turned on the light and ran cold water into the bowl. He thought to himself, that there was a little bitch in all women. Gerta was no exception. After getting up she had bathed. The tile floor was paved with wet towels. The room had the warm intimate smell of soap and water applied to bare female flesh. After bathing, as if to taunt him with what he'd missed, she'd washed out her fragile stockings and pants and bra and left them hanging over the shower rail to dry.

As he splashed cold water on his face and hair and used his pocket comb, Hart eyed the intimate garments thoughtfully. He wished he knew what he was going to do about Gerta. Man was a peculiar creature, almost as peculiar as woman. The girl was his if he wanted her. But did he? He'd taken Peggy without question. Being factual, she'd been just another body, a receptical in which to expend two months of desire. But with Gerta it was different. He liked her. He wanted her to be sure she knew what she was doing. He didn't want her to have any regrets.

It was a problem he was going to have to solve and soon. Meanwhile it was time to call Kelly again but not from the motel. He didn't want to be picked up; he didn't want the police to interfere with him until he'd examined the yacht.

Carrying his coat over his arm, Hart left the unit and crossed the street to the bar. As he recalled, there was a telephone booth near the cashier's counter.

Despite the late hour, the lachrymose tenor was still having twins and three young couples were walking around the small dance floor, more or less in time to the music. Three seamen in one booth and two fishermen in another were absorbed in Gerta who was sitting alone at the bar, moodily stirring a cup of villainous looking coffee. She looked up, sullen-eyed, as Hart took the stool next to hers.

"Well, so you finally came to."

"Finally," Hart said. He laid a five dollar bill on the bar and told the barman, "A double bourbon and water for me and whatever the young lady wants."

The barman leaned toward Gerta and asked protectively, "You know this guy?"

She continued to stir her coffee. "Yes."

Hart drank his drink. It helped. At least he could no longer taste anchovies. "Having a good time?" he asked Gerta.

She continued to pout. "What do you think?"

Hart shrugged and scooped up his change. He made his way to the telephone booth situated right in the window and gave the long distance operator his lawyer's number. From where he was standing he could look down the row of fishing boats and just see the ornate bowsprit of the Deering yacht. It was one of the few unlighted boats in the basin. Berthed at a comparatively isolated slip, it shouldn't be too difficult to board, if there was no watchman. He surely meant to try to get as far as the inside of the master's cabin.

There had to be some way for Bonnie to have left or been taken off the ship, with or without the crew's knowledge. Peggy had sworn she'd seen her alive and, if his assumption was correct, had been killed because she'd told him about it. He had to know. He was morally responsible for the girl's death. If he hadn't gone to her apartment, if in a state of emotional and sexual excitement, she hadn't entrusted the information to him, the chances were that she would still be alive. He was also responsible to Harry Cotton. He'd been the one out of eleven male jurors to talk Mrs. Slagle into changing her vote. Then there was his own neck to think of.

Hart had closed the folding door of the booth for privacy. He opened it so he could breathe. If he or Kelly or the private agency men Kelly had hired couldn't come up with some reasonable proof why someone else might have wanted to murder Peggy, by this time tomorrow morning he would probably be sitting in a cell awaiting trial for murder.

He perspired even harder. Merely because he was male, merely because he'd picked up a girl at a bus stop.

When Kelly answered his phone he sounded tired but not as if he'd been sleeping. Before Hart could speak, the lawyer said in a guarded voice, "If this is who I think it is, don't mention any names and be careful what you say. Things are not so hot at this end and it may be this phone is bugged."

Hart closed the folding door again. "What do you mean, things aren't so hot?"

"Just that. Have you read the evening papers?"

"No."

"They're putting pressure on Manson and Inspector Garcia. And it looks like a warrant will be issued sometime tomorrow morning, even before a true bill is voted."

Hart felt a hard lump form in the pit of his stomach. "I see."

"Have you found out anything?"

"Not yet. I'm going to go aboard in a few minutes. What have Masterson's men come up with?"

"Quite a few things. All of them bad as far as we're concerned."

"They checked the insurance angle?"

"Thoroughly. And the company is all pro-Deering. He hasn't even put in a claim of death, merely a notification."

"But they are going to pay off on Bonnie?"

"A quarter of a million, cash. They can't very well refuse. After all, the State has just convicted Cotton of killing her."

With the door closed Hart found his breathing was painful. With it open he couldn't hear Kelly, for the blare of the jukebox. He compromised by cracking it a few inches. "How about Deering's personal finances?"

"Seemingly as solid as the Bank of America," the lawyer said. "I talked to two of his fellow brokers after I talked to you this afternoon. And they say the feeling in local financial circles is that Deering's clients have cleaned up during the last few months."

"On what?"

"Mostly jet aircraft and guided missiles and electronics. That is, on the stocks of those firms either under contract to or working for the government in those fields."

"How about Cotton's claim that Bonnie was acting strange."

Kelly was impatient with him. "Look, Doc. Be reasonable. Why would she behave strangely? An animated mattress whose brains were already half rotted away by taking in too much whiskey at one end and too many men at the other. But at that she wasn't too frightened to go on a three-day spree with Cotton."

"I know," Hart said dryly. "I was on the jury, remember? But Peggy swore she saw Bonnie in Ensenada four months after Cotton is supposed to have killed her."

"The Ensenada police say not," Kelly said. Then he added, "There's more."

"What?"

"When you phoned before, on your way down to where you are now, you inferred that from the way they acted with you, you thought Mr. Deering or his chauffeur or both of them might have followed you to Peggy's place."

"That's right."

"Forget it."

The jukebox was blaring so loudly that Hart could barely hear Kelly. He cupped the palm of his free hand over his other ear. "What did you say?"

"Forget it."

"Why?"

"One of Masterson's men checked with the Beverly Hills police. I have his report in front of me now. And Deering's chauffeur was arrested for speeding about five miles from Mrs. Cotton's apartment, at the same time you say you went back to the store to get something to sober her up."

"Was Deering in the car?"

"He was. He tried to throw his weight around and the cop got sore and added an 'attempting to interfere with an officer in the performance of his duty' on the ticket." Kelly went on, "And while I'm at it, you might as well know the rest of it."

"Go on."

"One of Inspector Garcia's men prowled Mrs. Cotton's neighborhood and came up with the inevitable insomniac."

"Yes—?"

"Some old biddy who lives directly across the street. She says she couldn't sleep last night and she was sitting looking out her window when you brought Peggy home. She said she recognized you immediately, you having filled four or five prescriptions for her."

"Go on."

"This is what she told Garcia's man, understand."

"I understand."

"She said after you entered the building with young Mrs. Cotton, nee Jones, you stayed inside for perhaps a half hour. Then you came out and looked around, as if trying to determine if anyone was watching you."

"I remember that."

"Then you got into your car and drove off and were gone approximately ten minutes before you returned and re-entered the building."

"That's about the way it happened. What's so bad about that?"

"She claims she didn't leave her window. And that all the time she was sitting there she didn't see anyone but you go in or come out from the time you first drove up until the police arrived."

Hart's knees felt suddenly weak. His hand was so slippery with sweat it was all he could do to hold the receiver. He leaned against the folding door and realized Gerta had left the bar stool and was standing outside the booth, watching him with a worried expression on her face.

"Well," Hart said, finally. "Well. That makes everything just fine. When are they going to arrest me?"

"Probably in the morning. As soon as you get back to town." A long moment of silence followed. Then Kelly's voice came over the wire again. "Look, Doc."

"Yes—"

"I'm your lawyer. You know you can trust me. I'll do everything I can. It may take time and money but we'll whip this thing. But I can't formulate a proper defense unless you level with me."

Hart realized he was gripping the receiver so hard that his knuckles had turned white. "What are you getting at?"

Kelly laid it on the line. "You *are* leveling with me, aren't you, Doc? You didn't, well, shall we say get over-excited last night and lose your head when the babe tried to put the bite on you because she knew you had money and couldn't afford a scandal? Or because she said no to an encore? You didn't dream up this stuff about a pillow on the floor and someone tapping you on the head. Are you sure Peggy claimed to have seen Bonnie in Ensenada?"

Hart began a hot retort and couldn't get it out of his mouth. Instead, he cradled the receiver.

Gerta pushed open the folding door and laid her hand on his arm. "Are you all right, Doc?"

Hart patted his face with a sodden handkerchief, then rolled it between the palms of his hands before returning it to his pocket. "I'm all right, I guess."

Gerta was concerned. "You don't look like it. You look like someone just kicked you in the teeth."

"Someone just did."

"Mr. Kelly?"

"Yes."

"What's with him?"

Hart swept his change from the shelf under the phone, called to the barman to bring them two beers and sat in one of the booths next to the window.

Gerta sat across from him. "What's with Mr. Kelly?"

Hart waited until the barman had brought their beer. "It seems both Mr. Deering and his chauffeur are in the clear. They couldn't have killed Mrs. Cotton. There's nothing suspicious about Bonnie's insurance. Some woman who couldn't sleep claims she was looking out her window and didn't see anyone but me go into the building. The State's Attorney is ready to swear out a warrant. And—"

Gerta laid a small hand on his. "And Mr. Kelly has cold feet. He doesn't want to be on the losing side. He suddenly doesn't know whether he believes your story."

Hart sipped his beer. The cold liquid tasted good. "That's about it."

"I believe you."

Leaning forward as she was, the girl's entire upper body came into view. It looked cool and virginal and inviting, but strangely not immodest. Hart became mildly excited as he admired her. Kelly must be right in his claim that everywhere you go people, especially younger people, are living just for today. Right now.

It made sense. Despite the veneer of surface normalcy the underlying tension was apparent in almost everything: in modern music, art, pornographic books and nude girlie magazines flooding the newsstands. Cocktails and tail. No particular stratum of society was involved. Rich men, poor men, beggar men, thieves, doctors, lawyers, merchants, chiefs, and their wives and girl friends. It almost seemed as if the whole world, not only the young people in it, was feverishly trying to drink and screw itself to death in one last frenetic copulation.

Hart looked away from Gerta and out the window and up at the sky. Why not? Who knew? The end of the world could be at hand, wrapped in a nuclear warhead on the next object that streaked across the sky.

How long was eternity?

How many seconds to forever?

SEPTEMBER 3, 1958
1:55 A.M.

"What are you going to do?" Gerta asked.

Hart thought a moment. "Get aboard the yacht, if I can. And even if I don't find anything there to substantiate the theory that Bonnie could have left it alive, we're still going down to Ensenada and see if we can find any trace of her there."

"After what Kelly just told you?"

"Because of what Kelly told me."

"I don't understand."

"Now Bonnie *has* to be alive. Because if she isn't, I'm dead." Hart added grimly, "If my own lawyer doesn't believe me I can imagine how a jury will react. And there may not be a young Mrs. Slagle on it."

He laid some change on the table to pay for the beer and stood up. "You go back to the motel and wait for me. And while you're there, you'd better put on those things you washed out."

Gerta was contrite. "I'm sorry, Doc. I've been acting like a little bitch, haven't I?"

Hart was frank with her. "Yes."

"I'm sorry," the blonde girl repeated. "It's just that—" She shrugged her slim shoulders. "Forget it. But I'm not going back to the motel. No matter what you think of me, I do want to help you. And while you're on the yacht, at least I can stand on the pier and warn you if anyone comes."

"That might be a good idea."

As they left the cafe a blue and white local police car drew up and parked in front of the building and two youthful policemen got out and entered the bar and grill.

Hart wondered if the captain, Enrico Morales, would be on board the Deering yacht. He wished he'd paid more attention to Captain Morales while he'd been on the stand. All he remembered about him was his looks and the fact that he and his fellow jurors had decided that the man was not only a disinterested but a trustworthy witness.

After walking about a hundred yards, Hart looked back the way they had come. Up at the end of the basin the power winches of the commercial fishing boats still chugged noisily but here where the Deering yacht was berthed, there were no sounds but the suck and surge of the tide, the creaking of the heavy mooring hawsers and the plaintive cry of a sea bird, startled from its perch by the passing of the night boats.

As he watched, the floodlights in the parking area and around the rim of the basin winked out. From now on until six o'clock when the day boats began to leave for the fishing grounds closer by, the basin would be practically deserted.

Gerta's voice was small. "I'm frightened." She laid her hand on Hart's arm. "Why don't we drive back to L.A.? If Mr. Kelly doesn't believe you we can hire a lawyer who does. And if you didn't kill that girl they can't do anything to you."

Hart was tempted. The morning fog was beginning to roll in off the ocean and half-hidden in the mists, the big, unlighted yacht looked ominous. This really wasn't his dish of tea. He didn't know anything more about boats than he did about detecting. He wiped his face with the sleeve of his coat. Still, unless he could prove Bonnie was alive and that someone had killed Peggy for telling him, the chances were that Harry Cotton and he would wind up in the same mortar. A mortar minus a pestle, but equipped with peep holes so the warden and the official witnesses could make certain the cyanide pellets had dropped.

One. Two. Three. Take a deep breath and hold it and—*Good morning, Jesus.*

"You stay here," he told Gerta. "It shouldn't take me too long."

She protested. "But you don't know what you're looking for."

Hart disagreed with her. "Yes, that I do know. The way Bonnie could have gotten out of that cabin alive."

A narrow, steeply slanted gangplank led up from the pier to the deck of the yacht. Hart walked up a few cleats, then shined the flashlight he'd taken from Kelly's car over the superstructure of the yacht. He wished he knew more about yachts than he did. He wondered if it was customary for a decommissioned vessel to have a watchman, if the captain slept ashore or aboard.

He ventured a few cleats higher and flashed his light over the deck and into the wheel house. Everything movable was lashed and battened down. The awning over the fantail had been removed. There were no deck chairs or any other signs of human occupancy. The deck was filthy with gull droppings and accumulated grime and salt rime. As little as he knew about these things, it seemed reasonable to Hart that if Captain Morales was living aboard he would have made some attempt to keep the boat shipshape.

The fog was growing thicker. He waded waist deep in the swirling mist to the door of the captain's cabin and knocked lightly. If Morales or a watchman were aboard, it would be better to be ordered off the yacht as a trespasser than to be caught prowling in the cabin.

He closed the door behind him and stood with his back to it, wondering what to do next. In the books he'd read and in the motion pictures he'd seen, the hero, usually a wise-cracking private detective or sober-faced inspector of detectives methodically tapped on the walls of the room and sooner or later a fortuitous knock and the resulting hollow sound revealed the presence of a secret passageway leading down to the basement of the old deserted house. Unfortunately, yachts had no basements. More, it would do little good to sound the wood-paneled walls. It was a simple matter of mathematics. There couldn't possibly be more than a few inches of air space between the paneling and the steel hull and ribs of a vessel.

All the portholes were closed. Hart unfastened one of them and thrust his head through it. It was ample to admit his head and shoulders. As the State had alleged and proven, there was nothing under the opening but water. He turned and looked up. An active man could possibly work his way through the porthole and pull himself up onto the forward deck. He doubted that a drunken woman could do it, especially in a heavy sea.

He closed the port and sweeping a path ahead of him with his flashlight, he examined the bathroom next. In the few small boats and power-cruisers he'd been on, the head had always been well forward, usually a tiny, cramped compartment, strictly utilitarian. The Deering bathroom was something else. There was a tub and shower and the walls were lined with orchid tile. Hart rapped half-heartedly on the wall separating the bathroom of the owners suite from the captain's cabin, then flashed and held his light on a square of wood about fifteen inches wide and seventeen inches high. It started flush with the floor and was held in place with two round-headed chrome screws. He didn't remember such an aperture being mentioned during the trial and the scale model had been too small to show it. It was obviously a trap, common to all bathrooms, for the convenience of the plumber when it became necessary to work on the pipes feeding the tub and shower. Most such traps were usually at the head of the tub, in the wall of the opposite room.

Intrigued, Hart took a coin from his pocket and unscrewed the screws and lifted out the panel. Instead of pipes there was only a dark opening. He lay flat on the floor and shined his light through it. The opening led into a much smaller bathroom, obviously connected with the captain's cabin.

Lying as he was, Hart could feel the pound of his heart throbbing against the floor. He'd found what he'd been looking for. And whoever was involved in this thing had felt so secure that no attempt had been made to replace the panel on the other side. But he'd made it. He'd found out what he wanted to know. It could be done. The porthole was not the only exit from the locked cabin.

He stood up and brushed the dust and lint from his suit. The room he was in, more of a head than a bathroom, was one-fifth the size of the one on the far side of the wall. Hart shined his light through the opening of the door and saw a desk with a sextant and some books on it.

He opened the door and continued on into the captain's cabin. All the portholes were closed. The air was stale and foul and spiced with the lingering smell of pungent chili peppers. Hart found the door to the deck and started toward it, eager to get back to Los Angeles and tell State's Attorney Manson and Inspector Garcia what he'd found. Then, just as his hand closed on the door knob, somewhere in the dark of the room behind him, a man said, *"Buenos días, señor. ¿Como está usted?* You are looking for something?"

Hart turned slowly, the beam of his light turning with him. Pinned in its beam, Captain Enrico Morales was sitting on the edge of the bunk, holding a forty-five caliber automatic pistol in one hand and an unlighted cigarette in the other.

When Hart could speak, he said, "You were in this from the start. When Bonnie left Cotton she came in here. Peggy was right. She really did see her. Bonnie is alive."

"Bonnie?" Morales queried. He put the cigarette to his lips and thumbed a silver cigarette lighter into flame. *"Sí.* Of course. You are referring to Señora Deering." He drew smoke into his lungs, then expelled it with obvious enjoyment. "But no, *señor.* How could she be alive? I, myself, was in court last night when the jury of which you were a member found Señor Harry Cotton guilty of killing her and fixed his punishment at death."

Hart studied the big man sitting on the bunk. He was immaculate in a white Irish linen suit. The gaily ribboned Panama on his head had cost at least a hundred dollars. A large diamond glittered on a finger of the hand holding the gun. It was difficult for Hart to force the words past the constriction in his throat. "Morales, I don't know what this is all about or what your part in it is. But I can tell you one thing."

"Sí—?"

"There is a pair of Newport policemen sitting up in the cafe right now. And when I bring them down here and show them that hole in the bathroom wall both you and Mr. Deering are going to have a lot to explain."

Morales' excessively white teeth brightened his face as he smiled. "And just how do you propose to contact them, *señor?* You realize, of course, that you are guilty of breaking and entering and that as captain of this vessel I am empowered to shoot you to protect the property of my employer."

Hart exhaled sharply. "I don't think you'll do that."

Morales continued to smile. "Why not?"

It was a good question. Why not?

Hart leaned against the door beside the wall, then straightened again and his already tense body grew more tense as someone knocked lightly on the door. Hart hoped it wasn't Gerta. He hoped she hadn't grown tired of waiting and followed him aboard.

"Who is it?" Morales asked.

"Tumaco," a man's voice answered.

Morales used the barrel of the pistol he was holding to motion Hart to the other side of the cabin. Then, without looking away from Hart, he lighted a small oil lamp and stood up and unlocked the door.

One of the seamen who had testified at the trial was standing in the doorway with Gerta standing in front of him. One muscular arm was locked around the girl's waist, half holding, half carrying her. The palm of his other hand was clamped over her mouth to keep her from screaming.

"The little bitch," he complained, "bit me twice."

Hart swallowed the rising lump in his throat as he looked at Gerta. The eyes above the hand were terrified. In her struggle to free herself, she'd lost both of her shoes and her dress had worked up to her thighs. Shamed, she tried to twist sideways and couldn't.

Morales admired her for a moment. Then taking the cigarette from his mouth, he said, quietly, "Well, don't just stand there. Someone might see you. Bring her inside so I can close the door."

SEPTEMBER 3, 1958
2:28 A.M.

The seaman carried Gerta struggling and kicking into the cabin. Then, as Morales closed the door behind them, he suddenly shifted his hands and pushed the girl away from him with such force that she stumbled across the room and sprawled, face down, on the bunk. But not for long. Whimpering and gasping for breath, she got to her feet, clawing her dress into place and darted across the room to where Hart was standing.

Morales was amused. "How touching. The little blonde swallow fluttering back to the dubious sanctuary of her male Capistrano."

Gerta pressed even closer to Hart. "What are they going to do to us?"

Hart tightened his arm around her waist. "I don't know."

Seemingly he and his friends on the jury had been led down a devious path. Seemingly, during the course of the Cotton trial, a good many supposedly disinterested witnesses had put their hands on the Bible and sworn to tell the truth, the whole truth, and nothing but the truth, but only when it was convenient. Tumaco was the steward who allegedly served Cotton and Bonnie her last meal.

"Did anyone see you bring her aboard?" Morales asked.

Tumaco stopped sucking the bite wounds on his hand. "No. The fog is in."

"Good. Now what to do with them."

Despite the physical realities of the stifling heat in the cabin and the feeble glow of the oil lamp, there was something terribly unreal about the scene. It was like a page out of a poorly written play, a caricature of a gaslight melodrama, complete with the stilted dialogue of the era.

"Did anyone see you bring her aboard?"

"No. The fog is in."

"Good. Now what to do with them."

Hart wanted to laugh. He didn't dare. He knew the sound would be a sob.

Morales lighted a cigarette from the stub he was smoking. "How long would it take to round up the rest of the crew and get the yacht ready to put to sea?"

"An hour," Tumaco said. "Perhaps a little longer." He added, thoughtfully, "But wouldn't that be risking our necks?"

Morales shrugged. "I doubt it. The evening papers have already convicted Señor Hart of killing the Cotton girl. And when both he and the *señorita* turn up missing, it will be logical for the police to assume that rather than stand trial, our so nosy apothecary has run away with his pretty employee. And she is very pretty."

Tumaco admired Gerta. *"Sí."*

Morales added, wryly, "Señor Hart is a virile man. He has proven that. And, after all, with so little time left, with the end of the world so imminent, rather than wait for eternity in a cell, it is only natural he would like to continue to pursue the known pleasures of this world." He caressed Gerta with his eyes. "And in this instance, I think we shall help him."

Tumaco stopped sucking his hand. *"Sí."*

Hart didn't feel brave. He wasn't. But he meant what he said. It was the way he felt. "You'll have to kill me first."

"That can be arranged," Morales said. "Quite easily." He nodded to Tumaco. "Get the crew together. Tell them we sail in an hour."

Tumaco nodded and left the cabin after a sly look at Gerta.

A strained silence followed his departure. Hart broke it by asking, "I suppose Mr. Deering tipped you that I asked about the yacht and told you I might be on my way down here."

Morales returned to the bunk and made himself comfortable. "You are hardly in a position to ask questions, *señor.* Let us just say it is unfortunate for you both that you and the young lady chose to be so curious."

Hart mentally calculated the distance between them. Small as it was, Morales could empty his gun into him before he could take two steps. And it seemed he was perfectly willing to. But at least while he was rushing Morales, Gerta would have a chance to get out of the cabin.

As if sensing what he was about to try, Gerta tightened her fingers on his arm. "No. Don't try it, Doc. He'll kill you."

Morales showed his teeth in a mirthless smile. "If you are thinking of trying to rush me, *señor,* the young lady is right." He continued to smile. "And after you are dead, I assure you I will do my best to console the *señorita.*"

Gerta swayed as if she was about to faint. Her voice was small. "I don't feel well. I wonder if I might sit down."

Morales was the gallant Latin. "But certainly, *señorita.*" He stood up and offered her his free hand as if to guide her to the bunk.

Gerta took a few uncertain steps under his guidance, then fell heavily against him and wrapped her arms around his. "Now, Doc," she shrilled. "Hit him now."

Hart came away from the wall, moving faster than he had in years, and swung a hard punch that connected with the captain's temple. The blow stunned the other man but failed to knock him out. It did turn him around enough to give Hart the chance to rabbit punch him. Morales cried out in pain and the pistol dropped from his numbed fingers. Before he could recover it from the floor, Gerta picked it up and pistol-whipped him viciously.

"Help Doc, will you?" she screamed. "Console me, will you?"

Hart caught her arm. "You're killing him."

"I'm trying to," Gerta said.

Hart took the pistol away from her and allowed Morales to fall, unconscious, to the floor.

"No," Hart said, sharply. "The thing for us to do now is get the local police. And to do that we have to get out of here before Tumaco and the rest of the crew return."

Still breathing hard, Gerta said, "If you say so."

It had happened so fast it was difficult for Hart to reorient himself. One minute Morales had been top dog. Now he was just so much inanimate flesh. It seemed too easy, as if it were all a part of the same poorly written play. Hero enters left upper center and he and heroine beat villain unconscious. It seemed contrived. It was as though the captain wanted them to escape. Still, that didn't make any more sense than the rest of the affair.

He opened the cabin door and a wraith of fog swirled in. It was impossible to see more than a few feet. Holding Gerta by one hand he led her down the narrow gangplank. At the foot of it they found one of her shoes but not the other. The planking was rough and splintered.

"I'll have to carry you," Hart said.

Gerta felt small and warm in his arms and good. Now the immediate danger was over, she was softly crying. Her lips close to his ear, she asked, "Did you mean what you said in the cabin, Doc?"

"What did I say?"

"That they'd have to kill you first. You did mean that, didn't you?"

"Yes."

Gerta snuggled closer. "I could tell by the way you said it."

The fog was so thick that Hart had to feel his way up the pier. What few lights there were appeared haloed or distorted. When he got close enough to see through the windows of the all night bar and grill at the head of the basin, he stopped well back in the protection of the fog to make certain Tumaco wasn't inside. The two policemen and the seamen who'd been drinking in the booths had left but two of the three couples, barely moving now, were still walking around the small dance floor.

Hart carried Gerta inside and up to the bar. As he lowered her to the stool the barman stopped toweling glasses and gaped first at her tear-stained face and then at her bare feet.

"For God's sake, what happened to her?"

"We had an accident," Hart said, dryly. "Where would I find those two policemen who were in here when we left?"

"Making their tour, I suppose," the barman said. "You want the cops,

Mister?"

Hart nodded. "As fast as you can get them here." Reaction had set in and Gerta was having trouble controlling her facial muscles and the movements of her arms and legs. "But before you phone, set out a bottle. The young lady has had a very nasty experience."

The barman protested, "Look, Mister. It's after hours. I could lose my license. I—" He shrugged, set a bottle of whiskey and two glasses on the bar and continued on to the phone.

Hart poured a stiff drink of whiskey and made Gerta drink it. She stopped shivering and said, "I needed that."

Hart wished she'd used some other expression. Peggy had said the same thing. Under different circumstances, true. But the nuances were the same. Whiskey and sex and the end of the world. He hoped something would begin to make sense soon.

The couples had stopped dancing and were crowded around them. One of the girls asked, "What happened to the kid? What's she bawling about?"

Hart poured himself a drink. "You know the Deering yacht?"

"The big power and sail job at the lower end of the basin. The one that strip-teaser got killed on?"

"That's the one."

"What about it?"

Before Hart could answer, the barman returned. "The cops will be here in a minute. Is the young lady all right now?"

Gerta used a paper napkin to wipe her wet cheeks. "I'm fine. But I hope I killed the bastard."

The other girl asked, "Who?"

"That big Mexican. The captain of the Deering yacht."

"You mean Captain Morales?"

"Yes."

"He's not Mexican. He's from Panama or Chile or Venezuela, anyway some place in South America."

"Wherever he's from."

"What did he do?"

Hart stopped Gerta from answering. "Let's wait until the police get here."

The barman had been studying Hart's face. "I make you now," he said. "You're Hart. You're that druggist whose picture is in all the papers."

Hart admitted his identity. "That's right."

"I thought your face was familiar when you were in here before." He started a question and stopped talking as the door of the cafe opened and the two young policemen Hart had seen before came in. "Here's Greer and Hanson now," he said.

"I'm Greer," the radio car man who'd taken the paper from the bundle said. "What's going on here?"

"He was going to kill us," Gerta said.

Hanson pushed his uniform cap to the back of his head. "Who was going to kill you, Miss?"

"Captain Morales."

The officer looked dubious. "Enrico?"

"If that's his first name."

"Why?"

"Why what?"

"Why was he going to kill you?"

"The guy is Doc Hart," the barman offered. "You know. The Hollywood druggist the police think killed that Cotton woman."

"I see he is," Greer said. He unbuttoned the flap of his holster. "Okay. Let's have it. You wanted the cops. You have 'em. What's the story, Hart? You drunk or something? And what are you doing here? I should think the spot you're in, you wouldn't want to attract attention to yourself."

"I don't, particularly," Hart said. "I just want you to arrest Morales and hold him for the Los Angeles police."

"On what charge?"

Hart forced himself to be patient. "It's too long a story to go into the details now. But Peggy Cotton *did* tell me she'd seen Bonnie Tempest alive."

"We read your statement."

"To prove it was possible I drove down here to see if I could find some way that Mrs. Deering could have gotten out of the cabin of the Deering yacht alive. And I found there was. I found a crawl hole in the bathroom wall, between the owner's suite and the captain's cabin. And to make certain Mrs. Deering could have done the same thing, I crawled through it, myself."

"With Mr. Deering's permission?"

"No."

"Go on."

"And Morales was waiting on the other side of the wall with a gun. Then a moment later his steward, a man by the name of Tumaco, grabbed Miss Nielsen here out on the pier and carried her aboard the yacht."

Gerta explained, "He crept up on me in the fog and grabbed me." She added, bitterly, "And he wasn't at all careful where he grabbed me."

Hanson glanced at the bottle and the glasses on the bar. "Look, folks. You sure you know what you're talking about? You just haven't been drinking too much, have you?"

Hart was indignant. "Of course not. And it's easy enough to prove we're telling the truth."

"How?"

"After Tumaco left to round up the rest of the crew, Gerta tricked Morales off guard and I rabbit punched him. Then Gerta knocked him out with his own gun and right now he's lying unconscious on the floor in his cabin."

Greer was skeptical. "You rabbit punched Enrico Morales and she beat him unconscious with his own gun? I don't believe it."

"Take us down to the yacht and we'll show you." Hart added, "I'll show you the opening Bonnie crawled through, leaving Cotton framed for her murder."

"Why?" Greer asked. "I mean, why should she do anything like that?"

"I don't know," Hart admitted. "I haven't the least idea. That's what I'm trying to find out."

The officers looked at each other. Then Greer said, "It's your funeral, Mister, and I hope you have a healthy bank account. Mr. Morales and Mr. Deering could sue you for plenty for making up a yarn like this." He nodded toward the door. "Okay. Let's go down and talk to Enrico."

Gerta got down off the stool and looked at her bare feet. "I can't go."

"Why not?" Hanson asked her.

She held up a bare foot. "I lost my shoes when Tumaco grabbed me."

"I think I can help out there," the barman said. "Some of the waitresses keep spares in the employees' lounge. Wait just a minute. I'll see if I can find a pair to fit you."

SEPTEMBER 3, 1958
2:59 A.M.

When they reached the yacht, Greer motioned for him and Gerta to precede them up the gangplank.

The officers were carrying powerful torches that cut through the fog and laid a yellow runner of light up the gangplank and down the deck.

Outside the closed door of the cabin, Hanson asked, "Did you leave the door open or shut?"

"I don't remember," Hart said. "I was too anxious to get out."

"It's shut now," the officer said. "You're sure Morales is inside, unconscious on the floor?"

"I'm positive," Hart said.

Greer tried the door, then rattled, the knob and rapped loudly. "Inside there. Morales! Open up! It's Greer and Hanson."

There was a long moment of silence, then the sound of movement in the cabin and Morales unlocked and opened the door.

"*Sí*—? What is it, gentlemen?" he asked.

Hart stared at the man. Morales was no longer wearing the white linen suit and Panama. He'd changed into a pair of violently purple pajamas. His sleek black hair was neatly combed. Other than a little puffing, his face bore no signs of the pistol whipping Gerta had given him. Behind him all the portholes were open. The spread on the bunk was turned down and there was a paper-back novel on the sheet, lying open, face down, as if Morales had been reading when he'd been disturbed.

He looked at Greer and smiled. "What gives, Jerry?"

Greer looked uncertain. "You were in bed?"

Morales simulated amused surprise. "*Sí*." He glanced at the watch on his wrist. "Aren't most people usually in bed at three o'clock in the morning?"

Now Greer looked more uncertain. He turned the beam of his flashlight on Hart's face. "You ever see this guy before, Enrico?"

Morales nodded, "*Sí*. In the courtroom in Los Angeles. His name is Señor Hart. He is that druggist from Beverly Hills who was a juror in the Cotton trial. I have seen him a number of times."

Greer turned his light on Gerta. "How about her?" Morales studied Gerta's face, then moved his head from side to side. "I'm sorry. The young lady is unknown to me." His white-toothed smile returned. "A pity."

"But you've never seen her before?"

Morales repeated what he'd said before. "I'm sorry."

"They say they just beat you unconscious and left you here on the floor of your cabin."

"They what?"

Greer repeated what he'd just said and Morales shook his head again.

"I'm afraid I do not understand." He stepped aside to allow them to enter. "But I am forgetting my manners. Please to come in. The fog is thick this morning."

Hart walked into the cabin and turned to face Morales. "Don't tell me," he said hotly, "that you are going to have the gall to deny you held a gun on me a few minutes ago? And that a few minutes after that, one of your bully boys didn't carry Gerta in here, kicking and crying, with her skirt halfway up to her waist?"

Morales looked at Gerta again. "That should have been a most intriguing vision. I'm very sorry I missed it." He turned to the officers. "The *señor* is intoxicated, perhaps?"

"I'm beginning to wonder," Hanson said.

Greer said, sourly, "I did, right from the start."

"Now wait just a minute," Hart said. "I can prove every word I've said. I'll show you the hole I crawled through to get in here."

"Hole?" Morales puzzled.

Hart opened the door of the head and pointed to the fifteen by seventeen inch wooden panel in the wall. "I don't see any hole," Greer said.

Hart smiled wryly. "No. After we left he came to and he knew we'd come back with the police. So he replaced the panel on this side." He took a coin from his pocket. "I'll show you."

Working as rapidly as he could, Hart unscrewed the two round headed chrome screws holding the panel in place, then, sat back on his heels, staring at the opening he'd crawled through. Where, a few minutes before, there'd been a clear opening, there were three one inch copper pipes, so spaced that at no point was there more than two or three inches clearing. What was more, the panel on the far side of the wall had also been replaced.

"Oh, come now, fellow," Hanson said. "You don't expect us to believe either you or Mrs. Deering crawled through there."

"Mrs. Deering?" Morales asked.

Greer took off his uniform cap and wiped the leather band with his handkerchief. "You see, it's this way, Enrico."

"Sí—?"

"The yarn he told us was he got onto the yacht and into the owner's cabin someway and crawled through a hole into here. And you were waiting for him with a gun. And a minute later one of your boys brought in the dame. Then he got brave and rabbit punched you and she beat you unconscious."

Morales was sympathetic. "The poor *señor.*" He described a circle on his temple with his finger.

Greer nodded. "I'm beginning to think the same thing. He's either crazy or he's drunk. Perhaps he's crazy drunk."

Hart gripped the copper pipes with both hands and pulled as hard as he could. They were completely immovable.

"It's a trick," Gerta said indignantly. In her borrowed sneakers she seemed tinier than she was. The top of her head barely reached Morales' chest as she stood in front of him and looked up into his face. "Do you mean to stand there and deny that you told that thug who grabbed me out on the pier to go round up the rest of the crew and be ready to sail in an hour because you had to get rid of Doc and me? And I suppose you didn't say that the evening papers had already convicted him of murder and that when we turned up missing the police would think he'd run away with me?"

Morales spread his hands. "*Señorita.* Please. I did not even read the evening papers. As for telling any member of my crew to get ready to put out to sea, have you any idea, after it has stood idle as long as this ship has, how long it would take to put a yacht this size in condition to sail? Not a matter of an hour or hours but more a matter of days."

Both Greer and Hanson nodded.

Gerta persisted. "You didn't say that Doc looked like a virile man and infer he would get a much bigger kick out of going to bed with me than he would out of waiting for eternity in a cell? And that after you got us out to sea, you were all going to *help* him. Console me was the way you put it." Hot tears filled her eyes and spilled over her cheeks. "You didn't hint that it didn't matter what happened to me, because the end of the world was just around the corner?"

Greer returned his cap to his head and looked at his partner. "That does it. How about you, Swen?"

Hanson nodded. He inclined his head toward the door of the cabin. "Let's go, Hart. You, too, Miss."

Gerta protested, "But it happened just like Doc said. And Morales did and said everything I said he did."

"Yeah, sure," Greer agreed with her. "Anything you say, Miss." He looked at Morales. "You want to prefer charges, Enrico?"

Morales considered the matter. "No. I think not. If I preferred such charges, it would only reflect on my owner and *Señor* Deering has had enough trouble. No." He shrugged. "It seems that the *señor* and *señorita* have had hallucinations of some kind. Besides what would I charge them with?"

Hart lit a cigarette and offered Gerta a puff. "Thanks," he said quietly. "Thanks for nothing, fellow. I still don't get it, but I should have known from that corny dialogue the whole thing was an act, that you wouldn't be that easy to knock out." He added, "But a five will get you fifty that there is a ring coupling at both ends of those pipes, the kind they use on a wash basin trap. There has to be for you to have gotten them back in that hole as fast as you did."

Hanson pushed him toward the door. "I said let's go."

Either the weather had broken or Hart was angrier than he'd ever been in his life. The morning mist felt cool, almost cold on his flushed face.

Neither of the officers spoke again until they were in front of the bar and grill. Then Hanson asked, "Where's your car?"

Hart nodded across the street to where the red neon motel sign was still flicking on and off. "Across the street. In front of the motel."

"You're checked in there?"

"Yes."

"How?"

"As Mr. and Mrs. Hart," Hart admitted. "But we didn't—that is we just wanted some place to hole up until it was dark enough to go aboard the yacht."

"I'll bet," Greer said. "You just wanted a place to hold hands. What unit are you in?"

"Number ten."

"Did you pay in advance?"

"Yes."

"That's good. Because you are checking out right now. Did you leave anything in the unit?"

"No," Hart said. He tried to signal Gerta but she spoke before he could stop her.

"I did," she said. "In the bathroom."

"Then let's get it, whatever it is," Greer said. He opened the door of the unit and motioned them in.

Hanson walked into the bathroom, then came out and looked at Gerta. "How old are you, Miss?"

"Eighteen."

The officer looked from the girl to Hart. "That saves you a contributing to the delinquency of a minor rap. We could charge you with lewd and lascivious conduct."

"No," Gerta said.

"Why not?"

"Because Doc hasn't ever—" She realized what she'd been about to say and blushed. "Anyway, we didn't. He went to sleep in the chair."

"I'll bet. I'll just bet," Hanson said. "But before he gets sleepy again, you'd better go on into the bathroom and put on those things hanging on the shower rail."

When he was alone with the officers, Hart asked, "Would it do any good to swear to you fellows that you're making a big mistake, not only about Miss Nielsen and myself but about Morales?"

"No," Greer said.

Hart accepted the inevitable. "What happens now?"

"I'm trying to make up my mind."

"I think we should take them in," Hanson said.

"On what charge?" his partner asked him. "The girl's legally old enough. Neither of them are drunk. All we have is a possible disorderly conduct and disturbing the peace. And we don't even have that if Morales refuses to press any charges."

"Just the same."

Greer shrugged. "You may be right. I'll go over and get the cruiser and ask the lieutenant for instructions." He turned toward the doorway and walked out.

The cigarette tasted bitter. Hart snuffed it out in a tray. The deeper into this thing he dug, the more angles he found. He'd learned one thing. Whatever was back of this, whatever they hoped to gain, both Mr. Deering and Morales were involved to their eyebrows. He had inquired the whereabouts of the yacht from Mr. Deering, who immediately let Morales know by phone to expect Hart. Hart's face still felt hot when he thought of the scene aboard the yacht. He had been conned and taken in like a back country yokel being sold a "solid gold" brick.

On the other hand, if Bonnie was alive, why had Morales allowed him to see the crawl hole as it must have existed on the night of the alleged murder?

Now this. He and Gerta might or might not be booked and fined on some minor charge. Either way, the affair was certain to get into the newspapers. Greer and Hanson would talk and the local news service correspondent would pick up the story and file it. Hart could see the headlines—

PROMINENT L.A. DRUGGIST CAUGHT
IN SEASIDE LOVE NEST WITH
BLONDE TEEN-AGE EMPLOYEE!

Hart patted his face with his handkerchief. Coming on top of the Peggy Cotton affair, even a minor scandal would ruin him. If the grand jury did vote a true bill, if he had to stand trial for Peggy's death, any sensible jury, at least any jury as gullible as he and his fellow jurors had been, would do one of two things: find him guilty on the first ballot, or find him innocent by reason of sexual insanity and recommend he be committed to an asylum for the balance of his natural life.

He looked up as Gerta came out of the bathroom.

She'd washed her face and re-combed her hair. Without make-up she looked even younger than she was but at the same time, more mature. Hart's mind raced on. Thirty-two wasn't old. Thousands of thirty-two-year-old men married eighteen-year-old women. Marriage to Gerta would solve at least one of his problems. It was something to think about.

A car drove up outside and Hanson looked out the open door. "Okay. Here's Jerry. Let's go."

Greer had stopped the police car beside Kelly's sedan. He rested his elbow on the window and called out, "You ride in the car with them, Swen."

"Are we taking them in?"

"No."

"What then?"

"The lieutenant says to take them out to the city limits and point them north and turn them loose. He says why should we bother? The L.A. cops are going to take care of Hart in the morning anyway."

Hanson was disappointed. "He gives the orders."

Hart helped Gerta into the car, then walked around it and got behind the wheel. He had to drive slowly because of the fog. When he reached the northern corporate limits of the village, Hanson ordered him to stop and got out of the car.

"Keep right on the way you're headed," the youthful officer said curtly. "And don't come back. If you do, I don't care what the lieutenant says, I, personally, will find some way to jug you."

For a long while after they'd gone, Hart sat staring at the swirling fog isolating himself and Gerta in a sterile white world of their own. He felt cheap and shamed. In a mildly eventful life he'd had a number of unpleasant things happen to him. This was the first time he'd ever been escorted out of town and told to stay out.

He felt worse for Gerta than he did for himself. She might claim she didn't care what people thought of her but she did. And once this thing got into the Los Angeles papers and was blown up and exaggerated by the local scandal sheets, she wouldn't have enough reputation left to make a leotard for a one-legged parakeet.

He lit two cigarettes. "Look, Gerta."

She accepted one of the cigarettes. "Yes—?"

"Will you marry me?"

"Oh... yes."

Hart swung the car in a wide U turn and parked on the far shoulder of the road and turned off the headlights. "Good. We'll give Hanson and

Greer a few minutes to get out of our way. Then we're heading south to Ensenada."

"You think Mrs. Deering is there?"

"No. But now we know she could be alive. I want to know if she really is before we go back to Los Angeles, before I'm arrested for something I didn't do. And if Bonnie was in Ensenada when Peggy claimed she saw her, someone should remember her." He added, almost as an afterthought, "And on our way, we'll stop in Tijuana and get married."

Hart realized Gerta was crying and slipped his arm around her waist. "Honey. What's the matter?"

"You don't know?"

"No."

Gerta wiped at her cheeks with the back of her hand. "Then nothing's the matter. But I'm glad you at least called me honey. I know. I'm being silly. It's just that these things always turn out so different from the way a girl thinks they're going to." She stopped crying and became practical. "But after the way I threw myself at you and considering the spot we're in, I don't suppose I can expect you to bring roses or play a guitar under my balcony." She put her arms around Hart's neck and brushed his cheek with her lips. "You're a good guy, Doc. Even if you do need a shave. And I'll make you a good wife. You'll see."

Hart kissed her. "You're trembling."

Without moving her arms, Gerta turned her head and tried to see through the opaque white curtain just beyond the open window of the car. "I'm frightened." Her firm young breasts moved pleasantly against Hart's chest as they rose and fell with her breathing.

Hart kissed her again. He was glad he'd made the decision he had. He had no sense of immediate need. It was good to feel her body against his. He wished they could forget the entire Cotton-Deering-Morales mess.

But they couldn't. Through no fault of their own, he and Gerta were caught in the middle of something; something big and vital and potentially tragic. And time was running out on them.

SEPTEMBER 3, 1958
8:30 P.M.

Between Tijuana and Ensenada there are only three towns large enough to be shown on the map: Agua Caliente, Rosarito, and El Descanso. The speeding car behind them had appeared shortly after they'd passed through Rosarito. When Hart slowed his car, the car behind them slowed. When he put on more speed, they increased theirs just enough to keep about a quarter of a mile behind his car.

During the daylight hours when there'd been other cars on the road, Hart hadn't paid much attention to it. Now he was beginning to wonder.

Gerta rode with her hands in her lap, alternately looking at the ring on the third finger of her left hand and in the rear vision mirror. Her voice was small as she asked, "Do you think they're following us?"

Hart glanced at the mirror. "Frankly, I don't know."

He was hot. He was tired. He was worried. The stop in Tijuana had taken hours longer than he'd figured. There'd been the license to buy. He'd had to locate a judge. At the last minute, Gerta had refused to be married in the rumpled dress she was wearing and he'd had to give her a substantial amount from his rapidly dwindling supply of cash to get herself a complete new outfit.

The more he thought about it, the more insane it seemed for him to be doing what he was. He was a businessman, not a detective. If the car behind was following them, if it should crowd his car off the road and stop it, he was utterly defenseless. He had nothing with which to defend himself. Even if it would help, he couldn't roll a pill to throw at whoever might be after him.

Gerta, practical as always, said, "This is a hell of a honeymoon, isn't it, Doc?"

"Isn't it, though?" Hart agreed with her.

The highway was excellent, for the most part bisecting a level desert but they were climbing now. If Hart remembered the road, the basin in which Ensenada lay was just the other side of this hill. On impulse, when he reached the crest he turned off onto the shoulder of the road and braked in a cloud of dust. He half expected the other car to do the same. It didn't. It sped on by without even slackening its speed. It was too dark to see the occupants, but he could see California license plates.

Hart grinned at Gerta. "Just another pair of cheaters."

Gerta held up her left hand. "Just a pair of cheaters," she corrected him smugly. "And that's not the sort of language for a man to use in front of his wife."

Hart continued to smile. "I'm sorry, Mrs. Hart."

The longer he was married to Gerta the better he liked the idea. It was the one bright spot in the entire affair. She was trying to be very blasé and sophisticated about it but she was frightened. Hart doubted that despite all her talk, a man had ever put his hand on her.

He pointed to the town spread out below them. "There it is."

Seen from the crest of the hill, even by moonlight, Ensenada was far from attractive. The plain on which it lay was low and flat and treeless. The scattered business section was poorly lighted and looked shabby. Differing from most Mexican towns it had neither a market place nor a plaza. The sea was its main attraction and what money had been spent had been used to build ornate hotels along the beach.

Hart debated a moment and drove on. As far as he and Gerta were concerned, the beach was out. He might meet someone he knew. That would mean explanations and he was in no mood to explain anything to anyone. A town hotel, patronized by locals would have to do for the night.

The one he finally chose was old and painted a violent pink. There were some tired artificial palms and worn leather chairs in the lobby. The clerk was surprised and pleased. But to be sure he had a room for the *señor* and *señora*. At the moment, the best room in the house was unoccupied.

The room was on the second floor, in front. It was in keeping with the lobby and exterior. The furnishings were dark mahogany and massive. Torn but clean and stiffly starched curtains fluttered in the window. Through the open door of the one-story *cantina* directly across the street, a brightly lighted Tower Of Music poured a constant blare of plucked strings and rhythm.

From the window Hart could see the brightly lighted chain of Las Vegas-type hotels and motels rimming Todos Santos Bay, all them complete with every modern convenience, including tiled swimming pools and futuristic bars. Beyond them were the lighted and paved streets between the homes of the permanent English speaking community. Most beautiful of all—the sea.

He turned and sat on the sill. "Maybe we should have gone out to the beach."

Gerta sat admiring her ring. She said in a soft voice, "You've been there before, haven't you?"

"Yes."

"With other girls?"

"Yes."

"Then I prefer this." She looked up and met Hart's eyes. "Not that it's any of my business what you did before this afternoon. I'm not going to be a nagging wife, honest, Doc. But—" She didn't quite know how to say what she felt. "But, well, I—I want tonight to be sort of special, for both of us."

"I know."

"This is fine if it has a bath."

Hart got up from the sill. "I'll see."

The bathroom was old fashioned but adequate. It had a tub and shower as well as the other facilities. "Do you want me to run a tub for you?" he called.

"Please."

Hart plugged in the stopper and ran water into the tub. While he waited for it to fill, he took off his coat and washed his face and hands in the basin.

It was an odd sensation. He could still feel wheels under him. He was still in motion, standing still. It seemed incredible that so much could happen in so short a time. At this time, two days ago on Labor Day, he'd still been in the jury room, wondering how anyone could be as dumb as Mrs. Slagle, how anyone could have listened to the evidence and not know Cotton was guilty. Now Peggy Cotton was dead. And here he was in Ensenada, married to Gerta.

He dried his hands and face and used his pocket comb and returned to the bedroom. While he'd been gone, Gerta had turned down the heavy bed spread and the top sheet and laid a clean blouse and skirt and some underthings on the bed.

As he entered the room, she was standing with the hem of her dress in both hands, about to pull it over her head. When she saw him she stopped. Then, compressing her lips, she completed taking off her dress and hung it over the back of a chair.

She seemed puzzled. "I don't know why I'm suddenly so modest. Not after the way I acted last night. Doc, you do like me, don't you? You didn't marry me just on account of what happened back there in Newport, to avoid any possible bad publicity?"

Hart admired her. "No."

"And I do, well, attract you? You know how I mean?"

Hart was amused. In the always unequal contest between soft flesh and hard, the male of the species seldom won. If he were any more attracted he would take off like a guided missile, without benefit of launching pad. "Yes, very much," he assured her.

Gerta unhooked her bra and laid it on top of her dress. Her voice continued small. "Just be patient with me, please, Doc. I know I've talked awfully big. But—"

Hart forced her to say it. "But what?"

Gerta met his eyes. "I've never. This will be the first time." She was, as always, perfectly honest. "Not that I've been an angel. I haven't. I've let boys put their hands on me and I've put my hand on them and we've done that. Most of the girls I know go that far. The boys won't take you out unless you do. But I've never gone all the way."

Hart took her in his arms and kissed her, then fondled and kissed the rounded flesh she'd exposed, gently, without passion. He could afford to be patient. This wasn't a one night stand. This was the big one. This one was for keeps. And most marriages were made or broken on the bridal bed.

He continued to kiss and caress her, deftly, expertly. Gerta, like a good many modern girls, to go along with the crowd, to keep from being considered squares, permitted a certain amount of juvenile fumbling. They wanted to be good sports. But they came to their husbands as virgins. They knew the position and general procedure but the finer nuances of sex were still unexplored mysteries.

And that was when the trouble began. It was only natural that a woman, with a woman's finer sensibilities, introduced to a practice that was to say the least, new to her, should resent and be revolted by having that portion of her body she'd always been taught to regard as her very private parts entered and forced and invaded without any compensation. Most grooms didn't make love to their brides, they raped them. Time after time, without even trying to rouse them. Then they complained that their wives were frigid or wondered why. If such a bride was a normal, passionate woman she eventually turned to some other man who was intelligent enough to realize that sexual response in a woman was as much mental and emotional and even spiritual, as it was physical.

Gerta pressed Hart's cheek to her flesh. "I like that."

Hart kissed her lips. "So do I. But that's as far as we're going right now." He cupped the back of her head in his hands. "Now I tell you what you do. You go on in and take your bath, then put on your pretty new clothes. Meanwhile, I'll go downstairs and see if I can get a line on Bonnie. Then when I come back we'll go out and eat and have a few drinks to celebrate being married."

"Before—?"

"Before." Hart patted one of her silk-covered buttocks lightly. "Now stop trembling."

"I can't help it," Gerta said, big-eyed. "I'm scared." She was eager to please him. "But don't pay any attention to me, Doc. If you want me, take me."

Hart kissed her eyes. "I intend to. Later. But when I do, I want you to want it as much as I do. Now go on in and take your bath. There's no hurry. We have all the rest of our lives. This time it's for keeps."

Gerta repeated the two words, "For keeps. Sounds good." She wriggled out of her scanties and walked on into the bath. "Don't be long, please."

"I won't," Hart promised. "Believe me."

He left the room quickly and locked the door. It was difficult to walk down the stairs. Reading a two day old Mexico City paper, the clerk looked up. When Hart laid a five dollar bill on the counter he put down the paper.

"For some information," Hart said.

"*Sí, señor—?*"

Hart said, "I doubt if she was registered here but did you ever hear of a Señora Alveredo Montez? A pretty girl, well-built, with dyed black hair. This would be four, five months ago."

The clerk shrugged. "*Señor.* That is a long time ago. And in a tourist town such as this, people come, people go." He thought a moment. "The name however is familiar. Why do you not inquire in the *cantina* across the street?"

"Thanks," Hart said, "I will."

The *cantina* was small but well patronized. The trade was strictly local. There were six or seven couples at the tables. As Hart leaned against the bar a slip of a girl, not more than fifteen or sixteen, sidled up to him and smiled.

"You would buy me a drink, perhaps, *señor?*"

"Sure," Hart said. "Why not?"

He ordered tequila for both of them, mildly amused. B-girls were much the same, north or south of the border. This one thought she'd spotted a live one. She proved it by bending farther forward than need be to give him a glimpse of the delights that could be his for a fee.

Hart was curt with her. "Look, honey. You're wasting your time." He tucked a bill in the cleft between her *café-con-leche*-colored breasts. "But that's yours for the answer to one question."

"*Sí—?*"

"Did you ever hear of a Señora Alveredo Montez?"

The girl spoke in rapid Spanish to the barman. When she turned back she was smiling. "But *sí, señor.* She is one ver' grand *señora.* Francisco say her 'usband was one of Coronel Marcos Perez Jimenez's chief *tenientes.* Of Venezuela, you know. And when *el dictator* was deposed, she was given political refuge in this country."

It was, Hart thought, about the type of story a strip-teaser with delusions of grandeur would invent. His feeling of breathlessness returned. He said, "Ask him if he knows whether she is in Ensenada and if so where she is living."

This time, when she turned back to him from the barman, she was not smiling. "Francisco says for a time she was living in one of the grand *casas* on the beach but he does not know where she is now. He says it is unwise to meddle in such matters and will the *señor* please take his questions elsewhere."

Hart thought a moment. He'd done all he could alone. The local police might or might not have been notified about him. It was a chance he had to take. But now he knew that Peggy had been telling the truth. Such a person as Señora Alveredo Montez really existed.

SEPTEMBER 3, 2958
9:25 P.M.

The police station smelled like all police stations, of cheap tobacco and despair and unwashed male bodies. It was difficult to determine from his uniform if Captain Rafael Cabrera was of the federal or local police. An alert, clean-shaven man in his middle thirties, he listened politely to what Hart had to say, then nodded.

"That is correct, *señor*. The Los Angeles police did contact us two days ago and we informed them that on the dates they mentioned no such woman as they described was checked into any of the hotels or motels in Ensenada."

Hart protested, "But that can't be, Captain. I've only been in town less than an hour and the only three persons I talked to recognized the name. The clerk at the hotel, a bar *muchacha* and a barman."

Cabrera shrugged. "I'm sorry. Now may I ask you a question, *señor?* What is your interest in this matter?"

"Let's just say I'm vitally interested."

"You have some official standing? You are with the Los Angeles police? Perhaps the F.B.I.? Maybe the United States Secret Service?"

"No. I'm just a private citizen."

Captain Cabrera stood up to indicate the interview was over. "Then I am very sorry, *señor*, but I will not be able to assist you. Now if you will excuse me—"

Hart debated offering him money and decided it would be unwise. Captain Cabrera didn't look like that kind of an officer. If he offered the captain a bribe he would probably spend his wedding night in jail.

As he left the station a big man lounging in the doorway took an unlighted cigar from his mouth and said, *"Perdóneome.* Do you have a light, *señor?"*

Hart thumbed his lighter into flame and held it to the man's cigar. *"Gracias."*

"Think nothing of it," Hart said, sourly. "I like to light cigars for plain-clothes cops."

He'd developed a headache. He was back in the same old rut of everything failing to make sense. He could imagine Bonnie hiding out in Ensenada for a few days. But dumb as she was, he couldn't picture her staying there. Too many theatrical people used it as a playground, people who knew her and had worked with her.

Hart walked slowly back toward the hotel. Halfway there, he stopped in front of the mullioned windows of a dimly-lighted shop, his attention attracted by a pair of familiar red and green globes in the window and a weathered gold-lettered sign bearing the legend *Farmacia.*

He forced himself to think constructively. It had been brought out at the trial that along with her excessive drinking Bonnie, in order to sleep, had taken a large number of Seconal tablets and other barbiturates used as sedatives and hypnotics.

Judging from the size of the town he felt sure this was the only *farmacia* in it. It was worth a try. A bell on the door tinkled as Hart opened it. He hadn't been in a store like this for years. It was a typical old time pharmacy. There was no soda fountain, no cosmetic or cigar counters, no candy case, no wire racks filled with lurid magazines, nothing but neatly kept shelves of bottled drugs and herbs and packaged patent nostrums. The store was an anachronism, an isolated island in time, a relic of an older, less swiftly paced, perhaps better world.

A pleasant-faced elderly man smiled at him from behind a small wooden counter. *"Buenas tardes, señor. ¿En que puedo ser a usted agradable?"*

Good evening, sir. How can I be useful to you? Hart made a mental note of the phrase. A good many druggists, himself included, could dignify their profession by emulating the elderly Mexican.

He felt his way in faulty Spanish. "May I ask a favor of you?" He took his wallet from his pocket and laid the various cards identifying him as a fellow pharmacist on the counter. "But first let me introduce myself."

The elderly Mexican spoke no English. Hart's Spanish was elementary. It was sufficient. When he left the shop, fifteen minutes later, he knew what he wanted to know. Not only was the Señora Alveredo Montez still in the general Ensenada area, she was a valued patron of Señor Aguello's.

Every week, at her request, his assistant delivered to the de Medoza ranch, some six miles south of Ensenada on the road to Santo Tomas, where the *señora* was currently residing, three dozen one and one half grain Seconal capsules, one small bottle of black hair dye, a various assortment of aspirin, Anacin and similar remedies and one large bottle of a patent reducing formula.

The hotel clerk was still reading the Mexico City paper. He lowered it as Hart started up the stairs. "You were successful in your inquiries, *señor?"*

"I made out just fine," Hart told him.

He unlocked the door of his and Gerta's room, then closed it and leaned against it. Instead of being dressed to go out, Gerta was lying on the bed completely nude.

"What's the idea?" he asked her. "I thought you were going to fix yourself up to go out and eat?"

Gerta studied him with sullen eyes. She'd fluffed a pillow against the head of the bed and was lying with one knee raised, her other leg extended. Her straw-colored hair was still damp at the roots from her bath. Instead of combing it in its usual ponytail she'd allowed it to fall loose. Lying as she was, a lock of it hung down and partially covered one of her eyes. Her hands were pressed to her upper body, the crinkled, coral-hard peaks of her breasts thrusting out from between her splayed fingers.

When she spoke, her voice was barely audible. "Are you hungry?"

"No," Hart admitted. "Not now."

"Then why don't you come to bed?" Her lower lip quivered. "Sure, I'm scared. But I want to be married to you. Really married. You can understand that."

"Yes," Hart said. "I can."

He took off his coat and hung it on the hook on the door. Then he unbuttoned and took off his shirt and unbuckled his belt. Bonnie could wait. According to the proprietor of the *farmacia*, Señora Montez had been at the de Medoza ranch since shortly after the first of the year. A few more hours wouldn't make much difference.

As he crossed the room and lay down on the bed beside Gerta the night noises outside the window seemed to intensify. The blare of the jukebox in the *cantina* across the street seemed very loud. Through and above it, he could hear a woman laughing, the faint jangling of a ship's bell and the far-off howling of a dog.

Gerta scrunched lower in the bed. Her voice was low but fierce. "Just tell me what to do."

Hart stroked one of her rounded white hips, then ran his hand over her upper body. He should feel elated but he didn't. Perhaps he'd been a bachelor too long. He was ashamed of himself as he thought it but there was nothing different about Gerta from any of the other girls he'd known. She excited him, yes. But so had other women. To know the ultimate in sex women had to combine it with love. Not so with men. Most men, if sufficiently hard put, would lay a mongoose, if the mongoose would hold still.

"What are you thinking about?" Gerta whispered.

Hart was truthful with her. "Us."

He wished sincerely this whole thing hadn't happened. But how to explain that to Gerta? She was his wife. For better or for worse. Through sickness and in health. Until death did them two part. He'd put a ring on her finger. He'd promised.

Because he was dubious of his own emotions he was very gentle with her as he first fingered, then kissed her eyes, her throat, the deep hollow between her breasts, the aureoles of her breasts, her nipples.

"You're very lovely."

"Thank you."

Hart became more intimate as he kneaded the soft flesh of her thighs. Then his caresses became more insistent as he said what he knew she wanted him to say. "And I love you."

"I hoped you'd say that," she panted.

I love you.

A little thing.

Three words.

But not to a woman in love. Love made everything right.

The change in the girl was immediate. She was no longer afraid. Her body rocked in active co-operation as it rose and fell in the ageless rhythm of copulation. The words were an animal sound in her throat. "Are you ready?"

"God, yes."

Gerta scrunched lower in the bed. "Then do it," she groaned.

Hart thought for a moment she was going to know her climax immediately. She didn't. She seemed to want it to last. Hart hoped it lasted forever. All his doubts were gone. He hadn't lied to Gerta. He was in love with this child. He'd been looking for her all his life. Even this first time their bodies were perfectly mated. Holding Gerta was like holding living flame.

"You tell me when," he whispered.

She cupped his face between her hands and kissed him. "I will. I will."

Seconds short of their joint goal her rocking body went limp and she cried out again, not in ecstasy, but in shock, as a heavy hand pounded on the door and filled the room with new sound.

"Señor, señora," a man called.

Gerta lay with her fists clenched at her sides. Her eyes were agonized. "Tell him to go away," she whispered.

"Go away," Hart called.

"I am sorry, *señor,*" the man on the far side of the door said. "But you and the *señora* will have to admit me. I am from the police."

Gerta's flesh twitched spasmodically. She put her hands on Hart's chest and gave one last little despairing push. Then she turned on her side and cried.

The perspiration trickling into his eyes half blinding him, Hart swung to his feet and reached for his trousers. "What do you want?"

"You are the *Norte Americano señor* who just inquired for the Señora Alveredo Montez?"

"Yes."

"Then open the door."

Hart opened the door an inch and tried, vainly, to close it. The big man whose cigar he'd lighted was standing in the hallway and directly behind him was Mr. Deering's chauffeur.

"Don't try anything foolish, Hart," the chauffeur said. "If you do we'll kill the two of you right here."

Hart looked from the barrel of the gun poking him in the stomach to the face of the man holding it. "You're not a policeman."

"That's right," the man grinned. "I guess you might call me just a little extra insurance." He laughed.

Gerta got to her feet, trying to cover herself with her hands. "Excuse me," she said, as she walked uncertainly toward the bathroom. "I think I'm going to be ill."

SEPTEMBER 3, 1958
10:09 P.M.

The chauffeur watched Gerta go into the bathroom. "Nice. I guess I should have been a druggist. You do get around, don't you, Hart. First the pretty Cotton girl, now her. How was she, Hart? Cherry?"

Hart's reaction was instinctive. Ignoring the gun, he hit the chauffeur as hard as he could. While the man was still on the floor he tried to kick him with his bare foot and the big man who looked like an Ensenada detective knocked him to the floor beside the bed with a vicious swipe of the gun barrel.

"You shouldn't have said that," the man reproved the chauffeur. "After all, the young lady is his wife and that was a very personal question."

The chauffeur got to his feet. "It's going to be a pleasure," he informed Hart. "Up until now, I was just doing a job, but now you've made it personal."

All Hart had on was his trousers. He felt almost as naked as Gerta. Sitting on the floor, he put on his socks and shoes. Then pulling himself up by the foot board of the disordered bed, he put on his shirt and buttoned it. There was an ugly red welt across his face but he was too angry to feel any pain.

"You followed us from Rosarito. You were in the car that passed us on the crest of the hill."

"That's right," the chauffeur admitted. "It seems Luis and I got to Newport too late to stop you from nosing around the yacht. But when you took time out in Tijuana to make an honest woman of Miss Nielsen, it gave us a chance to catch up."

"Look," Hart asked. "What's this all about? What have I gotten into?"

Luis lighted a cigarette. "That, *señor,* is a long story."

"A long one," the chauffeur agreed.

Hart waited for one of them to say more. They didn't. He was damned if he'd ask again. The chances were that now Deering had come out into the open, he would find out what it was all about—at the multi-millionaire's convenience.

Hart picked up Gerta's new underthings and skirt and blouse from a chair. "Is it all right if I take these to my wife?"

Luis leered. "It might be wise. Unless you want the Ensenada police to arrest her for indecent exposure."

The chauffeur glanced into the bathroom. "Her exposure indecent? Not to me. I could use a little of that, myself."

"And screw up everything else?" Luis asked him.

"No," the chauffeur said. "I don't want her that bad. Okay, Hart. Take her clothes to her."

Gerta was standing with her back to the door, clinging to the rim of the wash bowl. "How do you feel?" Hart asked her.

"Terrible," she said. "I'm all sick and mixed up inside."

"I know."

"Everything was so beautiful. And now—"

Hart was afraid she was going to become hysterical. He turned her around and slapped her, lightly. "Hold on."

She touched his face with her fingers. "They hurt you."

"I'll live." Hart led her to the facility and closed the cover. "Now sit down and I'll help you dress."

It was like dressing a limp rag doll. He managed, after a fashion, to fit her stockings to her legs. Then he started her scanties for her and stood her up while he snugged them over her hips and fitted her breasts into the cups of her bra.

"I love you, Doc," she whispered. "So much."

Hart gave her a gentle kiss on the lips. "I love you."

He slipped her skirt over her head and helped her into her blouse. As he did, the chauffeur called from the other room, "You were just going to take her clothes to her, remember?"

"We're just about ready," Hart said.

"What are they going to do with us?" Gerta asked.

Hart shook his head. "I don't know."

The window was open. Hart looked out and down. It was twenty feet to the alley, too far for Gerta to drop. He searched the bathroom for a weapon. The only thing he could find was the heavy metal plunger type stopper in the old fashioned bath tub. He lifted it from the drain as silently as he could and put it in his side pants pocket.

He'd barely succeeded in concealing it when Luis came into the bathroom. "Come on. Let's go. Time's wasting."

Holding her small chin high, Gerta walked past him into the bedroom.

Mr. Deering's chauffeur had emptied the pockets of Hart's coat and the contents of his wallet on the rumpled sheet. "Of all the guys in L.A.," he said, "they would pick this one for jury duty. Then he would have to meet the Cotton girl."

"That's past history," Luis said. "But, by the way, Hart, why did you kill her?"

Gerta sat in a chair and put on her shoes. "He didn't."

Luis shrugged. "That's not the way I heard it." He picked Hart's paper money from the bed and put the bills in his own pocket. "A good thing we caught you, chum. You were running short of folding."

"Where are you taking us?" Hart asked.

"To see Mr. Deering," the servant said. "Mr. Deering wants to have another talk with you."

Hart was relieved. It was sixty-five miles from Ensenada to Tijuana, sixteen miles from Tijuana to San Diego and one hundred and twenty-one miles from San Diego to Los Angeles. A lot could happen in two hundred and two miles. He meant to see that something did.

"You boys have the guns," he said, quietly. "How do we travel?"

"By car."

"Your car or mine?"

"Yours," the chauffeur said. "With me driving." He put his gun in the side pocket of his coat. "But don't try to play the hero. Don't get any wild ideas. I can get at this in hardly any time. I can even shoot through my pocket. Besides, Luis will be in the back seat with his gun pointed at your head."

"And between here and the car?"

"What do you mean by that?"

"You have to take us through the lobby. What if I tell the clerk we're being kidnapped and ask him to call the police?"

"That's up to you," the chauffeur said. He pointed the gun in his pocket at Gerta. "But if you do she gets it." He was deliberately obscene as he told Hart the exact anatomical portion of her body in which he intended to shoot her. He opened the room door. "You first, Hart. Your wife right behind you."

Hart's knees felt stiff as he descended the stairs. The clerk was still reading the paper. He was pleased to see the Harts had company. *"Señora, señores."*

Luis bowed graciously. *"Señor."*

A stiff breeze was blowing off the ocean. The night was cool. Perhaps because it was growing late, the tempo of the music in the *cantina* had changed. The strident strings had ceased strumming. Accompanying the disjointed, random plucking of his guitar a lachrymose Spanish tenor was singing *Vaya con Dios,* my darling. Go with God.

"You and the girl get in front with me," the chauffeur said.

The moon was beginning to wane. There were no street lights. They drove through the dark in silence for a few minutes. Then Hart said, sharply, "Just a minute. This is not the road to Los Angeles. You're headed out toward the beach."

"That's right," the chauffeur nodded.

Luis said pleasantly from the back seat, "With a gun at your head, *señor.* It is to be regretted but it would seem in your country not only *poco* pitchers have big ears."

"Little pitchers, is that what he means, Doc?" Gerta asked.

"Yes," Hart told her. "In other words, we know too much."

He debated asking the two men to let Gerta go and knew it would be futile. Neither of them made policy. They were just hired hands. They were merely doing what they were paid to do. A few minutes later the chauffeur braked the car in front of a deserted section of beach. Peering through the windshield Hart could see a neglected wooden fishing pier and moored to the pier the bobbing silhouette of a small power cruiser.

"This is it," the chauffeur said.

Hart got out of the car slowly and helped Gerta out. One read about such things but they always happened to strangers. They never happened to anyone you knew or to you. He would have done much better to have made a stand in the hotel. The chauffeur and Luis weren't taking them to Mr. Deering. They were headed for the small boat and the open sea.

A half mile away he could see the lights of a motel. People were sitting in the patio and around the pool, talking, drinking and making love. Here there was only the night and the beach and the sea. Hart took an awkward step forward, pretended to stumble in the dry sand and threw himself at the chauffeur and wrapped his arms around him.

"Run," he called to Gerta. "Run. Go to the police."

In the darkness behind him he could hear Gerta breathing heavily. Her voice was semi-hysterical and poignant with frustration. "I can't," she called back. "The other one is holding me."

It was difficult to keep his footing in the loose sand. The other man was stronger than he was. Hart could feel his grip slipping. Then the chauffeur pulled his gun hand free and wrenched his gun from his pocket and beat down at Hart's head with it.

"I warned you not to try to be a hero," he panted. He continued to beat at Hart's head. "But if this is the way you want it, okay. When the police find what the sharks leave of your body, if they ever do, you're going to look like you bumped into a lot of rocks."

As Hart slipped to his knees, he thought he heard Gerta crying. Then the sound of the girl's sobbing voice and the surge and the suck of the sea exploded in a blinding flash of pain and only the dry sand in his mouth was real....

When Hart became conscious again he was lying in the open cockpit of the cruiser he'd seen. His aching head was pillowed in Gerta's lap. The shore lights of Ensenada were a misty blur in the distance.

As far as he could tell there were only the four of them aboard. Luis was forward at the wheel. The chauffeur was leaning against the transom, alternating admiring the wake of the vessel and Gerta. As Hart watched him, he drank from a pint bottle of whiskey and decided Gerta was the more attractive.

"You know, you're a very pretty girl," he informed her. "I noticed that when you came to the house with Hart the other afternoon. Then when

I saw you up in that crummy hotel room—" He sucked in his breath at the memory. "Jesus."

"Cut it," Luis said from the wheel. "I warned you."

The chauffeur was just drunk enough to be cocky. "So you warned me."

Luis sounded a little sick. "If we're going to dump them let's get it over with and get back to L.A. Frankly, I don't feel too good about the girl."

"That's what I mean," the chauffeur said. "Why waste her? Who's to know?" Without moving from the transom he reached down and gripped Gerta's arm and pulled her, struggling, to her feet. "How about a little for me before you go swimming, honey?"

What followed happened so fast Hart was never quite clear as to the details. He remembered kneeling, resting his weight on his knuckles, still working the sand out of his mouth. Then his body was hurtling through space and his fists were battering at the off-guard chauffeur's face and body. Caught off-balance, the small of his back to the sharp edge of the transom, the chauffeur cried out and was gone. Where he'd been there was only empty transom, some broken glass in the cockpit and a torn fragment of his coat.

"The beast," Gerta panted. "The filth."

She stared a moment at the screaming black dot bobbing in the phosphorescent wake of the cruiser, then snatched at the torn fragment of coat.

Luis closed the throttle and left the wheel and came aft. "For a druggist, you're a tough *hombre,* at that," he complimented Hart. "And that's one more share for me." He pointed the barrel of the gun in his hand at Hart's middle. "I'm sorry, *señor,* believe me," he said softly. "But—"

He stopped short, puzzled, and slapped his free hand to his chest as if he were slapping at a mosquito as a bright finger of flame pointed from the corner of the cockpit in which Gerta was crouched.

The hysterical girl continued to pull the trigger of the revolver she'd recovered from the pocket in the torn fragment of coat and Luis suddenly had too many bites to attend to. His body buffeted by the impact of the bullets was slapped back against the engine housing. He stood a moment longer, clinging to it, rubber-kneed, unbelieving, then slumped to the deck and lay still.

When Hart could find his voice he said, "You've killed him."

Gerta dropped the empty gun. "I meant to."

The cruiser with no seaway was wallowing and shipping water. It was almost impossible to stand. Hart fought his way forward to the wheel and shoved the throttle ahead.

Gerta came and stood beside him. She had to shout to make herself heard above the throb of the engine and the wind. "Are you all right,

Doc?"

Hart's smile was tight. "I'm fine. And you—?"

Her lips moved as if she was trying to work a bad taste out of her mouth. "All right, I guess. I still feel sort of queasy."

Hart put his free arm around her. "Forget it. You had to do what you did."

"I know."

Hart spun the wheel of the cruiser and circled back toward the distant lights on shore.

"Now, what are we going to do?" she asked him.

"That," Hart said, "is the problem."

He knew too much and nothing. Except for the fact that he and Gerta were still alive, he wasn't any better off than he'd been when he'd driven into Ensenada. He did not even dare to appeal to the local police. Captain Cabrera had refused to assist him before. Now, with two dead men to account for, Cabrera certainly wouldn't believe a fantastic story about the two men kidnapping himself and Gerta. He didn't even know the men's names. What could he tell Cabrera?

"One of them, the one in the boat, was called Luis. The other was Mr. Deering's chauffeur."

Captain Cabrera would laugh, politely. He would laugh and laugh and laugh. Then he would charge him with murder. Hart forced himself to think constructively.

Bonnie was still the crux of the matter. Until he had some tangible proof that Peggy Cotton could have seen Bonnie and been killed because she had, until he could prove Bonnie was alive, this nightmare could go on indefinitely.

"We don't seem to have much choice," he said, finally. "If I can get this thing back to shore, about the only thing we can do is call on Señora Alveredo Montez and see if we can force her to tell us what this is all about, why she wants to be dead, why she framed Harry Cotton for murder."

"Now? Tonight?"

"As soon as we can."

"We can't even go back to the hotel?"

"No."

Gerta leaned her head on Hart's shoulder. "Well, one thing is certain, that's for sure."

Hart altered his course a degree. "What's that?"

Gerta sighed. "I'll have a beaut of a story to tell my grandchildren. That is," the blonde girl added wryly, "if I ever have any."

SEPTEMBER 4, 1958
1:17 A.M.

At exactly six miles on the trip meter of Kelly's car, Hart pulled over onto the shoulder of the road and switched off the headlights. So far so good. The elderly Mexican pharmacist had been right about the mileage. The de Medoza ranch was exactly six miles from Ensenada. From what he could see of it in the dark it looked much more like a working spread than the type of dude ranch where a girl like Bonnie Tempest would be content to hide out.

Gerta studied the crude gateway on the far side of the road. "Aren't you going to drive in?"

Hart shook his head. "No. After that business back there on the boat, I don't want to attract any more attention to us than we have to. If possible, I want to talk to Bonnie and be back across the border by daylight."

He opened the door on his side of the car and got out. "Maybe you'd better wait here."

Gerta slid out under the wheel and joined him in the deep dust on the shoulder of the road. "No." She attempted to recover some of her flippancy. "We're married, remember? And like it says in the Bible, where you go I go."

The ranch road was graded but not surfaced. The buildings Hart could see were a quarter of a mile back from the highway. Before he and Gerta had gone two hundred feet they were joined by a brace of friendly dogs who sniffed curiously at their ankles, then romped along beside them.

"Nice doggies," Gerta said.

Hart made sure the revolver he'd taken from the cockpit of the cruiser, Luis' gun, was still in his pocket. It could well be he was being foolish in doing what he was doing but he couldn't see that he had any choice. Even his own lawyer didn't believe him. Proof that Bonnie was alive was the only thing that would save both his and Harry Cotton's life.

He'd been right about it being a working ranch. There were the usual outbuildings and open sheds and corrals. The ranch yard smelled of dust and hay and animal droppings. The house was long and low, one-story whitewashed adobe, with an immense open gallery running the length of the building.

Walking quietly, Hart tiptoed along the gallery and looked in through the one lighted window. It was a typical ranch house living room, complete with Indian rugs and rawhide chairs and gun racks on the walls. At the far end of the big room an expensive hi-fi combination record player and radio was playing Sibelius' *Valse Triste*. It was a strange choice for Bonnie. Obviously her musical tastes had changed since the days when she bumped her G-string in time to *I Can't Give You Anything But Love, Baby* and *Only a Paper Moon*. The chair in which the listening girl was sitting had a high back, so high that all Hart could see of her was one slim ankle and the back of her dyed hair.

"There she is," he whispered to Gerta.

"You can see her?"

"Just the back of her head."

He reached for the knob of the door beside the window, then straightened slowly as a round hard object pressed into the small of his back. It was an effort for him to turn his head to look over his shoulder.

The middle-aged Mexican who'd materialized out of the night stared back coldly. "As you have observed," he said, "I am holding a *pistola* to your back, *señor* and it would be most unwise of you to make any sudden move." He added, with a sober expression, "You see, the good Captain Cabrera informed me earlier this evening that there was someone in town looking for the *señora* and that we might have company."

Hart felt a drop of perspiration escape the pit of his arm and trickle down his side. It felt cold. "It seems," he admitted wryly, "I'm not much of a prowler."

The Mexican was factual about it. "Permit me to agree with you, *señor*. You are the *Norte Americano* who was inquiring for the Señora Alveredo Montez?"

"That's right."

The man pressed the barrel still deeper into Hart's back. "Then allow me to introduce myself. I am Jaime de Medoza. Just what is it you wish of my sister? And why should you concern yourself in a purely political affair?"

Hart felt the short hairs on the back of his neck rise. Something was radically wrong here. Bonnie Tempest had been a lot of things to a lot of men but as far as he knew she'd never been anyone's sister.

"Now, look. *Un momento,*" he began. "I—"

Before he could finish what he'd been about to say, the door beside the window opened and the escaping light rolled a yellow runner across the gallery.

"What is it, Jaime?" the woman who'd opened the door asked in liquid Spanish. "Was Captain Cabrera correct? Do we have a caller?"

"Callers," de Medoza said. "A gentleman who looks like he has just been very badly beaten." He glanced at Gerta. "And a pretty *señorita.*"

"*Señora,*" Gerta corrected him.

Still keeping his palms shoulder high, Hart made a slow turn and looked at the woman standing in the lighted doorway. As a girl she must have been very beautiful. Even now, in her forties, with obviously dyed hair and inclined to be more than a little plump, she was very lovely and gracious. But whoever she was, she was not Bonnie Tempest.

"You," Hart asked, "are the Señora Alveredo Montez?"

"*Sí,*" the woman smiled. "But I am forgetting my manners. Please to come in while you explain what possible reason my late husband's political enemies can have for wishing me harm. I thought that when the Republica de Mejico so graciously granted me political refuge and I came here to live with my brother that I would be finished with all that business."

De Medoza prodded Hart with his gun. "My sister asks you to enter." He bowed to Gerta. *"Por favor."*

Hart felt like a fool. "What can I say," he said. "Only that I've made a mistake. And that I have no wish to harm you, *señora.* I thought you were Mrs. John R. Deering, Bonnie Tempest."

Gerta sat in one of the rawhide chairs with her hands folded primly in her lap. "She's a night club entertainer from Los Angeles," she explained. "She did a strip tease for the better night clubs." Her eyes were thoughtful as she looked at Hart. "And another girl told my husband she saw her here in Ensenada about four months ago." With a slight edge to her voice she went on, "At least Mr. Hart *says* this girl told him she saw Bonnie."

The plump women was pleased. "You hear that, Jaime? Someone mistook me for a night club entertainer."

De Medoza wasn't amused. "How long ago was this?"

Hart fought down a wave of nausea. This was it. He'd reached the end of the line. Peggy had lied to him. There was nothing left for him to do now but return to Los Angeles and give himself up. If he could get that far. If he wasn't arrested before he reached the border and charged with the murders of Luis and the chauffeur. He answered the rancher's question. "The middle of last April. Why?"

Señora Montez answered for her brother. "I believe Jaime is thinking of a house guest we had at that time." She described her with her hands. "A very generously proportioned young lady. A very beautiful girl who for some foolish reason persisted in dyeing her naturally red hair black."

Hart leaned forward and rested his head in his hands. He'd never been so relieved. He felt like a man who, about to walk the last few feet to the lethal chamber, had just been granted a full pardon.

Gerta came over and sat on the arm of his chair. "I'm sorry, Doc," she was contrite. "I never should have doubted you. And I won't ever again. It's just that whenever I think of what happened that night I get jealous."

Señora Montez was concerned. "You are ill, *señor?* Perhaps a glass of brandy?"

Hart smiled at her. "Thanks, no. I'm fine. I'm just fine now." He chose his words carefully. "First let me apologize for blundering in here and alarming you the way I did. And let me assure you I wish no harm to the *señora* and there is absolutely nothing political about my being here."

De Medoza laid the revolver he was holding on a table and bowed stiffly. "I am inclined to believe you, *señora*. Please proceed."

Hart thought a moment. "If I may ask, just what was your connection with this girl?"

The woman shrugged. "It is rather complicated, I'm afraid. This girl of whom we speak was never quite coherent during the week or so she was with us. But I gathered that her husband had some business with the late Señor Montez, something about some money he had hoped to invest in my country before the recent unpleasantness and this girl of whom we speak wished to test the veracity of statements made to her by her husband." Señora Montez fluttered her hands. "It was all very confusing."

"What name did she give you?" Hart asked.

De Medoza smiled wryly, "Marie Garcia. Mary Smith in your country, *señor*. She arrived from Ensenada one day in a taxi, in a very intoxicated condition. I would have turned her away." He looked at his sister. "But Bianca, having no children of her own, is always mothering someone."

Señora Montez made a sound like a clucking hen. "She was so frightened, so confused, so pale. I thought perhaps I could help her."

Tight-lipped, de Medoza said, "But I may say that in this instance, my sister's kindness was wasted. This girl was not only basically immoral, she was a psychotic."

Hart, wondering at the rancher's command of the language, asked, "In what way?"

The other man cleared his throat. "She not only drank constantly but before she had been here two days she behaved in a most improper manner with my head vaquero. On the evening of the second day I caught them together in one of my box stalls in a very delicate situation."

He added dryly, "This is not customary."

"I don't suppose you know where she is now?" Hart asked.

"This was four months ago, *señor*."

Señora Montez was apologetic. "Her husband came and took her away. At least he said he was her husband."

"She went with him willingly?"

"Willingly. He was a big man, dark and very handsome, with an air of the sea about him."

That would be Captain Morales. Morales was in this up to his neck. More, the Mexican woman had specifically mentioned Bonnie being pale. Hart considered the statement. That could mean that until she'd come to Ensenada in April, Bonnie had been kept out of sight, willingly or not, either aboard the Deering yacht or in the Deering mansion immediately following her disappearance.

He got to his feet. *"Gracias. Muchisimas gracias.* Now if we have convinced you that I did not come here to harm the *señora,* Mrs. Hart and I had better be on our way."

"You are returning to Ensenada?"

"No. Los Angeles." Hart went on, with a shrug, "If we can get there. I want to see a man about something. Also a lot of money. To be exact, two hundred and fifty thousand dollars."

Gerta stood up and smoothed her skirt. "Before we leave, could I ask two questions, Doc?"

"Of course."

"Why did Bonnie come here? What possible sort of business could Mr. Deering have had with Señor Montez?"

Hart shook his head. "I'm afraid that is one of the things the police are going to have to ask Mr. Deering."

"Also tell me this."

"Yes?"

"You say Peggy Cotton told you she saw Bonnie in Ensenada and that Bonnie was using the name Señora Montez and posing as the widow of a wealthy South American."

"That's right."

"How could she possibly confuse the two of them?"

De Medoza raised his hand in a Latin gesture and said, "Possibly I can explain that. The girl of whom you speak, the one who confused my sister with this person who descended upon us, was she Norte Americano, young, intense and very pretty?"

"Yes," Hart said. "That would describe Peggy."

The rancher nodded. "Then I must be to blame. During the week she was with us, one day while my sister and this Bonnie were shopping in Ensenada and I was walking a few paces behind them, such a young *turista* seemed to take much interest in them. She finally approached me and asked me if I knew who the pretty black-haired lady was. I assumed she meant Bianca and I told her proudly she was the Señora Alveredo Montez."

The little things, Hart thought. The human reactions that pleased women, confused the destiny of nations, sent killers to the gas chamber.

His hand on the knob of the door, he said, "Just one more question. Did you mention the incident to the two women, perhaps point out the girl to them?"

"Sí," de Medoza said. "As a matter of fact, I did."

SEPTEMBER 5, 1958
12:12 A.M.

The freeway hadn't changed during the last forty-eight hours. It was still eight lanes wide, four lanes in each direction, each lane filled with speeding cars; young men taking girls home, eager to kiss them good-night, lay them in the back seat, sit holding hands and drinking coffee while they planned a dubious future filled with possible recessions and depressions and atomic war; older men, family men with tired eyes, the first fierce fire gone from their loins, their minds on mortgage payments and their wives and children and above all on their jobs; pick-up trucks and lonely girls willing to be picked up; sober old men and skylarking teen-agers; con men and preachers and squares; all of them in a rush to get where they were going and not knowing just what to do when they got there.

Hart's beaten head ached. His fingers were cramped from gripping the wheel. His eyes felt hot and gritty. He'd never been so tired. He'd driven five hundred miles in two days, in very few hours of actual driving time, with two beatings, one boat ride, two dead men and a bad case of sexual frustration thrown in for lagniappe. He hadn't been normal since.

His face settled into bleak lines as he relived the past few hours.

"Are you all right, Doc?" Gerta asked him.

"I'll make it," he assured her.

"Are we going to the store first?"

"If the police don't have it staked out."

"And then—?"

"Out to call on Deering."

"You think Bonnie might be there?"

"I don't know," Hart said. "I hope so. It can be by now she's dead. In that case, we're sunk."

He sighed as he left the freeway and turned west on Sunset Boulevard. When he and Gerta had left Ensenada, everything had seemed so simple, so close to a solution. He had reasoned if he and Gerta could get out of Mexico safely and return to Los Angeles before Luis and the chauffeur's bodies were discovered, all he would have to do would be to go to State's Attorney Manson and Inspector Garcia and tell him the story.

"This is the way it is. Harry Cotton didn't kill Mrs. Deering. He was framed. For some reason Bonnie assisted in faking her own death. There's a crawl hole in the Deering yacht to prove it. What's more, after I discovered the hole and Mrs. Hart and I drove on down to Ensenada to try to substantiate Peggy Cotton's story that she had seen Bonnie alive four months after Cotton was supposed to have killed her, Mr. Deering, tipped off by Captain Morales, sent his chauffeur and another thug down there to kill us. They tried but didn't succeed. Before we left to come home we found a woman and her brother, substantial people in the community who are willing to swear that Bonnie or a reasonable facsimile, was in Ensenada at that time."

The rest would be up to the police. It would be up to them to examine the yacht, to question Morales, to try to determine who killed Peggy, to locate Bonnie, to sweat Mr. Deering until he broke down and told them the truth.

Now all that was changed. They were more on the defensive than they had been. Hart glanced at the folded newspaper Gerta was holding, the paper they'd bought in Laguna Beach on their way north. "Read me that story again, honey," he said.

Gerta unfolded the paper and held it under the faint light from the dashboard. "Well," she began, "the headline says, 'Grand Jury Indicts Druggist.'"

She drew one knee up under her and turned sideways on the seat to get more light on the paper. "Under that it says 'Late this afternoon, despite an impassioned plea by the missing John Hart's lawyer, the blue ribbon grand jury, impaneled to hear the evidence in the vicious sex murder of Mrs. Peggy Cotton, sometimes known as Peggy Jones, voted unanimously that the girl had come to her death at the hands of the prominent Sunset Strip businessman. State's Attorney Manson immediately issued a warrant charging Hart with suspicion of murder.'"

Hart braked for a red traffic light. "Now skip on down to that business about us and the Deering yacht."

Gerta ran her finger down the column of newsprint. "'When interviewed by this reporter, Inspector Garcia of the metropolitan Los Angeles homicide squad said it is his considered opinion that Hart, in company with a pretty blonde employee, Gerta Nielsen, has fled to Mexico to evade prosecution for murder. Additional credence is given to this theory by the Newport Police who report that Hart and Miss Nielsen appeared in that city last night in a highly intoxicated condition and after spending some hours together in a nearby motel made such a scene aboard the Deering yacht that the police were forced to escort them to the city limits and warn them to leave town. It is now believed, however, that instead of leaving Newport, for reasons known only to themselves, the couple returned to the boat basin and set fire to the Deering yacht which burned to the water line, in spite of the heroic effort of the local fire department.'"

Gerta looked up from the paper. "I'm scared, Doc."

"So am I," Hart admitted.

He was. Now that he'd been indicted, now that the yacht had burned, he didn't dare go to the police. The police would have no choice but to put him in a cell. Separate cells for him and Gerta. Whatever was done he would have to do himself.

The one bright spot was Kelly. The lawyer must have had a change of heart. Kelly evidently didn't believe he was guilty. Kelly had made an impassioned plea to the jury.

When he reached his store he drove past it slowly. As usual, the night lights were on but as far as he could tell, there was no stake-out. The police had no reason to watch the store. They thought he was still in Mexico. To be on the safe side, however, he drove around the block and parked on an unlighted side street and entered the shop through the rear service door.

It was good to be home after the long journey. The big store was pleasantly cool and fragrant with the aroma of its expensive wares and the clean cut smell of life-preserving drugs and herbs. Hart knew differently, but for the first time in days he felt secure. He glanced into the front of the store but refrained from going in. Instead, with Gerta close behind him, he walked on into the employee's lounge and turned on a floor lamp. It was a large, pleasant room with several couches, a make-up table, a phone booth, a small bank of metal lockers and a toilet and shower stall.

Gerta was apprehensive. "Isn't this dangerous? Why have we come here, Doc?"

Hart told her. "A number of reasons. One, I want to work on these cuts on my face and head. You're just as dead if you die from infection as you are from cyanide. Then let's clean up a bit if we can. If and when we are arrested, I don't want our pictures smeared all over the front page of every newspaper in town with both of us looking like we just crawled out of some rat's nest."

Gerta sat on the edge of one of the couches. "I thought only women were vain."

Hart gave her a sad smile. "This isn't a matter of vanity. You remember that picture of Harry Cotton, the one taken when he was picked up at the border, unshaven, tousled, still wearing the pants of his tuxedo, the same ones he'd been wearing when he and Bonnie left Ciro's?"

"Yes."

"It was one of the things that convicted him. He *looked* guilty. And there wasn't a juror on the case who hadn't seen the picture."

"I see what you mean."

"Have you another dress in your locker?"

Like Hart's other young hopeful would-be leading men and women, Gerta always kept several changes of costume in her locker, just in case a rush call should come in from Central Casting or one of the studios during store hours. "Yes," she said. "I have. Several, in fact."

"Then doll up to the nines. Gloves, hat, everything. If we are arrested, I want to be proud of you."

"Whatever you say, Doc," Gerta said. She unbuttoned the soiled white blouse she'd bought in Tijuana. "But I think I'll start with a shower. I feel sticky." She rested her fingers on his shoulders and lifted her face to be kissed. "You still love me?"

Hart wondered why he'd ever been in doubt. Gerta was the nicest thing that had ever happened to him, that could ever happen to a man. "Very much," he assured her as he kissed her.

The broad aisles and windows of the store were lighted but the prescription section was dark. It didn't matter. Hart knew where the things he wanted were. He felt through the dark for a bottle of antiseptic, a one thousand unit ampule of tetanus antitoxin and a sterile hypodermic needle and carried them into his office. There was a washroom and shower in connection that he shared with his male help.

It was awkward to inject the antitoxin. First he took off his trousers. Then, using his reflection in the mirror as a guide, he first cleaned, then antisepticized the wounds on his face and head. They were painful but not deep.

When he finished he shaved. Then, after making certain there was a freshly pressed suit in his closet, he stripped off the rest of his clothes and turned on the shower.

The hot water felt good on his flesh. He stood a long moment enjoying it, then stepped back and had just finished generously soaping his face and body, when over the pelt of the shower, he was conscious of a new sound. Somewhere in the store a phone was ringing. It took a minute to place it. It was the phone in the booth in the employees' lounge.

Fearful that Gerta might automatically answer it, he stepped out of the shower without stopping to rinse off the soap and ran into the lounge. Gerta had been having a shower also. With a towel around her waist she was standing just outside the shower stall, dripping water, staring round eyed at the ringing phone.

"Don't answer that," Hart said.

The phone in the booth continued to ring, loudly and insistently.

All the good feeling from the shower disappeared. It was a creepy thing, this being hunted. He could smell his own fear. It was a sour, stinking, feral smell.

Gerta swallowed the lump in her throat. "But who could it be? Who could possibly know we're here?"

Hart wiped soap out of his eyes. "I haven't any idea." He changed his mind about answering the phone. "Maybe we'd better find out. You answer it. If it should be the police you can say you're one of the cleaning women and there's no one but you in the store."

Clutching her towel with one hand, Gerta stepped into the booth and picked up the receiver. "Yah—?" she asked, affecting a Swedish accent. She turned quickly and looked at Hart. "It's Mr. Kelly."

Some of Hart's fear left him. Of course. The phone in the lounge was unlisted. The police would have used one of the listed phones. He crowded into the booth with his wife and took the receiver from her. "Hello—?"

The lawyer sounded relieved. "Thank God I've found you. I thought you might show up there. I've been calling on the half hour ever since the store closed. Are you all right, Doc?"

"Relatively speaking," Hart said.

More soap ran into his eyes and bothered him and Gerta took the towel from around her hips and wiped his face with it. "What does he want, sweetheart?"

Hart shook his head. "I don't know."

Kelly continued. "I've been trying to contact you ever since you hung up on me in Newport. You have me all wrong, Doc. I'm with you all the way. I was just making certain you were telling me everything."

"I realize that now," Hart said. "As soon as I read tonight's paper. Thanks."

He started to say more and was suddenly conscious that without the towel, jammed together facing each other as they were in the booth, the entire length of his and Gerta's bodies were touching. His reaction was immediate and normal. Instead of being embarrassed, Gerta grinned at him.

"Are you still there, Doc?" Kelly asked.

"I'm here."

"What did you find out in Newport?"

"There was a way for Bonnie to get off the yacht, at least out of the owner's suite, a crawl hole between the bathroom and the captain's cabin."

Kelly didn't seem surprised. "I figured it was something like that as soon as I heard they'd torched the yacht. You and Gerta went on to Mexico from there, I suppose."

"We just got back. And Bonnie was in Ensenada when Peggy said she was."

"Good," Kelly enthused. "Now here is the reason why I've been trying to get hold of you. There are warrants out for both of you. So whatever you do stay out of sight and don't give yourselves up for the next few hours."

Hart had no intention of giving himself up but he wanted to know Kelly's reason. "Why?"

Kelly told him. "Because there is a lot of pressure on Manson and Garcia and it's a lot easier to keep a client out of jail than to get him out. I told you I was hiring Jim Masterson."

"Yes."

"Well, it paid off. Jim and his boys have come up with a number of things. Such as Deering looting his customers' accounts over a period of the last nine months. And this morning he accepted payment from the insurance company for the policy on Bonnie, in cash. And what with his burning the yacht and other signs of activity around the house we figure he's getting ready to skip. Jim has had two men watching the house for days. And now that I know where you are he and I are going out and have a showdown with Deering."

"I'm going, too," Hart said. In answer to the lawyer's protest, he added, "Why not? It's my neck that's involved. And it's more than Peggy now." He told Kelly what had happened in Ensenada.

The lawyer whistled. "Well, when I pick a client, I pick a good one. In that case, I'll see you outside of Deering's house in half an hour."

"In half an hour."

Hart cradled the receiver. His breathing was shallow. Illusion or not, Gerta's flesh was burning his.

As she pressed closer to him the tips of the fingers of one of her small hands butterflied lightly over his chest. She wanted to know, "Am I bad because I feel this way, Doc?"

"No," he assured her.

"Then, please, Doc."

"In here?"

"What difference does it make where?"

"None."

Her fingers left his chest and moved between them. "How long have you felt this way about me?"

"You know."

"I know." Gerta's need was imperative, urgent. "I nearly died back in that room."

"At least let's go out into the lounge."

Gerta's lips parted. Her teeth showed. "No. Now. Here." Her slight body moved experimentally. "I told you. Any time after the first week. In the stock room. On the duck boards behind the fountain. On the corner of Hollywood and Vine. Let me prove it."

"How?"

"I'll show you."

Accommodating herself to him she did show him, until she cried in ecstasy and was still.

Hart continued to hold her as if she was something precious. She was. To him. Then he felt Gerta's wet lips move moistly on his chest.

"My husband," she said, simply.

SEPTEMBER 5, 1958
1:30 A.M.

Here and there Hart could see a lighted window but for the most part the big houses scattered through the wooded hills were dark. He parked the car under a flowering acacia tree a block from the Deering house and turned off the lights.

"Do you want to wait here?" he asked Gerta.

She shook her head. "No. You know what I told you in Mexico. Even if she did say it to her mother-in-law."

"Whither?"

"Whither."

Hart walked around the car and helped her out. So much depended on the next few minutes. He wished they were over. He held her, briefly, then kissed the tip of her nose. "I like you. You're cute."

She was frightened but for the sake of his morale she tried to be flip. "You'd better be careful. After what happened back there in the store, flattery will get you anything."

Hart went along with the gag by pretending to be shocked. "In Beverly Hills?"

"Even in Beverly Hills."

They walked up the dimly lighted street together in search of Kelly and Masterson and his men. Neither of them spoke again until they neared the gate in the big stone wall enclosing the Deering grounds. Then Hart said, puzzled, "That's funny."

Gerta's fingers bit into his arm. "What's funny?"

"I don't see Kelly's car. In fact I don't see any cars." He looked at the luminous dial of his watch. "He said in half an hour."

He walked through the gate and looked up the tree-shaded drive. The windows of the Deering living room were lighted but the rest of the house was dark. There was a car parked in the drive, the identity of which he couldn't tell at the distance.

Gerta suggested, "Maybe they've gone in. Maybe they are already talking to Mr. Deering."

"Could be."

"But what if Mr. Deering won't confess? What if he refuses to say anything? What happens then?"

"I don't know," Hart answered her.

He was at a loss. After talking to the lawyer on the phone, his interlude with Gerta had happened so fast he hadn't had time to evaluate everything Kelly had said. So Jim Masterson's men had found out that Deering had been looting his customers' accounts. He'd accepted the insurance money. That still didn't prove Bonnie was alive or tell them who'd killed Peggy Cotton. Then there was the matter of legality. A lawyer, a private detective and a druggist couldn't just walk into a multimillionaire's home and beat the truth out of him.

"You're worried, aren't you, Doc?"

"Yes," Hart said. "I am. I don't like it. Kelly not waiting for us, I mean. We could be walking into a trap."

"But Mr. Kelly wouldn't do that to you, would he?"

"I really don't know," Hart said. "Considering the amount of money involved and after all that has happened to us, I don't trust anyone but you."

"Maybe we'd better go back to the store."

"No."

"Why not?"

Hart was factual. "At least we aren't any worse off than we were before. I was coming here, anyway. Making our friends talk is the only chance we have of getting off the hook."

He walked slowly on up the drive. The car parked in front of the house was the same big black limousine in which Deering had been riding when the chauffeur had honked at his car in front of the Criminal Court Building. Hart left the drive and crossed the lawn to a point from which he could look into the living room windows.

Neither Kelly nor Masterson were in the room. Deering was sitting in a tall-backed chair with wooden arms, his own arms extended along those of the chair, his thin white fingers drumming nervously on the wood. As far as Hart could tell, the investment counselor was alone in the room and in the house.

He waited another ten minutes for Kelly and Masterson. Then when they hadn't arrived, impelled by a feeling of haste, he tugged the gun from his pocket. "Well, here goes."

Gerta put her hand on his arm. "But what if it is a trap?"

Hart assumed a confidence he didn't feel. "Maybe we will come out all right. Anyway, the way I see it, getting Deering to talk is our only chance."

He opened one of the tall French windows as quietly as he could and entered the huge room at a point behind Deering's chair. As quietly as he'd entered, Deering heard him. Without lifting his arms from the chair or turning his head, he asked, "Is that you, Luis? Sam?"

Hart walked past the display of model rockets. "I'm afraid not, Mr. Deering. If Sam is your chauffeur's name, both he and Luis are dead."

He walked around the chair and faced Deering. The other man had aged ten years in three days. He looked like a very tired and very sick old man. "Oh, no," Deering said. "That can't be." Then, surprisingly, his chin fell forward on his chest and a dry sob shook his body.

"What's the matter with him?" Gerta asked.

Hart started to answer her and realized why Deering hadn't moved or gotten to his feet. He couldn't. His ankles and wrists were tied to the legs and the arms of the chair with a stout cord.

"What's the matter?" Gerta repeated.

"Everything, I'm afraid," Hart said.

The voice came from the dark hallway behind him. "That's right. For you and the girl, but not for us. Lay your gun on the table, Hart. Very gently. No sudden moves."

"And if I don't?"

"I think you think more of the girl than that."

Hart laid his gun on the table beside Deering's chair.

"You fool," the older man said, thickly. "They're mad, both of them. Now they'll kill you, too."

Captain Morales' smile was mocking. As he entered the room, he asked, "You say Sam and Luis are dead?"

"That's right."

"How dead?"

"I shot one of them," Gerta said, hotly. "And Doc pushed the other one into the ocean, after they kidnapped and tried to kill us."

Morales sat on the edge of a sofa in a position to watch all three of them and allowed the revolver in his hand to dangle between his knees. "Good." He looked at Deering. "I told you. You'd have been much better off if you'd upped my cut after I put the squeeze on you by letting Hart find out Bonnie could have left that cabin without Cotton pushing her through a porthole. But no. You had to be greedy." He indicated an oversized attaché case Hart hadn't seen before. "You wanted everything. And if Luis and Sam had gotten away with killing the pill roller and his girl friend and we hadn't come back to town when we did, the three of you would have been gone by now."

"I swear," Deering said.

Morales shrugged. "You already have. And we told you we didn't believe you."

Hart looked at the attaché case. "What's in it?"

"Money," Morales smiled. "A lot of money." Despite the air conditioning in the room he was perspiring. He drew a silk handkerchief from his pocket and patted his face with his free hand. "Funny the way the breaks fall. Everything went so wrong for a while. But now it looks like it's going to work out after all."

Deering strained at the cord on his wrists as he looked at Hart. "And it's all your fault. If only you hadn't been on that jury."

"I'll buy that," Hart said. "I haven't enjoyed this any more than you have. But now that we are exchanging confidences, I wonder if one of you would tell me two things."

"What?" Morales sneered.

"Was Kelly in on this? Did he sell me down the river? Was that why he made that phone call? To trick me here?"

Morales and Deering looked blank. "Who's Kelly?" the captain asked. Then it came to him. "Oh, yes. He's your lawyer. He's the boy wonder who pleaded with the grand jury not to indict you." He fumbled a package of cigarettes from his pocket. "But what's this about a phone call?"

Hart kept his face expressionless. "That's immaterial. What I really want to know is who killed Peggy Cotton."

"I did," a girl's voice said.

Gerta gasped, "She is alive."

"That's right, honey," the girl said.

Hart turned. Except for her dyed hair, Bonnie Tempest looked much the same as she had the last time he'd seen her in his store. The former night club entertainer and strip tease artiste was wearing a simple, expensive white sports dress cut in a plunging V to show the upper rounds of her much-publicized breasts. The lighted cigarette bobbling in one corner of her mouth made her look incredibly evil and wanton. No. Not quite the same, Hart thought. All of her sins and excesses were beginning to show in her face. A psychotic, de Medoza had called her. Hart was inclined to agree with him. The girl couldn't be really sane.

"Hello, Bonnie," he greeted her casually. "Welcome back from the dead. You know, of course, you can't get away with this."

She sat on the sofa beside Morales. "Don't try to kid me, Hart. I can do anything I want, including killing you and your little blonde broad and the law can't do a thing to me." The thought amused her. "I'm dead. A guy named Harry Cotton killed me." She noticed Deering looking at her legs and her smile faded. "Pretty, aren't they, pappy?" she taunted him. "A shame you couldn't do anything about them." She amended her statement. "That is, any more than you did do." Bonnie transferred her attention to Gerta. "If you were going to live long enough to use the advice, darling, I'd warn you never to get mixed up with an old man. They have some of the damnedest ideas of fun."

Gerta wondered what the girl meant. She had enough of an idea to make her blush.

Stalling for time, hoping Kelly and Masterson would show up, Hart tried to keep Bonnie talking. "You say you killed Peggy?"

"Don't bother answering him," Morales told her. "Let's get it over with and get out of here, now that we know Luis and Sam won't try to stop us."

Bonnie protested, "But, darling. Hart and his pretty little friend are the only two people in the world I'm ever going to be able to tell. I'm dead, remember?" She ran her fingers through her dyed hair, then got up and moved restlessly around the room. "Yes, I killed the Cotton girl. I did it with my little pillow," she explained. "You see, the original idea was for me to fly down to Caracas and wait until my dear husband could collect my insurance and finish cleaning out the accounts of his trusting clients before he, too, brokenhearted over my death and not really realizing what he was doing, disappeared."

Deering cursed her. "Shut up."

The 'dead' girl ignored him. "But when President Jimmy-whatever-his-name-was got the sack and he and his top boys had to leave a few steps ahead of a posse, the fix was no longer in. I had to keep out of sight where I could." Her voice was plaintive. "And after all, a girl gets tired of looking at ceilings, whether they are in a cabin of a yacht, some crumby water-front hotel or in one of the upper rooms here. She wants a little sunshine. She wants to be able to move around. So that's why I went to Ensenada."

"Why?" Hart asked her.

The girl looked at him as if he was stupid. "To see Montez's widow. She wasn't in on the deal but her husband was. And I wanted to make certain he was dead and couldn't deliver what he'd promised."

"I see."

"Then while I was down there, of all the people in the world, that one little bitch had to see and recognize me. I knew her as soon as I saw her. She used to do something in the office when I was under contract to Associated Artists."

"Then why did you wait so long to kill her?"

Bonnie picked a decanter from a table and poured herself a drink. "Because I didn't know who she was in relation to Cotton. I didn't know until the last night of the trial. Enrico and I followed you to her apartment and did a little eavesdropping."

"But why follow us?"

"Because Enrico said every time he'd attended the trial she was there. I'd seen her several times myself. We were curious."

Hart asked, incredulous, "You attended the trial?"

Bonnie drank the drink she'd poured. "Four or five times. I got a big blast out of it. Then that last night, when you picked her up at the bus stop, something clicked. I remembered Cotton had told me he had a wife named Peggy." She was even more amused. "So we followed you and heard you stud the truth out of her." She mimicked the dead girl's voice. *"Don't you see? I crucified him. Because Bonnie isn't dead. I saw her four months ago in Ensenada. With her red hair dyed black. And these pulled in real tight to make her look flat where she isn't. Using the name of Señora Alveredo Montez. Now come on. Let's get even with Harry again.'"*

"You were there," Hart said.

Morales was as amused as Bonnie. "In the hall for a time. Then in the living room. You should be more careful to lock the door whenever you have an assignation."

Hart protested, "But why kill Peggy? She was going to let Cotton go to the lethal chamber."

Morales shrugged. "We couldn't take a chance on her changing her mind at the last minute. I wanted to kill both of you. I still think I should have. But Bonnie said no."

Bonnie walked to the bank of tall French windows opening onto the lawn and looked out and up at the night sky. "It's better this way," she said without turning. "My dear husband and Sam were the only two witnesses to see the girl get into Hart's car. And when the police find them all dead in the morning they'll think—" She shrugged. "Frankly, I don't care what they think. I mean to be far away from here by then."

Deering struggled to free his wrists. "You can't do this to me, Bonnie. This was my idea."

Bonnie continued to study the darkened sky. "That's right."

Hart put his arm around Gerta's waist.

Bonnie's ability to imitate voices was uncanny. If Hart hadn't been watching her lips he could have sworn Deering was speaking.

"I've been unfortunate in the market, my dear, and not wanting either of us to suffer poverty, I have a little plan. Here is what we will do." Bonnie reversed her hand and pressed the back of it to her forehead as she resumed her own voice. "And I did it. I agreed to let myself be murdered, like a good little girl." Her voice gained strength. "And to make it look good I slept with Harry Cotton for three days. No hardship. I rather liked the guy. He admitted he was a heel. Then I crawled through that damn hole in the cabin wall and let Enrico pick up right where Cotton had left off." She lighted a cigarette with fingers that were trembling so badly she had trouble making flame and tobacco meet. "Scared half crazy most of the time. What my dear husband forgot was that I like a good man and Enrico's a better man than Deering anytime."

"Shut up," Deering shouted. "Shut up."

The girl smoothed the fabric over her half exposed breasts. She sounded a little sad. "The hell of it is, I was going to give you a break. I was flattered because a man like you was willing to marry a girl like me. I meant to make you a good wife. I tried, even after I found you couldn't be a good husband. For two years, with only a couple of slips, I gave up drinking and taking off my clothes for anyone but you. I was going to be a goddamn lady if it killed me." She made a futile gesture with the hand holding the cigarette and smoke trailed through the still air. "But you didn't want it that way. You've probably been stealing so long it's a disease with you. To get the lousy money that would get you out of the country and keep you out of jail you didn't care how many men I went to bed with. You were willing to wallow in their leavings." She nudged the bulging attaché case with the toe of her shoe. "All right. I earned the money. I have it. I'm going to enjoy it with Enrico." She turned to Morales. "You have the plane tickets?"

"Two on the aisle to Tangiers."

Hart glanced at the open French window through which he'd entered and tried desperately to regain Bonnie's attention. "Then that whole binge with Cotton, you picking him up in Ciro's and that scene on the yacht was staged?"

"That's right: With a hundred thousand dollars worth of diamonds as bait. Uninsured diamonds. So the insurance company wouldn't come into the case prematurely."

"And the blood in the cabin? The blood that helped convict him?"

Bonnie sucked her cigarette to a red glow. "My type blood. Bought by my dear husband from one of the hole-in-the-wall blood donor services in Hollywood. It was easy for him. He's on the board of directors of two hospitals." She started to laugh and couldn't stop. It was insane, blood-chilling laughter. "And if the police ever do catch up with me, what can they do? I'm not only dead, I'm crazy."

Morales got to his feet and took a pen knife from his pocket. "All right. You've told Hart how it was. You've had your audience." He cut one of Deering's wrists free. "Now let's get out of here. So the police aren't looking for us. They are looking for Hart and his girl friend."

Bonnie snuffed her cigarette and picked up the brief case. "I'm ready. But why cut him loose?"

Morales explained. "I'm going to try to make it look like he and Hart and the girl had a fight. Then when the police find them—" He caught a glimpse of movement in the French window and stopped talking. It took him a long time to stand up straight. He managed, finally, and gaped at the long bank of such windows opening on the lawn. In each one, open now, was an armed man.

"Go on, Morales," Inspector Garcia said. "You were just coming to the interesting part. I've always wanted to see a triple murder committed. See any murder committed, for that matter. In the twenty years I've been on the force I've never been that lucky. Usually I have to mess around for days with clues and things like that."

SEPTEMBER 5, 1958
1:55 A.M.

Bonnie took her cigarette from her mouth and replaced it with one of her thumbs. "You tricked us," she reproached Hart. "You brought the police with you."

Hart was truthful with her. "No. But I was expecting my lawyer and a private agency man." He looked back at the inspector. "And was I glad to see you standing outside that window a few minutes ago."

Inspector Garcia sounded tired. "You should have been. Because Kelly and Masterson didn't make it. They're outside now in a police car under technical arrest for withholding information pertinent to the solution of a crime."

The detective came a few steps into the room. His voice was almost as plaintive as Bonnie's had been. "I don't know why the general public always seems to think the police are stupid. My men are just as smart as any private agency men. Once they had reason to check, they found Deering's accounts were short. They found the blood bank that sold him the blood. And this should interest you, Hart. They also got the old dame across the street from the Cotton girl's place, the one who swore that no one but you and Peggy entered or left the building, to admit that she'd gone to the bathroom a few times."

Garcia continued. "Then there was the matter of torching the yacht to conceal the crawl hole." He looked at Morales. "I imagine we'll pin that on you, Captain. We know Hart didn't do it because at the time it was burned he was spotted passing through San Diego, some fifty miles to the south."

"I see," Hart said. "You've been keeping tabs on me."

"Most of the time."

"You've been using me as a cat's paw to pull your chestnuts out of the fire."

"You could put it that way. With the co-operation of the newspaper boys and the Mexican police." Inspector Garcia added, "But what really paid off was tapping your phones. You see, every phone in your store, including the one in the booth in the lounge, has been tapped for a week. And your conversation with Kelly was very enlightening. It not only confirmed what we were already beginning to suspect, it told us you were coming here. So we came on ahead and listened."

Bonnie was indignant. "You shouldn't have done that. It wasn't right. Phone tapping is illegal."

Garcia agreed with her. "That's right, Mrs. Deering." He removed one of the cushions from the sofa and picked up a cleverly concealed microphone. "A lot of things are illegal. Like wiring this house for sound. Like—murder. 'With my little pillow,' I believe you said."

Deering spoke for the first time since he'd yelled at Bonnie to shut up. It was a statement, not a question. "Then you heard everything that was said in this room."

"It's on tape," Inspector Garcia assured him. He spoke into the microphone. "You can turn it off and wrap it, boys. We may not be able to use the tape in court but I doubt if we'll have to. I have a very strong feeling one or more canaries are just about to sing."

The resurrected girl's breathing was shallow as she looked at Morales. "Well, don't just stand there. Protect me. Shoot him and get me out of here."

Morales looked from Bonnie to the expressionless faces of the detectives standing in the open window and dropped his gun on the sofa. "Not me. I've just grown a full set of feathers."

Bonnie called him an obscene name. Then clutching the attaché case to the deep V of her dress she took a few quick steps toward the hallway and stopped. Her voice brittle, she said, "Well, the place seems to be lousy with cops. But you're not going to send me to prison. I won't be locked up. I won't be, I've had nine months of that."

Still clutching the brief case, she turned with a dancer's grace and fled up the stairs leading to the second floor.

"Let her go, for now," the inspector said. "She's not going anywhere."

Then the men stood watching the girl. Gerta was watching Deering. "Stop him," she cried, too late.

Before anyone could move, Deering's freed hand snaked across his body and snatched up the revolver Hart had laid on the table. His face was mottled with shame and anger.

"For everything, darling," he called. And as he spoke he emptied the gun.

The bullets, striking the girl in the back, added to her forward motion, their impact hurtling her into the rail at the top landing. The rail cracked under her weight. The bulging attaché case sprang open.

Bonnie stood a moment, puzzled, gripping the rail with both hands. It gave way and she fell with it, momentarily hanging suspended, as the hem of her dress caught on one of the splintered balusters. Then the cloth came away from her body and she fell in a shower of fluttering green bills, each bill kissing and caressing the nude flesh it was following.

Who live by the sword, Hart thought.

A long moment of silence followed the thud. Even Inspector Garcia looked sick. Then Hart felt Gerta's fingers biting into his arm. Her voice barely audible she said, "I wonder, please, if we could go outside."

Hart looked at Garcia.

Garcia handed the gun he'd taken from Deering to one of his men. "I don't see why not," he said. "Of course, there are still some technical details to clear up. You both will have to answer some questions and make some depositions for us and the Mexican authorities. The warrants against you will have to be quashed. But—yes, you can go outside. As far as any charge is concerned, you're as good as back of your counter, Hart, rolling little pink pills."

"Thank you. Thank you very much," Hart said. When they reached the French window, Garcia called after them. "And, Doc—"

Hart turned, "Yes—?"

"If I were you, in the future, I'd stick to pills."

"I intend to," Hart assured him.

It was pleasant out on the lawn. The night was cool. The moon had set but the sky was filled with stars. As Hart stood holding Gerta, still shaken by the presence of violent death, he looked up at the sky and saw a shooting star.

It flashed across the heavens leaving a bright trail behind it.

Out of all evil some good was born. He'd found his good, he'd found Gerta. As long as their forever might be, wherever it might be, he and Gerta would spend it together.

Gerta was warm and soft in his arms as she rested her cheek on his chest. "Do you think they'll let us go home soon?"

"I hope so," Hart said quietly.

THE END

HUNT THE KILLER
BY DAY KEENE

CHAPTER ONE

It was hot. It was dark. The cell block smelled of men sleeping with dreams. Men without women for years. Of fear and despair and frustration. Night after night, alone. Three walls, a high window, iron bars. A hard, narrow cot—and you. With disinfectant replacing affection. A small squirrel in a big cage. Staring hot-eyed into the dark. Wanting a drink. Wanting a woman. Trying not to blow your top. Hysteria building up inside you.

Can you go down to the corner for a beer? Can you catch a mess of shrimp and go fishing? Can you pat your wife and say, "Tonight, huh, babe?"

No. You do what you're told. And like it.

I hadn't slept all night. And morning was slow in coming. I'd waited for it a long time. Four years the man had said. Four years I had done. Without any nonsense about parole or time off for good behavior.

I was washed and dressed and waiting when the rising siren blew. McKenny, the guard on the tier, paused in front of my cell on his way to pull the master switch.

"This is the big day, eh, Charlie?"

The lump in my throat was so big all I could do was nod.

Then he pulled the switch and my cell door opened for the last time and I lined up on the catwalk with the others. The guys who still had days, weeks, months, and years to do. Wishing me luck from the corners of their mouths as we marched down to breakfast. Not meaning it. Nothing personal. But hating my guts. For one reason. I was going out and they were staying.

I tried to eat, and couldn't. I was too excited. Then, too, the pock marks in the plaster of the mess hall bothered me. I knew them for what they were. I'd heard the machine guns make them. And if it hadn't been for Swede I could be dead instead of walking out. I could be with Mickey and Saltz. I could be in solitary. I could even be with Swede.

The thought cost me what little appetite I had.

A front-of-the-prison guard was standing in the mess hall door as we filed out. As I passed him, he asked:

"You Charlie White?"

"I am."

"Then step out of line and follow me."

I followed him down a long corridor, across the yard, and into a small room in the administration building. The clothes I'd signed for the day before were hanging on a wire hanger.

The guard said, "When you're dressed turn the things you're wearing now over to the supply clerk."

"Yes, sir."

"Then go to the warden's office."

"Yes, sir."

A sallow-faced cracker with jaundiced eyes, he lighted a cigarette and blew smoke in my face. "That is, unless you want to keep your denim as a souvenir."

I shook my head at him. "No, thank you. All I want out of this is a faint recollection."

He didn't laugh. "Then if I were you, I'd keep out of trouble."

"Yes, sir."

The sun lifted out of the Florida scrub and beat in through the window. I stripped and stood in it a minute, naked, letting the sun burn the prison stink off me. It was going to take a lot of sun. Then I put on the suit of clothes, turned my denims into the supply clerk, and walked into the warden's office.

He had my dossier on his desk. "So you're going out this morning, White?"

"Yes, sir."

"And glad to be leaving us, eh?"

It was as hot in the warden's office as it had been in my cell. Sweat trickled down my spine and tickled me. It was difficult to breathe. How much did they think a man could take? I'd done my time. I wanted out. By swallowing hard I managed to gulp out another, "Yes, sir."

The warden looked from my papers to me. "Fishing boat captain, weren't you, White?"

"Yes, sir."

"Your own boat?"

"Yes, sir."

He looked back at my papers. "Hmm. Four years. With no time off for good behavior." A touch of color crept into his fat jowls. "As a matter of fact you're lucky to be going out at all. You know that, don't you, White?"

I gave him the, "Yes, sir," routine again, leaning on it this time. So what could he do to me?

More color came into his face. He started to get sore, and changed his mind. "Okay. If that's the way you want it, White. You're several cuts above the average prisoner we get here. I wouldn't want to see you come back. But right now you're so stinking filled with self-pity that anything I might say wouldn't do a bit of good."

I wiped my face with the sleeve of my new coat. "Then why bother to say it?"

He laid a typed receipt, a sealed envelope, a small sheaf of bills, and some silver on the corner of his desk. "I don't intend to. If you'll sign a receipt for the one hundred and twenty-six dollars and fifty cents that is credited to your account, I'll let someone else do the talking."

That would be Father Reilly. The priest had given me the only news I'd had of Beth in four years. I knew she knew about Zo. But if Beth had filed suit for divorce, I hadn't been served with the papers.

He tucked the receipt in a corner of his blotter. I wadded the bills and the envelope into my pocket.

"Good-bye and good luck, White," the warden concluded the interview.

He pushed a buzzer on his desk and a new guard took me in tow. But we weren't headed for the chaplain's office. It was the first time I'd been in the death house. I didn't like it.

Swede was sitting on the edge of a desk in a small windowless conference room. He was barefoot, wearing nothing but pants and a skivy, looking much the same as he always had, except that his tan was gone, the lines in his face were deeper, and his eyes seemed even bluer.

"You've ten minutes, White," the guard said.

He closed and locked the door behind him. The lump in my throat almost choked me. Ten minutes wasn't long enough to even start thanking Swede for what he'd done for me. I'd have been in the attempted break up to my eyes if Swede hadn't belted me unconscious.

"Stay out of this, kid," he'd bellowed. "You've only got six months to go. With me, it's different. I've got life and ninety-nine years."

It hadn't been much of a riot. When I'd come to, the machine guns had stopped chattering. Mickey and Saltz were dead. And Swede had picked up the big tab for caving in a guard's head.

"Cigarette?" Swede asked.

I took one from the pack he offered. "Thanks."

Swede sucked hard at his own cigarette, as if with time running out on him he wanted to enjoy every puff to the maximum. I had a lot of respect for the old man. A charter boat captain who knew both the Gulf and the Caribbean like most men know the streets in the town they live in. If anyone knew the score, Swede did.

"Ten minutes," he said, "isn't long. So let me do the talking, kid. Would you say I was a Holy Joe?"

The lump in my throat let go. I laughed.

"Then keep that in mind," Swede said. "Except for our age, you and me are a lot alike, Charlie. We both love the water. We've both made a good living on and out of it. But were we content with that? No." He gestured with his cigarette.

"That's why I asked the warden if I could talk to you. A man does a lot of thinking when he gets in one of these quick fry joints. And it all boils down to this: a guy hauls in the fish he baits for and at the depth at which he fishes."

He let me think it over while he lighted a fresh cigarette from the butt of the one he was smoking.

"In the old days it was different. A man had to depend on himself. There was a lot of uncharted sea for him to sail as he saw goddamn fit. But times have changed. After years of sailing by guess and by God, society has set out certain buoys and markers. You got a silver dollar, kid?"

There was one in the money the warden had given me. I gave it to Swede.

He traced the lettering on the head side with his finger. *"E Pluribus Unum.* Know what that means, Charlie?"

I said, "Something about one for all or all for one."

Swede shook his head. "Naw. It means *one out of many.* And that's you and me, Charlie. And the guard who brought you here. And the warden. And the guy's who's going to fry me tonight. We're all just one of many. And you've got to swim with the school or—well, look what's happened to me. Look what happened to you when you tried to sail on your own.

"As rackets go, you had a good one. But let's add up the score. On the debit side it cost you your wife, your boat, and got you four years in the can. On the profit side you had a few roaring good drunks in Habana, a fancy, oversexed dame and the false knowledge that you were smarter than your fellow fishing boat captains. There were no lulls in your business. You brought in a good catch every time. Okay. How much dough you got?"

I told him, "One hundred and twenty-six dollars and fifty cents."

Swede hooted. "For four years of your time. Hell. There are guys netting mullet out of Naples, and Palmetto City for that matter, who are making that much every night. But netting mullet is hard work. So is fishing the snapper banks. Or running a charter boat. And you and me had to be wise guys. Your wife waiting outside?"

I admitted I didn't know.

"I don't know why she should be," Swede said. "A man can starve a dame. He can get drunk and beat her every night and twice on Sunday and she'll still think he's her personal Marshall Plan in a silver champagne bucket. But only if she knows she's the only woman in his life."

He went on before I could speak.

"Sort of looks like you got a little off course, eh, Charlie?"

I hesitated. "Well—"

Swede spat his cigarette on the floor. "Naw. You still don't think so. You still aren't willing to admit you made a mistake and cut bait or fish. You're still feeling too damn sorry for yourself."

He lighted a third cigarette, his blue eyes probing my face. "I know how you feel, kid. I've got a temper, too. That's one of the reasons I'm here. But don't do it, Charlie."

Even thinking of *Señor Peso* choked me. "Don't do what?"

Swede said, "You know damn well what I'm talking about. But killing your former partner because he ran out on you when the law stepped in will only bring you back here." Swede patted the wall of the death house. "And I mean here. Building up another dividend for the stockholders of Florida Power."

I wiped the sweat tangled in the hairs on the back of my right hand with the palm of my left.

Swede sucked at his cigarette. "Look. When you came back from that mess in '45 or '46 you'd been living in a bloody tide for four years. Life meant nothing. A thousand lives meant nothing. That right?"

I said it was.

Swede got up from the desk and began to pace the floor. "Well, we had a similar tide in the Gulf while you were gone. We called it the red tide. Fish died by the tens of millions. The shores and the tide flats from Apalachee Bay to Cape Sable were heaped so high with dead fish you could smell them for ten miles inland. Everyone swore things would never be the same again."

"I heard about it."

"But they are." Swede's eyes were surprisingly blue and clear and unafraid. "I mean the same. The water gradually cleared. The shrimp came back to the grass flats. The fish began to spawn again. Oh, maybe not quite as many as before. But nature is gradually building back."

My throat tight, I asked him, "So what's all this got to do with me?"

Swede said, "You're in clear water again, Charlie. If you're smart you'll stay there. Get a job fishing on shares. Swab out a charter boat and bait tourists' hooks if you have to. Then when you get something to offer her, find your wife. Get down on your knees if you have to and beg her to forgive you and come home."

I said, "That sounds like good advice, Swede."

He looked at me a long minute, then snuffed his cigarette. "But you aren't going to take a damn word of it. Okay, kid. It's your funeral."

The guard opened the door. "That's it."

"I've been wasting my time," Swede complained. He walked to the door without offering to shake hands. Then he turned in the doorway and said, "I won't bother to say good-bye. As long as you feel the way you do, it's just *auf Wiedersehen.* Till we meet again. I'll try to save a quart and a brunette for you, Charlie." His smile was wry. "But I'm afraid the whiskey is going to be hotter than the dame."

CHAPTER TWO

Life. A funny proposition. The things it does to a guy.

I walked back through the yard with the guard. Inside the administration building again, he pointed at the front door.

"Okay. You're on your own, White."

I nodded. "Thanks."

He turned into one of the doors. And I was alone in the hall, without any supervision for the first time in four years. I stood looking at the front door, afraid to walk out on the stoop. Was Beth waiting, or wasn't she?

She knew I was getting out. Father Reilly had written her. So where did we go from here?

There was a cigarette machine in the hall. I bought a deck of Camels, my fingers shaking so badly I could hardly get the quarter in the slot.

And what to do about *Señor Peso?*

Señor Peso. The name sounded like a gag. But it was the only name I had. Outside of Zo's.

I leaned against the wall, waiting for my hands to stop shaking, thinking about Beth, about Zo. About the mysterious *Señor Peso.*

The big veins in my temple began to pound. It had been his voice on the phone that had started all the fireworks. If it hadn't been for a guy I'd never met, the past four years wouldn't ever have been. I'd still be operating the Beth II out of Bill's Boat Basin. He'd cost me four years in the can, my boat, and more important, Beth. And now Swede wanted me to kiss him off the record.

A trusty I knew walked down the hall on an errand. When he saw me, he said, "I thought they turned you loose this morning?"

I said, "They did."

"Then what are you hanging around for?"

What could I tell the guy? That I was afraid to walk out the door? Not physically. In my mind. Afraid of what I might do. "I'm waiting for my wife," I lied.

He sucked in his breath through his teeth. "Geez. Would I like to be waiting for my wife."

And he went on about his errand. I walked a few feet closer to the front door. Past a sort of alcove. With a sofa for visitors. And a mirror on the wall. A big mirror with beveled edges. Like the one Beth had wanted for the parlor of the old home place on the island.

I stopped and looked in the mirror. Four years hadn't changed me. I was still a big, freckled face, red-haired cracker fishing guide. One hundred and ninety pounds of beef and about two ounces of brains.

"This is Señor Peso, Captain White. How would you like to make two thousand dollars?"

That had been the first time. Over the phone. With just a trace of an Ybor City accent. The time I'd been behind in the payments on my new boat, the season three months off, and Beth sick to boot. Because of me. Because of a miscarriage.

How would I like to make two thousand dollars? How would I like to drop a mullet net around ten ton of pompano?

And all I had to do for the dough was meet the *Andros Ancropolis,* a converted sponge boat, eighty miles out in the Gulf, and bring in a few small, waterproofed packages that fit easily into my bait well. I didn't know what was in them. I didn't bother to ask. All I knew was that they were gone when I looked in the well the next morning. Replaced by the two thousand in cash *Señor Peso* had promised would be there.

So it was wrong. So I knew it. So Beth cried all night when I told her. It was money. Big money for me. The kind of money I'd always wanted.

Money to fix up the house. Money to live like the tourists lived. Money to buy Beth the pretties I'd always promised her she'd wear. If only she'd stop her goddamn crying.

A trip to Veracruz had followed. Then one to Pinar del Rio. I'd had my boat paid for by then. Then the trip to Habana where somehow I'd met Zo. After that I was in so deep that it hadn't mattered. I went where I was ordered to go, met whom I was told to meet, got what I was ordered to get. And brought it back to Palmetto City.

Every trip a good one. No lulls in my business. Getting in deeper and deeper with Zo. Beginning to drown my conscience in rum. A big shot. Me.

I'd only made one restriction. I'd refused to run wetbacks. And after the one proposition along that line, *Señor Peso* hadn't mentioned the subject again.

It had been a lead pipe cinch. All the boys in the Coast Guard knew me. The older officers had known my father. I'd had no trouble with clearance papers. No one had ever stopped me. Until that last time.

And that trip my bait wells had to be filthy with forty thousand dollars worth of Swiss watches and French perfumes—on which no duty had been paid.

I still hadn't met *Señor Peso.* My instructions came by phone. My money came in the mail, in cash. And, once the Coast Guard lowered the boom, he had walked out on me cold.

"And whom," the federal prosecutor in Tampa had asked, "were you running this stuff for, White?"

I told him. "Señor Peso."

The judge almost bust his gut from laughing. And fined me five thousand dollars. Confiscated my boat. And sent me away for four years. Away from Beth. Away from Zo.

To learn how to hate *Señor Peso.*

I dropped my cigarette and snuffed it with the toe of my shoe. It all depended on Beth. If Beth were waiting for me, I'd follow Swede's advice. I'd start all over again.

If Beth had decided to call it quits, the hell with everything. So I was a big dumb cracker. No guy ran out on Charlie White. I'd identify and kill *Señor Peso* if I had to call for the quart and the dame that Swede had promised to save.

I walked out the front door. It was the same sun that had shone on me in the yard. But different somehow. Hotter. Brighter.

I shaded my eyes with my hand. Beth wasn't in the parking lot. Beth had called it quits. But Zo was waiting. Zo had stuck by me.

I stood a minute just looking at her. Leaning against a canary yellow jeepster. Her head bare. Her black hair shining in the sun. Wearing a white strapless sundress that made her shoulders look like they were made of cream. The dress cut low in front. Her breasts straining against the cloth. Reminding me.

I walked over to the jeepster and Zo's voice reached out and caressed me. Stroking me where it hurt. After four years without her. Without any woman.

"Hello, honey. Am I glad to see you." Zo lifted her lips to be kissed. "I've been waiting out here since daybreak."

Her lips clung to mine. Fiercely. Her fingers dug into my back.

I thought, *To hell with Swede. To hell with everything.* It was nice to hold her in my arms.

I said, "You shouldn't kiss strange men like that. You won't go to heaven."

Zo wrinkled her nose at me. "Who wants to go to heaven?"

I kissed her again. "You devil. You cute little she-devil!"

Zo understood. Zo knew how I felt. She cupped my face between her hands. "Right here, if we could. But they'd jug both of us, Charlie." She handed me the key to the jeepster. "Here. You drive."

I got in back of the wheel. "Where to?"

Instead of answering, Zo lighted a cigarette, sucked smoke into her lungs, then put the cigarette between my lips. "Let's get one thing straight first, Charlie?"

"What?"

"No one let you down."

I started to get out of the jeep. Zo put her hand on my arm. "I mean it. The *Señor* you-know-who couldn't afford to show at your trial. It would have jeopardized the whole set-up."

"So he threw me to the wolves."

Zo smiled, white-toothed. "Let's say the sharks." She dug in her purse and came up with a bank passbook. Mine. "But you haven't done too bad."

I opened the book and looked at the figures. I'd lied to Swede. I wasn't broke. I was filthy. For every month I'd spent in a cell, someone, *Señor Peso* presumably, had deposited one thousand dollars, American, to my Habana bank account. The last figure showed I had $48,546.00 on deposit.

I put the book in my pocket. "How come?"

Zo showed more of her teeth. "Perhaps I had something to do with it." Her smile faded slightly. "You are all mine now? Or do I still share you?"

I named her what she was.

Zo continued to smile. "Even so. Sluts have been known to love their man." Her Spanish accent grew more pronounced. "Even as much as a wife." She looked around the parking lot. "And I do not see any wife waiting for you."

It was hot in the parking lot. The top of the jeepster was down. The sun burned like a blow torch. I took off my coat and laid it in the back seat. And the devil climbed in with us.

I thought, The hell with Beth. She didn't even care enough to show. To hell with everything. To hell with trying to kill Señor Peso. It wasn't his fault I was caught. And in his way the guy has tried to play square with me. Forty-eight thousand bucks is a fortune.

I tilted Zo's chin and kissed her.

Suspicious, she asked, "Why?"

I said, "I'm sorry I called you that name. But my nerves are shot." I jerked my head at the pile of stone. "A few more months in that joint and I'd have gone over the blue wall."

Zo smiled through a mist of tears. She called me by her pet name. "You are nice, Captain Charlie. I like you. And now shall we go?"

I eased the jeepster out of the lot. "You tell me where."

Zo said, "Straight across the state. To Cross City. I've engaged a cabin on Dead Man's Bay. Just us for two or three days. Then one of the boys will put in and take us on to Habana. That all right with you?"

After four years in a cell? The sky and palm trees, the pound of surf on the beach, and Zo. "You kidding me?" I asked her. Swede had been wrong. Wrong about a lot of things.

Zo sat closer to me on the seat. "You still like me a little bit."

"I like you a lot."

"Only like?"

"Well, love then."

She sat even closer to me. "You thought of me once in a while?"

"A thousand times."

"In a nice way?"

"No."

My answer seemed to please her. "I'm glad." She was breathing hard, her breasts rising and falling with each breath.

"Why should you be glad about that?"

The devil leaned over the seat and lighted twin candles in her eyes. "Because I am not a nice girl. Being nice would bore me very much, I think."

She was all Cuban now. The two words came out, "I theenk." I laughed at her.

She was hurt. "Why are you laughing at me?"

I said, "Because you're cute."

"As cute as Beth?"

I fought a sick feeling in my stomach. "Don't mention her goddamn name."

Zo smiled like the bitch she was. "Whatever you say, my darling. You would like a drink perhaps?"

"I would."

She took a fifth of Bacardi rum from a paper bag, uncorked it, and handed it to me. I let it trickle down my throat like wine. Perhaps a half a pint before I handed it back. She put it on the seat beside her.

After being away from the stuff so long it hit me almost as hard as Zo's kisses. There was little or no traffic on the road. I let the rum spread through my body until my nerve ends were tingling. Then on a lonely stretch of highway I pulled the jeepster off the road onto a grassy spot and in under a clump of palmettos.

Zo made no protest as I took her in my arms. She didn't call it 'foolishness' as Beth might have done. Sweat was trickling down her cheeks, staining her dress, under her arm pits, across her stomach. From an inner fire.

"I hoped you would, darling," she panted. "Four years is a long time."

I said, "You're kidding me."

"No," she protested. "I'm not."

Cupping my face in her hands, she plastered her lips to mine. I touched her and caught on fire. And after that we had no need for words.

CHAPTER THREE

It was late afternoon when we reached the cabin. On the shore of Dead Man's Bay. We'd stopped three more times. Once to eat. Once to pick up more rum. In Gainesville and Cross City. And once along the road.

Both of us were fairly high. Zo filled with plans for the future. Me satisfied with the status quo. Zo, a bottle, a cabin. What more could any man want after four years in a cell?

The cabin, when we reached it, was a pleasant blur in a stand of slash pine on an isolated white beach that looked as if a careful housekeeper had swept it. A rutted sand road led back from the Highway to the Gulf. As nearly as I could tell, the nearest house, and that a fishing shack, was over a mile away.

The Gulf looked the same as it always had. Blue and darkly mysterious in the brief afterglow of the sun. Stretching out to hell and gone. To Yucatan. And through the channel to the Caribbean.

It looked good to me.

Zo understood. "You like?"

"I like," I admitted.

She unlocked the door of the cabin. A two room shack with a combination living room and kitchen and a bedroom. "Then why don't you go for a swim, sweetheart? While I put on some coffee and get us some supper."

Between the rum and emotion she'd gone all Cuban now and supper came out *suppair.*

I put the groceries we'd bought in Cross City on a table. It was a good idea. After four years away from it, the rum was hitting me hard. If I wanted to stay with the party I had to lay off the stuff for a while.

I said, "Swell," and peeled off my clothes where I stood, Zo laughing like mad but fending me off when I tried to get amorous.

"Later, sweetheart."

I left her to the coffee and padded down to the water barefooted. I swam out until the shore line was a blur in the deepening dusk. Then I turned on my back and floated, looking up at the first faint stars. Thinking how much I'd missed them. How much I'd missed the water. Yes, and how much I'd missed Zo.

Almost glad Beth hadn't met me. Thinking how different mistresses were from wives. It was marriage without restrictions. Zo never cried when I got drunk. Zo got drunk with me. Zo always wanted to do whatever I wanted to do, whenever I wanted to do it. Zo didn't give a damn what people thought. So I'd been in jail, I was out. And that was the end of it. More, Swede had been wrong about the location of her heart. Sure she liked me that way. But if her affection hadn't been deeper than that, she wouldn't have shown up at the prison with the forty-eight grand. And turned it over to me. When a dame like Zo loved a guy, she stuck.

I turned over and swam back to shore slowly, leaving a phosphorescent wake. Hungry for Zo again. Normally now. Without any immediate need. So I was a heel. So I'd been born fifty years too late. So I should have lived before society set up the buoys and markers that Swede had yapped about. What the hell? I couldn't turn back the clock. All I could do was live.

I stood a moment on the beach, squeegeeing water from my body with my hands, looking out to sea, sucking in the salt air, imagining being out there on the water again. In a Diesel powered fifty-footer. Or a sloop-rigged ketch. Or even a kicker-powered rowboat. Any damn thing that would float.

Then I walked back along the path to the cabin.

Zo had lighted two lamps. One in the kitchen. One in the bedroom. I followed the yellow carpet into the kitchen. There was coffee water boiling on the battered old kerosene stove. And a pot of black-eyed peas. And a heavy iron spider put to heat for the big steak we'd bought in Cross City.

"You have fun?" Zo called from the bedroom.

"It was swell," I called back.

There was an opened bottle of rum on the table. I took a swig from the neck of the bottle. Then started into the next room to see what Zo was doing and I tripped over the clothes I'd dropped and damn near broke my neck.

Zo heard me laughing and asked what was so funny.

Still sprawled on the floor I laughed, "Your housekeeping. Why didn't you hang up my clothes?"

I could imagine her slim shoulders shrugging. "How do I know but what you *like* to hang your clothes on the floor?"

She'd been hitting the bottle while I swam and her chicken and yellow rice accent was even more pronounced. "And when I am a little girl my mother told me. 'Zo, always remember this. To please a man you should always let him do what he likes.' You like?"

Still sitting on the floor, I whooped, "You bet I like."

Then I picked up the bills and the crumpled envelope that had fallen out of my coat when I'd kicked it. The envelope was the one the warden had given me, along with what money I'd had coming. With my name typed on the front. Along with my number.

Charles A. White, 34408133.

It was probably a song and dance about keeping my nose clean in the future. Or a religious tract. I started to throw it away. Into the trash box by the stove. Then remembered that since the riot all incoming mail had been retyped.

I ripped it open. Two tens and a five dollar bill fell out. All the good from my swim gone, my skin suddenly felt cold and clammy, I got to my feet and held the letter under the lamplight. It read in Beth's precise phrasing—

My Dear Charles:

If it were at all possible I would be waiting for you when you have finished your penal term. Unfortunately, one of us has to work. So, as a substitute, since you are probably without funds, I am enclosing twenty-five dollars for train fare.

If you are sober when you reach Palmetto City, ready to settle down and be the type of man I thought I married, I will be glad to discuss the matter with you.

All my love,
Beth

Then, as an afterthought, she'd added:
P. S. We will start all over.

It was the type of letter Beth would write. She'd been a school teacher when I married her. And her family had looked down their noses when she'd married a charter boat captain. Who didn't go to church. Who drank. Who lived in a run-down old mansion on an island.

But Beth loved me. She'd sent me train fare to come to her. She was ready to start all over. And here I was—all mixed up with Zo again.

Zo called from the bedroom. "What is the matter, Captain Charlie?" She added a liquid love phrase in Spanish. "I thought we had an appointment while the coffee water was boiling."

I took another drink of rum and tried to do some straight thinking. I'd promised Beth it was for always. I loved her. She loved me. And with Beth and her slim blonde beauty out of my life forever, nothing would ever be quite right again. The money, the excitement, Zo, were just poor substitutes for what I really wanted. Beth to love me. Love me like Zo loved me. To the point where nothing else mattered.

Maybe with forty-eight grand she would. I could build her a nice house. In a nice section of Palmetto City. Get a job she approved of. Maybe in a store. Maybe selling real estate. Be the type of man she wanted.

Zo called again. "Is something the matter, honey?"

I told her the truth. "Yeah. Plenty."

I padded into the bedroom carrying the letter and the bottle of rum.

Her hair a black frame against the white of the propped up pillow, Zo was lying on the bed smoking a cigarette.

"Now what?"

I sat down on the bed beside her, wishing she weren't so lovely, wishing I'd never met her.

"Now what?" she repeated.

I said, "So I'm a heel. I'm sorry. But you and I are washed up. As of now. I'm going back to Palmetto City and my wife."

Zo laughed. "You are kidding." She reached out a hand to caress me. "You are having a joke with me. No?"

I shook my head. "No."

Zo withdrew her hand. "But why?"

I handed her the letter from Beth. She read it, the hand holding her cigarette resting on her concave stomach. White smoke curling up like incense rising in front of an idol. A very lovely idol.

Finished, she looked at me. "This is a *love* letter?"

I said, "It's just Beth's way of writing."

For some reason I was embarrassed for Beth. She could have been more demonstrative. Not that she ever had been.

Zo looked at the letter again. "Where did you get this?"

I said, "The warden gave it to me. It's been in my pocket all the time. But I didn't open it until now."

The letter seemed to fascinate Zo. She read it through again.

"After four years she writes you this. After four years without you, she is willing to *discuss* the matter?"

I made more excuses for Beth. "Beth isn't a tramp. Going to bed with a man means something to her."

"Bah." Zo dropped the letter on the floor. "This woman with whom I used to share you does not love you, Captain Charlie." Crimson fingernails bit into my forearm. Zo's voice was as fierce as her eyes. "I am a woman. I know." She raised her left palm breast high. As if she were taking an oath. "And I would have been at that gate this morning to offer myself to you if to raise the fare to get there I had to sleep with every man between here and Habana." Hot tears filled her eyes. She shook them away. "It would have meant nothing to me. Your love would have made me clean again. Pleasing you would have been all that mattered."

I slapped her. Hard. "Stop talking like a slut."

Her eyes turned sullen. She wiped her cheeks with the back of her hand. "Why should I? You seem to think I am one."

I tried to explain how I felt, and couldn't. I was all twisted up inside.

"Have I asked for any money from you?"

"No," I admitted. "You haven't."

Zo lighted a cigarette from the butt of the one she was smoking, reminding me of Swede. As if time were running out on her, too. "Let's have a drink," she suggested.

I handed her the bottle. She sipped a drink from the neck and handed it back to me. I wet my lips and put it on the floor by the bed.

Calmer now, Zo said, "Be reasonable, sweetheart. How much could you possibly make commercial fishing or running a charter boat?"

"I could do something else."

"What?"

"Sell real estate."

"I laugh."

I got a little sore. "Even so. I'm going back to Palmetto City. Now. Tonight. And get a job. And make Beth proud of me. And remodel the old house. Or buy a new one. And raise five or six red-headed kids. And be disgustingly honest."

Zo took my hand. "I could have children for you."

"Little bastards."

"Would that make you love them less? If they were your children?"

"No."

Zo moved my hand a few inches. "Love me."

I cursed her. "You devil. You black-eyed devil."

"But cute?"

"But cute," I admitted.

Then she was in my arms again, her body straining against mine, chanting, "I love you, I love you, I love you."

Beth, the letter, nothing, mattered for the time being. Nothing at all.

It went on for what seemed like hours. Then Zo's eyes suddenly went wide. The corners of her lips turned down. I thought in passion. She opened her mouth and screamed.

"No! Please, God!"

Her fingers left my hair and spread across the back of my head as if trying to protect it.

I thought she was screaming at me. She wasn't. The blow came from one side and behind me, crashing through her fingers to my head.

Zo screamed again. In pain now. I turned my head in time to see a blur of white face through the fog of unconsciousness that was reaching up to engulf me. A faceless face. A face like a man with removed cataracts might see without his glasses. A shapeless, featureless face, topped by a blob of dark hair.

Then the leaded butt of the gaff hook the killer was using as a club landed a second time. And still clinging to Zo, I floated out into a sea of space. On a red flood tide.

As if from a great distance away, Zo whispered, "I love you, Captain Charlie."

Then the flood tide swept us out to sea, turning, twisting, buffeted by huge waves. Then just as we passed the last buoy marking the channel of consciousness, I thought I heard the flat slap of a pistol. And Zo's body relaxed in my arms.

CHAPTER FOUR

I came to lying face down in a tangle of wet seaweed, wondering why it was so dark, and where I was.

I tried to lift my head. I couldn't. The pain was too intense. Then one by one the shattered pieces of reality began to fall in place. Like the curlicues of some monstrous jigsaw puzzle.

I was in a two room cabin on Dead Man's Bay. With the oil lamp in the bedroom turned out. The wet seaweed was Zo's hair. The yielding substance was her body. Still soft but cold now. Her passion spent for all time.

I lifted my face from her hair, rolled to the far side of the bed and was sick. Between the bed and the wall.

I'd read the letter from Beth. I'd told Zo I was through, that I was going back to Palmetto City. I'd taken Zo in my arms. For the last time. Then what had happened?

Then Zo had cried out, "No. Please, God."

But it hadn't been God who had slugged me. Rolling back across Zo's cold legs I felt on the floor for the bottle of rum. The rum tasted good. It washed the taste of Zo's hair from my mouth. I took a second drink, then forced myself to feel through the dark until I found her heart. There was no beat. Zo was dead, had been dead as long as I'd been unconscious.

I felt through the dark for the lamp. It was still intact, still on the table beside the bed. With a package of book matches beside it. I struck a match. Then sitting on the side of the bed I lifted the chimney of the lamp and lighted it.

A yellow glow spread through the room as I replaced the chimney. A moth attracted by the flame batted its body against the glass. The drone of mosquitoes outside the screened window grew louder.

All I could see of Zo, without turning, was one white arm and hand. Dangling over the edge of the bed. Her fingers barely touching the bloody handle of the gaff hook with which I had been slugged.

I picked up the gaff and weighed it in one hand. The handle was loaded with lead. Whoever had slugged me had meant to kill me.

But why?

I took another drink of rum, studying the pattern of the rag rug. I had no illusions concerning Zo. I'd met her in a Habana night club. She was in the rackets up to her eyes. And, for all she had sweet-talked me, I doubted she had remained physically true during the four years I'd been in prison. For one thing she had to eat. A jealous boy friend was the obvious answer. One of my successors had slugged me and killed her. But how had he known where we were?

A flight of mosquitoes found their way through a hole in the screen and settled on my bare back. The ticking of a clock annoyed me. I looked up and around the room and saw a battered alarm clock on the dresser. I had been out for hours. It had been seven when we reached the cabin. Now, if the clock were right, it was five minutes of twelve.

Still without looking at Zo I carried the lamp and the bottle into the kitchen. It smelled of burned peas and hot metal. The black eyed peas were a charred mess in the pan. The coffee pot had long since boiled dry. The heavy iron spider glowed red.

I turned off the burners of the stove and set the lamp and the bottle on the table beside the groceries we'd bought in Cross City. My clothes were still lying on the floor. Where I had dropped them to go swimming. I walked to the screen door and looked out. The clearing lay snuggled in the hot Florida night. The Gulf lay placid in the moonlight, a silver streak stretching to Yucatan. The canary yellow jeepster was still parked under a slash pine. There lay the Gulf of Mexico. There lay the road to the highway. A lump formed in my throat. But I wasn't going anywhere. After sixteen hours of freedom, I'd been.

I picked up the lamp again and walked back into the bedroom. Zo was lying on her back, her eyes open and staring at the rain-streaked beaver-board ceiling, a small, puckered, brown hole in her left temple.

I sat on the bed beside her and picked up her dangling hand. All four fingers on it were broken. Had been broken when she'd tried to protect me by cupping her hands on the back of my head. I looked at her left hand. It was the same as the right. Zo's hands had taken the full force of the blow. If it hadn't been for Zo, I'd be dead.

I sat holding the lamp, looking around the room. It might have been a stage set for a movie. A chair was tipped over just so. A torn shade dangled in the window. A shattered rum bottle drained of its contents lay on the rag rug.

"I'm sorry, Zo," I told her.

Then I walked back in the other room and picked my coat from the floor. It was heavier than it had been. An automatic pistol, undoubtedly the one with which Zo had been killed, sagged the right hand pocket. I put the gun back in my pocket, dropped the coat back on the floor, and put on my shorts and socks. Then I put on my pants and shoes. And had another drink.

I could see the scene as the newspapers would describe it. A recently released ex-convict and his girl had rented an isolated cabin to celebrate his release. A drunken brawl had followed. Zo had clubbed me with the gaff. And I had shot her.

I put a cigarette in my mouth and struck a match. But I forgot to inhale. My cigarette still unlighted, the match burned down and burned my fingers. Without me feeling it.

The lump in my throat choked me. This was murder. And I was tagged. I couldn't prove that I hadn't killed Zo. All the evidence was against me.

A half dozen prison guards had seen me get into the yellow jeepster. The waitress in Gainesville who'd served us a meal would identify me as the man who had been with Zo. The liquor store man in Cross City would testify that he had seen us together and I had been drinking heavily. So would the grocery clerk.

No one would believe my story. My money was still in my pocket. Zo hadn't been attacked. I couldn't describe the faceless man I'd seen. He was as vague as my testimony concerning *Señor Peso*. There was no known reason for him to have done what he had.

I thought of what I'd told Zo:

"Even so. I'm going back to Palmetto City. Now. Tonight. And get a job. Make Beth proud of me. And remodel the old house. Or buy a new one. Raise five or six red-headed kids. And be disgustingly honest."

That was a laugh.

What breeze there had been had died. It was stifling hot in the I cabin. I picked my shirt from the floor, used it to wipe the sweat from the hair of my chest and threw it into a corner. Then picked it up and put it on. Not that it made any difference. My fingerprints were all over the cabin. On the tables, the bedstead, on Zo.

I took another drink, thinking about *Señor Peso*. I wondered if Zo had known him. I wished I'd asked her who he was. If Zo had known, she'd have told me. Still, if he hadn't come forward before, I couldn't expect him to step up now. Now only the devil could save me.

What had Zo told me? Not much. She'd told me not to jump to false conclusions. That no one had let me down. That *Señor Peso* couldn't show at my trial without jeopardizing the whole set-up.

It sounded logical when Zo said it. It still did. *Peso* had backed his talk with cash. He'd put up $48,000.00. A thousand a month for every month that I'd spent in a cell. That put him in the big time. International, no doubt. I was only a small cog in his wheel. But I was valuable to him. Why? I knew two dozen fishing boat captains who knew the Gulf and the Caribbean as well as I did. What had he planned for me? Why should he go to the trouble to order a converted sponger to put in and carry Zo and me to Habana?

Not that it mattered now.

Restless, my shirt sodden with sweat, I walked into the bedroom again and looked at Zo. She looked cool and somehow at peace. I hoped there were virile men, thick steaks, and aged rum wherever she was.

Then back of me something metallic 'pinged.' Twisting, I threw myself flat on the floor. Only to hear a bell ring and realize it was the alarm clock. That someone had set for twelve.

I got up and shut it off, thinking about Swede. The old man had been right about a lot of things. If I had listened to him I wouldn't be in this mess. If I'd opened Beth's letter in the warden's office I wouldn't have cared if ten Zo's were waiting.

I'd be in Palmetto City. I'd be in Beth's arms. Or would I? I wished I were smarter than I was. I wished I knew as much about women as I did about fish.

Doubt crept in to torment me. Along with the fear needling my nerves. I closed my eyes and saw Zo drop the letter beside the bed.

"Bah. This woman with whom I used to share you does not love you, Captain Charlie. I am a woman. I know."

I found the letter on the floor and reread it. It was a hell of a letter for a woman to write a man. A man with whom she was supposed to be in love. Setting up covenants and restrictions. If I were sober, if I were ready to settle down, Beth was willing to discuss the matter. Even the 'we'll start all over' had been an afterthought.

I crumpled the letter into a ball and dropped it back on the floor. Then I looked at the clock again. The hour hand had snipped the day from time.

A hundred and some odd miles away, Swede was slipping his hook. At the State's request. Swede was setting out on the big cruise. Swede knew all the answers now.

Not that it would do me any good.

Swede had called this one, too.

"Here, and I mean right here," he'd told me. *"Building up another dividend for the stockholders of Florida Power."*

But why stay to be burned? I hadn't killed Zo. I didn't know who had. I fingered the passbook Zo had given me. I had $48,000.00 in cash. In the National Bank of Habana. That the law didn't know about. If I could get that far, the chances were that I could get farther.

I tightened my belt a notch. The thing for me to do was run. My decision made, I felt better. The law might get me. It might not. But before it did it would have to put on the damnedest man-hunt the Florida west coast had ever seen.

CHAPTER FIVE

As it was, I'd delayed too long. A faint light swept across the screen window. There was only one thing it could be. A pair of headlights bobbing down the sand road leading to the highway.

I blew out the lamp and walked outside. It had been headlights I had seen. Less than a quarter of a mile away. I walked fifty feet from the cabin and stood with my hand in my pocket, in the shadow of a big slash pine. I hoped it was the killer returning.

It wasn't. It was a black and white state police car. With two uniformed troopers in it. The driver slowed as he passed the yellow jeepster and parked in front of the cabin.

His partner got out with his revolver in his hand. "Looks quiet enough to me. Probably a false alarm."

"Probably," the driver agreed. He flicked the car's searchlight around, missing me by inches. "Who lives here?"

"The sergeant didn't have a name. As I get it, it's a rental unit owned by some guy in Cross City."

The driver pointed the searchlight at the shoreline. "Lonely sort of place." He was a bit impatient with his partner. "Well, go ahead. Bang on the door. Wake 'em up and ask 'em if anyone screamed."

His partner banged the screen door. "State Police."

When no one answered, he banged again. Then he opened the screen and walked in, sweeping a path before him with his flashlight. A moment later he whistled. Then light showed in the bedroom window as he lighted the lamp.

"Find something?" the driver called.

"Plenty," the guy inside called back. "That fisherman who called the barracks wasn't whoofing. Some dame was screaming all right. But she isn't screaming now. She's dead."

"How dead?"

"Shot through the head."

"I'll be damned."

"After taking a hell of a beating. And boy is she a little honey."

My whole body drenched with sweat, I waited for the driver to get out of the car so I could sneak away. Instead he talked rapidly into his two-way radio.

"Kaniss and Phillips reporting. On that call to Dead Man's Bay. A dead woman in the cabin where the woman was heard screaming. Shot through the head, Phillips says."

So much was clear. There wasn't another house within a mile of the cabin. No one could have heard Zo scream, if she had screamed. And she'd only screamed three words.

"No. Please, God."

Whoever had killed her had called the police. He really wanted to pin this thing on me. And he hadn't wanted me to get too far away before the law stepped in.

The two-way crackled something and the driver called to the lad in the cabin.

"Any sign of a man?"

"Plenty," the lad inside called back. "Looks like they did plenty. And there's a broken rum bottle on the floor. And a chair tipped over. You know, the usual drunken party." There was a wistful note in the trooper's voice. "I don't know why I never get in on any of these drunken parties. At least not with dames like this one." He repeated, "Boy, is she a little honey."

"Describe her."

"Five feet two, one hundred and ten, well-stacked, black hair, black eyes. Not more than twenty-five. A small mole under her right breast. Probably Cuban."

The driver repeated the description into the two-way, then said, "Check the cottage for her purse, while I call in the plate on the jeep. Funny the guy didn't blow in the car."

"Maybe he's lyin' around drunk somewhere."

"Could be. We'll have a look."

The driver called in the number of the license plate and by that time the trooper in the cottage had found Zo's purse. He called:

"I was right about her being Cuban. Her name is Zo Palmyra. According to an Eastern Air Line stub, one way Habana to Palmetto City."

"Anything else?"

"That's all."

The driver repeated the information into the two-way. Then he got out of the car. "Okay. You've seen women before. They're all built just alike. Only some more so than others. Come on out and help me look around until the other boys get here."

The trooper in the cottage opened the screen door lighting a cigarette. "You think he hung around?"

"It's hard to tell what a drunk will do. You think he was drunk?"

"I'd say he was stinking. There's an empty bottle in the bedroom and two more in the kitchen."

They stood a moment in indecision, flicking their lights between the trees. Then I got my first break.

The driver of the car, an older man, said, "I tell you what, Joe. You take a look at the beach. I'll comb the ground around the cottage. You didn't find the gun?"

"No."

"Then watch yourself. And if you spot the bastard let him have it if he even looks like he's going for a gun."

The young trooper followed the path toward the shore. The older man began a wide circle that would bring him directly in front of the tree under which I was standing. Taking the gun from my pocket I stepped back of the tree and pressed my body into the bark.

Then as he passed me I stepped out and rammed the gun into the small of his back. "Don't try to turn and don't yell. And maybe nothing will happen to you."

He played it smart and stood still. "Don't be foolish, chum. I'm the law."

I said, "I know who you are. Drop your hands to your side. I'm going to take your gun."

Sweat starting on his cheeks, he hesitated.

I said, "Or I can plug you first. It doesn't much matter to me."

He dropped his gun. I picked it up and put it in the pocket of my coat. He said, "Now what?"

I said, "Now walk slowly to the cruiser, raise the hood, and rip the ignition wires loose."

He shook his head. "You can't get away with it, fellow. There are more cops on the way. Three cars full of them."

"I heard you reporting," I told him. "Walk."

He walked slowly toward the cruiser. His back as straight as a Burma rod. Still sweating. But a good copper. "Why did you kill her, fellow?"

"I didn't."

"Then who did?"

I told him, "I don't know. Just some guy who walked in."

"You expect me to believe that?"

"No."

"Why not put that gun away and let's talk it over."

"No. Just do what I told you to do."

He lifted the hood of the police car then hesitated again. I reached in and did it for him, ripping loose all the wires I could find.

He said, "All you're doing is building up more trouble for yourself."

I told him the truth. "Brother, I couldn't be in any more trouble than I am. Now walk on over to the jeepster."

"What if I yell for my partner instead?"

"I'll blow your spine in two."

"You say that like you mean it."

"I do."

He walked over to the jeepster. I felt the dash with my left hand to make certain the keys were in the ignition. They were.

"Now what?" he asked.

I considered taking him with me and decided against it. "Now lie down on your face."

There was enough moonlight for me to see the back of his ears turn red. "I'll be goddamned if I will," he said.

He turned, yelling, "Joe!" at the top of his voice, sinking his right fist into my guts as he yelled.

I could have killed him. I didn't. I had nothing against the guy. All he was doing was his job. I brought up the gun instead and laid it alongside of his head. He went down dragging me with him, shouting "Joe" again.

I fell on top of him, the trooper beating at my head with his fists, blinding me with pain. Forgetting the gun in my hand I swung a hard left to his jaw. Then sunk my knee in his stomach.

He gasped, "Oh, Jeez," and lost all interest in trying to hold on to me.

I wanted to be sick, and hadn't time. I scrambled to my feet and back of the wheel of the jeepster and kicked the motor over. Just as the young trooper pounded up the path from the beach, his gun in his hand but afraid to shoot for fear of hitting his partner.

"Sing out, Ben," he shouted.

Ben managed to get to his knees, vomit dribbling from his mouth. "Shoot the son of a bitch," he wheezed.

A slug starred the windshield of the jeepster. Then another. As sick as the trooper I'd kneed, I swung the jeep in a wide U-turn. The older trooper, on his feet now, showed briefly in the headlights I'd turned on from force of habit. He screamed as the bumper hit him.

There was a crashing in the brush. Then I turned off the lights and bumped down the rutted road to the highway. At sixty miles an hour. Swaying from side to side. Sideswiping trees. Scrunched down in the seat. The young trooper spraying the back of the car and the windshield with lead.

I made the highway and stopped to be sick. Then started on again. I had at most a five or ten minute start. I'd put the patrol car out of action but the chances were its two-way radio was still working. According to the trooper I'd slugged, three more cars were on their way. I hadn't the least idea which direction they would come from. It would only be a matter of minutes before road blocks would be set up. Before every law enforcement officer in every county on the Florida west coast would be alerted for a killer driving a new yellow jeepster with the license tag 4-1153.

As I remembered, there was a little town five miles down the road on the north bank of a river. I had remembered correctly. The business houses, except for one filling station, were dark.

I'd slowed down for the town. As I passed the filling station a tired-looking elderly tourist driving a mud-splattered '51 Buick with Iowa license plates pulled out and gave me a dirty look as I passed him.

Driving faster now, I drove on to the edge of town and the bridge across the river. There was a small gap perhaps eight feet wide between the black and white guard rail leading up the small ramp and the wooden bridge proper.

Pointing the jeepster at the gap, I rammed down on the gas and hopped out, hitting the road hard, skidding thirty feet, winding up panting with my nose buried in sand. The jeepster crashed through the gap, splintering the guard rail. A moment later it hit the water with a sullen thud, showering water as high as the bridge.

I sat up and held my head as the '51 Buick I'd seen braked on the approach to the bridge and the elderly tourist stuck his head out the partly-opened window.

"Holy smoke, fellow," he gasped. "I thought you were going pretty fast when you passed me. But not that fast. What happened? Did your car go out of control?"

I got to my feet and limped over to the car. "No," I told him. "I did."

I yanked open the door and climbed in beside him, ramming the nose of the gun that had killed Zo in his ribs.

"Let's roll. How fast will this crate go?"

He looked at the gun and swallowed hard. "Well, I've had it up to sixty."

I shook my head at him. "Uh uh. Let's open it all the way up. This make and model will do a hundred easy. And I have a date with a road block where this road joins U.S. 19. And there's apt to be some shooting. Unless we get there first."

The old man looked from the gun in his ribs to me. I knew what he was thinking. He didn't want to lose his car. He didn't want to die. If he did as he was told the odds were that he wouldn't.

"I don't seem to have much choice."

"None."

The old man stepped down on the gas. He was frightened but curious. Also a damn good driver. "The law's after you, huh?"

"That's right."

"What did you do?"

It was futile to try to explain. "I killed a woman," I told him. The old man was philosophical about it as he took a tight S-curve at seventy miles an hour. "Well, of course I don't know the details. But lots of women need killing."

CHAPTER SIX

There was no road block at U.S. 19. We'd beaten the law to the junction.

The old man slowed the Buick and looked down at the gun in his ribs. "Now, what?"

I said, "Turn south on 19."

He grumbled but did as he was told. He was frightened. He was nervous. But behind his fear and nervousness, he was having a hell of a time. For the first time in his life, he was bucking the law. Deep down inside him, he liked it. The buoys and the markers Swede talked about are swell. But most men would rather be on their own. There's a little pirate in every one of us. It's part of being male to *like* to live dangerously.

I added, "But keep it down to sixty from here on. Unless I tell you to step on it."

He asked, "From here on to where?"

I said, "I'll tell you when we get there."

Except for a few night lights in the business houses and filling stations, both Shamrock and Cross City were dark. A lump came into my throat as we passed the grocery store in Cross City. When I'd been in it a few hours before, Zo had been alive, thinking of me. She hated black-eye peas, but she had bought them because I liked them.

Now the peas were burned to a crisp on the stove in the cabin on the shore of Dead Man's Bay and Zo was dead. It still seemed incredible that anyone so vital could die.

"No. Please, God," Zo had screamed, her fragile hands protecting my head. Then, as the red tide had carried us out to sea, her last words had been whispered, *"I love you, Captain Charlie."*

I wiped my eyes with the back of my hand.

"What's the matter?" the old man asked.

I told him the truth. "I'm bawling."

"You loved her, huh?"

"Yeah. I guess I did."

Eugene, Old Town, Fannin fell under the exhaust. Still without a block. But luck couldn't go on forever. Behind and ahead of me, wires were crackling. Alert state troopers were making plans. Sleepy-eyed small town constables were backing their heaps out of carports. The air waves were filled with me:

'Red-haired... freckles on face... six feet... two hundred pounds... driving a canary yellow jeepster... wanted for murder and assaulting a state trooper... exercise care in apprehending this man.... He is armed and will

shoot!'

Troopers were swarming over the cabin by now. Technicians were dusting fingerprints. In a few hours my name and record would be added to the information on the air.

'Wanted for murder, Charles White... released from Raiford yesterday morning after serving a four year term.... He may be heading for Palmetto City.... This man is armed and dangerous....'

I fiddled with the radio of the Buick but all I could get was Cuban stations and a glib Texas border announcer who was peddling a vitalized vitamin pill, that, according to him, would cure everything from an inferiority complex to failing manhood.

The old man glanced sideways at me. "You can't get the police band."

"So I see," I told him and switched off the radio.

I rode, looking out the window, watching a south-moon-under skip from the top of one tall slash pine to another. I was still a long way from palm trees. I tried to make some concrete plan and couldn't.

I knew I wanted to get to Habana. I *had* to get to Habana. I had forty-eight thousand dollars waiting for me. More, if and when I reached Habana, *Señor Peso* would probably contact me. If I had been valuable to him before, I was invaluable now. Men who were wanted for murder didn't ask questions about their pay-load. They had nothing to lose.

Chiefland, Otter Creek, Lebanon Station, Lebanon, joined Eugene, Old Town and Fannin as misty blurs in the flat darkness behind the twin tail lights of the Buick. But time was beginning to squeeze me. As we passed through Lebanon the lights in the sub-sheriff's station were on and a yawning fat deputy, buckling on his gun belt, looked up sharply as we passed. The news was beginning to spread. I could expect a block at Inglis. Other eyes had undoubtedly spotted the Buick. All that had saved me so far was getting rid of the jeepster.

I realized, for the first time, that I was still breathing hard.

The old man rubbed it in. "Time's running out on you, huh?"

I yelled at him. "Shut up. Goddamn it, keep your mouth shut."

He returned his attention to his driving. "You don't need to get sore at me. I just made a statement."

I forced myself to think. I couldn't stay in the Buick much longer. Once we came to a block, it wouldn't make any difference what kind of a car I was in.

If I could reach the Palmetto City waterfront, I knew a half dozen charter boat captains who would be glad to sail me to Habana for a price. The same held true of Sarasota and Fort Myers. Because Beth lived in Palmetto City, the search for me would be concentrated there. My best bet would be to cut into the middle of the state, then west again after I'd passed Tampa Bay.

There was a blue road east out of Inglis. Also a short spur west to Yankeetown and Withlacahoochee Bay. I'd put in there to ice a couple of times when I'd been commercial fishing.

"Not far now, old man," I panted.

He cocked a gray eyebrow at me.

I lied, "I've got a boat waiting in Withlacahoochee Bay."

"Oh," he said. "I see." He tried to keep his voice level. "Which way when I come to the crossroad?"

We were coming into Inglis now. It's a little town, not more than two hundred people, but there is an overhead light at its main intersection and beyond the light I could see the glistening broad side of a black and white state police car.

"We stop right here," I told him. "Pull over on the shoulder of the road and turn off your lights."

He did as he was told. The strain had begun to tell on him. He was panting, too. "Now, what?"

"Now you get out," I said. "You'll find your car unharmed in Yankeetown. That's three miles to your right, at the mouth of the Withlacahoochee River."

He protested, "But—"

I rammed the gun in his side. "Out." There was no use telling him to keep his mouth shut. He'd lie and promise that he would. But he wouldn't.

The old man got out unwillingly, showing his first surface trace of emotion. "You bastard. You dirty, woman-killing bastard. I hope they catch you and burn you."

Like they'd burned Swede at midnight.

The palms of my hands slippery with sweat, I slid under the wheel the old man had vacated and rolled forward without lights, looking for a turn-off. I began to think there wasn't any. I was within two blocks of the black and white patrol car before I found one. It was a narrow dirt lane, flanked by high weeds, leading back toward a clump of live oaks. I parked the car under the oaks and listened. There was no disturbance on the highway. No one had seen me turn off. I took a step away from the car and a cold nose nuzzled my hand. I knew it was a dog. It had to be a dog, but my neck hurt as I craned it to look down. It was a friendly, mildly curious hound. I scratched his ears and walked back to the highway through the croaking of the tree frogs.

As I reached the mouth of the lane, the headlights of a rapidly moving car picked out the frail figure of the Iowa tourist, walking down the middle of the highway toward the road block. The car braked to a screaming stop beside him, and the big deputy I'd seen in Lebanon got out and threw a gun on the old man.

I was too far away to hear them, but from the way the old man was gesturing and pointing, I knew he was telling the deputy about the boat. The officer ordered him into his car. When it had passed me, I followed it toward the block, keeping well in the shadows of the trees and buildings.

I hoped the state patrolman would act on the information. He did. He transferred the Iowa tourist to his car and roared off toward Yankeetown. But he was a smart cop. On the chance that I might double back, he left the fat deputy sheriff guarding U.S. 19. Standing beside his parked car under the overhead light, the deputy looked enormous. His shadow was fourteen feet long.

I wriggled across the highway on my belly and skirted the back of a combination grocery and filling station until I was close enough to hear the radio in his car. The lad back of the microphone still didn't know if I had gone north or south and was dispatching his cars accordingly. Then the trooper on his way to Yankeetown radioed in, and the police announcer enthused:

"He's been sighted. At Inglis. On 19. He stopped an Iowa tourist north of Shamrock and forced him to drive him south. Cars 21 and 36 go to Yankeetown and back up Schaefer in 28. He is reputed to have a boat in Withlacahoochee Bay."

I smoked a cigarette in the shadow of a flame vine, listening. Then, moving as quietly as I could, I cut across lots and came out on the blue road headed west. On the road, I turned for a last look at the intersection. From this angle, the deputy wasn't so huge, but three townsmen, armed with rifles had joined him. It was an eerie feeling, being hunted.

For the moment I was safe. Possibly until dawn. With dawn, someone would find the Buick and the hunt would spread out again. There could be only so many boats on Withlacahoochee Bay. By morning, my name and record would be known. I strode on down the state road toward Dunnellon, fifteen miles away. There was always a lot of traffic on U.S. 41. Truck traffic. If I was lucky I might get a ride. If not, I'd steal a car.

I walked on through the moonlight, thinking how a man's sense of values change. Twenty-four hours ago, thinking of stealing a car would have shocked me. Even while I was sitting in a cell doing four years for smuggling. Now it was merely a matter of self-preservation. I was damned if I was going to the chair for a murder I hadn't committed.

It was hot and muggy this far inland. I took off my coat and carried it over my arm. Then I put it on again as protection against the mosquitoes that spewed out of the swamp on both sides of the road.

Sweat trickled into my shoes. The cool, clean freshness of the Gulf was memory along with Zo.

Now and then I passed a farm house. Twice dogs ran out and barked at me. I slogged on through the heat. I couldn't stop. I didn't dare. Then, topping a small rise, I spotted a car with one light and lay down in the ditch that paralleled the road. The car came on with agonizing slowness. It was a battered pick-up truck with two beered-up farm hands in it. They zig-zagged on down the road, happily ignorant that they were about to be pinched for drunken driving; two minor casualties of the murder in the cabin.

The grass was tall and wet and held an illusion of coolness. I lay a long time after the truck had passed, wondering if a man could love two women. Remembering Beth's dainty blonde beauty, trying to feel ashamed for wanting her physically after what had happened, thinking how happy we could have been if Beth had only let herself go the same way Zo had.

But Beth had always been reserved with me. Sex was something that happened after the lights went out, on Tuesdays and Friday nights. I buried my face on my arms and could hear her prim voice in the darkness, "You know I have to work in the morning."

I felt a little sick.

Maybe it was my fault. Maybe a woman couldn't let herself go with a man she didn't respect. Beth had always been slightly ashamed of having married a charter boat captain. Her folks had lived "nice." The material things of life had meant everything to her. A modern house with expensive furnishings, the solid respect of her neighbors, a substantial bank account. A big order for a cracker boy. Until I'd tied in with *Señor Peso,* all I had been able to give her was a forty-year-old frame house on a palmetto and snake-infested island. A three-inch steak at one of the best hotels in town one night and grits the next. She'd even had to take a job with Mr. Cliffton to be able to buy the kind of clothes she insisted on wearing.

It was a wonder she'd written to me at all. Still she had. So she hadn't been over-demonstrative. So what? Why should she be? What more did I want? She'd said we'd start all over. She'd sent me twenty-five dollars to come to her. I'd read her letter roaring drunk with a girl waiting for me. Now the girl was dead and I was running away. I was honest with myself. I was running away, not so much because I was afraid to die, but because I felt put upon, because I wanted one last hell of a good time on the forty-eight thousand dollars I had waiting in Habana.

I began to sweat even harder. What kind of a guy was I?

I wished I could talk to Ken Gilly. Ken was a lieutenant of detectives on the Palmetto City force. He and I had been friends since we'd been yard babies together. In those days his family had lived on the island, too. Ken was smart. He'd gone away to college. He was almost as smart as Swede. Ken could tell me what would be best for Zo, what would be best for Beth. The law wasn't hunting me, personally. The law was tracking down a killer. If I gave myself up and told the story as it happened, they might possibly believe me, find the man who'd killed Zo. I'd promised to love and support Beth. If I turned the forty-eight thousand dollars over to her, she'd never have to worry about money again.

The mosquitoes drove me out of the wet grass. I got to my feet and walked on, starting at unexpected sounds rising above the muted night noises of the swamp.

Then I thought of the bars of my cell. The sweat on my body turned cold. I had trouble getting my breath. I began to walk a little faster, looking back over my shoulder now and then. Right or wrong, I knew what I was going to do. I couldn't stand even one more night back of bars. I'd taken all of prison I could. Right or wrong, I was going to try to reach Habana.

It wouldn't be easy. By morning every patrolman, sheriff, deputy and constable in the state of Florida would be hunting the killer. They would have my name, my habits, my description. If one of them killed me, he'd be a hero. If I killed one of them, I'd be a double killer in the eyes of the law.

There were five hundred and seventy-two hot, hunted miles between me and Key West, and ninety miles of water beyond that to Cuba.

I walked still faster, with my hand on the gun in my pocket, the gun that had killed Zo.

CHAPTER SEVEN

The sign read:

WELCOME TO DUNNELLON Pop. 1344

I stood leaning on the sign, panting, watching dawn smear the eastern sky a dirty red. Morning was close. I could sense it in the sudden hush. I could smell it in the air.

I looked at the darkness behind me. I couldn't take another step. I had to stop. I didn't dare stop. I'd killed a girl named Zo Palmyra in a cabin on Dead Man's Bay. At least so the law believed.

My prison-made shoes had rubbed blisters on my feet. I took off my shoes and socks and limped on, barefooted through the silent residential streets, looking for a car I could steal. Most of Dunnellon still slept but, here and there, lights were winking on.

There was a Pontiac parked in front of a white frame house two blocks from the city limits. I tried to jump the ignition, but my fingers shook so badly that I couldn't make a connection. I tried three times. By then, my fingers were slimy with sweat, a family of awakened squirrels were scolding in the tree under which the car was parked, and the street was gray with dawn.

I limped on, breathing hard, carrying my shoes in my hands, looking back over my shoulder, acting guilty as hell, avoiding the business district, trying to find a car with the keys in the ignition. There weren't any. More houses were lighted now. Solid, substantial home men, the type Beth had wanted me to be, yawned their way out onto their lawns wearing pajamas and robes, to pick up the morning paper.

Then the residential street I was on pinched out and I was on a side road again. I started to turn back, walked on. The road led past a dump—and came out on U.S. 41, a mile south of town, not far from an all-night truck stop.

There were two cars with out-of-town plates parked in front of it. There were also four big trailer trucks. Three of them had nationally known trucking names and the I.C.C. stamp of approval on their sides. The fourth was a battered gypsy with the name "Jim Kelly—Elyria, Ohio," stenciled on the doors of the tractor.

Just this side of the truck stop there was a small creek under a culvert. I soaked my feet in the water. Then I put on my shoes and socks and looked in both of the cars. The keys weren't in the ignition. I could smell frying ham and eggs and coffee. I hadn't eaten since noon the day before. I fingered the money in my pocket, wondering if I dared stop.

As I looked in the second car, the door of the restaurant opened and an unshaven little man in khaki pants and shirt came out and kicked reflectively at one of the worn tires of the battered truck. His eyes were puffed and red-rimmed from lack of sleep. He looked tired.

The trucker assumed that I'd gotten out of the car into which I was looking and nodded a curt "Good morning."

I nodded back as curtly and walked on into the truck stop. Even if I could keep on walking, I couldn't stay on the road any longer. The first police car that passed would spot me.

A big exhaust fan was making a lot of noise inside the combination filling station, restaurant and bar, but it was even hotter than it had been outside. Three truckers and their relief drivers were sitting on stools in front of a white tile counter, eating heartily. A little farther down the counter, two well-dressed couples were toying with their food. They looked like they were sorry they had stopped.

The lad behind the counter was as big as the deputy in Inglis. His sleeves were rolled up above his elbows. His shirt was open at the neck exposing a tattooed eagle hiding in a mat of red hair.

I ordered ham and eggs and grits, and walked on back to the washroom to try and freshen up a bit. The back of my head was still clotted with blood. I washed most of it off, washed my face and slicked down my hair with water. My feet hurt. My head throbbed. But I didn't look too bad. I looked like I'd been on a bat. I limped back and sat down at the counter and the big lad back of it slid a plate of ham and eggs and grits in front of me. It was swimming in grease but it looked and tasted good. It was just what I needed.

The tourists stopped picking at their food, paid their checks and left. The red-haired lad spat after them.

"Goddamn tourists. I wish they'd stop coming in here." He picked an almost untouched plate of ham and eggs and grits from the counter and pushed it under my nose. "What's the matter with that, mister?"

I said I couldn't see anything wrong with it.

He scowled, "Nor me. Goddamn such picky eaters. What do they think this is, the 'Ronny Plaza'? They make me tired."

One of the truckers winked at me.

The counterman gave him a dirty look and went out to service a car that was honking in front of the gas pumps. I finished the food on my plate and sopped up the eggjuice with my bread. I felt better, but my insides were still quivering. Habana. That was a laugh. After walking all night I was stuck in Dunnellon. The Buick would be found any minute and the search would be extended to all highways.

The counterman finished gassing the car. I ordered another cup of coffee. The trucker in the khaki pants and shirt came in and dropped some silver in the phone. The other three truckers and their helpers finished their breakfasts and left.

The counterman picked six quarters from the tile and jingled them in his palm. "See what I mean? Them kinda guys are real. Two bits every time, even for pie and coffee. And they eat what you put on their plates. Some of them damn tourists ought to take lessons in etiquette from you truckers."

The lad in khaki didn't seem much interested. I'm certain I wasn't. Despite the heat in the truck-stop my undershirt felt cold and clammy. It was all very well to talk about beating your way through a cordon of police. Doing it was another matter.

"Here. Right here," Swede had said. "Building up another dividend for the stockholders of Florida Power."

The little khaki clad man ordered another cup of coffee.

"No load, yet, eh, Kelly?" the counterman asked him.

Kelly shook his head. "Naw." He looked at his watch. "I'll give Ocala ten more minutes to make up a load. Then I'm going to dead-head on into Fort Myers. I ought to be able to pick up a load of early cukes or tomatoes and make a market run." He jerked his thumb at the rapidly graying window. "Them big trucking firms is putting us gypsies out of business. I'm working for United Rubber and the finance company."

The red-haired counterman laughed where the cuff of his sleeve would have been if his sleeve had been rolled down. "I should have your money."

I gripped the edge of the counter. If I could get to Fort Myers, I could get to Habana. Both Skip and Harvey berthed in Fort Myers. Either man would sail me to Cuba for five hundred dollars.

"Just come down?" I asked the trucker.

Kelly nodded. "Yeah. From Chicago to Lake City. I was supposed to have a load waiting in Ocala. But I've had trouble with that guy before, so I stuck to 41, figuring something like this would happen."

He ordered and drank another cup of coffee.

I said, "It happens that I'm going to Fort Myers. I'll be glad to pay you whatever you think it's worth to let me ride along."

The little man rubbed his red-rimmed eyes. "Can you drive that rig of mine?"

I was honest. "I've never driven one," I admitted. "But—"

He lost interest. "Sorry."

He finished the dregs of his coffee and dropped more silver in the phone. He was little but he was tough. "All right, nuts to you, then," he concluded his conversation. "I'm not shoving off for New York with half a load for no one. Hell. It wouldn't pay for my ice and gas."

He slammed up the phone, paid his check, laid a half dollar beside his cup and walked out. I followed him into the morning. "I'll give you fifty bucks to take me to Fort Myers."

Kelly opened the door of his tractor. "Why don't you take a bus?"

I said, "Because I'd rather ride with you."

His shrewd eyes took in the prison made suit and crew cut. "Just got out, eh, son?"

He was my last chance. I laid it on the line. "That's right. Yesterday morning."

"And you're hot already?"

"A little." I answered.

"You kidding about being willing to pay fifty bucks to get to Fort Myers?"

I wiped the sweat from my forehead. "No."

"Let's see your money."

I took out my slim roll and counted out five tens.

Kelly weighed them on his palm. Fifty bucks would pay for his gas. It would buy a third of a tire.

"How hot are you, fellow?"

I lied. "Not very. Just a little caper. But I'm out on parole, see? And I don't want to go back."

He put the money in his shirt pocket. "Okay. I'll take a chance on you." He jerked his thumb at the shelf back of the seat. "But you better ride in the sleeper until we get down the road a piece."

I ducked back in the truck-stop and paid my check, then climbed up on the shelf before Kelly could change his mind. As he turned the motor over, he said:

"I don't think much of cops anyway. 'Overweight, overweight, overweight.' That's all they can yak about, especially in Alabama, Florida and Georgia. I get clipped every time I make this run. It's either pay off or be fined."

He rolled the big tractor and trailer out onto the highway, the seven gears forward whining as he shifted, picking up speed. "And for Pete's sake talk to me," he added. "I'd rather have that than your money. I came down without any sleep and I'll probably go back the same way."

I took off my shoes and asked him what he wanted to talk about.

He said, "If it ain't too personal, where did you do your time?"

I told him, "Raiford."

"How long?"

"Four years."

"For what?"

"For smuggling."

"I thought that was a Federal rap."

"It is."

"Then how come you do time in a state pen?"

I lay back on the pad. It felt good. "Because of a good war record and it being my first offense, they let me plead guilty to assaulting the Coast Guard officers who boarded me."

Kelly looked at me in the rear vision mirror that supplemented the one on the side of the tractor. "Who boarded you? You're a sailor, then, huh?"

"In a way. I owned my boat. A thirty-eight foot deep sea fishing cruiser with twin screws."

He said, "Well, I'll be damned. What happened to your boat?"

"They confiscated it."

For some reason, it made us friends. "Them sons-of-bitches," he swore. "The dirty sons." Kelly looked in the mirror again. "Like taking my rig away. Tough."

"Yeah. Damn tough," I agreed. "It cost me over ten thousand bucks."

The big job cruising at sixty miles an hour wasn't any worse than riding out a chop in the Gulf, except that the shelf bounced instead of pitched. The rising sun beating down on the metal roof was making me drowsy. I fought to stay awake. I couldn't afford to sleep.

I turned on my left side and elbow and the gun in my coat pocket bored into my hip. I eased my coat out from under me, then froze as a siren began to undulate somewhere on the highway behind us. The police cruiser came on fast and passed us at eighty miles an hour with its siren wide open.

I lay back on the pad, panting.

Kelly wasn't so friendly now. "They wouldn't by any chance be looking for you, would they, pal?"

I had trouble getting my breath. "No. I'm not that important."

"I'm beginning to wonder," he said. "What are you wanted for, chum?"

I asked him if he had a radio in the tractor. He said, "I have. But I never turn it on. The damn thing puts me to sleep."

"Turn it on," I ordered. "See what you can get."

He fiddled with the dial on the dash and tuned in the six o'clock Ocala newscast. The announcer sounded as if he was bug-eyed:

"...so if you see this man contact the nearest policeman or sheriff's office or call the state patrol. I will repeat his description. He has red hair. He is six feet tall. He weighs two hundred pounds. When last seen, he was wearing a prison made blue serge suit, a white shirt and a green tie. He has no hat. His hat was found in the cabin in which he killed his sweetheart. But he is known to be armed. And this is important. Please pay attention." The announcer stressed the words. "Do not try to apprehend this man yourself. *He has killed once and will, in the opinion of the state police, kill again, before he permits himself to be captured.*

Please keep tuned to your local station for further developments in the manhunt. We will interrupt our regular programs to bring you bulletins as we get them...."

Kelly switched off the radio and met my eyes in the rear vision mirror. He no longer looked tired. He was breathing through his mouth, but he was hurt more than frightened, as he looked from my eyes to the gun in the back of his head, then back at my eyes again.

"Cripes," he whispered softly. "And when I ask him how hot he is, he tells me, 'Not very. Just a little caper.'"

CHAPTER EIGHT

It was still short of nine o'clock when we raised Tampa. We had passed two road blocks. One at the junction of Florida 48 at Floral City, eighteen miles south of Dunnellon. The other just outside Tampa. Both times officers had questioned Kelly.

"Have you seen the man we're looking for? Red hair. Six feet tall. Around two hundred pounds. Probably still wearing a blue serge suit and a white shirt. No hat. Did he try to hitch a ride with you?"

Both times Kelly had pointed to the *No Riders* sign on the windshield of the tractor. Both times he had lied, with my gun at the back of his head. Neither officer had thought to look in the sleeper.

The hunt was still unorganized. The law was still confused. The Buick had been found under the clump of oaks at the end of the lane in Inglis, but the law still didn't know if I had left U.S. 19 or whether I'd headed north or south. It did know my name and record and, according to the patrolman who stopped us last, the Palmetto City police had been alerted.

"Not that I think he'll go there," the officer told Kelly. "White would be a fool if he did. The chances are he doubled back and he's somewhere in Georgia by now."

I almost wished I was. Tampa was much too close to Palmetto City. I wouldn't begin to even hope until we'd rounded the bay.

Kelly drove, looking straight ahead, cursing the traffic lights under his breath, damning all dumb drivers, damning me. Twice he almost sideswiped parked cars. The second time I warned him to be careful.

The backs of his ears got red. The muscles of his jaw set. He sat erect in the seat, meeting my eyes in the mirror, coming to a decision. Then, in the first clear space he came to, he pulled over to the curb and cut his motor.

"All right. Goddamn it. You drive."

I said, "Start the motor and get going."

He said, "To hell with you." He opened the door of the cab and got out. In the street, he turned and looked at me. "Why don't you shoot?" He answered his own question before I could speak. "I'll tell you why. Because you only think you're tough. It's taken me a hundred and nineteen miles to make up my mind. Now I know. So lay up there and roast, or try to drive the rig, or get out and walk. I don't care what you do. You've gone as far as you're going with me."

He started across the street toward a bar. I called after him. "Kelly."

He called back, "To hell with you. I'm going to have a beer. Maybe two beers. On you. I got 'em coming."

He disappeared into the saloon. I climbed down off the shelf and got out of the truck on the far side. Kelly meant what he said. I'd gone as far as I was going with him.

The sun reflecting off the red bricks turned the street into a furnace. The metal door of the cab burned my fingers. I crossed the street and looked in the window of the saloon to see if Kelly was telephoning. He wasn't. The little trucker was sitting at the bar drinking a glass of beer.

The bar looked dark and cool and inviting. I walked on down the hot street wondering if Kelly would notify the police. I doubted it. It would mean more delay for him. Every hour his outfit stood idle cost him money.

At the end of the block, I looked back. Kelly was just coming out of the bar. He crossed the street to the tractor and got in. A few minutes later, he drove by without even looking at me.

It was hot with my coat on. It made me conspicuous. Every other male on the street was in his shirt sleeves. I took off my coat and carried it over my arm. It helped some, but not much. I looked like a guy carrying a blue serge coat over his arm. And the police were looking for a guy, Charles White, wearing a blue serge suit, white shirt, and a green tie. I took off my tie and put it in my pocket. The gun in the pocket of my coat was heavy. It banged against my knees. Taking off my tie didn't disguise the fact that I was carrying a blue serge coat.

I stopped in the washroom of the next filling station I came to, and locked the door of the men's room behind me. I wanted to get rid of the coat but keep the gun if I could. I tried stuffing it under my belt between my belly and my shirt. The butt showed between the buttons of my shirt and would show unless I wore the coat. Besides, my belly was wet with sweat and I couldn't tighten my belt enough to keep the gun from slipping down.

Some Joe turned the knob of the washroom door. My heart began to pound. I called "Just a minute." I unbuttoned and dropped my pants and tried to anchor the gun to the inside of my thigh with my tie. It looked like I had a gun tied to my leg. Then the gun slipped out of the tie and clattered on the cement floor.

"What the hell are you doing in there?" the Joe outside asked.

Breathing hard, sweat dripping from my forehead, I put the gun and tie back in the pocket of the coat, rolled up the coat and laid it on the bottom of the oil drum acting as a refuse container. Then I stuffed the soiled paper towels back into the drum. Judging from the general filth of the washroom, it would probably be days before the coat was discovered.

Outside in the street again, I limped on acutely conscious of my red hair. There was a sporting goods store in the next block. I spent a buck and a half for a khaki-colored long-billed fisherman's cap, the kind four out of five tourists buy. I felt like a fool in it, but it hid my hair. It also gave me an idea.

Kelly had stopped close to the heart of town. I walked on, into the main business section and bought a twenty dollar tan gabardine shirt and a pair of twenty-five dollar fawn-colored slacks, in separate stores. I spent five more in still another store for a pair of thick-soled sneakers and a dollar in a drugstore for a pair of dark sun glasses. Counting the dollar I'd spent for breakfast, the four bits I'd left as a tip hoping the fat boy would think of me as a trucker when the police got around to him, plus the fifty I'd given Kelly, it left me thirty-three dollars and fifty cents of my original stake. But the money didn't matter. If I didn't make Fort Myers, I wouldn't need any money. If I did, either Skip or Harvey would trust me until we got to Habana.

I put the pants and shirt and sneakers on in the washroom of a saloon and stuffed my old pants and shirt and shoes in the bag that the shirt had come in. The new clothes were worth the investment. I still had red hair. I was still six feet tall. I still weighed two hundred pounds. But I looked a lot more like a northern tourist than I did like a cracker fishing guide.

I bought a beer at the bar and sat listening to the conversation. The two men on my right were talking about Joe DiMaggio. The lad on my left was arguing politics with the bartender. I listened for perhaps ten minutes. The names White or Zo Palmyra weren't even mentioned. It gave me a lot of confidence, more than I'd had. I wasn't important except to myself and the police.

To the general public I was just a small stick in the morning paper. An ex-convict had killed his sweetheart during a drunken brawl. So what? As the old man from Iowa had said, "A lot of women need killing."

Back in the heat of the street, I bought a noon edition of the Tampa evening paper. Then I crossed the street to a drugstore, bought a small canvas duffle bag and put the paper bag in it.

The strain was beginning to tell. I couldn't go on without sleep. I'd make some fool mistake if I did. I was so tired the kettledrums of fatigue were booming in my head. Despite the lift I'd gotten in the bar, I had a feeling everyone was looking at me.

I stopped on a corner and watched the passers-by. The feeling was all in my mind. No one was paying the slightest attention to me. Unless I called attention to myself I was safe for the time being.

At a liquor store near the bus station, I bought a fifth of rum and put it in the canvas bag with my clothes. I wanted a drink and I knew I'd need one to help me to go to sleep. Then I checked into the nearest hotel, using the name of Ben Benson and signing my home address as

Chicago.

The desk clerk wasn't even mildly curious. He took my three and a half, racked the registry card and gave a bellboy my key—410.

I followed the boy to the elevator and down the hall to my room. He put the bag on a bench and opened the windows. I gave him a dollar tip and told him to bring up some ice. When he had left the second time, I stripped and showered, wishing I'd bought a razor. I'd forgotten about my beard. It was as red as my hair. I considered having the boy go out and buy me a razor and some blades. Then I thought—to hell with it. I wasn't going to bed with anyone. I'd been.

I opened the bottle of rum and lay down on the bed naked and read the afternoon paper. I'd made a small headline in this one. It read:

EX-CONVICT MURDERS SWEETHEART

The story was about what I'd expected. I'd been traced back to Raiford through my fingerprints and Beth's letter. I remembered now. I had balled and dropped the letter on the floor of the bedroom.

I read on down the story. Two prison guards and the trusty to whom I'd spoken in the hall, had seen me get into a yellow jeepster with a beautiful black-haired girl. We had, so the newspaper account read, kissed passionately, before we'd driven away. Whoever had done the backtracking had missed the restaurant in Gainesville, but both the liquor store man and the grocer in Cross City had identified me as the man who had been with Zo. The grocer said I was drunk. The liquor man protected his license by saying that we'd both been drinking but neither of us was drunk. He, too, had seen us kiss before we'd driven away.

The trooper I'd tangled with at the cabin had a broken leg, but was otherwise okay. He admitted I'd told him that I hadn't killed Zo, that I didn't know who had, but that angle was played down. The way the state patrol and the Marion County Sheriff figured it, Zo and I had staged a drunken party to celebrate my release. During it, we had quarreled over the letter from Beth. Zo had slugged me with the gaff and I had shot her.

I'd told the Iowa tourist as much. The paper quoted him verbatim:

"I said, 'The law's after you, huh?' He said, 'That's right.' Then I said 'What did you do?' And he said, 'I killed a woman.'"

I was, variously reported, seen on the upper rim of the Gulf near Apalachicola, boarding a Tarpon Springs sponge boat in Withlacahoochee Bay, hopping a southbound freight train at Dunnellon.

I washed my mouth with rum and spit it out. The law was merely confused, not stupid. The manhunt had just begun. Once they sifted out the false reports and the hysterical telephone calls, the net would begin to tighten.

I would be traced to Dunnellon. The lad who lived in the white frame house would report that someone had tried to jump the ignition on his Pontiac. One of the solid substantial men yawning out to pick up his paper from the lawn would remember seeing me. The fat lad at the truck stop would be questioned. He would admit that a man answering my description had been in his place that morning and had left with a gypsy trucker named Kelly who was heading for Fort Myers in the hope of picking up a load of early cukes and tomatoes.

The officers who had stopped Kelly would remember him. Kelly would be located and whether he wanted to or not, he would be forced to talk. He would admit calling my bluff in Tampa. He would name the street and corner where he had stopped his rig. The Tampa police would take up from there.

My coat and tie and the gun that had killed Zo would be found in the refuse barrel. They would learn that I'd bought a long-billed fisherman's cap, a tan gabardine shirt and a pair of expensive slacks. They'd find the bar where I'd changed my clothes. They'd follow me to the bus station. I stopped it there before the cops knocked on the door. Shuddering, I drank from the neck of the bottle, looking at the newspaper picture of Beth's letter, knowing she was reading this, too.

"We'll start all over," she'd written.

I drank from the bottle again. Then I dipped my hand in the pitcher and rubbed cracked ice on my chest, my neck, my head.

"We'll start all over."

I wished I were with Zo. I wished I were dead.

Finally, I slept.

CHAPTER NINE

It was early evening when I woke up. A blue bottle fly was droning on the screen. I lay a long time listening to the fly, tasting the sweetness of rum in my mouth. It would be dark in a few more minutes. It was time for me to move on.

I had another drink and washed it down with a swig of the lukewarm water in the ice pitcher. Then I called down for a bellboy and sent him out for a razor, some blades, four hamburgers, a quart of coffee and the evening paper.

He grinned at the almost empty bottle on the dresser, when he brought back the things I had ordered. "Kinda pitchin' a little one, eh, Captain?"

"Yeah, kinda," I admitted.

"It does a man good," he said sagely. He added sadly, from the doorway, "That's what I try to tell my wife. But Maybelle don't hold much with drinking."

When he'd gone, I counted my money. I had twenty-three dollars. I walked to the open window and looked out and down. A Greyhound bus marked Tallahassee was loading. As I watched, the street lights came on. Men and women and boys and girls walked into the station. Men and women and boys and girls came out; none of them worried about the law, just going somewhere, coming back, killing time. Still other folks crowded the walk, shopping, walking, talking, laughing, following each other in and out of the stores. They looked like a bunch of ants.

I smeared my bristle with hand soap, put a blade in the razor and shaved. Then I filled the tub with cold water and sat in it while I ate the hamburgers and drank the coffee and read the evening paper.

The state patrol had traced me to Dunnellon. The big lad in the all night truck stop had talked. I read his statement to the reporter who interviewed him after the law had:

"Yeah. Sure I seen him. He was in my place about six o'clock this morning. I thought he was just another trucker, see? But, come to think of it, there were only four trucks around that time. Three of them left before he did. So he must have pulled out with that gypsy trucker named Kelly. But he don't act like no killer to me. He ate every bit of what I served and left me a four bit tip."

I wondered how a killer acted.

Officers Clausen and Dew of the state patrol remembered stopping a thirty-two foot trailer truck driven by a man named Kelly. Both officers admitted I might have been riding on the sleeper shelf, holding a gun at Kelly's head. The Manatee, Sarasota and Charlotte county police were looking for Kelly.

When they found him, I was cooked.

I got out of the tub and toweled. It had been a mistake to stop in Tampa. I should have gone straight on. It was too late to think of that now. The thing to do was to get out of Tampa before the local cops dropped a gill net around the city and netted me along with a lot of hot and bothered small fry. I doubted that the law would figure I'd head for Fort Myers. Once they learned Kelly had dropped me in Tampa, with Palmetto City only forty miles away, they would undoubtedly reason that I would try to see Beth, before I shoved on. Or was that wishful thinking?

My fingers felt thick and blunted. I had trouble buttoning my shirt. The gabardine was hot and scratched my skin. I wished I'd bought a cotton one.

Dressed, I weighted the hamburgers and coffee with the rum left in the bottle and looked at myself in the mirror on the dresser.

I was kidding no one but myself. I looked as much like a northern tourist as a red fish looks like a grouper. I looked like a big, raw-boned, red-haired, freckle-faced fishing guide wearing a silly looking cap, a pair of pleated sissy pants and shirt that was inches too small across the shoulders. No wonder the bell boy had called me "captain." He'd seen me in my hide. He knew me for what I was. I put the dark glasses on. They only made it worse. They made me look like a damn fool.

I threw the glasses in the wastebasket, picked up the canvas duffle bag and rode the cage down to the lobby. There was a new clerk at the desk. He glanced at me, then back at the dog track entries he was reading. I slid the key across the marble and walked on.

The weather hadn't changed. It was still hot. My body perspiration was turning the tan shirt black. I stood a moment in front of the hotel, debating whether to push on for Fort Myers or buy a ticket for West Palm Beach, and then cut back across the state. I decided it didn't make any difference what I did. It hadn't been shrewdness or brains that had gotten me this far. If my luck held, I'd make Fort Myers and, eventually, Habana. If it pooped out, I'd be pinched.

I crossed the street to the bus station. A uniformed policeman was standing in front of one of the entrances. I walked past him into the lunchroom and cut through it to the ticket counter. There didn't seem to be any stake-out in the waiting room. I bought a ticket for Bonita Springs, three stops beyond Fort Myers and asked the lad back of the wicket what time the bus left.

He said, "Seven-thirty."

I had fifteen minutes to wait. There was a magazine rack in the lunchroom. I bought two magazines I didn't want, to kill a little time.

Then I walked back and looked at the policeman.

His hands clasped behind him at parade rest, he was rocking heel and toe, admiring the south landfall of a pretty Cuban girl walking north.

She was small but well-stacked with a piquant face and a shining mass of long black hair curling around her shoulders. The way she walked, the bobble of her hips, the proud way she held her head, reminded me of Zo. I watched her up the street, with butterflies hatching in my stomach. I didn't want to hide. All I wanted to do was to sit down some place and bawl.

The Cuban girl merged with the crowd on the walk. I lighted a cigarette and started back into the bus station and stopped. A police car swung into the curb in front of the entrance where the patrolman was standing.

Four plainclothesmen got out. One stood beside the car. One walked directly to the ramp where a bus for Palmetto City was loading. One went into the station. The fourth man, his face vaguely familiar, stopped to talk to the patrolman. He had a deep voice that carried. I heard him say:

"...six feet, red hair, around two hundred pounds."

The patrolman shook his head. "No. I can't say that I have."

My heart began to pound. I tried to swallow. I couldn't. My mouth and throat were too dry. The police had found Kelly. He'd talked. The police knew I was in Tampa, at least that I had been in Tampa as late as nine o'clock that morning. Then I recognized the plainclothesman. He wasn't a Tampa detective. He was a Palmetto City man, the bailiff of the court in which I had been tried. All he had to do was look up and recognize me.

A group of small boys laughing at some wisecrack one of them made came out of the bus station and started up the street. I walked up the street with them looking back over my shoulder.

The detective who'd entered the station came out faster than he'd gone in. The ticket seller had remembered me.

"Why, yes," he'd told the detective. "I sold a ticket to Bonita Springs to a guy answering that description, not five minutes ago."

The detective said something to the bailiff. He gave the uniformed cop a dirty look, then walked up to the corner where I'd been standing a minute before and looked in the other entrance. The cop standing beside the police car reached over and kicked open the siren. It sounded like all the trumps in the world were wailing because Zo was dead.

The small boys stopped laughing. They looked at each other, then at me. They stopped walking and pressed themselves against the wall of the hotel. I was in the middle of the walk, alone. I'd never felt so lonely.

Somewhere up in the business district a siren answered the wail of the police cruiser in front of the bus station.

"You there," the Palmetto City bailiff called. "You. The big guy in the tan shirt and cap. The one carrying the bag. Turn around and let me look at your face."

I dropped the bag and ran.

The bailiff fired a shot into the air. "Stop."

I kept on running. The bailiff shot again. One of the women on the walk began to scream. A man tried to trip me. I hit at him with a clenched fist. The crowded walk behind me was filled with shouts now.

"There he goes. Stop him. Stop him, somebody."

A second, a third, then a fourth shot rang out and rocked the street. One of the detectives was shooting now. He wasn't shooting into the air. A bullet ricocheted off the wall beside me and a plate glass window starred, then shattered.

I ran on, panting, sweat making my freshly shaven cheeks burn as if they were on fire.

The cries behind me doubled. I could hear the slap of running feet. "Get the son of a bitch. Stop him, one of you guys."

The hue and cry. They hadn't the least idea who I was or what I'd done. It didn't make any difference. I was running. Get me. A fish had swum out of the school. I was no longer one out of many. I was one. I stood out. Get me. It was normal. It was natural. It was nasty.

More sirens began to wail. I rounded the corner, ripped off the long-billed cap and dropped it in the gutter. Then I angled across the street, cutting in between a steady stream of cars and buses. It was Saturday night. The main drag of Tampa was crowded with shoppers, theater-goers, strollers. I forced myself to walk at a normal pace with the crowd on the far side of the walk.

Then the chase boiled around the corner. I turned with the others to look. A girl standing next to me said: "Something must have happened."

I tried not to pant. "Yeah. It must have."

The traffic and the crowd on Franklin Street effectively blocked the pursuit as far as the mob was concerned. Then the police cruiser, its siren wailing, nosed around the corner against the light. The bailiff and the detective were standing on the front bumper. Both of them had their guns in their hands. Both of them were damning the crowd.

"A stick-up, I'll bet you," the girl said.

"Probably," I agreed.

Some of the crowd stopped to watch. I walked on with the girl, glancing back over my shoulder now and then, idly curious. The Palmetto City bailiff and the Tampa detective were standing on the hood of the cruiser, trying to pick me out of the crowd. Not having any success. Both sides of the walk were jammed with people trying to escape the heat.

The light at the next corner was green. I touched the girl's elbow, helped her across the street. She was young. Not bad looking. Willing to be friendly.

"A guy is nuts," she said, "trying to beat the law."

We were walking past the brightly lighted windows of a drugstore. As she spoke, she looked up at me. The smile faded from her face. She looked at my red hair. Then at my freckles. Then at my sweat-stained shirt and heaving chest. Her upper lip curled away from her teeth. Her eyes went round. She opened her mouth to say something, changed her mind and walked into the drugstore.

To buy a chocolate soda? To phone her boy friend? To open her goddamn pretty little mouth and scream:

"I saw him. I saw Charlie White. There he goes. There. That big red-haired man without a cap."

I had no way of knowing. I suddenly didn't care. My feet hurt. I was tired. My head began to ache again. It was an effort to think, to move one foot in front of the other. I'd run as far as I could. I couldn't run any more. I'd run out of places to run to.

My hand shook as I lighted a cigarette. By this time, the detectives on foot were weaving through the crowd, looking at faces, asking questions. The bus station was plugged. So was Union Station and the airport. Every road out of town was blocked, or would be. With one possible exception—the causeway to Palmetto City. The police would probably leave that open. Like an inverted fish trap. To tempt me to try to go to Beth.

That was all right with me. If I couldn't make Fort Myers and Habana, I wanted to talk to Ken Gilly, tell him I hadn't killed Zo, ask him to keep an open mind regardless of what happened to me. I wanted to talk to Beth. I wanted to tell her how sweet it had been of her to write, how sorry I was that I'd messed up both our lives. Before they took me back to Raiford and put me in the little white house. The one Swede was no longer using.

"Here. And I mean here," he told me.

There was an empty taxi parked in the cab zone a few feet from the corner. I got in and leaned back against the cushion. The driver flipped his flag. "Where to, chum?"

I said, "Palmetto City."

CHAPTER TEN

I'd been right about the causeway being open. There was no block at either end of it. There was also no way out of Palmetto City except by water or back across the causeways. Three causeways. The manhunt was over. The law had me where it wanted me, now. All it had to do was draw in the net.

Passing the dog track, the cab driver asked, "Whereabouts in Palmetto City, fellow?"

I blew smoke at the ceiling of the cab. I wanted to talk to Ken. But friend or not, Ken would have to arrest me. Ken was the law. And I wanted to talk to Beth before I was locked up. I said, "Just let me off at the mole."

Palmetto City hadn't changed. The green benches lining both sides of Center Street were crowded with northern tourists. A band was playing in the shell in Phillips Park. Dig Davis, a kid I'd soldiered with, was directing traffic at Fourth Avenue. For some reason he made me think of Matt Heely. Matt owed me a thousand dollars. Matt had a boat capable of raising Cuba. It could be that I could get Matt to sail me to Habana, if I could contact him before I was picked up. I began to hope a little, but not much. After I'd talked to Beth, I might see Matt. It would depend on what Beth advised me to do.

The mole was dark and crowded as usual, with northern tourists fishing for grunts and pig fish about the size of the ones I usually used as bait for snook. I paid off the cab driver with my last ten dollar bill and lighted my last cigarette, while I watched him pull away.

The cops seldom patrolled the mole. I was safe for the time being. I almost wished they had caught me before I'd gotten this far. I wanted to talk to Beth and dreaded to. She would be pleased to get the money. But telling her about Zo would hurt her.

I stalled for a few minutes watching the fishermen. The tide was coming in. The moon was right. You could have caught fish with a bent pin and a doughball. I watched the excited tourists for a moment, glad to have a chance to feel superior about something. Then I cut across Waterfront Park, under the royal palms, toward the return address that had been typed on Beth's letter.

The street was shabby and run-down, on the edge of colored town, not far from Cliffton's store. The address on the letter proved to be a white frame garage apartment on a bougainvillea-tangled alley, behind a square frame rooming house. It was a hell of a place for the wife of a man who'd made the money I had. Shame made me sweat even harder.

There was no police car in front of the rooming house nor, as far as I could tell, any stake-out in the alley. But neither was there any light in the apartment. Then I remembered it was Saturday night. Cliffton's stayed open until midnight. Even working in the office, Beth probably wouldn't be home until after ten o'clock.

I walked back down the silent street toward the mole. Swede had been right about the bloody tide, too. I must have been out of my mind to treat Beth the way I had.

I tried to salve my conscience. Of course, she could be living in the big old house on the island across the deep water channel from the mainland. But she couldn't live there and work in town. At least, not with me in prison. The only way the old house could be reached was by boat. I'd had to run her across every morning when I'd been home. When I'd been away on trips or out fishing the banks she'd always stayed with her folks.

I hoped she'd rented the old place to bring in a little extra income. But the chances were she hadn't. It wasn't flossy enough for tourists. It needed too many repairs. The odds were that nothing but snakes and raccoons and rabbits and field mice had lived on the island for four years.

I watched the fishermen for another hour and walked back. There was a light in the apartment now. As I watched, it winked out. I reconnoitered both the street and the alley more carefully this time. There didn't seem to be a stake-out.

My heart pounding, I walked down the alley. No one stepped out of the shadows to stop me. No one said, "Just a minute, killer."

The stairs leading up to the apartment were on the outside of the building, profusely covered with flame vine. I inched up, step by step, keeping my back to the wall. At the head of the stairs, I reached out and ran my knuckles across the wooden frame of the screen door.

On the other side of the screen, Beth gasped, "Who's there?"

I said, "It's Charlie. Please don't scream. And please don't turn on the light."

Bare feet padded across the floor until only the screen door separated us. After four long years. There was a hole in the flame vine behind me. Moonlight flooded through it, spotlighting Beth's face and slim young figure.

I began to breathe hard again. Not from fear. I'd lied to Zo. This is what I'd dreamed of. But I'd forgotten that Beth was so pretty. Even with her cheeks stained with tears and deep shadows under her eyes, she was beautiful. And at one time she had loved me.

Beth snatched a thin robe from a chair. Then she pressed her nose against the screen. She was almost as breathless as I was. "You shouldn't have come here, Charlie. The police were at the store not half an hour ago. I promised Ken Gilly I'd call him if you tried to contact me."

She slipped the robe over her shoulders but the front of it gaped open.

I said, stupidly, "Then you know?"

Beth brushed a lock of straw-colored hair away from her forehead, her right breast rising with her arm. "How could I help knowing? It was in both the morning and the evening paper." Her mouth began to work. Tears rolled down her cheeks. "Everybody at the store, except Mr. Cliffton, has been 'sorry' for me all day."

I got it off my chest with a rush. "I didn't do it, Beth."

"You didn't do what?"

"I didn't kill Zo."

"It says in the papers you did."

"I don't care what it says in the papers. I didn't kill her. And I didn't open your letter, I didn't realize what it was, until it was too late. I thought you were through with me. I didn't read your letter until after I'd reached the cabin. When I did read it, I told Zo I was through with her, for good. I told her I was coming back to Palmetto City and you. That's when it happened."

Beth stopped crying. "You mean you didn't kill that girl?"

I panted. "No. Someone I didn't see, some man, slugged me with a gaff hook and shot Zo. He meant to kill me, too."

"Who?"

"I don't know who he was. I didn't see his face."

She pressed her nose still more tightly to the screen. Her voice was a breathless whisper. "You expect me to believe that?"

"Have I ever lied to you?"

Beth thought a moment. "No." She shook her blonde curls against the other side of the screen. "No. That's one thing you've never done, Charlie. You've never lied to me." She stepped back and unhooked the door. "Come in," she said softly. "Before the neighbors see you."

Inside the room I tried to take her in my arms.

Beth pushed me away. "No, I want time to think. This may change things for both of us. You swear you didn't kill that girl?"

"I swear it."

From what I could see in the moonlight, it was a one room efficiency apartment with a small kitchenette and bath. Beth sat on the edge of the bed. "Please light me a cigarette, Charlie."

I said I didn't have any. She said there were some on the table. I lighted one and gave it to her. Beth had changed in one respect. It was the first time I'd ever seen her smoke. I sat on the bed beside her. It squeaked slightly under my weight.

"Why did you come here?" she asked me.

I told her the truth. "I didn't intend to at first. I didn't think you'd want anything to do with me. I was going to try to make Habana, but they blocked me off at Tampa."

The bar in the screen door so divided the moonlight that all I could see of her were two small white feet. It was like looking at a surrealist painting. I couldn't see her face but I could feel the scorn in her eyes.

"In other words, if you could evade the law and get out of the country, you were going right back into the same vicious racket that wrecked our marriage. You were going to work for *Señor Peso* again."

I cracked my knuckles. "That's right." I didn't know how much time I'd have with her. I didn't want to waste it trying to explain my involved reasoning. I made it as short as I could. "I made up my mind that if you were waiting for me when I was released, I'd go straight. If not, I'd identify and kill *Señor Peso* for not helping me during my trial."

Beth turned toward me and her warm body brushed my arm. "Then you still don't know who *Señor Peso* is?"

"No."

"Then what happened?"

"When I was released, you weren't waiting for me, but Zo was. She told me *Señor Peso* hadn't let me down and proved it by giving me my Habana bank book with a thousand dollars deposited to my account for every month I'd been in prison. She said a boat would put in at Dead Man's Bay and take us to Habana. So I thought 'What the hell' and went with Zo."

Beth protested, "But I would have been there if I could have gotten away. I sent you train fare to come to me." Sobs shook her shoulders. "I wrote you I was waiting. I said we'd start all over."

There was a note of rising hysteria in her voice. I put my arm around her waist. "For Gosh sake, Beth, don't blow your top. Please."

She said, "I'm not going to blow my top." She moved away from me. "But I did write you, Charlie, I did."

I continued to crack my knuckles. "I know. And if I'd read your letter at the prison, none of this would have happened."

"Why did you come to me now, Charlie?"

"To turn the money over to you."

"I don't want it. It's dirty money."

"To say good-bye then. To tell you I was sorry I'd been such a heel."

"Is that the only reason?" Her hand was on my knee.

"To tell you I love you."

"But you loved this other woman, too? This Zo?"

I looked at the small feet in the moonlight. I'd never lied to Beth. I continued to be truthful. "Yes. I did. I loved both of you, I guess."

Beth's fingers tightened on my knee. She began to cry softly. "What will they do to you when they catch you, Charlie?"

I took the cigarette from her fingers and sucked it to a small red torch. "What we're doing to this cigarette."

She sobbed, "I won't let them. If you didn't kill that girl, there must be some way we can prove it."

I snuffed the cigarette. "How?"

Beth shook her head. She was sitting so close that her hair brushed my face. It smelled sweet and clean. The small apartment was hot and filled with the smell of her. I was acutely conscious of her body.

"I don't know," she admitted. "There must be *some* way." She clutched at a straw. "Perhaps Mr. Cliffton could help us."

Cliffton was the merchant for whom she worked. She'd been his confidential secretary for years. Beth liked him. I never had. A cocky little cracker from the middle of the state, he had built an idea into the biggest business in town. He boasted that he would not be undersold. To my knowledge, he never had been. He was a shrewd merchandiser, a good showman. He wasn't afraid to spend money on advertising. As a result, he'd built a hole in the wall drugstore into a block square, four story high merchandise carnival, handling everything from apples to zithers. If you couldn't buy it at Cliffton's, it wasn't for sale.

I asked, "Why should Mr. Cliffton help us?"

Beth took her hand off my knee and folded her hands in her lap. "Mr. Cliffton is in love with me. He's asked me to marry him. He even offered to buy the old house on the island so I'd have money to live on and wouldn't have to work while I made up my mind whether or not to divorce you."

I said, "That's a hell of a note."

Beth said, hotly, "Your own hands are clean?"

The strain was beginning to get me. Too much had happened too fast. I buried my face in my hands. "No. I guess they aren't. I'm sorry. I have no right to say anything. Not after the way I've messed up our lives."

Beth pulled my hands away from my face. I couldn't see her now. She was too close. But I could feel her. "Kiss me, Charlie," she demanded.

I said, "I shouldn't think you'd want me to. After the way I treated you."

Her breath was sweet in my face. "Kiss me," she repeated.

I took her face in my hands and kissed her. Not the way I had kissed Zo. Without passion. Like I had kissed Beth at the altar. After Reverend Paul had finished marrying us. When the world had still been our oyster. Beth was something sweet and beautiful and good. She was something that had been missing from my life for a long time.

When I lifted my head, the shaft of moonlight had risen so I could see her face. Her eyes were shining. Her lips brushed mine, again. "It's going to be all right, Charlie. Believe me. I don't know how we're going to do it. But somehow, we'll *make* it right."

I sat, afraid to move, afraid to touch her. The next move was up to Beth. She sat a long time, just fondling my face with her fingers. Then she leaned back, with her hands cupped under her head. Her eyes were cat-green in the dark.

"Prove that you love me, Charlie."

Prove that I loved her.

I kissed her throat, her lips, her lovely shoulders. Her flesh was hot and quivered under my lips. I touched her and she whimpered.

"It's been so long. I've wanted you so badly."

I rolled over and she kissed me fiercely. Her fingers tangled in my hair.

"Love me. Love me," she panted.

Then a car drove up the alley and stopped. A revolving red police spotlight found the screen door and settled, replacing the moonlight with a bloody glow. Two pairs of heavy feet began to climb the stairs.

CHAPTER ELEVEN

Beth twisted away from me and stood panting in the red glow of the spotlight, fighting for breath, as she felt frantically for her robe.

I started to get up.

She stopped me. "Stay there," she whispered.

The climbing feet reached the landing. A man's bulk cut off the red glow. Knuckles drummed on the wood of the screen. Beth finished wrapping her robe around her. "Yes—?"

"It's Ken again, Beth," Gilly told her. "And Sergeant Strawn."

"Yes—?" Beth repeated. "I've gone to bed."

Gilly sounded tired. "We presumed that, Beth, and we're sorry to disturb you. But we thought you ought to know."

Beth was still having trouble with her breathing. "You thought I ought to know what?"

Bill Strawn said, "Charlie's been spotted in Tampa, Mrs. White. He bought a ticket for Fort Myers, but some of the boys jumped him at the bus station and he ran."

"Oh," Beth said. "I see."

I felt like a fool, crouched on the bed, while Beth fronted for me.

"That was two hours ago," Sergeant Strawn added. "Tampa immediately blocked all roads except the causeways, figuring on funneling him here. And it seems to have worked. They've just picked up a cab driver who says he drove a man answering Charlie's description down to the south mole."

"Oh," Beth said. "I see." She found her mules and slipped her feet in them. Then, reaching behind her, she squeezed my hand and scuffed over to the door. "I'm sorry I can't ask you in, but I'm not dressed."

"That's quite all right, Mrs. White," Strawn said. "We just thought you ought to know."

Ken said, "I wish Charlie hadn't headed back this way. God knows I don't want to make the pinch."

Beth was in control of her breathing again. Her voice sounded cool, almost casual. "Maybe he didn't do it, Ken. Maybe Charlie didn't kill that girl."

Ken said, "Don't be silly, Beth. Of course he killed her. You read the papers, didn't you? They staged a drunken party to celebrate his release. Sometime during it, they quarreled. Maybe over your letter. She hit him with a gaff hook and he shot her."

Strawn said, "That's the way the evidence stacks up. You want us to post a guard in the alley, Mrs. White?"

Beth's shoulders raised as she took a deep breath. "Thank you,

Sergeant. I don't think that will be necessary. I doubt if Charlie would be fool enough to come here. Even if he should, I doubt if he'd hurt me."

"No," Ken agreed. "I don't think so, either. I don't think he'll come here. Now that he's gotten this far, he'll probably try to get away by water. And if he should get down to the Glades or the Thousand Islands, we'd never find the guy. What was the name of that guide you once told me owed Charlie money?"

I held my breath.

Beth lifted her hair up and away from her neck. "I don't remember," she said. "I'm too upset to think straight. This has all been a nightmare to me."

Sergeant Strawn was sympathetic. "Of course. You get on back to sleep now if you can, Mrs. White. But you will let us know if Charlie should try to contact you?"

"Of course I will," Beth lied.

Ken fixed it good for me. "Remember, you don't owe Charlie a thing, Beth. He and that Cuban girl did plenty before he shot her."

Heavy feet clumped down the stairs. I was still crouched on my hands and knees. I lay down on the bed, my body bathed in cold sweat. Now everything was wrong again.

Down at the foot of the stairs, a car door opened and slammed. A motor purred. The red light moved away. Beth scuffed into the bathroom and closed the door. After a long time she came out and sat on the edge of the bed. She didn't take off her robe or make any move to lie down beside me. She just sat staring at the screen door.

Swede had been right about so many things. He'd said, "A man can starve a dame. He can get drunk and beat her every night and twice on Sunday and she'll still think he's her personal Marshall Plan in a silver champagne bucket. But only if she knows that she's the only woman in his life."

"I'd better go," I said, finally.

Beth seemed to come to some decision. She came down beside me. "No. I don't want you to go. Besides, you're safer here than you would be anywhere else. At least for the time being."

She'd forgotten to take off her scuffs. She inserted the toe of one foot under the sole of the other and the motion brought one of her legs in contact with my body.

"Pardon me," she said.

I said, "That's quite all right."

I was beginning to want her again, knowing she was thinking about Zo. I laid my hand on her arm. "I love you, Beth."

She put her hand in mine. "I love you, Charlie. But you've made it so difficult."

I said, "I know. Maybe I'd better go. I don't want to involve you."

Beth sighed. "No. Why shouldn't I be involved? You're my husband." Her free hand fondled my face. Then her body began to shake as if she were crying or giggling. I decided she was giggling.

"What's so funny?" I asked her.

She said, "You know what I was thinking about when we were so rudely interrupted?"

"What?"

"That you better stay right here in the apartment until after I talk to Mr. Cliffton. No one ever comes here but me. But now that's out. When you don't show up at the police blocks and none of your old friends on the waterfront see you, someone is bound to get nasty-minded and suggest that Ken search my apartment."

I kissed the tip of her nose. "Then the best thing I can do is give up."

Beth shook her hair in my face. "No," she said. She seemed to have a lot of faith in the guy. "Not until after I've talked to Mr. Cliffton. But there's only one logical place for you to hide."

I asked her where that was.

Beth said, "Out at the old house. You know it and the island better than anyone else. An army couldn't find you there, if you didn't want them to." She moved closer to me. "Now tell me just what happened in that cabin, Charlie. And don't try to spare my feelings. My knowing exactly what went on can be very important to us both." She rolled away from me and to her feet. "But first, let's have a cigarette."

She lighted one for both of us, then came back beside me.

Wanting her became a pain. I tried to take my hands away from her. I couldn't. Beth was holding them against her. I blew smoke at the ceiling.

"There isn't too much to tell. We hit the cabin just before dark. Both of us were pretty drunk. We'd stopped in Cross City for groceries and more rum. The Gulf looked good to me. I thought I'd have a swim while Zo got supper, and I did. But I stayed in the water longer than I'd figured and it was dark when I got back to the cabin. Zo had lighted two lamps. One in the kitchen. The other in the bedroom. The coffee water was boiling along with the pot of peas. I'd stripped in the kitchen before I'd gone in the Gulf. My clothes were still lying on the floor. I was still so drunk that I tripped over them. Then I saw your letter and remembered that since the riot all incoming mail had been retyped."

Beth's hand tightened on mine. "That's why you didn't read it at the prison?"

"That's right. When I did read it, I was sick. I walked on into the next room and told Zo we were through, that I was coming back to Palmetto City."

"What was she doing?"

"Nothing. She was in bed."

"What did she say when you told her you were through?"

"She thought I was joking."

"Then what happened?"

"She wanted to read your letter."

"You let her read my letter?"

"Yes. I did."

I could feel Beth's body stiffen. "What did she say when she'd read it?" she asked.

"She said you didn't love me."

Beth kneaded her arm with my fingers. "If I didn't love you, do you think you'd be here now?"

"No," I admitted. "I don't. I knew you loved me then, I think. But I was still half drunk, confused. And Zo pointed out that all I knew was the water, that I couldn't make a dime on land."

I began to sweat again. "Well—"

There was enough moonlight to see Beth's eyes. They were cat-green and slitted. "She persuaded you to make love to her."

"Yeah. Yeah. That's what happened."

"Then where did the quarrel come in?"

"There was no quarrel. All of a sudden the corners of Zo's mouth turned down. She screamed, 'No. Please, God.' She clasped her hands on the back of my head and the next instant the whole ceiling fell on me. I turned, but all I could see was a white blur. Then the guy hit me again. As I passed out, I remember hearing a shot. When I came to, Zo was dead."

"But it was a man who hit you?"

"Yeah. It was a man. I'm positive of that."

The name was distasteful to Beth. "This Zo person had mentioned some other man?"

"No. She said there'd been no other man since I'd gone to prison."

Beth's lips twisted in the moonlight. "I can imagine."

I didn't say anything.

Her free hand caressed my face again. "You've told me the truth now, Charlie?"

"Exactly as it happened."

"You didn't kill her?"

"No."

Beth was suddenly crisp and businesslike again. She might have been fully dressed and sitting behind her typewriter in Mr. Cliffton's office. "All right. I'll tell Mr. Cliffton everything you've told me in the morning."

I still didn't like the Cliffton angle. I said so. "You say the guy loves you.

You say he's asked you to divorce me and marry him. What's his reaction going to be when you tell him you've talked to me. Cliffton's going to reach for his phone and call Ken. The guy is a bargain hunter. And it's a lot cheaper for him to turn me in to be burned than it is for him to pay for a divorce."

Beth put her fingers on my lips. "You're doing Joe, Mr. Cliffton, a big injustice, Charlie. He's really a very fine man. An honorable man."

"I'll bet."

"I mean it. You might as well accuse Mr. Cliffton of being *Señor Peso* as of being capable of doing such a thing as you just said. Besides, I'm not going to tell him where you're hiding. You have to admit he is smart."

"Yeah. He's that, all right."

"All I'm going to tell him is that I don't think you killed the girl and ask his advice on how to go about hiring a private detective to prove it. This Zo was a Cuban, wasn't she?"

"Yes."

"Pretty?"

"Very."

"Then maybe it was some lover who followed her from Habana. I mean who killed her and left you framed for her murder. The police won't believe us. Not even Ken. I realize that. But if a private agency man could uncover some jealous lover, we'd at least have something tangible on which to base our contention."

I kissed her eyes. "Thanks for believing me, Beth."

"You're my husband. It's my duty to stand by you."

My fingers crawled down her back. "That your only reason?"

She began to have trouble with her breathing. "No. I love you. You should know that by now, Charlie. And you'll hide out on the island until after I've talked to Mr. Cliffton?"

"I will. But how will you contact me?"

She gasped as I touched her. "I'll find some way. I have a right to go out there anytime I want to. Maybe I want to put the house in order, to be sold." She turned on her side and nibbled at my lower lip.

I continued to caress her. "When do you think I'd better go out?"

Beth panted. "About four o'clock this morning. There won't be any moon then. The searchers will be tired."

"And until then?"

"Do I have to say?"

She didn't.

CHAPTER TWELVE

I dressed in the hot sticky silence. I couldn't find one of my shoes. Beth found it under the bed. She handed it to me. I put it on and lighted a cigarette.

I'd wanted to see Beth. I had seen her. Even with every cop in Florida looking for me, I should feel a glow. I didn't.

Beth had changed.

There'd been some other man in her life while I'd been gone. She wasn't the same girl I'd left. Beth knew all the answers now.

"Why so silent?" she whispered.

"Just thinking," I whispered back.

She kissed the lobe of my ear.

I fought the queasy feeling in my stomach. I had no right to be jealous. I'd forfeited all rights. And Beth had given them back again.

I forced myself to put on my shirt. I wanted to stay. I felt as though Beth wanted me to. But Ken Gilly was nobody's fool. When I wasn't picked up by morning they'd know I was holed up somewhere. Beth was my wife. Her apartment was the first place they'd look.

I walked to the screen door. Beth padded barefoot beside me. "Have you a gun, Charlie?"

"No."

"Wait."

She padded back through the dark. I heard a dresser drawer open. Beth pressed a gun into my hand. From the feel, it was a .32 Colt automatic. I put it in my side pants pocket.

"Don't use it unless you have to."

"No."

"How about cigarettes?"

"I took two packs from the table."

"Good." Beth stood on her tiptoes and kissed me. "I'll be out tonight or tomorrow night at the latest."

"What if you're followed?"

"I won't be. I'll make certain I'm not."

"Ken is going to be suspicious."

My shirt was open at the neck. Beth twisted a tuft of the hair on my chest until it formed a tiny peak. "Pooh for Ken Gilly. I can twist Ken around my fingers."

I wondered if Ken was the man in her life. I took her bare shoulders in my hands and kissed her. "Be careful."

Beth kissed me without passion, pressing the length of her body against mine. "You be careful. Please."

My fingers bit into her shoulders. "Say it."

Her lips brushed mine again. "I love you, Charlie."

"I love you, Beth," I told her. Then I unhooked the screen and keeping my back to the wall I sidestepped slowly down the stairs.

The moon had set. It was even hotter than it had been. It was like moving through warm black ink. The only sound was the drip of condensation and the occasional rustic of a dry palm frond.

At the foot of the stairs, I stood with my back pressed to the wall, wondering if it was worth it to try to make the island. My body felt like an empty rain barrel. I was emotionally and physically drained. Instead of feeling free and eager to run on, somehow I felt trapped.

I moved cautiously up the alley, feeling my way toward the distant street light I could see. A hundred feet from the foot of the stairs I stopped, poised on the balls of my feet, as a man stepped out from behind the squat bole of a pineapple palm and flashed an electric torch in my face.

His voice was a husky whisper. "Just a minute. What's your name? What are you prowling this alley for at four o'clock in the morning?"

My stomach turned over slowly. Sergeant Strawn and Ken had been humoring Beth. Despite the fact that she'd refused one, they had posted a guard. It was the logical thing to do. I looked at the man back of the flashlight. I couldn't see his face. All I could tell was that he was big. But he was obviously new to the force, at least since I'd been away. Otherwise he would know me. My only chance was bluff and run.

"Why, my name is Fred Davis," I told him. "And I'm not prowling the alley. I live five houses back. I'm on my way down to the bay to fish the morning tide. Why? What's the big idea of popping out from behind a tree and scaring a guy to death?"

"Wise guy," he whispered. "Wise guy."

I caught a glint of silver back of the light. I thought at first he was drawing a gun. Then his arm swung down and back. I knew then what he had in his hand. I backed a step and allowed the weapon to rip air. Then before he could set himself again, I stepped in fast and swung a hard right to his jaw. The flashlight flew from his hand and winked out. He stood a moment, a darker blob against the night. Then, as his knees collapsed, he grew smaller and smaller until he melted into the dark of the alley.

I struck a match and leaned over him. His face didn't tell me a thing. He was a stranger to me. But, whoever he was, he was not a plainclothesman. A plainclothesman would have no reason to whisper. Besides, if he was a cop, he was the first one I'd ever seen armed with a six-inch fish knife.

I struck another match, intending to go through his pockets for some clue to his identity, but blew it out as a light came on in a window of the garage apartment under which I was standing. The voice was feminine, thin with sleep and crotchety with age.

"Who struck that match? Who's down there in the alley?"

I purred, "Me-arrh."

"Oh," the old lady said. "Bad kitty."

The light in the window went out. I tiptoed up the alley before the old lady, composing herself for sleep, realized that cats don't strike matches. When I reached the corner, I looked back. As I turned, the light in the window came on again, and the old lady looked out and down. She began to scream.

A low-lying fog hugged the water. The tide was still full, but beginning to ebb. I lay a long time in the sea oats along the shore studying the situation. Here, back of the string of bait camps and boat slips, I was on familiar ground. I knew every pile, every piece of planking, extending out over the tide flats.

Cook's and Robert's were dark. But there was a light in McNeely's bait shanty. As I watched, a young cop, his blue shirt wet with sweat, his cap pushed back on his head, walked out on the pier slapping at mosquitoes and peering into the dark and fog. I moved up the shore toward Frenchman's Bayou and Bill's boat basin, where most of the fishing guides berthed their boats. Four of the cabin cruisers were lighted as late poker games continued or charter boat captains checked over their gear and tackle.

I felt even more trapped than I had at the foot of Beth's stairs. I was back in a cell again. This one of my own making. There were a half dozen boats in the basin capable of reaching Habana. Their captains would sail me there if I offered them sufficient inducement for them to thumb their noses at the Coast Guard. But I'd promised Beth that I'd wait on the island until she talked to Mr. Cliffton.

The more I thought of it the screwier it sounded. Why should Mr. Cliffton do anything for Charlie White? He didn't want to go to bed with me. He wanted to go to bed with my wife. Or had he already been?

I rounded the bayou to Frazer's camp. A dozen rental row boats bobbed at their ropes, as the outgoing tide sucked and gurgled around the piling. I considered stealing a boat, but I didn't. For two reasons. One, a boat would be missed. The only way I could hide it after I reached the island would be to stave in the bottom and sink it. I knew how most bait men felt about their boats. Frazer was no exception. He would raise hell if a boat turned up missing. He'd rather lose his wife than a boat. A good boat cost a hundred dollars. He could get married for five.

Two, a boat crossing the channel might be spotted.

I stripped off my clothes and piled them on a dry plank. Then picking up the plank, I waded out in the water until it was up to my chest. The water was as warm as the air. I swam out into the bay pushing the plank ahead of me.

It felt good to be back in the water. I swam for a long time, then turned on my back and floated, one hand on the plank.

The knife man worried me. Who was he? How had he known that I would be coming down the alley? Why had he tried to kill me? At whose orders? I wondered if he'd been the man who had killed Zo.

My heart began to pound. I should have kicked the son of a bitch in the teeth, made him confess. On the other hand, if he'd been the man in the cabin, he'd have known me on sight. He'd have ripped out my guts with his knife without bothering to ask questions.

I turned over on my face and swam. The morning sky was gray when I sighted the mangrove trees fringing the island. I felt for the bottom. There wasn't any. The storms of the last four years hadn't changed the coastline. Deep water extended to within a few feet of the shore. I pushed the plank up on the beach, then squeegeed and slapped my body dry before I dressed. Sometime during the crossing, my sneakers had fallen off the plank.

Dressed, I sat under a cabbage palm and smoked a cigarette before going up to the house. Now I was really home. My rotting nets, unused since before I'd gone into the army, still hung on their long cypress drying racks, not worth stealing. A half dozen hulks and stove-in row boats lay half-buried in the sand, including the bare ribs of the fifty-footer that had been my father's boat. I was glad the old man was dead.

I looked back toward the mainland. There were no running lights in the channel. As far as I could tell, my passage had been unobserved. When I wasn't picked up by morning, Ken and Sergeant Strawn would undoubtedly make a perfunctory search of the island. But I knew it from one end to the other, all five hundred tangled acres of it. I could hide out for a month, if need be. I could live on rabbits and fish.

I no longer felt tired or depressed. I was home. I'd been with my wife. I had plenty of smokes. Nuts to the law. Let them try to find me.

I got to my feet and padded up the weed-grown path to the house. The path was a jungle of tangled vines. I wriggled through them being careful not to disturb them any more than I had to. I hoped I wouldn't step on a snake.

The old mansion was still picturesque although even in the half-light of dawn, I could see the twenty-foot wide front porch was sagging badly in spots, its pillars rotted away. Its only support was the thick-trunked purple bougainvillea vine that had been old when I was born.

I picked an orange from a gnarled tree, cut a hole in it with my pocket knife and tried to suck it. The grove was as sour as the soil. I spat out the juice and looked at the house again. Beth had never liked it. She'd hated living on the island. She said it was 'cracker.'

I walked up the sagging stairs and onto the wide front porch, watching a flock of white heron wading in the shallows, trying not to think of Zo.

Zo would have clapped her hands and said, *"How lovely."* Zo would have loved the old house as I loved it. So it was 'cracker.' My people had never asked a thing of anyone except to be left alone. The old house represented a people and a way of life that would never exist again. A free, self-sufficient life before society, in an attempt to weaken the strong and strengthen the weak, had set up the goddamn buoys and markers that Swede had talked about.

In the death house it had sounded good. Swede had thought he meant it. But if the clock could have been turned back, and Swede could have started all over again, the chances are he'd have led the same life that he had. Some guys just didn't fit into the new pattern. Some guys were born to take chances.

I sat on the rotting canvas of a chaise lounge and watched the mainland grow out of the channel. I didn't want any part of Mr. Cliffton. I'd been a fool to agree to let Beth talk to him. No private detective could prove that I hadn't killed Zo.

When Beth contacted me, I'd tell her to arrange passage for me with Matt Heely or one of the other guides. To my original destination, Habana. Beth could join me later. I could change my name and buy a house and a boat in Habana. Or Santiago de Cuba or one of the smaller towns. Fish out there. I didn't have to contact *Señor Peso.* We could live well and legally for years on my forty-eight thousand dollars. If Beth loved me, she'd agree. I breathed hard, just thinking of her. And Beth did love me. She'd proved that.

Thinking of Beth made me restless. I tried the big front door. It was closed but not locked. I opened it and walked in. Closing the door behind me, I took two steps into the dusty silence and stopped.

I think even then I knew. But all I thought at the time was—*I'm not alone in this house.*

CHAPTER THIRTEEN

I slipped the gun Beth had given me from my pocket. It was on safety. The clip was full, but there was no shell in the chamber. I pumped a shell into the chamber and padded barefoot through the big living room down the long hall to the kitchen. The kitchen was festooned with cobwebs and as dusty as the front of the house. The sun was high enough now for me to see there were no tracks in the dust except the ones I was making.

I looked through the back door. Flame-vine practically covered the glass. The island vegetation had encroached on the rear of the house until the backyard was a jungle of wild grape, live oak, flowering yucca, and re-leafed poison ivy. I tried to open the door and found it was stuck fast by the flame-vine that had grown around the knob and anchored it.

I walked across the kitchen to the rear stairs and plowed a pine sliver with my big toe. I stuffed the gun in the waist band of my slacks and sat down on the floor to dig at the sliver with my knife. I'd have to find shoes of some kind. They'd made me wear shoes at Raiford. All the time. The quarter-inch callouses on my feet were gone.

I extracted the sliver and limped up the back stairs. There was no one in the bedroom that Beth and I had used. Dust lay thick and undisturbed on the floor. The bed was as Beth had left it, stripped to the bare mattress. It was the same with the other three bedrooms. Nothing had been touched. Nothing had been stolen. That was because I was Charlie White. If I'd been a northern tourist who had built a new home on the island and then gone away for four years, the boys would have 'borrowed' everything down to and including the plumbing and the foundation blocks.

I sat on the bed in the front room. The feeling that I wasn't alone persisted. But not as strongly. I put the gun back in my pocket and lighted a cigarette. Nerves did funny things to a man.

I finished the cigarette and snuffed it. It was time for me to think of a place to hide. When I wasn't picked up in town or found at Beth's apartment, Gilly and Strawn would either hook up a kicker or get the Coast Guard to run them over to the island. I'd want a vantage point from which to see them coming.

I thought of the captain's walk and dismissed it. It was exposed to the weather. I doubted that the rotted floor boards would hold me. Besides, if I were seen on the walk I'd be trapped. The best place to hide would be out on the island itself. But I'd have to have shoes of some kind.

Then I thought of the old pair of sneakers I'd discarded on my last trip down to Shrimp Bay. I'd left them in the bedroom. I'd told Beth to throw them out. They were probably up in the attic along with the other junk she saved. The attic was the only feature of the house Beth liked. She never threw anything away on the theory that sometime she might find a use for it. This was one of the times.

I got off the bed and looked through the shutter to the mainland. I could see it plainly now. There were three boats in the channel, all of them headed out into the open gulf, probably with charter parties. I wondered what was running. It was too late for king or tarpon. But the gulf was filled with fish. They could be out for almost anything.

As I climbed the stairs, I wondered if there were a hell and if there were what it was like. *"I'll save you a brunette,"* Swede had offered. He didn't need to bother now. I had Zo waiting.

Man. A funny proposition. I'd just spent hours with my wife. Beth had done everything a woman could to prove that she loved me. And here I was thinking of Zo again, almost as much as I was of Beth. Maybe I was a born heel.

The house had been built by my grandfather's father when the law had finally driven the wreckers out of Key West. Both labor and lumber were cheap. Rumpus rooms hadn't been heard of in his day, but the old man had finished the attic as a ballroom so he and his friends could dance when a fleet of small boats had sailed out from the mainland or a rare passenger boat on its way to Cedar Keys, which had been a world port in those days, had dropped anchor in the deep channel to broach a few casks of rum and pay its respects to old Captain White, the last unreconstructed rebel.

The finished section of the attic was thirty by forty feet with two large dormer windows on each side and two smaller windows on each end. But the windows had been boarded up for years. Even when my father had been a small boy, the attic had become a family catch-all and a place to play on rainy days.

It would be dark in the attic. There was a lamp on the dresser. I shook it. It still had some oil in it. I wiped the dust from the bowl and chimney and touched a match to the wick.

Holding the lamp ahead of me, I climbed the narrow stairs to the attic and pushed open the heavy door. A sudden gust of wind slammed the door shut behind me. I took a step into the attic and stopped.

I had been right. I wasn't alone in the house. There was no wind in the attic. A human hand had closed the door. I smelled them, then, the sour stench of unwashed bodies. The smell of men who had lived with fear for a long time.

I was holding the lamp in my right hand. I set it on the floor and reached for the gun in my pocket. From behind me, muscular hands closed around my wrist and shoved my hand deeper into my pocket, making it impossible to draw the gun.

I looked out beyond the faint glow of the lamp. Sitting on folding cots against the wall, a dozen men looked back somberly. I'd seen their faces before. Many times. Always covered with a fine sheen of sweat. On the quays and in the bars of Habana, Port au Prince, Tiburon, Roseau. The faces of men without countries and passports. Hunted, worried, harried men. Men who begged you to name your own price to sail them to the States.

Wetbacks on the grand scale. The most profitable item in the trade. The one thing I'd refused to run for *Señor Peso.*

I tugged at my wrist. "What the hell?"

A thin-faced man with a heavy accent said, "Make out that light."

They were the only words spoken. A man scampered across the floor like a rat, scooped up the lamp and blew down the chimney.

I beat at the man holding my wrist with my free hand. He whimpered with pain, but held on. There was a scurrying sound in the darkness. A wave of men swept over me. Hitting, clawing, kicking. I got the gun out of my pocket and managed to fire one shot. Then the gun thudded to the floor, as a dozen fists pounded at me. I went to my knees, fought back to my feet, then doubled up screaming in agony, as a pointed shoe caught me between the legs. I sensed the circle of men move back to let me fall. Then another foot found my jaw.

I came to, lying in semi-darkness. My nose was pressed into dank earth. There was a rope around one of my wrists and a foul tasting gag in my mouth. I rolled over on my back and spat out the gag. Heavy feet walked over my head. I turned my head to one side. Twenty feet away a trickle of bright sunshine was forcing itself through a thick tangle of vegetation. I'd been in the attic when I'd been slugged. Now I was lying under the house.

I slipped the rope from my wrist and lay listening to Sergeant Strawn's voice, muffled by the double flooring.

"Charlie's been here, all right. We should have come out last night. The dust is thick with his tracks. Barefooted, too. He must have swum over from the mainland."

"He must have," Ken Gilly agreed.

The feet tramped through the house. I started to crawl out, thought better of it, and lay waiting for the shouts and burst of shots when they discovered the men in the attic. I waited a long time. There were no shots. There were no shouts. There could be only one explanation. The men in the attic were gone.

I looked at the length of rope. Then feet tramped over my head again and out onto the sagging front porch. The voices were plainer now.

"Damnedest thing I ever saw," Ken said. He sounded puzzled and a little worried. "I don't get it. I don't get it at all."

From down on the shore, someone called, "White been here?"

"It looks like it," Ken called back. "But that's only half of it. There are a dozen cots up in the attic."

"Cots?"

The lad on the shore said he would be damned.

Strawn said, "It looks to me like some of the boys have been using the house as a drop for wetbacks."

There was the scratch of a kitchen match as one of the two men lighted a cigarette. Then Ken admitted, "Could be. Some of these damn fishing guides will do anything for money. Either way, Beth's going to have a fit when she hears this."

"Yeah. Probably." Strawn said. "But you never can tell about a woman. You think Mrs. White was leveling with us last night?"

"How do you mean?"

"I mean it's funny we didn't pick White up last night. It's only a few blocks from where the Tampa cab man dropped him over to her apartment. Maybe he was in the apartment while we were talking to her. It wouldn't have taken a minute to slip into something and invite us in. But she didn't. She didn't even turn on the light. Then this morning there was that fracas in the alley not a hundred feet from her stairs. So there was no one there when the prowl car answered the call. It could have been White and one of his pals that old Mrs. Pilley heard."

"I don't know what to think," Ken said. "Beth's sworn right along that she'd never have anything more to do with Charlie on account of that Cuban girl. Then she writes him a letter saying she's willing to start all over. Like you say, you never can tell about a woman."

The lad down on the beach called, "So what do we do now?"

"I'll be damned if I know," Ken admitted. "If I know Charlie, and I do, he's long gone by now. But while we're here, we'll look around."

He walked down the sagging stairs and kicked at the tangled vegetation growing up around the house. I pressed my belly to the sand. A moment later, he squatted and looked under the house. I could see Gilly but he couldn't see me. Ken hadn't changed. He was still round-faced and over-plump. He still wore rimless glasses. He still looked more like a bank teller or a preacher than he did like a lieutenant of detectives.

Sergeant Strawn was a little smug. "We should have come out last night. Remember, I said Charlie would probably head for the old house."

Ken had always had a temper, even when we were boys. He still had one. Releasing the vegetation his hands were parting, he stood up. "All right. You told me. You thought he might head out here. I didn't. I didn't think he'd be that big a fool. So you were right and I was wrong. *If* those footprints do belong to Charlie. Can you prove they do?"

Sergeant Strawn attempted to placate him. "No. I can't, lieutenant. And last night was just a lucky guess on my part. *If* it was Charlie who made those footprints in the dust."

A moment of silence followed. Then Ken said, "Well, I suppose we'd better go back and get some of the boys and search the island. But personally, I think it's a waste of time."

"How come?" the voice from the shore called.

Ken told him. "Charlie would be a fool to stick around so close where everybody knows him. If there is any truth in that *Señor Peso* gag he sprang at his trial, some of *Peso's* boys were probably waiting for him here. That would explain the cots. Charlie buying a ticket for Fort Myers could have been a red herring. He could have been headed here all the time. There are three coves on the other side of the island where I know a good sized boat could anchor. And the chances are, when he got here, he took off with the party waiting for him."

Sergeant Strawn continued to butter his stripes. "Could be. Sounds logical, lieutenant."

Ken allowed himself to be placated. "Well, let's get back to the mainland and ask the chief what he thinks we ought to do. If there's any chance that the island has been used as a port of illegal entry, he may want to call in the Federal men."

Their voices trailed off as they walked down the path to the shore. A few minutes later a kicker roared as it caught, then settled down to a high-pitched drone as they pointed the boat toward the mainland.

I crawled to the edge of the house and looked out. They were using one of McNeely's boats. Strawn and Gilly were sitting on the middle thwart with a youthful uniformed policeman handling the outboard motor.

I lay watching the boat grow small. The attack on me in the attic was easily explained. So it was my house. I wasn't supposed to be here. I was supposed to be in police custody by this time, accused of murdering Zo Palmyra. I'd poked my nose in where it didn't belong. Being alive was another matter. The only way I could explain that was that the men who had attacked me had been about to tie and weight me and drop me into the channel, when they had been interrupted by the arrival of Strawn and Gilly. In panic, they had rolled me under the house and scattered into the brush.

I picked up a rock and waited. I waited for half an hour. Then I crawled out and went inside the house. It was as silent as it had been the first time, but the feeling I'd had before was gone. I tiptoed up the stairs to the attic.

The door was open. There was no one in the attic. Except for a dozen canvas cots there was no sign that anyone ever had been there.

I climbed the ladder to the top and muscled myself up onto the captain's walk. From where I stood, I could see every section of the island. There was no wind. The palm fronds drooped in the sun. There was no sign of movement or motion. As far as I could tell, there was no one on the island but me. But on the far side, nosing its way out of one of the coves Ken had mentioned, was a white thirty-eight foot double cabin cruiser with a flying bridge. The boat was new to me. I wished I had a glass so I could read its name and registration number. Out in the gulf proper, it headed north toward Tarpon Springs. I wondered if my friends in the attic were on it. I hoped so.

CHAPTER FOURTEEN

The morning sun got hotter. I stood letting it bake my sore muscles, looking alternately at the gulf and across the channel to Palmetto City. I should have been depressed. I wasn't. For some reason I felt fine. I wanted to contact Beth; tell her to stay off the island. But I was stuck where I was until night.

The thirty-eight foot cruiser became a white dot in the distance and disappeared. The channel was filled with boats now, outboard powered rowboats, sea skiffs, cabin cruisers, sailboats. There was even one ketch-rigged sloop beating south. It looked like a scene on a picture postcard. The kind the tourists send home.

I sorted the buildings on the mainland until I located Cliffton's store. It wasn't difficult to find. A half dozen of the hotels and as many office buildings were twice as tall. But Cliffton's was white, a block square, four stories high, with a big flag whipping atop a slim pole.

I visualized the man as I remembered him. He was a dapper little man with widespread alert eyes. I'd never seen him in repose. He was always on the go, thinking, scheming, planning. As far as I knew he'd never married, although scuttlebutt along the waterfront had established him as something of a stud. If so, he was probably as good at it as he was at everything else.

Now Cliffton wanted to marry Beth. He'd advised her to divorce me and marry him. He'd offered to buy the island. I knew why he wanted to marry Beth. She was lovely. For the past four years she'd been alone. It could be that he'd been getting samples. The more I thought about it, the more certain I was someone had. Beth had changed. But why did Cliffton want to buy the island?

I took off the gabardine shirt and kneaded sweat into my sore shoulder muscles. I wondered how I could have been so blind so long. I'd asked Beth what Cliffton's reaction was going to be when she told him she'd talked to me. I'd warned her that he'd probably reach for his phone and call Ken. That was probably what was happening right now.

Beth had slipped right there. She'd called him by his first name. Then she'd corrected herself. She'd said, "You're doing Joe, Mr. Cliffton, a big injustice, Charlie. He's really a very fine and honorable man. You might as well accuse him of being Señor Peso as being capable of doing such a thing as you've just said."

Well, why not? I should have thought of him in the first place. Men of his type lived to make money. They never had enough. He could well be *Señor Peso*. The more I thought of it the more logical it seemed. He'd built his business on cut prices. He had a store that sold everything from perfume to watches, from guava jelly to drugs, from imported cigars to the best in whiskies and wines. He had a Cuban agent in Habana. I knew that. I remembered hearing Beth say so. More, he had the merchandising connections in the States to get rid of anything too hot for him to handle.

Cliffton had known that I'd been having trouble meeting the payments on my boat. He'd known Beth had had a miscarriage. What would have been simpler than for him to pick up his phone and call me.

"This is Señor Peso, Captain White. How would you like to make two thousand dollars?"

Then, when he had decided that Beth was more valuable to him than I was, all he'd had to do was pick up his phone again and tip the Coast Guard.

How dumb could a man be? I wanted to talk to Mr. Cliffton. If I weren't picked up and jugged before I could.

I dropped back into the attic and found the sneakers I'd remembered. Beth had saved them. She'd also saved an old pair of dungarees, a blue chambray shirt, and one of my old white caps. I put them on and felt like myself again.

I walked down to the kitchen. One thing we'd forgotten was food. There was a can of beans in the pantry. That was all. I took them back to the captain's walk and ate them with my knife, watching the channel and the mainland. The beans tasted good.

Around eleven o'clock there was a stir of movement in Bill's boat basin. Also in the Coast Guard base on the point. A few minutes later, a cabin cruiser put out from the basin. It was joined in mid-channel by a Coast Guard boat.

I closed the trap and went downstairs. Then, wrapping the bean can in the shirt and pants I'd discarded, I walked outside and down the beach. From behind a tangle of mangrove trees, I watched the approaching boats.

Frenchy Gorman was running the cruiser. I'd fished as his partner lots of times. From the expression on Frenchy's face, I gathered his boat had been requisitioned. As far as he personally was concerned, he hoped they never found me. So I'd killed a woman. So what? A lot of women needed killing. He swung his boat alongside the shelf, cut his motor and dropped his anchor. Then he sat down on his bait box and rolled a cigarette.

Their faces red with the heat, their shirts already stained with sweat, Ken and Sergeant Strawn and a half-dozen uniformed Palmetto City patrolmen scrambled over the side and waded ashore in water up to their knees. An efficient young lieutenant j.g. followed them ashore from the Coast Guard boat. Four unenthusiastic enlisted men in fatigues came after him.

Ken was beginning to age. He was no longer just plump. He was beginning to look gross. There were dark bags under his eyes and indulgence lines in his face that hadn't been there four years before. I was glad I hadn't gone to see him before I talked to Beth. Ken was not my friend anymore. He was just another cop. A cop who looked like a preacher. A renegade preacher who liked his whiskey and women.

I felt a little sick just looking at him. Remembering. Remembering he'd been in love with Beth as long as I had, that Beth had made her choice between us. And I'd left Beth wide open when I'd gotten tied up with *Señor Peso* and Zo, and been sent away for four years.

Was it Ken? Was it Cliffton? Who? I had no right to be jealous. I was. While I'd been tucked away in a cell, someone had had a lot of fun teaching Beth the new tricks she had learned.

Ken and Strawn and the lieutenant j.g. walked up the stairs and into the house. The cops and the enlisted men squatted on the sand. Frenchy lighted his cigarette. I stood sweating, waiting. Five minutes passed. Then the three men came out.

The lieutenant j.g. admitted the obvious. "Someone's been here all right. And someone's been using that attic. Could be kids. Could be someone else." He looked at Ken. "Who did you say owns the old house, lieutenant?"

Gilly said, "Charlie White. The guy we're looking for."

The lieutenant j.g. wiped the sweat band of his cap. "Well, we'll keep a little closer watch on the island from now on. In fact, we'll swing around it right now. But outside of those cots in the attic, I don't see any sign that the house has been used as a port of illegal entry. We'd have to have more than a few cots on which to base an official investigation."

It was the old game of passing the buck. The future admiral was good at it.

"As far as White is concerned, you want him. We don't. Until he breaks some federal law that comes under our jurisdiction, we haven't any interest in him. So I guess that bows us out."

He waded back to his boat. The enlisted men followed him, relieved.

Ken scratched his fat rear end. "The educated son of a bitch." He shrugged. "But I agree with him that a few cots in an attic don't mean anything. I think them high school kids have been holding parties out here."

One of the patrolmen said, "Boy. Would I like to go to one of them parties."

Ken gave him a sour look. "Well, let's get it over." He looked at the tangle of vegetation back of the house and along the shore without enthusiasm. "Fan out and we'll walk across it. You stay here, Scott, in case Charlie is still on the island and should try to double back."

One of the patrolmen got to his feet and walked up in the shade of the porch. "Yes, sir," he acknowledged.

Ken placed his men. "You take the left flank, Bill. Keep pretty well to the shore line. You do the same on the right, Pete. I'll take the middle. You other guys bird-dog between us." Ken's face got even redder. "This is a lot of crap as far as I'm concerned. Eight guys to search five hundred acres. But the chief says we search so we search."

He was wearing his gun stuffed into the tight waist band of his trousers. He tugged it out and broke it. There was no shell under the hammer. He thumbed a shell into the empty chamber. "If you should see White, don't take any chances. Shoot. You fellows understand that?"

The men said, "Yes, sir," soberly, in unison.

I moved back from the tangle of mangrove and faded into the thicker vegetation, being careful not to step on anything brittle. The heavy summer rains helped me. But it wasn't going to be as easy as I had thought. Sweat dripped from my face, ran down my legs. The three or four really safe hiding places I'd had in mind were out. Ken wanted me—dead. And Ken knew the island almost as well as I did. Ken had been born on it, too. On the far side. In a squatter's shack on one of the coves.

I walked faster, ducking under low-hanging branches, sucking in my guts as I slipped past wild lemon trees, hung with knobby lemons as big as footballs and studded with inch-long thorns. I realized I was still carrying the rolled up pants and shirt and bean can. I burrowed a hole in a pile of leaves, buried the bundle and walked on.

There was or had been a small five-acre cypress swamp in the middle of the island. It was, as I remembered, surrounded by a savannah of tall grass. At this time of the year, both the savannah and the swamp should be filled with water. It wasn't one of the hiding places I'd planned. But if I could reach the swamp, the only way they could flush me out, would be to bring one or more small boats to the island. By the time they could return with a boat it would be night. I angled toward the swamp.

The thrashing in the scrub behind me grew louder. "Charlie," Ken called softly. "Charlie."

There was a lulling, soothing quality to his voice. It was as if the one word meant much, meant: *This is your old friend, Ken. Don't be afraid. Trust me. I want to help you, Charlie.*

It was darker here. The trees were thicker, their branches laced over my head. There was less underbrush. I stepped back of a tree and waited until I could see Ken in the small clearing I'd just raced across.

He'd outdistanced the man on either side of him by three hundred yards. His face was scarlet with exertion as he walked with the light fast tread some fat men have. His soft hat was tugged over his eyes to shield them. He was holding his gun shoulder high, the muzzle tilted. As I watched, he stopped and called again.

"Charlie. I know you're in here. Answer me."

There was the same lying smile in his voice as he paused with his gun barrel lifted. He waited licking his thick lips. His grey eyes darted from side to side.

The sweat draining down my spine turned cold. For some reason Ken hated my guts. He wanted to kill me. Personally. Why? Because he was a cop? Because he had a guilty conscience? Because he'd been two-timing me with Beth?

He called a third time, "Answer me, Charlie. I want to help you."

I thought, "You lying fat cracker," and slipped on to the next tree. I could see the saw-grass now. The water was knee-deep. I waded out into the grass trying to keep from splashing and went through the grass to the swamp. There was a deep hole in the far side of the grass. I forgot it and went under. I broke water spitting and clawing at a thick cypress root. The root lifted its head and opened its mouth at me. Its mouth was a dirty cotton white. I jerked back my hand, caught at another root, pulled myself out of the hole and waded as swiftly as I could on into the swamp. I waded on through the silent greyness for two hundred feet and threw myself down behind a cypress elbow. Most of the trees were dead with long beards of Spanish moss entangled in their bare branches, blotting out the sun. The water was cool. I lay panting silently, looking back at the tall saw-grass.

Something white was bobbing in the deep hole. I realized it was my cap with a school of small fish nibbling at it.

Then Ken parted the saw-grass cautiously with his left arm and saw the cap. At first glance it looked like a drowning man. The gun in his hand swung down. The cap bobbed, then bobbed again, under the impact of two shots before he realized there was nothing under it but water.

Ken wiped the sweat from his face with his left arm. Looking out into the swamp, he fired again, at the snake this time. Then, as the snake writhed on the root, Ken hooked the cap with his toe, glanced at it quickly and tossed it out of sight into the grass, just as a uniformed patrolman splashed up beside him.

Gilly thrust out an arm to stop him. "Careful. There's a deep hole there."

The man panted, "You spot him, lieutenant?"

Ken looked out into the moss-hung swamp again. "No." He pointed at the dead cottonmouth. "I was shooting at a snake."

"Geez," the patrolman admired. "Right through the head."

Ken took off his hat and fanned at his beet-red face. "I still think what I thought in the first place. What I told the chief this morning. That some of Charlie's Cuban friends were waiting at the house for him and he left with them during the night."

"Could be," the patrolman agreed. He remembered to whom he was speaking. "I mean probably, sir." He looked at the twilight silence under the dead trees with distaste. "Do we have to go through that, lieutenant?"

Ken adjusted his rimless glasses. "Not me. At least, I don't recall reading anything in the civil service regulations that says I have to know how to swim." He looked at the swamp a last time, then shrugged. "Come on. We'll go around it."

"Yes, sir," the patrolman said. "Whatever you say, lieutenant."

CHAPTER FIFTEEN

Night was long in coming. When it did come, I crawled out of the swamp and made my way, cautiously, back to the shore. No one tried to stop me. No one stepped out from behind a tree. Frenchy's boat was gone. I watched the house for a long time. There was no giveaway glow of a cigar or cigarette tip.

I was tired. I was hungry. My arms and shoulders were on fire with insect bites. Time was when sand flies and mosquitoes didn't bother me. After four years in a cell, I'd lost my immunity. The bugs had been bad during the day. With night they had become unbearable. I chewed a wet cigarette, wishing I had a dry smoke.

The tide was at full ebb but starting to come in. I waded out to the edge of the shelf and, squatting in the saw grass, I rubbed salt water and wet sand on the bites. It helped some, but not much.

I walked to the house and sat on the steps. I'd been all right while it was still daylight. Now I was beginning to panic, to start at sounds. I wasn't afraid of the dark. I was afraid of what might come out of it.

Hiding on the island had become like hiding in a fish bowl. The wetbacks in the attic hadn't gotten there by themselves. Someone had brought them to the island. Someone had taken them off. That someone knew I had seen them.

Then there was Ken. Ken knew I was on the island. Alone. For some reason Ken hated me. For some reason he'd made the manhunt personal. Was it because of Beth? Or was there another reason? But of one thing I was sure… Ken wanted to empty his gun in my guts!

I thought of the white cap bobbing on the pool and shuddered. My head ached. I was confused. I wished I was smarter than I was. Beth had promised to come out tonight or tomorrow night at the latest. I couldn't let her come to the island. I had to warn her somehow. I had to get off the island myself before the moon rose. But where to go?

The sound of tolling church bells on the mainland reminded me it was Sunday night. Outside of the drone of the mosquitoes and the gentle lapping of the tide, the night was a great black vacuum, filled only with the far-off tolling of the bells. Tolling for me. Tolling for Zo.

"I love you, Captain Charlie."

How long ago had Zo died? How long had I been running? It seemed that I'd been running all my life. I'd never felt so sorry for myself. A man made one mistake. And he paid. He paid for it all his life. Until he was dead.

If I hadn't listened to *Señor Peso,* I could be going to church tonight. I could be sitting beside Beth, listening to Reverend Paul. After church, we could stop in at the drugstore for a cup of coffee and a sandwich. We could laugh and kid a bit with other couples. We could walk home together openly. We wouldn't need to hide in darkness. I could watch Beth undress. We could go to bed together. I wouldn't have to wonder who'd been the other man in her life. I could get up in the morning and go out to the snapper banks, or take out a deep sea charter party, or—

I stopped it there. With the tolling of the bells I was thinking a lot of crap. A man was what he was. Like he either drank or he didn't. If I could, I wouldn't go to church. I wouldn't stop for coffee and sandwiches on our way home. I'd be more apt to stop in at the Jockey Club bar or at Sally's. Beth would look primly disapproving while I washed down a few shots with beers. And when we got home, we'd argue. What did I think this was, Tuesday night?

If it hadn't been for the phone call from *Señor Peso,* it would have been something else. Sure I'd needed the money. But after that first scared trip, when I'd met the *Andros Ancropolis* eighty miles out in the gulf, when I'd realized what I was in, I'd gotten as big a kick out of the excitement as I had out of the money. I was, it would seem, a born bastard. What I needed right now, was more of what I'd had the night before, a three-inch steak and about a half a fifth of rum. Zo had summed it up when I'd told her I was going back to Palmetto City to sell real estate or something. All she had said was:

"I laugh."

The mosquitoes and sand flies were making the steps unbearable. I searched the channel for the running light of a boat. There wasn't any. I got up and went into the house. The rusted screens would be some protection. I might even find a cigarette butt I could smoke. If I could find a match to light it.

The house was darker than the night. I started back toward the kitchen, stopped as a floor board squeaked. Then I twisted frantically to one side and flung myself forward, rolling, as a shot rattled the windows of the living room. Bullets followed me as I rolled, pecking at the floor boards behind me like so many angry redheaded woodpeckers tracking down an elusive worm.

The first shot burned across my ribs. The others had come close, but not quite close enough. I lay at the end of my roll, holding my breath, waiting for Ken to speak.

A moment of deep silence followed. Somewhere on the mainland a belated church bell began to toll after the others had stopped. Then I heard hoarse, subdued breathing and a stealthy snick of metal as the man who had fired attempted to slip the clip from his gun and insert a new one without me hearing him.

It was like hitting a wall head on. He grunted and dropped one of the clips he was handling. From the thud it sounded like the full one. Then he reversed the gun and tried to use it as a club.

I crowded him still closer, beating at his ribs and kidneys. He whimpered and gave ground, but continued to flail at me with the gun. A blow to the back of my ear dropped me. As I went to my knees, I wrapped my arms around his legs and heaved him over my back. A bone snapped as he landed. He screamed and clawed his way across the floor away from me. I followed him on my knees, feeling for him in the dark.

He screamed again and kicked at me. His shoe landed low on my chest. Then he was on his feet again and above me, racing up the stairs. I clawed after him. On the top stair, he turned and kicked again, more of a thrust of his leg than a kick. I caught at his ankle as I fell and he went over my head again. I fell grabbing for the rail with my left hand.

Both of us were cursing. I caught the rail. It swung me around with my back to the hard wood spindles. With such force, the spindles cracked and I went through them. He landed somewhere below me in the darkness and stopped cursing.

My backside pushed through the spindles like a yard baby stuck on his potty. I clung to the rail gasping for breath, blood mixed with sweat on my face. Then I pulled myself back on the stairs.

The lad at the foot of the stairs hadn't moved since he landed.

I felt my way down a step at a time toward the sprawled blob of deeper black. Trying to save himself, he had turned in mid-air and landed on his back. I stepped over his legs, felt the palm of a hand under the heel of my sneaker and stomped it hard before the fingers could close.

"You son of a bitch."

The hand rocked under my heel. He continued to lie motionless, silent. Still panting, I knelt beside him and patted his pockets for matches. There was a book in his shirt pocket. I wanted to find the gun and the full clip before he came to. I struck a match and turned. Then very quickly I turned back again.

The man on the floor wasn't Ken. It was the big lad who'd tried to knife me in the alley behind Beth's apartment. I studied his face, the match rising and falling with my breathing until it burned my fingers. I dropped it and lit another.

His face was in no way familiar. He was wearing blue slacks and thick-soled sneakers and a blue sports shirt. There was a pack of cigarettes in one of his shirt pockets. I slipped it out and touched the match to one of them. Then I dropped the pack in my own pocket. He didn't need it any more. He'd quit smoking. Suddenly. When the back of his neck made contact with the riser of the first step.

I found the gun and the full clip he'd dropped. Then I walked back and, squatting beside him again, I went through his pockets carefully. They didn't tell me any more than his face. All I found was another clip of shells to fit the gun, thirty-five dollars in bills and a small handful of silver. I gave him back the bills and silver and kept the clip. Then I went out into the kitchen and washed.

The hand pump on the sink was still in prime. I filled the sink with water and bathed my face and head. The water was lukewarm and smelled of sulphur, but it was better than what I had on my face. Finished, I used the tail of my shirt as a towel and walked back and looked at the dead man.

I wished I knew who the bastard was and why he'd wanted to kill me; who had sent him to kill me.

A touch of silver crossed the doorway. The moon was beginning to rise. I snuffed my cigarette and went out on the porch. More time had elapsed than I'd realized. I limped down the weed grown path to the shore.

The voice came off the water—faintly.

"Ahoy, the island. Charlie."

Just the four words. No more. A full minute of silence followed. Then I heard the muffled snort of an underwater exhaust and the sound of an idled marine motor. Whoever it was, was running without lights, not very far off shore. The voice came again. Slightly louder this time.

"Ahoy, the island. Charlie."

I waded out onto the flat, keeping well in the shadows of the mangroves and squatted down, straining my eyes to see the craft. It glided by, fifty feet off shore and I recognized the silhouette of Frenchy Gorman's thirty footer.

Frenchy's eyes were as good as mine. The idling screw reversed. The snortle of the exhaust became more pronounced. His voice was a low-pitched whisper. "That you squatting in them shallows, Charlie?"

I debated a moment before I answered. "Yeah."

Frenchy sounded relieved. "Good. I 'most give you out. I been cruising this goddamn island since dusk-dark."

I took the gun from my pocket and slipped the safety. "You alone?"

Frenchy sounded hurt. "You think I'd call out if I wasn't?"

I was still breathing hard from what had happened at the house. Washing my face had been a waste of time. The cuts on my face were still bleeding. I doubted I'd ever stop sweating. Until I was like the guy in the parlor. Like Swede. Still, if I could trust anyone beside Beth, I could trust Frenchy. "No," I admitted. "I don't."

I put the gun back in my pocket and stood up.

He called softly, "Then come aboard. You'd better swim out. I don't want to make any more noise than I have to."

I stepped off the shelf into deep water and swam out to the cruiser. Still keeping his voice down to a whisper Frenchy added, "There's a line hanging over the stern."

I found the rope and muscled myself up over the fish box into the open cockpit. It felt good to be on a boat again. I wished I was on one of my own. A hundred miles out in the Gulf. With its nose pointed at the Dry Tortugas and points south. With Beth in the galley getting supper.

Frenchy hadn't changed. He still smelled of good rum and cheap tobacco. A bald little man in his middle forties, with a wisp of black mustache etched in the saddle leather of his face, under perpetually twinkling black eyes and a hooked nose, he got a big bang out of life. He was a good fisherman. He was also a good friend. If he liked you, you could do no wrong. If he didn't like you, you were a no-good Yankee bastard. No matter where you were born. Surprisingly, nine times out of ten he was right.

I tried to control my breathing. "How did you know I was on the island?"

He showed me his white teeth. They were all I could see of his face. "I seen you."

"When?"

Frenchy was amused. "This morning."

"This morning?"

"Yeah. When I brought Strawn and Gilly out. You were standing down the shore, say maybe two hundred feet from the path. Back of some mangrove. With a bundle under your arm."

"That's right."

"You're damn right that's right."

"Why didn't you tell Ken?"

Frenchy spat over the side of the boat and took his makings from his pocket. "That no good Yankee-bastid." He spilled tobacco in a paper. "'Run me out to the island,' he says. 'Police business.'"

I felt my way. "Ken's a cop."

"So what?"

I didn't say anything. I couldn't. I'd reached the end of my rope. The lights on the mainland were revolving slowly. My knees began to shake. I tried to stop them by bracing my feet. It didn't help. My whole body began to shake.

His back to the mainland, Frenchy lighted a match to touch off his cigarette, the flame cupped in his palms. He saw my face. He exhaled slowly. "Cripes. What happened to you, Charlie?"

I told him. Through chattering teeth. "I just killed a man."

"In a fight?"

"Yeah."

"Why?"

"Because he tried to kill me."

"Where?"

"In the house."

"Who?"

"I don't know. I don't know who he is. I only saw him once before. Last night. When he tried to knife me outside of Beth's apartment."

"Was he alone?"

"I don't know that, either."

Frenchy pinched his hooked nose in deep thought. "Well, in that case," he decided, as he reversed the screw and swung the cruiser in a wide arch away from the shore, "Maybe we better get out of here."

CHAPTER SIXTEEN

As we swung out away from the shelf, still running without lights, Frenchy reached in the wheel locker and handed me an unopened bottle of rum. "Get some of that in you before you try to talk anymore."

I peeled the plastic and pulled the cork with my teeth. The rum tasted good all the way down. When it reached my stomach, it spread out to my toes and fingers. I took another drink, the neck of the bottle clattering against my teeth. The shaking subsided gradually.

I corked the bottle and handed it back to Frenchy. He gave me a towel in exchange. "Now peel off those wet things. There's some dry pants and a shirt on my bunk. Also a cap and some sneakers. No thanks to me. Your missus brought 'em."

I caught his arm. "Beth sent you out to the island?"

"That's right."

"Why?"

"Because she's been nearly nuts all day, worrying about you. She came down to the basin right after I brought Gilly and Sergeant Strawn back, and them other dumb cops. She was going to rent a kicker from Frazer and go out, but she was afraid the cops were watching her. They were, too. It would have been a dead giveaway. Gilly made all the bait camp boys agree to keep a record of who they rented boats and kickers to today. They done it, too." Frenchy didn't like bait camp men on general principles. "Names and addresses. Just like he asked. Goddamn no-good-Yankee-bastids."

I stripped and toweled till I glowed. "Gilly isn't so dumb. He knew I was on the island."

"That ain't what he's saying along the water."

"What is he saying?"

"That you're probably on your way to Cuba."

"Ken hates my guts."

"That's why your missus was so worried."

I asked him flatly, "Why?"

Frenchy leaned out to make certain he was clearing the number six bouy. "She told me this afternoon. Ken's been after her ever since you got sent up. He wanted her to divorce you and marry him."

That made two of them. I stepped down into the cabin. There was a pair of socks and shorts and a tee shirt with the shirts and pants. All of them were new. In a Cliffton bag.

Frenchy gunned his engine a little. "As Beth told it he damn near went nuts when she'd told him she'd written you a letter saying she was willing to start all over. They had her down at the station two hours this morning trying to make her admit that you were in her apartment when Gilly and Strawn banged the door last night."

The cap fitted as well as the rest of the clothes. I stepped up into the cockpit again and nonchalantly leaned against the live-bait well. "How come, Frenchy?"

He knew what I meant. "Let's say you done me favors in the past."

"I'm awfully hot."

Frenchy wasn't perturbed. "You're telling me? I couldn't even get the baseball game today." He imitated a radio announcer. "'Now Minoso is stepping up to the batter's box. Now Vic Raschi is winding up. Here comes the pitch. Minoso swings at it hard—and we interrupt this broadcast to tell you that Charlie White, the ex-convict who is the object of the most intense manhunt this state has ever seen has just been spotted in a black Chevrolet coupe on Clearwater Causeway, drinking in the Tampa Terrace, picking up shell on Anna Maria beach, eating at a hot dog stand in Sarasota!' Believe me, Charlie. That goddamn no-good-Yankee-bastid may have known you were on the island. But you're driving the rest of the state nuts."

The cigarettes I'd taken off the dead man had gotten soaked swimming out to the boat. I borrowed Frenchy's makings and rolled a cigarette. "Okay. Go ahead and ask me."

"Ask you what?"

"Did I kill Zo?"

Frenchy idled his engine, barely maintaining seaway, letting the sweep of the incoming tide carry us past the boat basin, the string of bait camps and the Coast Guard base on the point. "Okay. Did you kill Zo?"

"No."

"I figured that," Frenchy said. "You know who did?"

"No."

He inclined his head at the island now lying astern. "How about this guy you told me about?"

"I don't know. I doubt it."

"Why?"

"It's just a feeling."

"What kind of a feeling?"

"That he was only a hired hand." I lighted the cigarette I'd rolled. "Who's running wetbacks, Frenchy?"

Frenchy was silent a long time. "That," he said, finally, "is something I don't know. And I'm not holding out. I've heard rumors from time to time. But never pinned on no one guy. You know how it is along the water."

"Yeah. I know."

"Then it's true about them cots in the attic?"

"Yeah. There was a dozen guys in it this morning. They jumped me when I opened the door. When I came to, I was under the house. The way I figure it, Ken and Strawn and that Coast Guard j.g. showing up to search the house was all that saved me. Whoever parked the merchandise didn't have time to kill me. They had to get their cattle off the island. They took them off the back way. Which one of the boys has a new thirty-eight foot, double cabin, twin screw with a flying bridge? Painted white?"

Past the point and the Number One light, Frenchy gunned his engine and relaxed on the stool. "There's only one boat around here that answers that description."

"Who owns it?"

"Who do you think? Cliffton."

I found the rum bottle and uncorked it and let the rum trickle down my throat, enjoying the taste. What Frenchy had just told me tied in with what I'd figured. With me tucked away so he could make his play for Beth, Cliffton would need a boat and someone to replace me. The rum on an empty stomach was making me light-headed. I'd need all the brains I had. I corked the bottle and put it back in the locker.

"Who's running it for Cliffton?"

"Matt Heely."

"What happened to Matt's boat?"

"He got drunk with the charter party he had aboard the last night of the tarpon round-up four years ago. Right after you were sent away. And coming back just before dawn in a fog, he missed the goddamn channel lights by sixty feet and piled up on the breakwater. Damn near drowned all his sports. From what I hear, they're still suing him for this and that."

The picture was familiar. A guy pacing the floor at night. Desperate. In a tight spot for money. All he knows is the water. The phone rings.

"This is Señor Peso, Captain Heely. How would you like to have a good job? One that will pay you real money? Put a wheel in your hands again?"

So what should the guy say? "No?"

Only Matt was in deeper than I'd been. If Matt were running Cliffton's boat, he knew who *Señor Peso* was.

"Why?" Frenchy asked. "You see Cliffton's boat this morning?"

"Or one just like it. Pulling out of one of the coves on the far side of the island. While Ken and Strawn were pulling up in front."

Frenchy took the bottle from the locker, took a big drink, held it up to the rising moon, then passed it on to me. "Kill it and bust the bottle. There's no stamp on it."

I killed it and smashed it on the rail and dropped the pieces over the side. It didn't set as well as the first drink I'd taken. I was suddenly sick of the whole mess. So Cliffton was *Señor Peso?* All I wanted was out. I wasn't mad at anybody. Not even Ken. With forty-eight thousand dollars, Beth and I could start all over again. I'd be any kind of a husband she wanted me to be. *If* I could get out.

I was almost afraid to ask. "Where are we headed now?"

"Across the bay to Sally's."

"Beth is waiting for me there?"

Frenchy nodded. "Yeah. I ran her over before I started looking for you. I figured if we were ordered to heave-to, you could go over the side. She couldn't."

I said, "Sally's is a hell of a place for her to be."

Frenchy got a little sore. "Where do you expect her to meet you? On the steps of the city hall? Or in front of the band shell in Phillips Park? As you remarked before, you are a little warm."

"Yeah. That's right," I admitted.

Few folks except commercial fishermen and guides even know about Sally's. There is a road of sorts, across the flats, but no one ever uses it. Not even delivery trucks. Sally brings in his own supplies by boat. Those he buys in Tampa or Palmetto City. The rest are dropped off in the dark of the moon. A big Portugee weighing three hundred pounds, Salvatore caters to an exclusive clientele. The bar and hotel are built on pilings at the end of a series of inlets and swash channels. It takes a guide who knows that particular section of water to navigate it. He serves good drinks and good food. There is gambling of course. And if a drunken commercial fisherman with a thousand pounds of pompano burning a hole in his pocket should happen to require feminine companionship, Sally's waitresses double in brass. For a price.

Contacting Matt Heely was out. I was glad I hadn't suggested it to Beth. If Matt were working for Cliffton and Cliffton were *Señor Peso,* Matt would probably have agreed to run me anywhere I wanted to go. Then dropped me off in forty-fathoms. With an anchor tied to my ankles.

I took off my cap and let the wind blow through my hair, relaxed for the first time in two days.

I thought it over, then asked it. "How's for you running me and Beth to Cuba, Frenchy? I can make it worth your while. Enough to buy a new boat."

He sounded genuinely regretful. "Geez, I'd like to, Charlie. I could use a new boat. But—"

"But what?"

He thumped the side of his boat. "But we'd never make it in this tub. She's going to twist to pieces on me some night, sure. She's rotten from the bottom up. More, she's got so many worms in her they keep me awake nights, listening to them eat up my bread and butter."

"How about Fort Myers?"

"I could make it to Myers, I guess. Hell, I go out to the banks every day."

I said, "I could get either Skip or Harvey to run us on from there."

"Yeah. You probably could," Frenchy said. He was silent for a long time. Then he said, quietly, "But keeping on running ain't going to do you a damn bit of good, Charlie. Even if you get to Cuba."

"Why won't it?"

Frenchy took a fresh bottle of rum from the locker and cracked the seal. He took a big drink, then handed the bottle to me. "I been thinking about that, ever since they been hunting for you."

I wet my lips and stood holding the bottle.

"Why won't it?" I repeated.

Frenchy eased the boat up an unmarked swash channel into a dark inlet, lined on both sides with mangroves. "You ain't got a chance in Cuba, Charlie."

"Why haven't I?"

"What was the name of the girl you're accused of killing? Her right name."

"Zo Palmyra."

"She was an American national?"

"No. Zo was Cuban. I met her in Habana."

Frenchy cut his engine still more. We were barely creeping now. The mangrove was so close I could have reached out with a boat hook and touched it. "So there you are," he said.

I shook my head. "I don't get it."

He leaned still farther out of the boat, keeping his eyes on a feeble yellow glow winking through the mangrove. It was the low watt bulb on Sally's pier, powered by his own generating plant.

Frenchy said. "Use your head, Charlie. After all the stink there's been in the papers and over the radio, with your name and description and hers spread all over the state, and beamed to Cuba, you think the Cuban cops are going to let you hole up there?"

Some of the rum glow faded. We scraped on a bar, slid over it.

Frenchy continued. "You think they're going to let you walk down the Prado just like nothing has happened, maybe even give you a charter boat permit? The hell they will."

The dream began to fade.

Frenchy angled through another swash channel into deep water again and gunned his engine. "The hell they will," he repeated. "If you get picked up in Cuba, and you will, the chances are you won't even be extradited. They won't take any chance you might get free after killing one of their nationals. Cuban cops are the same as any other cops. They'll take care of the matter themselves. I can't say I blame them."

I gripped the rail of the boat and lost the rum I'd swilled on an empty stomach. Frenchy was right. All I'd been doing was kidding myself. Swede had been right about so many things. The days of sailing by guess and by God were gone. There were no safe ports for a man accused of murder. I could change my name. I could change my mannerisms. I could even change my means of livelihood. But I couldn't change my hair or my face or my body. Or the charge against me.

"Wanted for murder, Charles White, red-haired, freckles on face, six feet tall, two hundred pounds," meant just the same in Spanish as it did in English.

Forty-eight thousand dollars. That was a laugh. I didn't have a dime. The chances were I wouldn't last long enough to get from the shore to the bank. The first Habana *policia* to see me would throw me in the jug. And cork it.

I began to shake again. The rum bottle dropped out of my hand into the boiling wake back of the screw.

It bobbed a moment. Then sank. I envied it.

CHAPTER SEVENTEEN

There were a half dozen boats made fast along the pier. All but one were commercial fishing boats. The exception was Cork Avers charter boat. I jumped up on the planking, caught the rope Frenchy threw me and dropped it over a piling. He made the stern fast and joined me.

The juke in the bar was blaring something about a moon. I asked Frenchy the name of the song.

He said, "I think it's *How High Is the Moon*. It came out since you've been away."

How high is the moon? How deep is down? Where did I go from here? The pier was long and narrow, with heaps of oyster and clam shells piled high on both sides. We walked back through the stink of the tide flats, the loose boards rattling under our feet.

The bar was sided with cypress slabs. Unpainted. Patched here and there with driftwood. With a crescent moon hovering over it, Sally's looked romantic. It wasn't. It was hot. Hot as only tide flats can be hot. It was dirty. It stank. The throb of the generator that supplied the electric power became a second pulse in the ears.

There were eight or nine men at the bar. All of them nodded at Frenchy. One or two said, "Hi."

None of them paid any attention to me. They weren't being unfriendly. They were minding their own business. It was the only house rule at Sally's.

A drunken little brunette, who was about to pop out of the bodice of her white off-the-shoulder blouse, was sitting at a table with Cork Avers. She managed to focus her eyes on me and gasped, "Migawd! Ain't that Charlie White? Ain't that the guy they're looking for on the radio?"

"Shut your goddamn mouth," Cork told her. And went on beating time to the music with the bottom of a half-full bottle of Old Angus.

I'd never known Sally to wear shoes. He wasn't now. He was behind the wood, barefooted. With no shirt. Wearing a pair of white duck pants. His belly bulged over the turned down waist band. Sally was getting old. The mat of black hair on his chest was flecked with gray. His face wasn't fat. It was flabby. He'd made a lot of money. On the wrong side of the law. He'd earned it.

"Gentlemen," he said. He set two sweaty bottles of beer on the bar. Then barely glancing at me, he inclined his head at the door, leading back to the rooms he rented, and his lips formed the figure seven.

"How they going, Sally?" Frenchy asked him.

"Fine. Just fine," Sally replied.

I wet my lips with the beer. Then I walked back down the hall and ran my knuckles across the louvered door of Number 7.

Beth's voice sounded small and frightened. "Who is it?"

"Charlie."

She unlocked the door. I closed and locked it behind me. The room was small. Square. With unpainted pine walls. There was a chair, a table, a bed. To keep her dress from getting stained with perspiration, Beth had taken it off and hung it on a hanger on the wall. All she had on was a pale nylon slip and a pair of low-heeled white sandals. The heat in the box of a room had tightened her curls into wet little ringlets. Sweat plastered the sheer slip to her lovely body.

"I was afraid to wait outside," she said. "So Mr. Salvaterra rented me this room."

A naked twenty-five watt bulb hung from the ceiling on a green cord. I held her at arm's length and looked at her. She was as lovely as I remembered her. By moonlight. But Beth, too, had aged. There were faint lines in her face and deep purple shadows under her eyes.

I tilted her chin. "You look like a bride."

She stood on tiptoe and kissed me feverishly. "I feel like one." Then she buried her face on my new shirt and cried. "I've been so worried."

I held her tight against me for a moment. Her body was sweet in my arms. Then she looked up again and touched the cuts and contusions on my face with the tips of her fingers. "Who hurt you?"

I said, "You wouldn't know the guy. It was a fellow out on the island."

"Who?"

"I never saw him before."

"Where is he now?"

"He's dead."

"Who killed him?"

"I did."

Beth began to cry again, holding her head back, looking at me through tears. "What have we gotten into?"

I told her. "Even more of a mess than the Zo business. Someone's been using the old house as a drop for wetbacks."

"Wetbacks?"

"Smuggled aliens."

Her voice was no longer small. It was fierce. "Who?"

My knees were still shaky. I patted her heinie and sat on the chair. "We'll come to that." There was a pack of cigarettes on the table. I lighted one and sucked the smoke into my lungs. It was menthol. But it made me think I felt better. "But first, I have to have some food."

"You haven't eaten?"

"Only a can of beans."

I unlocked the door and walked down the hall. Sally came to the end of the bar and raised one bushy eyebrow. I asked him what he had to eat. He said he could fix me almost anything. I settled on fresh smoked mullet, some cold hush puppies and some beer.

Beth was sitting on the bed when I got back. I put the tray on the table and locked the door again.

She talked as I wolfed the fish. "I talked to Mr. Cliffton today. And you were right about him. He laughed at me. He said there wasn't the least doubt that you'd killed Zo and that spending money on a private detective would be foolish."

I said, "We'll come to Cliffton. Right now, let's talk about Ken."

"What about him?"

"He came out to the island twice."

"I know. That's why I was so worried."

"What's more, he knew I was there. He had me trapped in the swamp. But he didn't want me arrested. He wants to kill me. He tried to. Not because he's a cop. Because he hates my intestines. Why?"

Beth looked at the floor. Then ran the hem of her slip between her fingers. "Well, you know how it is with Ken. He's always been in love with me. I—I suppose he's jealous."

The mullet was good but greasy. The towel on the table was there for another purpose. I wiped my hands on it. "He has reason to be?"

Beth dropped her slip and raised her eyes to meet mine. "You've no right to ask me that."

The *thump thump—thump thump* of the power plant seemed to expand the heat in the room until the walls bulged. It was difficult for me to breathe. I washed down the mullet with a swig of beer. "I'm asking it, Beth."

"Even after Zo?"

"Yeah. Even after Zo."

Beth's lower lip quivered. Her mouth screwed up as if she were going to cry again. She lifted her hair up and away from the back of her neck, her pointed breasts rising with her arms. "All right, if you must know. Yes. He had."

The mullet didn't taste as good. I forced more down my throat. It stuck halfway.

A single tear rolled down Beth's cheek. Her eyes continued to meet mine. "I could stand you being sent to prison. I could stand you disgracing me. But the thought of you having another woman was more than I could take. Ken was good to me. He used to come out to the house after you were sent away, then up to the apartment. And just talk." A note of hysteria crept into her voice. "Then one night—it happened. I didn't care. At the time I was glad. I was getting even with you." She ran her hands over her breasts. "I even liked it. For the first time in my life,

I liked it. It was as if some wall inside me had broken." More tears rolled down her cheeks. "That went on for about a month. Then I came to my senses. I realized what I was doing, how I was cheapening myself. I tried to stop it. I tried to break away from Ken." She sobbed hysterically. "But Ken wouldn't let me. He forced me to continue to have relations with him. He said he'd kill me if I didn't."

I got the morsel of mullet down. "The bastard." I was breathing as hard as she was. "The fat cracker bastard."

Beth continued to sob hysterically. "That's why he hates you. That's why he wants to kill you. He went crazy when I told him that I'd written you. That I'd sent you the fare to come to me. That I was going to start all over with you." She wiped her eyes with the back of her hand. "That's why I didn't write you a love letter. That's why I said we'd talk it over. I was going to tell you everything. Then you showed up at the door and all that mattered was that you were with me again."

I walked over to the bed and sat beside her. "Beth, honey. Sweetheart."

Beth twisted out of my arms. "No. Don't touch me. It's all your fault that it happened. I'm not that sort of a person. I've been living a lie for four years." Sobs shook her body. "I've even been ashamed to go to church. I have to turn my head away when I see Reverend Paul on the street." She stood up and peeled off her slip. There was an ugly bruise on her stomach, another on her left breast. "If you don't believe me, look."

Her body was inches from mine. I panted. "Who beat you?"

She sobbed, "Ken. He came back to the apartment this morning. Alone." She screamed the words at me. "And he beat me because I wouldn't. Because I couldn't. Not after I'd been with you."

Beth flung herself face down on the bed, her shoulders heaving. I sat beside her, my heart pounding. Breathing hard. Drenched with sweat. Afraid to touch her. Afraid to try to comfort her. I'd done this to Beth. Me. Mr. Charles White. First class heel.

"I'll kill him," I panted. "I'll kill him."

Beth continued to cry. For a long time, the only sounds were the *thump thump—thump thump* of the power plant and her sobbing. Then Beth rolled over on her side and wiped her eyes with a lock of hair. "So now you know."

I nodded. "Yeah. So now I know." What could I say? That I was sorry?

She sniffed. "Light me a cigarette. Please."

I lighted one and gave it to her. Beth lay on her back sucking at it in the awkward, feverish way some women smoke. When she spoke her voice was small again.

"What are you going to do, Charlie? I mean about Ken?"

"Kill the bastard."

"And then?"

"I don't know."

"You hate me, don't you?"

I bent and kissed her, "Why should I hate you for something that was my fault? You talked to Cliffton?"

"Yes."

"Just what did he say?"

Beth brushed her hair out of her eyes. "Joe was horrid. He said there wasn't a doubt in his mind that you'd killed Zo. He said I was a fool to even give you a second thought."

"He knew you'd seen me?"

"No."

After what she'd just told me about Ken, it was a difficult question to ask. I picked up Beth's hand from the bed and played with it. "What about Cliffton, Beth?"

"What do you mean, what about Joe?"

"You call him Joe. You must know Mr. Cliffton pretty well."

Beth turned her face to the wall. "Why shouldn't I? I've been his confidential secretary for five years."

"How confidential?"

I turned her face back to mine. "How confidential?"

Beth's shoulders shook. She began to cry again. Silently. "You've no right to question me."

"You've stayed with him, too?"

Her lower lip quivered. "No."

"Don't lie to me."

"Well, once then."

My nerves were keying higher with every word she spoke. Like the E string of a violin. "Where?"

"On his boat."

"When?"

"About six months ago." Her lips twisted in revulsion. "Oh, not because I wanted to. He's been after me for years. In a very gentlemanly manner. Then this night on the boat he got drunk. Off Anna Maria."

"What were you doing on his boat?"

"He *said* he wanted me to take some important dictation. Oh, it was awful, Charlie. I tried to fight him off. But I couldn't. He carried me into his cabin and tore off my clothes and—and—" She couldn't go on.

I choked out the words. "It's happened since?"

"No."

"Why did you keep on working for him?"

"I had to eat. Besides, when Mr. Cliffton sobered up, he was as sorry it had happened as I was. He said it wouldn't have happened if he hadn't wanted and loved me for years. He begged me to divorce you and marry him. He said he'd give me the kind of a life and home that I deserved."

"Why didn't you marry him?"

Beth made a hopeless gesture with one hand. "I told you. I love you. Besides, I was all mixed up with Ken." She sobbed harder. Hysterically. "Oh, dear God. I wish I were dead."

I slapped her. Lightly. "Stop that." The *thump thump—thump thump* of the power plant was a bass drum in my ears. I realized it wasn't the power plant. It was the pounding of my heart. I sounded like I was shouting at her. I was. "And stop blaming yourself. Everything that's happened is my fault. I exposed you to all of it by getting mixed up with *Señor Peso* and Zo in the first place. Cliffton has been persistent? I mean about you divorcing me and marrying him?"

"Very."

"It was Cliffton who suggested you move off the island?"

"Yes, I think it was."

"He knew you wrote me that letter?"

Beth rolled her head on the pillow. In torment. "I don't know. I don't know anything, Charlie. I'm not this sort of person. I don't want to be. All I know is that I want out of this trap. Why can't we go away somewhere? Anywhere. Away from here. Just so we're together."

The beer was lukewarm now, and sour. I rinsed my mouth with it and set the bottle back on the table. "Because we wouldn't get very far. Frenchy pointed that out on the way over here. I'd be arrested before I got to the bank in Habana."

"Then what are we going to do?"

I panted. "Have a show down. If I'm right, Cliffton is *Señor Peso.*"

Beth sat up on the bed and clung to me. She looked frightened. "You can prove it?"

"No," I admitted. "I can't. But it was Cliffton's boat that took those wetbacks off the island this morning. Cliffton has the connections to dispose of the stuff I brought in. He knew I needed money, needed it bad, four years ago. You say he's been after you for years. It was Cliffton who suggested that you move off the island."

Beth put the back of one hand to her forehead. "Of course. I should have realized that. I can see it all now. So plainly. It was Cliffton who gave Zo that money to keep you from coming back to me. Then, when he learned that I'd written you, he was afraid you might come back anyway. So he killed Zo and tried to kill you. It was Joe Cliffton's face you saw. Don't you see? He had to kill Zo. She knew who he was."

"He was out of town that night?"

"He was. He said on a business trip." Beth's eyes narrowed slightly. "What are you going to do about it, Charlie?"

I took the gun I'd taken from the hood out on the island out of my pocket and looked at it. "I don't know," I admitted. "I don't know, sweetheart. My brains weren't made for this kind of thinking. I'm just a dumb charter boat captain. I don't know what to do."

"I do," she said, quietly. Her eyes narrowed still more. There were glints of gold in them now. "I know just what we ought to do to get even with both Ken and Mr. Cliffton." She unbuttoned the top button of my shirt and twisted a tuft of hair into a little a peak.

"What?"

Beth evaded the question. "Would you be willing to take a chance, a big chance, sweetheart? If we could go away together. Fix it so your name would be cleared first? Be happy?"

I panted. "You know I would."

Beth moved still closer to me and ran the tip of her tongue around my lips. "And you know now that I love *you?*" She unbuttoned another button of my shirt.

"Yeah. Sure."

"And you still love me?"

"I do."

She unbuttoned two more buttons and patted my chest, her eyes searching mine. "You mean that, Charlie? You really love me? In spite of what I told you? About Ken? About Mr. Cliffton?"

The heat in the room was physical, tangible substance. Covering us like a wool blanket. Making it almost impossible to breathe. I could smell the raw pine, smell her. I gasped, "I told you it wasn't your fault."

Beth's eyes narrowed to mere slits. She sucked in her breath and held it as she massaged the sweaty flesh on my stomach. "And you forgive me?"

The E string was tuned to the snapping point. I swallowed. To relieve the pressure in my ears. "Of course. Come to the point, Beth. Tell me what you want me to do. What I can do."

"I'll tell you," she said. "In a minute." Her upper lip curled away from her teeth. "But first prove you forgive me."

Then the only sounds in the room were the *thump thump—thump thump* of the power plant, the pounding of my heart, as I proved that I forgave her.

CHAPTER EIGHTEEN

Beth rented the car. In her name. From the U-Drive-It firm near the basin. Frenchy stayed with me, talking in whispers, until Beth drove up to the tall royal palms under which we'd agreed to meet. Then Frenchy gripped my hand for luck and faded back into shadows. I got into the car with Beth.

It was a four door black Chevrolet.

Beth slid over as I got in. "You drive."

Rather than go around, I stepped over her legs and squeezed in back of the wheel. "What's the matter? Nervous?"

She bobbed her head. "I'll say." She opened her purse, took out a cigarette and lit it. "Look how my fingers are shaking."

I switched the ignition back on. "You're positive now you want to go through with this?"

Beth bobbed her head again. "It's the only possible way we can clear you, make things right for you and me again. You see that, don't you, Charlie?"

"Yeah. Sure." I agreed with her.

I started to let out the clutch. "No. Kiss me first," Beth insisted.

I kissed her. I felt good, and sad, at the same time. It was a funny feeling. I'd never had it before. It was as if I had died and come to life and was scheduled to die again at some specified time in the near future. And didn't give a damn.

As with most advice, Swede had been half right, half wrong. But he'd hit it on the head in at least one respect.

"A man hauls in the fish he baits for and at the level at which he fishes."

Beth was fiercely possessive. "Love me?"

"What do you think?" I asked her.

She smiled the self-satisfied little smile that women smile when they know they're sure of their men. "I know you do."

I eased the car into gear and drove slowly down the road rimming the waterfront. Cliffton's sleek thirty-eight footer was in its slip. There was a light in the aft cabin. As we drove past, I could see Matt Heely propped up on one of the bunks, reading.

"Probably the Sunday comics," Beth said.

"Probably," I answered.

There were few cars on the road and fewer pedestrians on the walk. Phillips Park was deserted. So was downtown Palmetto City. But Cliffton's, when we reached it, was still open and crowded. At ten-thirty on a Sunday night. Cliffton's was always crowded. Seven days a week. From eight o'clock in the morning until midnight. Sunday was one of his big days. Most of the back country people came in then to do their shopping. Along with cut-rate prices, Cliffton always gave them a free show. One week it was a free circus in the parking lot. The next a troupe of hill-billy singers.

There was an empty place in the line of cars on the Fourteenth street side of the building, across from the Atlantic Coast Line depot. I backed into the space and started to get out.

"No," Beth stopped me. "Let me go in alone. It being late as it is, Joe may not be here. If not, we'll have to drive out to his house."

"And if he's here?"

"I'll get him out to the car somehow."

I asked her if she wanted a gun.

Beth was scornful. "I won't need a gun. Meanwhile, you be careful you're not recognized."

I promised I'd be careful. Beth kissed me again. Then she strode off down the walk, crisp and cool and lovely in a pastel green dress. Her yellow hair spun gold in the light from the big plate glass windows. Looking like a dewy-eyed vestal virgin. On her way to light a torch. After what had happened at Sally's.

Women.

I sat watching the crowd for a few minutes, then reached for a cigarette. I was out. Fresh out.

Hub Conners was directing traffic on the corner, but no one seemed to be watching the crowd. I slipped into the side door of Cliffton's and bought a pack of Camels. As I waited for my change, the public address system announced the last special of the day would be a banana split for sixteen cents to the first hundred customers only.

The office was on a glassed-in mezzanine. As far as I could tell it was dark. I sifted the crowd with my eyes, looking for Beth, and saw her, finally, in one of the telephone booths. The girl back of the counter was trying to give me my change.

"Will there be anything else, sir?"

There was a stack of unsold Sunday papers near the counter. I told her to take out fifteen cents for a paper and walked back to the car. By tilting the paper sideways, I could read fairly well by the lights in the show windows.

I could see what Frenchy meant. According to that morning's headline, I was driving the cops nuts. Every crank in Florida had phoned in with information concerning me. I'd been seen in a dozen places, from Pensacola to Key West.

I read on down the story. The general public had been alerted to watch for me. I was known to be armed and dangerous. My description followed. I skipped it. I knew what I looked like. Of more interest was an item pertaining to Zo. Some bright boy in the state patrol lab had begun to wonder why her fingers were broken in the manner that they were and just what they had been clasping when they had been broken.

I turned the pages of the paper. Swede was on page four, in a one column two inch box. All it said about him was that Swen (Swede) Olson, former fishing guide and well-known West Coast Florida charter boat captain, had been executed, in the manner and at the time prescribed by law, for killing a prison guard during an abortive attempted prison break.

I wondered if Swede had met Zo by now. I hoped so. I was suddenly lonely. Lonelier than I'd ever been in my life.

I tossed the paper on the back seat of the car and smoked a cigarette while I waited for Beth. She came weaving swiftly through the crowd, looking as pretty coming toward me as she had walking away.

"Mr. Cliffton wasn't in the office."

"Oh."

"I could see it wasn't lighted. But I went upstairs to make certain. That's what took me so long."

I said, "I see."

Beth was breathing hard. As if she'd hurried. The emotional and physical strain was beginning to tell on her.

"So?"

"So now we drive out to his house," she said. "But stop at the apartment first. I want to pack a small bag. Just in case things go wrong."

"What if there's a stake-out?"

Beth shook her head. "There won't be."

"How do you know?"

"I know."

I didn't say anything. There didn't seem to be anything to say.

Beth added, "Ken thinks you're still out at the island."

I asked, "What do we do about Ken?"

Beth folded her hands in her lap. "That's—up to you. You know what he's done to me."

I circled the block her apartment was in. There didn't seem to be a stake-out. Beth got out the second time around and was waiting on the curb clutching a small overnight case when I came around again.

I asked her what was in it. She put the case between her feet. "Clothes," she said.

I hadn't any idea where Cliffton lived. Beth directed me to the house. It was in a swank section of town that was called Small Bayou. You have to have money to live there. But Cliffton's house was neither large nor pretentious. It was a low, rambling, hollow tile affair, set well back from the road at the end of a landscaped, winding drive.

Beth looked at the house, then at me. As if to say, "I could have lived here if I wanted to. If it hadn't been for you. See what I gave up for you, Charlie?"

I parked the car under the dangling feelers of a banyan tree and cut the lights. It was black under the tree and silent, except for the croak of the tree frogs and the humming drone of mosquitoes.

Beth sat breathing hard. "I'm frightened."

I gave her a chance to back out. "Now's the time to call this off. If you want to. I can always go down to the police station and surrender. Maybe I'm wrong. Maybe they'll believe my story."

Beth's fingers bit into my arm. "No. I won't let you do that. They won't believe you. They'll send you away from me again." Her voice was barely audible. "Besides—"

"Besides what?"

"There's Ken."

I could taste the smoked mullet. "Yeah. There's Ken."

I opened the door on my side. "Well, let's get it over with."

She got out on her side and joined me, still clutching the overnight bag. There was a light in the living room window. There was also a light in the room beyond it. I judged this room to be a bedroom or study. The rest of the house was dark. None of the blinds were drawn.

I'd been wrong about the size of the house. The living room was huge. There was no one in it. I looked in through the window of the room beyond it. I'd been right about it being a study. Still fully dressed, even to his coat, Cliffton was sitting at a big desk comparing what seemed to be bills of lading with entries in a huge loose-leaf ledger.

Beth's fingers bit into my arm. "Please."

"Please what?"

"Please kiss me for luck."

I kissed her. For luck. Her lips were hot and feverish. Not with passion. With fear. Her body trembled in my arms. I crushed her to me for a moment. "You're certain you want to go through with this?"

She bobbed her head. "I am. But, please. Not so tight, Charlie."

"Why?"

"You're mussing my dress."

I released her and pressed my back against the house, beside the door. "Okay. Go ahead. Ring the bell."

Beth pushed the button, chimes rang somewhere inside the house. A moment later, brisk footsteps crossed the parquet floor and the overhead porch light came on.

"Oh," Cliffton said. "It's you. What brings you here, this time of night, Beth?"

Beth lied, "I want to talk about Charlie."

I waited for the door to open. It didn't. Cliffton stood with the screen between them, making no effort to unhook it. "They've caught him?"

"No. Not yet," Beth said. "I hope they never do. Well, aren't you going to ask me in?"

"It's eleven o'clock, Beth."

"So what?"

"I'm alone in the house."

"I have to see you. Talk to you. Please, Joe."

From where I stood, it sounded as if Cliffton sighed. "I don't know whether I should or not, Beth. To be perfectly candid, I'm a little afraid of you."

Beth's lips twisted in a funny little smile. "Afraid of me?"

Cliffton had a crisp, staccato way of talking that matched his movements. "Afraid of my own reactions. So if it's about your husband, I'd rather you wouldn't come in. I'd like to help you. You know how I feel about you. But I'm really very busy, Beth. I might add, and a bit perturbed."

I watched Beth's breasts rise and fall. I imagined that Cliffton was watching them, too. Her voice had a certain quality to it that I'd never heard before. "You're perturbed about what?"

"I'd rather not say," Cliffton said. "And as far as White is concerned, as I told you this morning, I can't see that hiring a private agency man to snoop around would do a bit of good. I had a long talk with Lieutenant Gilly after I talked to you. And Gilly says there isn't a doubt that White killed that girl in Dead Man's Bay."

Beth ran her free hand over one of her breasts. "Perhaps Lieutenant Gilly isn't exactly impartial."

"Even so."

"Then you refuse to let me in?"

Time was running out on me. Fast. I'd waited as long as I could. I grasped the knob of the screen door and pulled. It opened with a rasp of metal pulling out of wood.

Cliffton was every inch as small and dapper as I remembered him, with widespread, intelligent eyes and hair so black it looked like it had been dyed. He backed slowly away from the door as I walked in with Beth crowding on my heels. He seemed more puzzled than frightened.

"Who are you?"

"You wouldn't know?"

He recognized me then. "Oh, yes. Of course. You're Charles White. You're the man for whom every law enforcement officer in Florida is looking."

He still wasn't frightened. He looked from me to Beth. "A rather shabby trick, my dear. What am I supposed to do now? How am I supposed to react? What do you want of me?"

I sat on the padded arm of an expensive overstuffed chair. "Beth tells me you're in love with her."

I expected him to deny it. He didn't. He met my eyes instead.

"That's right. Have been for some years. In fact, I've suggested a dozen times that she divorce you and marry me."

"She also tells me you want to buy the old house."

"That also is correct."

"Why?"

"Why what?"

"Why do you want to buy it?"

He got a little hot. "I don't consider that any of your business." Cliffton backed toward a long console table and sat on the edge of it.

I played out the string, exactly as Beth had suggested. "I intend to make it my business. Did you use your boat this morning?"

He lighted a cigarette. "No."

"You didn't send Heely out to the island to pick up the covey of wetbacks you had hiding out in the attic before Lieutenant Gilly and Sergeant Strawn happened on to them, searching the old house for me?"

He knew the meaning of the term. "You're out of your mind. No one would dare such a thing in Palmetto City."

I was holding the gun I'd taken in my right hand. I used my left to light a cigarette.

I pointed out, "Someone did."

His eyes were as black as his hair. They narrowed slightly as he asked, "You can prove this?"

"No," I admitted. "I can't. But they were there. I know. I happened in on them. They beat me half to death. The only thing that saved me was Gilly and Strawn showing up to search the island for me."

"Gilly and Strawn saw them?"

"No. Your boat took them off the other side of the island."

Cliffton looked at Beth. "You believe this, Beth?"

Beth's voice was as hot as her eyes. "I do. The old house is ideally situated for just such a nasty business. Charlie's been in prison. I haven't been out there for years. Not since you suggested I move into town. To be *closer* to my work. You send Matt to Cuba at least once a month. The way we see it, he brought them back and dropped them at the house. Later, one by one, they were landed on the mainland as tourists. And the law or no one else would ever be the wiser, unless one of them should be picked up accidentally." Tears streamed down Beth's cheeks. "It's been you. It's been you all the time."

Cliffton seemed sincerely puzzled. "It has been I who did what?"

Beth said, fiercely, "Who tempted Charlie in the first place. Who got him into running contraband." She was practically screaming now. "And then you had him sent to prison."

Cliffton ran a hand over his hair. "You're mad. You're out of your minds. Both of you." He opened the drawer of the console table. Casually. As if in search of a cigarette.

"I wouldn't if I were you," I warned him.

He dropped the gun back in the drawer and closed it.

"All right. I won't." He took a package of cigarettes from his pocket and lighted one. "Just what is it you want of me?"

I told him. "A confession."

Cliffton blew smoke at the ceiling. He still seemed more puzzled than frightened. "What do you want me to confess?"

Beth told him. "That you're *Señor Peso*. That you hired a knife man to try to kill Charlie this morning. That you either killed or had someone kill that Cuban girl Charlie is accused of killing."

Cliffton's fingers shook slightly as he lifted his cigarette to his mouth again. "I seem to be a pretty vicious sort of person. Just what could I hope to gain?"

Beth knew the answer to that one, too. She told him.

"Me."

CHAPTER NINETEEN

Cliffton was silent a long time. Then, looking at me, he asked, "I don't suppose it would do much good for me to deny these allegations that your wife's just made?"

"No," I admitted. "It wouldn't."

"You think I'm the mysterious *Señor Peso* that you mentioned at your trial?"

"We both do," Beth said.

Cliffton looked at her thoughtfully. "I didn't quite expect this from you, Beth. I guess it goes to prove that one lives and learns." He looked at me again. "Just what is your case against me, White?"

I told the truth. "I haven't any. Nothing but seemingly well-founded suspicions and the fact that it was your boat that took the wetbacks off the island this morning."

He suggested, "Maybe Heely is *Señor Peso*."

Beth's lips twisted in scorn. "Matt hasn't enough brains to be *Señor Peso*."

"No," I agreed with her. "He hasn't. *Peso* has been smart. Damn smart. But he slipped up in killing Zo and trying to kill me."

Cliffton pursed his lips. "It is your contention, then, that you didn't kill this Zo Palmyra?"

"It is."

"You think I did?"

"I do."

"You saw me do it?"

"No. The face of the man who slugged me and killed Zo was just a blur."

"And my motive?"

I said, "Beth told you that. She was the one thing you couldn't get at a bargain. But you could buy me. And you did. You brought me. With a phone conversation. *'This is Señor Peso, Captain White. How would you like to make two thousand dollars?'* And like a chump I fell for it. And made you and myself a lot of money until you tipped the Coast Guard and had me tucked away for four years. It was probably you who first sicked Zo on me. In Cuba. And it was you who sent Zo to meet me when I got out of prison. You were beginning to make a little time. You didn't want me back in Palmetto City. So you deposited forty-eight thousand dollars to my account in the National Bank of Habana."

"I did what?"

"You heard me. Beth was worth that much to you. Everything went fine until you learned that Beth had written me, offering to start all over."

Cliffton looked at Beth. "You did that?"

She pleated her handkerchief. "You know I did. I remember now. I told you. The morning I wrote it."

He nodded. "Yes. Now that you bring it up, I do recall you mentioned that you intended to write White."

I snuffed my cigarette. "You damn well remember. Because *Señor Peso* and Zo were the only two people who knew we were headed for that cabin. You followed us there. You were probably listening at the window when I read Beth's letter and told Zo we were through, that I was coming back to Palmetto City."

Cliffton shrugged. "Pure presumption on your part."

"You can prove where you were that night? You have an alibi?"

"This was what night?"

"Friday. Two nights ago."

Color crept into Cliffton's pale face. "No. I can't. At least I have no alibi I'd care to offer."

I continued. "You heard me read the letter. You heard what I said to Zo. And you saw another way out of your problem. It was you to whom Zo cried out just before you shot her and slugged me with that gaff hook. Maybe you meant to kill me. Maybe you didn't. It didn't make much difference one way or another. With me back in a cell at Raiford waiting to be burned for a murder I hadn't committed, I couldn't very well return to Beth. And you are a patient man. You could wait. You knew that in time you would get what you wanted."

Cliffton was plenty nervous now. All three of us were. For different reasons. He picked up a cigarette from the table and dropped it. Instead of picking it up from the floor, he squashed it with the toe of his shoe. "You're not mentally right. You can't be. A jury would howl at that story."

I laid my last card on the table. "Okay. Let's test it. Let's all three go down to the station. I'll tell my story. You tell yours."

Cliffton shook his head. "No. I'm afraid we can't do that. I can't afford to. I'm a prominent man in Palmetto City and my business enemies would be certain to try to make capital of this."

Beth's voice was shrill. Shriller than I'd ever heard it. "You mean you're afraid the federal men might look at your invoices and begin to wonder where you're getting some of your goods that you'll be able to sell for less than your fellow merchants pay for it wholesale. It's been right in front of my nose all the time. And I didn't have sense enough to see it. No one but you could be *Señor Peso.*"

The little man looked hurt. "You really believe that, Beth?"

"I do," she said, hotly.

"You think I'm that much of a heel?"

I said, coldly, "Any man who would rape another man's wife, force her against her consent, is capable of anything."

Cliffton looked from Beth to me. "Now I've raped someone. Who?"

I told him. "Beth."

He looked at Beth. She blushed and looked away.

It was a long time before he spoke. Then he said, quietly, "I see." He looked back at me. "Beth told you, eh?"

"She did."

"She told you where this attack took place?"

"In the cabin of your boat."

"When?"

"Six months ago." I brushed his excuse aside before he offered it. "Oh, I know what you're going to say. You were drunk. Beth told me that, too. That when you came to your senses you were as sorry as she that it had happened. That you begged her to divorce me and marry you."

Cliffton snuffed his cigarette. "I don't suppose it would do a bit of good to deny that I've ever had carnal knowledge of your wife, drunk or sober?"

I shook my head at him. "No. Naturally you'd deny it."

"Naturally," Beth said, shrilly.

"Naturally," Cliffton agreed.

We sounded like a bunch of goddamn parrots jabbering at each other. I was having all I could do to hold myself in. I was tired of being a gentleman. I wanted to pound on things and people. I wanted to smash my fists into faces. I wanted to get roaring drunk and forget the whole damn thing. But I couldn't. I had to keep my head. I had a date. Back at Raiford. With a chair. To pay for a life I hadn't taken. Zo's.

I love you, Captain Charlie, she'd told me. While she was dying. Because some son of a bitch had killed her. Killed her in my arms.

Cliffton took another cigarette from his pack and lighted it with steady fingers. "So what happens now?"

I followed the instructions Beth had given me. "So now we walk out of here. Out to the car we have waiting in the drive."

"And then?"

"We drive down to the basin and your boat."

Cliffton repeated, "And then?"

"We'll take care of that when we get there," I told him.

Outside in the night again, I asked Beth if she could drive. She said she could. I rode in the back seat with Cliffton, both of us looking at the back of Beth's head. Her shoulder length bob fit her like a golden helmet. Hiding what thoughts? Only she could answer that.

Cliffton spoke only once during the ride. "What if we should happen to pass a police car and I should happen to cry out?"

"I wouldn't if I were you," I advised him. "Believe me, Mr. Cliffton, I wouldn't."

A few minutes later we passed one. He had sense enough not to yell. Beth had never been a good driver. She hadn't improved. I rode with the feeling that I was on a balky merry-go-round that was gradually gathering momentum. If it went much faster, one of us was going to fly off into space.

The waterfront was dark and silent but here and there I could see a light in the cabin of a cruiser as the endless poker games and the caring for gear went on into the night. Matt Heely was still reading in the cabin of Cliffton's boat.

Beth parked the car a few boats down the mole.

"How did you get this far?" Cliffton asked me.

I told the truth. "God knows. I don't."

Beth got out of the car. She was breathing hard again. "All right. Take him out to the boat, Charlie."

I walked Cliffton down the mole with the gun in the small of his back. With my fingers crossed. Hoping we would not be stopped. We weren't. His boat had a private pier. I walked him out on it slowly. Heely heard us coming. He put down the paper he was reading and opened the screen door into the cockpit. A lean, hatchet-faced cracker with gimlet eyes, he stood with one hand to his forehead trying to see into the dark, as a swift scudding cloud crossed the moon.

"Ahoy, the pier."

I could take Heely or leave him alone. A hard drinker with a penchant for jail bait and an uncanny ability to find an ace when he needed one, he wasn't popular along the water. On the other hand he was a good guide and a good seaman.

Beth was walking a few steps ahead of us. "It's Beth White, Captain Heely," she answered the hail.

"Oh," he said, quietly. "I see. Who's with you?"

"Joe Cliffton," Cliffton told him. "With a gun in my back."

Heely swung as if to re-enter the cabin.

I stopped him. "Hold it right there, Matt. Let's not have any unnecessary shooting. I'm the guy with the gun."

Heely froze, half in, half out of the cabin and shielded his eyes again. "That sounds like Charlie White."

I said, "It is."

He said, "Well, I'll be damned."

The tide was in. The cruiser was riding high. It wasn't much of a jump. Beth jumped down into the cockpit and as the moon floated out from behind the cloud, I caught a glimpse of white thigh, before she could paw down her skirt. "We want to talk to you, Captain," she told Heely. "But not here."

"Where then?" he puzzled.

"Out on the water," Beth said. "Slip your lines, turn your engine over and head out toward the island."

Heely looked at Cliffton. Cliffton looked down at the gun I was holding. "I guess you'd better do as you're told," he said. "It would seem that Beth and Charles White have some wild idea that I'm *Señor Peso.*"

"I've heard the name," Heely said.

He turned one engine over and put the screw in reverse to hold the big cruiser against the tide.

Beth asked, slightly breathless, "Has Lieutenant Gilly been here?"

Heely shook his head. "No, he ain't, Mis' White. There ain't been no police around. Not lately, anyway. Not since it was rumored along the water that Charlie was headed for Cuba."

The merry-go-round was moving faster now. It was all I could do to keep from using the gun to smack the smirk off his thin face. I'd taken almost as much as I could, mentally, emotionally, physically. All I wanted was to get it over with. One way or another.

Cliffton asked if it was all right for him to sit in a deck chair. I said it was and sat in the chair beside him. Heely cast off the last line and walked back to his controls. There was a snortle in the water as the powerful screw took hold and eased the cruiser out of the slip. Clear of the slip and pier, Heely cut in his other engine and the big boat moved forward slowly, out into deep water, to the channel between the mainland and the island.

With deep water under him, Heely turned his head and looked at Cliffton again. "Now where?"

Cliffton's voice was crisp and bitter. "You'd better ask the Whites. It seems I haven't a thing to say."

"No. Not a thing," Beth said. Her breathlessness had left her. She seemed almost amused, but still a trifle frightened.

"Where?" Heely asked her.

She told him. "The island. Anchor in front of the house."

"Just as you say," he answered.

He gunned his engines a little and a tail of spray fanned out behind the cruiser.

Cliffton lighted a cigarette. "Were you out at the island this morning, Matt?"

Heely didn't bother to turn his head. "Why, yes. Come to think of it, I was."

Cliffton straightened in his chair. "What were you doing there?"

Heely turned and looked at him this time. "Why, as it so happens," he said, "I was taking a load of wetbacks off before the cops got to them. You ought to know. You told me to go get them and take them to the

Springs."

"I knew it," Beth cried. "I knew it." Her fingers dug into my arm. "Would you swear that in court, Captain?"

Heely shook his head. "No. I'm not putting my neck into a federal noose for anyone. But I don't mind telling you folks. I been running stuff for Cliffton for some time. Ever since I smashed my boat. I'm walking the floor one night, see? Wondering which way to turn. And the phone rings. *'This is Señor Peso, Captain Heely,'* a guy tells me. *'How would you like to make some fast money?'*"

Beth exulted, "You hear that, Charlie? You hear what Matt just said?"

"Yeah," I said. "I heard."

Cliffton stood up and walked to the rail. I stood up and walked with him. But he wasn't trying to escape. All he wanted was some place to be sick.

I didn't blame the guy. I knew just how he felt.

CHAPTER TWENTY

The moon slid out from behind a fast moving cloud and in behind another. In the brief flash of light Beth looked like an avenging angel. With yellow hair. And big breasts. And an overnight case in one hand. Clothes in it. She'd told me.

The moon came out and lighted her face again. It was contorted with anger, as she continued to beat the drum.

"There he is. The man who killed Zo and framed you for murder. The man who ruined our lives. The man who took four years of your life away from you. Because he wanted me."

I stood, unable to speak, the palm of my gun hand wet with sweat, having trouble breathing.

Beth looked at me, expectant. "Well, why don't you shoot him?"

I lifted the gun in my hand and looked from it to Cliffton. He stared back, his face white and haggard, but unafraid.

Beth continued to beat at me with her voice. "Well, go ahead. Don't just stand there. Shoot."

My throat was so contracted I had to squeeze the words out. Then they almost stuck in my mouth. "Yeah. But what happens then?"

Beth dropped her voice. "I told you, darling."

"Tell me again."

She might have been speaking to a slightly stupid child. "We take his body ashore and clear your name."

"How? By confessing to another murder?"

Beth stroked my arm. "But he's *Señor Peso*, Charlie. He killed Zo."

"How do we prove that if he's dead?"

"I'll show you. Just leave everything to me. Here. Let me have that gun."

I moved my gun hand away from her. "No. Why don't we take him ashore alive?"

"And have him lie out of it? You heard what Matt Heely said. He was willing to tell us but he wouldn't testify in court. Please let me have the gun."

I shook my head. "No dice. So Mr. Cliffton is *Señor Peso*. Why don't we take him ashore alive?"

Beth said, "Because—" and stopped there.

His back to the rail, Cliffton gripped it with both hands. "I can answer that," he said, quietly.

Heely had reached the far side of the channel and the narrow shelf in front of the old house. He reversed, then idled his engines and disappeared forward along the narrow catwalk to drop his anchor. But not until he had made certain there were no small boats pulled up on shore. We were still standing as he had left us, when he dropped into the cockpit again. None of us saying anything. All of us busy with our thoughts. None of them pleasant.

Then the moon came out from behind a cloud and stayed out. Beth's face was screwed up as if she were crying, but no sound was coming out.

"I told you," Heely panted. "I told you over the phone it wouldn't work." He glanced apprehensively at the shore. "I was a goddamn fool to let you talk me into this."

Beth made one last try. "But he—he *raped* me, Charlie."

I felt as sick as Cliffton had. "Yeah. So you told me. But then you told me so many things."

"You don't believe me?"

"No."

Cliffton's voice was sad. "I think I've known for some time. But then a man in love is a fool."

Heely spat the word. "Love. There ain't no such thing, it's all heat."

"I'm inclined to agree with you," Cliffton said.

I shook my head. "I'm not. I had a woman in love with me once. Her name was Zo."

Beth was breathing hard again. She gave me a dirty look and crossed the cockpit to Cliffton. "You do love me, don't you, Joe?"

The little man lighted a cigarette. "I suppose so. Having been in love with you for years, I don't suppose I'll ever be completely cured."

Beth rubbed her leg against his, like an amorous alley cat. On a back fence. Willing to rub more. "Then take me out of here. Take me to Cuba. Anywhere. I don't dare go back to the mainland."

He said, "You're forgetting your husband."

Beth turned on me. "I hate him."

I didn't say anything.

Cliffton said, "Even so. He has the gun. Besides, what's this deal with Heely?"

"You can count me out," Heely said. "All I was interested in was the money."

"What was the deal?" I asked him.

He started to tell me, "After you'd killed Cliffton—"

Beth turned on him. "Shut up."

Heely shrugged and leaned against the screen door of the aft cabin.

Beth went back to work on Cliffton. "You must love me, Joe. You asked me to divorce Charlie and marry you a dozen times."

Cliffton said, "But that was before I 'raped' you."

Beth began to cry. "So I was desperate enough to lie. To try anything to get out of the scrape I'm in." Hysteria was creeping into her voice. "I'll make you a good wife. I'll do anything you ask, Joe. Anything."

I felt like I was running again. On through an endless nightmare. Only before, I'd been running toward Beth. Now I was running away from her. This was the woman I'd dreamed of for four years. This was the woman who had lain in my arms, her breath in my mouth, panting that she loved me.

I said, "I've been away for four years. I wouldn't have contested a divorce. Why didn't you divorce me and marry Mr. Cliffton while your chances were still good?"

"Damn you, Charlie White," Beth cursed me. "I wish I'd never met you."

The words sounded strange in her mouth.

"I can tell you that, White," Cliffton said. "Beth knew I wouldn't permit my wife to work and by that time she was in so deep that she didn't dare quit her job."

"So deep in what?"

"Running contraband through my store and writing checks for it to non-existent jobbers. Dummy concerns that she set up in Tampa, Orlando, St. Petersburg, Miami. Even as far away as Chicago and New York. Checks that she cashed herself. God knows how much she got away with. She was my confidential secretary. Her signature is as good as mine at any of a dozen banks that I can name."

Beth continued to cry silently.

Cliffton dropped his cigarette over the side. When it hit the water it made a small sound. Like a baby snake, just learning to hiss. "As to the night I 'raped' her, I think I can explain that. Even that long ago, the house of cards she'd built was beginning to get shaky. Twice federal men traced merchandise, believed to have been brought into the country without going through customs, to my store. But it was all supposition. Nothing could be proved." The little man sounded sad. "But Beth wanted a better hold on me than she had. She couldn't marry me. She didn't dare. So she tried to become my mistress. I still don't know why she didn't succeed. I'm just another guy. I like pretty women. I was with one the night this Cuban girl was killed. That's why I couldn't offer you an alibi."

Cliffton lighted a fresh cigarette and sucked smoke deep into his lungs. "But with Beth it was different. I'm a rich man, but a lonely one. I've spent all my life making money. Dreaming, some day, I'd meet the girl. I did. It was Beth. I knew it the first day she came to work for me. But then she was a married woman. I didn't dare say anything. Later, when I did, after you'd been sent away, she was already in so deep from stealing pennies, that she didn't dare try for the jackpot."

My right hand was tired holding the gun. I shifted it to my left hand. "But why this sudden urgency? Why should she want me to kill you now?"

He said, "The federal men are due at the store in the morning. And this time, they have me dead to rights. Over a matter of some perfume. And with our set-up at the store, it has to be myself or Beth. This time it so happens that I can prove I didn't place the order. I was in New York on a buying trip when it was introduced into our stock."

Beth stopped crying and felt in the bodice of her dress for a handkerchief.

"If she's lucky," Cliffton said, "she ought to get off with ten years. Possibly as little as five. On the other hand Uncle Sam doesn't like to be clipped. The judge may throw the book at her."

I asked, "And *Señor Peso—?*"

Cliffton shook his head. "There you have me. It's a cinch Beth was working with someone. And I'm almost positive it's not Heely. Matt isn't smart enough."

"Thank you," Heely said.

Beth had lost the handkerchief out of her bodice. She put the overnight case on the stool in front of the cockpit control and unsnapped the clasps.

Cliffton added, "I imagine the wetback business you mention was a last desperate attempt to make a final killing. I've heard they'll pay a thousand or more apiece to be brought into the country."

I said, "I've been offered as high as five."

Then something hit my hand. I felt the sting before the report. It sounded like someone had snapped his fingers, loud. I looked from my bleeding hand to the gun on the deck of the cockpit, then across the cockpit at Beth.

She was standing with her feet spread to steady herself against the roll of the cruiser, a small, black, ugly looking twenty-five caliber automatic in her hand. In the moonlight, her face was a series of flat white planes, all of them ugly.

"Pick up his gun," she told Heely.

Matt scuttled across the cockpit and scooped up the gun. "I was hoping you had one." He grinned. "God knows I didn't." He leered at me. "But I have now."

"Like a pair of ducks," Cliffton breathed.

Beth's smile was as evil as her eyes. "Sitting ducks is the cliché," she corrected him. "Now I'll do some talking." Her eyes flicked over the side of the cruiser, across the shallows to the shore. "But not for long. What is there to say? Besides, *Señor Peso* is waiting for me. At the International Airport in Tampa, I trust."

Heely looked disappointed. "You'll never get away by plane."

Beth shrugged a slim white shoulder. "I don't intend to try. After we take care of Charlie and Mr. Cliffton, you're going to run me to Cuba."

Cliffton shook his head. "You'll never make it, Beth."

Her smile was superior. "Why not? Matt's cleared for his regular monthly trip to Cuba. And it won't make the least bit of difference to the Coast Guard if he starts a few hours early."

Heely looked toward Beth's breasts. "That's all right with me. That's fine. You have the money?"

Beth snapped the clasps on the overnight case. "I have." She looked at me. "And while we're on the subject of money, please give me that passbook, Charlie."

I tugged it from my hip pocket and handed it to her. "It's in my name. You can't collect it."

She put it between her breasts. "We'll see. You fool. I meant to go away with you, Charlie. I planned it that way. With you it wasn't pretense." Her smile was the twisted smile of every cheating wife in the world. "What's the matter? Didn't I please you? I tried so hard."

"Yes," I told her. "You did try. Too hard."

"And you didn't like your new wife?"

"Not enough to kill an innocent man for you."

"You knew," Beth accused.

"Not the first time," I admitted. "I thought maybe you really loved me. But I was pretty certain out at Sally's."

"How did you know?"

I told her. "You poured it on too thick. You tried too hard to be certain I was hooked."

"What did you know?"

"That everything you told me was a lie."

Beth squared her shoulders. "Light me a cigarette, Matt."

Heely lighted one and handed it to her. "And now—?"

"Get your anchor up and get underway."

"And Charlie and Mr. Cliffton?"

"We'll take care of them as soon as we're underway."

"Right." Heely tucked the gun he was holding in the waistband of his pants, started to pull himself up on the catwalk to go forward and froze in fear, as Ken Gilly, his heavy service gun in hand, looked down from the flying bridge.

"Going somewhere?" Ken asked.

But he wasn't talking to Matt Heely. He was talking to Beth.

She turned slowly at his voice. Then she began to scream. One scream following another. Each one seeming to tear a fresh layer of membrane from her throat.

CHAPTER TWENTY-ONE

When she could no longer scream, she panted, "You're at the airport in Tampa. Waiting for me. You have to be."

Ken had dropped into the cockpit by then. "You bitch," he named her. "You bitch." He was breathing as hard as she was. "You lying, two-timing bitch. You got me into this. And now you run out on me."

Heely went over the side. Ken didn't even see him go. He didn't know that Cliffton and I were pressed to the rail of the cockpit. Or didn't care. All he had eyes for was Beth.

He looked like a man who'd been through hell a long time. Tears streamed down his fat face, unnoticed.

"'I love you, Ken,' you told me. 'If you'll do what I say we can both be rich.' That was four years ago. And like a fool I listened to you. I slept in my best friend's bed. I helped you send him to prison because you were afraid he might find out about us, find out there was no *Señor Peso* but you."

"Please, Ken," Beth begged him.

He slapped her with his free hand. "No. It's all torn now." He knew we were in the cockpit. "It doesn't matter what Charlie or Cliffton hear. They have a right to know. Everyone will know by morning. You're not going anywhere. I'm not going anywhere. We've been."

Beth attempted to distract him. "How did you get on this boat?"

"I've been on it since it left the basin. In the fore cabin. I knew by the tone of your voice that you were lying when you phoned me to meet you at the airport. And I figured you'd try to use Matt and leave me holding the bag."

Beth attempted to explain.

Ken cut her short. "I know. I heard. If you could chump Charlie into killing Cliffton, you figured you'd be in the clear, that you could stay in Palmetto City."

"That *we'd* be in the clear," Beth panted.

Ken shook his head. "No. I never figured with you. Except as a willing stooge. A stooge you paid off with your body. And the fat cracker boy loved it. Loved it because he loved you. Because he's always loved you." Ken glanced at me briefly. "What did she tell you, Charlie? I mean about us."

I said, "That you, well, got together one night, shortly after I was sent away. And from then on, you forced your attentions on her, threatening to kill her when she tried to stop seeing you."

Ken continued to cry, great dry sobs racking his body. Did you ever see a man cry? A strong man? It's not nice. His tears weren't coming from tear ducts. They were being pumped out of his heart.

"I imagined it was something like that," he said. "But that wasn't the way it happened. It started long before you were sent away. I was the guy who called you on the phone." It was the voice I'd heard for four years, lying awake nights in my cell, staring up into the darkness. *"This is Señor Peso, Captain White. How would you like to make two thousand dollars?"*

I couldn't help it. I gasped, "You son of a bitch."

"I'm all of that," Ken nodded. "But all I ever was, was a voice. A voice on the phone. Except one time."

"And that one time?"

Ken wiped his fat cheeks with the back of his free hand.

"Was last Friday on Dead Man's Bay."

"It was you who killed Zo?"

He nodded. "That's right. I also tried to kill you. I thought I had."

"Why?"

"Because even then I knew that we'd played out our string, that time was running out on us." His fat face was a mask of tragedy. "And Beth was running out on me. I had Matt locate Zo on his last trip to Habana and advance her money to meet you. I arranged for a boat to pick you up and take you down to Cuba. The money was Beth's idea. She said the figures in a bankbook would make it look good. Then I learned that the figures were real. I learned she had written you and that she had sent you money to come to her."

"And if I didn't come to Palmetto City?"

"She planned to join you in Habana, cut out Zo, at least long enough to recover the money. The forty-eight grand was insurance. Oh, Beth was smart. She thought of everything. She covered every angle. But me. So I drove up to Dead Man's Bay and did what I had to do to make certain that you didn't come back, but you did. And somehow I'm not sorry. I'm glad that it's over."

Beth brushed her arm against his. "Don't talk like that, Ken. We still have a chance together."

He shook his head at her. "No. We had our chance."

She pressed even closer to him. "Don't talk like that."

Ken used his free hand to push her away from him. Gently. "No. It's gone. The boat's sailed. It sailed when you went to bed with Charlie. To find out how much he knew, to tuck him away as an ace. To use against me. In case I stepped out of line. But you almost slipped up there. When you sent him out to the island to hide. You forgot we hadn't had time to move the wetbacks in the attic. They almost killed Charlie. Then Matt got them off barely in time."

He glanced at me again, briefly. "You were in the swamp, weren't you,

Charlie?"

"I was."

"I knew. I tried to kill you. I wanted to kill you, then."

"And now?"

Ken looked at me again, longer this time. "I've done enough to you, fellow. Don't you think?"

I didn't say anything. What was there to say? Besides, he had a gun. All I had were my fists.

Ken continued, "Then, tonight out at Sally's tore it."

Beth stared in fear. "What do you know about Sally's? How do you know?"

Ken looked at her dull-eyed. "How does anyone know about anything along the water? I know you met Charlie in room seven. I know you were there an hour. There was only one thing you, being you, could be doing. You were paying him in advance for something you wanted him to do. Something clever that you'd schemed up in that pretty little head of yours."

Beth backed away as far from him as she could. "No. Don't look at me that way, Ken."

"How do you want me to look at you?"

Beth wet her dry lips with her tongue. "I'll go away with you now. We'll go away together." She picked up the overnight case. "Look. I have most of the money."

Ken slapped it out of her hand. "I've never been too interested in the money angle. You know that. All I wanted was you."

Beth pleaded with him. "And you can have me, Ken." She repeated, "I'll go away with you. We'll go away together."

"Where?"

"Anywhere you want to go."

"How?"

"On this boat."

"I can't run it and neither can you."

"By plane then. We'll go to the airport in Tampa."

Ken gestured out at the water. "And how do we get through that?"

Beth's eyes followed the gesture and her face screwed up again as if she were going to scream. The channel immediately offshore looked like a Christmas tree, hung with the red and green running lights of cruisers, half-cabins, power-boats.

There was a Coast Guard boat with the cocky young j.g. silhouetted against the moonlight.

"Ahoy, the cruiser," he called.

Beth screamed at me. "You did that. You didn't intend to go through with what you promised from the start. That's what you and Frenchy were whispering about. You warned him to alert the harbor."

"That's right," I answered.

She lifted her shoulder length yellow hair up and away from the back of her neck. "I won't be arrested. I won't." Then she realized she still had the small gun in her hand and pointed it at me. "Run this boat out of here, fast."

I shook my head at her. "I can't."

"Why not?"

"The hook's down. Remember? Matt was just going forward to lift it when Ken joined the party."

The j.g.'s voice was sharper this time. "Ahoy, the cruiser. Who's aboard?"

Cliffton spoke for the first time. "Cliffton, lieutenant," he called. "And I'd appreciate it if you'd board us. We're in a little trouble."

Beth emptied the small gun at him. "No!"

Lead smacked into the side of the cockpit, screaming off the metal it touched. Then, sobbing as if her heart were broken, Beth raced the few feet to the stern and a white thigh showed to her hip, as she straddled the wide fish box. "I won't be arrested. I won't."

"No, Beth," Ken said quietly. "Don't try it."

She ignored him and slithered over the stern, cursing as her dress caught on the raised metal burgee socket. There was a sound of tearing cloth. Then a splash. Then she was scrambling up on the shelf and stumbling across it toward shore. A big spotlight on the Coast Guard boat came on and pinned the scene against the night.

Beth's dress and slip were gone. She raced on, her blonde hair trailing behind her. Looking like the beautiful but evil creature that she was. Released from the hell of her own making.

"No," Ken panted beside me. "Not that."

His gun bucked in my ear. I tried to knock up his arm, too late. A red stain appeared on Beth's white back, just under her left shoulder blade. She took another uncertain step or two and fell face forward into the water and there was another splash as Ken went over the side and floundered through the shallows to her, his fat shoulders shaking again, calling softly, "Beth, darling, sweetheart."

Sergeant Strawn met him wading back, with Beth's white body in his arms, tears streaming down his fat face. I stood dry-eyed, watching. It was his right to carry her. She was his dead, not mine.

As they met, Ken held out his service revolver. "It's all right, Bill," he said. "I won't give you any trouble." He held Beth's body closer. "We won't give you any trouble any more...."

It was dawn when they let me leave the station. There wasn't much I could tell them. I told them what little I could. With the exception of the hood in the old house. Ken admitted that he'd hired the hood to kill me. Strawn said they would question me again later. I didn't see any sense in confessing something that couldn't be traced to me. I'd had all of cells that I wanted.

Cliffton and I walked down the worn steps together. He looked tired and old, much older than he had. The hunt for the killer was over. I'd been found and I wasn't wanted. But in dying, the way she had, Beth had killed a little something in all of us.

In forcing him to do what he'd done, she'd killed Ken outright. Something in Cliffton died. He would always be lonely now. I knew that I would be. But not for Beth. My love had died on Dead Man's Bay.

We stood in front of the station a moment, trying to find something to say to each other. There didn't seem to be anything.

"Well," Cliffton said, finally, "I'll see you around, White."

I said, "Yeah. Sure thing, Mr. Cliffton."

I watched him walk away, uptown toward his store. Then I walked slowly toward the water. Frenchy was waiting for me on the curb. He fell in step with me but didn't say anything.

I walked on, thinking of Swede. He'd been right. And he'd been wrong. Beth and Ken had swum out of the school. And look what happened to them. But on the other hand he'd called Zo a fancy dame. And it hadn't been like that at all. Zo had loved me. She'd died telling me so. I'd done the same things with her as I had with Beth. But there was a difference somehow. It wasn't just a matter of making love to a man that made a woman good or bad. Zo had probably had a lot more men than Beth. But Zo had known. She'd warned me. Zo had told me:

"This woman does not love you. I am a woman. I know."

Zo had been right. It made it difficult for a man. I hadn't known what to think or what to do. What was right? What was wrong? Which was the real? Which was the false?

At the edge of the basin, Frenchy stopped to roll a cigarette. "You got any dough, Charlie?" he asked me.

I shook my head. "No. I haven't got a dime."

He licked and lighted his cigarette. "Neither have I. But you're welcome to bunk on the boat as long as you care to, Charlie. I can always scrape up a meal and a bottle. And we can even fish partners again, if you want."

"I'd like that, Frenchy," I said. And borrowed his makings. I walked on with him to the battered half-cabin in the basin.

But long after he'd turned in, I sat on the live bait well. Smoking. Listening to the drip of the condensation off the roof of the cabin tinkle in the silence. Taking a drink from time to time. Looking out at the undulating water taking on color from the sun. The past was dead.

There was no use thinking about it. But the rising sun, shining on the water, gave me hope. Perhaps, somewhere out there beyond the horizon, there was another Zo. Waiting for me.

I hoped so.

THE END

TOO HOT TO HOLD
. . . .
BY DAY KEENE

ONE

Although his actual physical death didn't take place until two days later, Mike Scaffidi began to die the moment he picked up a fare in front of Grand Central Station at exactly 9:25 on the morning of November 3, 1958.

The day was gray and raw. A cold rain was falling. Scaffidi was late getting his cab on the street. His windshield wipers were giving him trouble. He barely glanced at the girl as she got into his cab. If he had thought of her at all as a woman, he would have compared her slight body unfavorably with that of big Serafina. *Jesu-Giuseppe e Mari.* There was a woman. All two hundred pounds of her.

Although she took no physical part in his murder—tried desperately, in fact, to prevent it—the frightened girl in the red plastic raincoat killed the good-natured cab driver as surely as if she'd triggered the gun.

A good many factors were involved. If Linda Lou hadn't been so frightened she wouldn't have bolted from Scaffidi's cab and run directly in front of the truck. If Brady hadn't quarreled with his wife he wouldn't have missed the 8:01 from Stamford. If Scaffidi had yielded to his amorous impulses, he would still have been burrowed between mounds of Serafina's fragrant flesh. And if the elder statesmen of the Mafia hadn't been pressing Lew Dix for an accounting, there would have been no need to transport the parcel in the first place.

Technically, it began as an accident report:

Female, white, blonde hair, gray eyes.

5'2"—110—19

The traffic officer's name was Coogan. While he was waiting for the ambulance to arrive he covered the girl with his slicker before adding the rest of the information he found in her wallet:

Illinois driver's license—Linda Lou Larson. Occupation, model. Clark Street Arms Hotel. Contents of wallet: $444.65 plus return half of round-trip ticket to Chicago.

Foremost in the circle of traffic-blocking, rain-drenched, morbidly curious onlookers, the driver of the truck was vehemently vocal in protesting his lack of blame.

"Ask anybody," he insisted. "The dame run right in front of my rig. On account of it being raining like it is and what with traffic this time of morning and all, I'm barely crawling along, see? Then all of a sudden, out of nowhere, there she is."

Several onlookers confirmed his statement.

The girl on the pavement would have been happy to do likewise. Despite all that had happened to her since she'd left Della's Place, she was an inherently decent and honest, if very frightened, girl. After all of Mr. Dix's warnings as to what was certain to happen to her if she failed to deliver the parcel, she had been terrified when the big man with one hand in the pocket of his rain-sodden trench coat had wrenched open the door of the cab. All she remembered was crying out, "No!" Then she was out in the rain and running until the hard grille of the truck had violently impeded her flight....

It had been bad enough to miss the 8:01. And now the 8:25, Stamford-to-New York, was ten minutes late. It was the second time in several days. When he reached the office there was certain to be a scene.

There were times when Brady wished he and May and the children still lived in a Manhattan apartment. He'd been out of his mind when he'd agreed to buy the G.I. resale in Stamford. True, the country was good for the children. So was fresh air.

As the commuter train limped past a ground crossing in a wet blur of clanging bells, Brady studied his reflection in the rain-silvered window beside him. The lines in his face were deepening. His black hair was beginning to gray. He was beginning to look like an old man. He was growing old at 34, just when he should be beginning to live.

Brady continued to study his face. Life hadn't turned out at all as he'd planned it. He'd intended to do big things, perhaps even have his own import-export firm. There were to have been buying trips to Paris, Seville, Milan. The Champs Elysées in the springtime. The Cathedral Santa Maria de la Sede at Easter. Snow on the Piazza del Duomo. The places he'd known as a child.

And here he was at 34, still working for Harper, Nelson and Ferrel, a $6500-a-year translator, afraid for his job because he was a few minutes late. His only traveling, besides the morning and evening commuter's train, was done via a 21-inch television set he couldn't afford and for the use of which he had to compete with a bored wife, a ten-year-old stepson with a pathological addiction to sports and a 15-year-old stepdaughter with a pathological addiction to him.

He had to do something about Alice and soon. But what? He couldn't confide in May. If he did, with her filthy mind, she would say it was all his fault, that he'd encouraged the child.

Brady stared down at his hands. Nothing ever happened to him. Nothing. Period. He got up. He ate. Unless he and May had a fight and he was delayed, as he'd been this morning, he caught the 8:01. He spent the days translating French, Italian and Spanish business letters. He caught the 5:15 back to Stamford. He ate again and then went to bed. When May was in the mood, they made love purely as a matter of mutual convenience. Then he set the damn alarm clock and the whole thing started all over again.

Brady clenched his fists. It wasn't fair. Where had he made a wrong turning? He glanced down at his shabby brief case, wondering why he bothered to carry it. There was seldom anything in it but bills.

His depression deepened. Both Jimmy and Alice needed new school clothes. May had to have a new coat. He'd promised her one last winter. More, it was time he had a new suit. No matter how little they paid them, Harper, Nelson and Ferrel demanded that their employees be well dressed at all times.

It wasn't fair. He was a capable linguist. He'd spent most of his childhood in Europe and he could read, write and speak four languages fluently. He was more than a translator. He was a public relations man for Harper, Nelson and Ferrel. Whenever a big-shot French, Italian, German or Spanish businessman came to New York, who had to show them around? Jim Brady. Who had to cement good relations? Good old reliable Brady. In the Velasquez affair alone he had saved the firm almost $40,000. And what had he gotten for it? Nothing. What he ought to do was to walk into Mr. Harper's office and pound his fist on the desk and demand a substantial raise.

Suppose Mr. Harper fired him instead? Who would make payments on the house and buy oil and groceries? Who would buy school clothes for the children? And pay for the refrigerator and the car and the television set? Who would keep up his insurance? What would happen to himself and May? It had taken him ten years to get as far as he had. He couldn't start all over. He was stuck.

Linguists and translators were a dime a dozen in New York. When the U.N. had sent out a call recently for interpreters, men who could speak four or more languages, the line of applicants had stretched for blocks. He knew. He'd spent his lunch hour in it.

Brady rode the rest of the way into New York glowering out the window. Just outside the train shed there was another short delay and word spread through the coach that it was because the Twentieth Century from Chicago was also late.

It was raining even harder in Manhattan and Grand Central smelled of plastic raincoats and wet wool. Brady's minor mental rebellion persisted. Instead of joining the rush for a cab, he walked out onto the street and into the nearest bar. He ordered a double rye. It was already past nine. A few more minutes wouldn't matter.

As he sipped his whiskey he stared through the rain-smeared window at the people scrambling for taxis in the main cab rank outside the station. A light-haired girl in a red plastic raincoat attracted his attention. The rain had molded the transparent fabric to her body. She was pert and pretty and worried. Her breasts thrust forward as she walked. Her small behind waved like a flag. Brady liked her. He liked her very much. She looked like the girls he used to see before he married May.

Brady paid for his drink and left the bar. It was raining too hard to walk to the office. The scramble for cabs was still going on in front of the station and Brady decided he'd stand a much better chance of getting one on the other side of 42nd Street. He started to weave his way through the traffic, only to step on a slick of oil and have his feet fly out from under him. Two cars narrowly missed running over him.

An irate Irish policeman helped him to his feet. "You drunk or something, Mister?" he demanded. "You trying to get yourself killed?"

Brady took his dripping hat from one bystander and his brief case from another. His trench coat was sodden with oily water. He'd torn a hole in the knee of his trousers. The wet brim of his hat dripped water in his eyes.

"No," he assured the policeman. "I like to roll in the street. I do it every rainy morning. It's part of my Yogi exercises."

The policeman wasn't happy with him. "If I had time I'd give you a ticket. I'd take you in myself," he promised. "Now get on with you while I clear up this mess you caused." He pushed Brady roughly back toward the curb and moved off into the rain blowing his whistle and waving his arms to get the stalled traffic started.

Brady stood on the curb and looked down at himself. His trench coat was a mess. He'd thrown out his right hand in an attempt to break his fall and his barked knuckles were streaming blood. He doubted that the tear in the knee of his trousers could be repaired. Now he'd have to buy a new suit. And there went another dent in the budget.

No longer caring how late he was, his brief case under one aim, Brady thrust his bleeding hand into the slash pocket of his trench coat and started to walk toward Fifth Avenue. He was immediately sorry for his decision. The rain was slanted from the west. It knifed into his eyes, almost blinding him. Then he saw a seemingly unoccupied cab at the curb. Its hood was raised and the cursing driver was trying to re-attach the small rubber hose feeding power to his balky windshield wipers.

Pressing his brief case to his side, Brady used his good hand to open the door of the cab and started to get in, only to realize it was occupied.

The girl in the red plastic raincoat was pressed as far as she could get against the side of the seat, staring at him with frightened eyes, while her numbed lips tried to scream.

Brady stopped awkwardly in the door of the cab, the rain dripping from the brim of his hat still partially blinding him, the raw flesh of his torn knuckles scraping against the pocket of his trench coat. He was annoyed with her, so annoyed that his apology came out more curtly than he intended it to sound.

"I'm sorry," he said. "But—"

The girl looked from his face to his hand bunched up in his trench coat pocket. "Oh, no," she pleaded. "Please don't."

Before Brady could back out of the cab she'd opened the door on the far side and scrambled out and was running across the street through the rain. A moment later there was the frenzied blast of an air horn and an even more frantic squeal of brakes and Brady thought he heard a scream, a scream quickly drowned out by the sounds of traffic and the shrill blare of a police whistle.

Brady eased his bleeding hand from his pocket to wipe the rain from his face as he fought down a desire to be sick. It wasn't his fault. It couldn't be.

He walked to the rear of the cab and stared across the street. It was raining too hard to see clearly but it looked as if two men, one a uniformed policeman, were kneeling on the wet pavement looking at someone or something lying in front of the high grille of a massive semi-trailer.

Mike Scaffidi closed the hood of his cab and joined Brady. "What gives, Mister?"

Brady was truthful. "I don't know. I thought the cab was empty and I started to get in, and a girl in a red raincoat begged me to please don't. Then before I could back out she opened the door on the far side and ran across the street and I'm afraid there's been an accident."

Scaffidi wiped the rain out of his eyes. "The things a guy runs into hacking. You know her, Mister?"

"I never saw her before."

"You want to talk to the cops?"

Brady considered his answer. He hadn't seen the accident. If he crossed the street and talked to the police, it would be another half-hour, perhaps longer, before he could get to the office. He might even have to appear in court. And Harper, Nelson and Ferrel didn't look kindly on employees who took time off for any reason. Besides, there was nothing he could tell the police. All he'd done was open the door of the cab.

"No, I guess not," he said finally.

He got into the cab and closed the door as the driver slid behind the wheel. "Me neither," Scaffidi admitted. "Yackity, yackity, yack. That's all them dumb cops know. And me, I got a living to make." He eyed the ticking meter sourly. "So the broad changes her mind about going to the Piccadilly and sticks me with a tripped meter. It's not the first time I been stuck." He raised the flag and lowered it again. "Where 'bouts for you, Mister?"

"Forty-sixth and Fifth Avenue."

As the cab pulled away from the curb and merged with the traffic Brady sat back on the seat and attempted to relax. Something sharp and pointed dug into his hip. It was a wonder, Brady thought, with the prices they charged, that the cab companies didn't check their cabs once in a while for broken springs.

TWO

Brady shifted in the back seat of the cab and felt around for the broken spring. Instead he found the package.

Neatly wrapped in silver paper and tied with baby blue ribbon, it was wedged between the cushion and the back of the seat. Of course it could have been in the cab for some time, but Brady felt it belonged to the girl in the red raincoat.

He leaned forward to speak to the driver and at the last moment changed his mind.

Brady wasn't proud of the way he'd acted. True, it had been raining. True, if he'd stopped he'd probably have been delayed for another half-hour. But he could have crossed the street and found out how badly the girl'd been hurt and why he'd frightened her so.

Surely after an accident like that, she'd be hospitalized and the story would be in the late afternoon and evening papers. A girl with a face and figure like hers couldn't help but make the papers. If the parcel belonged to her, he could deliver it in person and apologize at the same time. After all, he wasn't exactly the sort of man who went around frightening pretty girls.

He made a small tear in one corner of the silver paper to find what was in the parcel. There was a second layer of paper under the first. It looked like newsprint. He widened the tear and was certain. The underwrapping was a piece of newspaper. The bold-faced printing he could see read: CAGO TRIBU.

That could be the *Chicago Tribune*. Brady widened the tear still more. His guess was right. The inner wrapping was a section of the *Chicago Tribune*. Even more intrigued, he played detective. When the 8:25 from Stamford had been halted outside the train shed, the rumor had been it was because the Limited from Chicago was also late. Both trains had discharged their passengers at about the same time. If the girl in the red raincoat had been a passenger on the Limited, the parcel could certainly be hers.

Brady tore away the newsprint, then gasped and instinctively covered the parcel in his lap with his brief case. If his glimpse of the contents had been correct, he was holding a parcel of money—hundreds, perhaps thousands, of dollars, more money than he'd ever seen in his life.

It was almost cold in the cab but Brady could feel beads of perspiration on his face. He looked at the back of the cab driver's head, then at his framed license near the meter.

The driver's name was Mike Scaffidi. He was 42 years old, 5 feet 9 inches tall, weighing 170 pounds. He had black hair and black eyes.

Brady perspired harder. And Scaffidi hadn't seen the parcel. He didn't even know it was in his cab. He was too busy with traffic and the rain to even glance back at him.

Using the brief case to shield the parcel in the event Scaffidi should look around, Brady tore away still more newspaper. His first quick glimpse had been correct. The parcel held stacked sheaves of bills, none of them of less than 50-dollar denomination. There might be $10,000 in the parcel. There might be $100,000.

Brady swallowed the lump in his throat. The money was his. He temporized: at least the reward for finding the money was his. And there would surely be a reward, a substantial reward.

Brady barely managed to resist the temptation to rip open the parcel, spill the money on the seat and count it. The cab was crossing Forty-fourth Street now. He had less than two blocks to go. On impulse, he unzipped his empty brief case and stuffed the parcel inside. It was a tight fit. He had trouble getting the zipper shut.

When he'd finished and returned the case to his lap, Brady glanced at the driver again. Scaffidi hadn't even turned his head. He didn't have the least idea of what had gone on in the back of his cab.

Brady unwrapped the handkerchief from his knuckles and used it to pat at the perspiration on his face. He tried to tell himself this feeling like a thief was foolish. All he wanted was a reward. A little backlog. That was it. Say five hundred, possibly a thousand dollars. He had that much coming. His mind raced on. And if the money wasn't claimed, who was to know he had it? Even if the money was traced back to the cab, what could Scaffidi tell anyone?

"He was a man. He had two arms, two legs, one head. I picked him up near Grand Central Station. Out of 7,891,957 people in Greater New York I should describe one fare? On a rainy morning yet!"

When the cab stopped at Forty-sixth Street, Brady opened the door and thrust a dollar at the driver and left without waiting for his change. Once safe in the crowd on the walk, he looked back. An elderly man with gray hair was helping a younger woman into Scaffidi's cab. It was a perfect cover. No one but James A. Brady knew he had the parcel.

Brady waited until the cab moved on with the green light, then entered the foyer of his office.

Harper, Nelson and Ferrel occupied the entire sixteenth floor. As Brady got to the elevator, the receptionist gave him a conspiratorial smile and whispered, "A little late, aren't you, Mr. Brady?"

Brady returned the smile. "And wet."

"And bloody," the girl added as she surveyed his torn pants leg and barked knuckles.

"I fell down in front of Grand Central. Then when I couldn't get a cab,

I walked."

"You look it," the girl declared. She pushed an inter-office memo across her desk. "For you. You can guess from whom."

Brady looked at the memo. It read: Mr. Brady will report directly to my office.

Brady felt unimpressed. Instead of reporting directly to Harper's office, he walked to his desk and put his brief case in the bottom drawer. It seemed a very public place to leave so much money, but for the time being, it was the best he could do. Brady lit his third cigarette of the day and opened the door of Mr. Harper's private office without knocking.

"You wanted to see me?"

"I'd like to," Harper admitted, "I'd like to very much. But much closer to nine o'clock. You realize, of course, this is the second day in a week you've been late."

"Yes, sir," Brady answered. "I do."

"What's your excuse this time?"

"The same. My train was late."

The senior partner of Harper, Nelson and Ferrel was not impressed. "Very touching, Mr. Brady. Now let me tell you a few things, young man."

It was the brief case filled with money in the bottom drawer of his desk that did it. The words came out before he could stop them. "No," Brady said quietly. "Let me tell you a few things, Mr. Harper. I've been with this firm ten years with one brief break for the unpleasantness in Korea. And during those years I've only been late four times, two of them this week. Against that I've handled every account you've ever given me successfully. I've made money for the firm, a lot of money. I saved you almost $40,000 in the Velasquez deal alone. But every time some small thing comes up you proceed to eat off my tail. And I'm very tired of being pushed around. So if you're dissatisfied with me and my work, I think the best thing you can do is discharge me."

When Harper found his voice, it was surprisingly small. "No. No. Of course not. I assure you I'm perfectly satisfied with your work, Mr. Brady. Er, that will be all for now."

Brady closed the door behind him and swaggered slightly as he walked back to his desk, conscious that the conversation had been overheard and admiring eyes were following his progress.

One of the men spoke from the corner of his mouth. "Brother, was that telling him. What did May do? Feed you raw meat for breakfast this morning?"

Brady tried to work on a new French perfume account and was too excited to concentrate. Nothing mattered except the brief case full of money in the bottom drawer of his desk.

He knew now that he'd meant to keep the money from the start. It was his. He'd found it.

Brady closed his eyes briefly and saw the rows of tightly stacked sheaves again. He wondered how much they totaled. Not that it mattered greatly. There was enough. There was plenty. And however much there was, it was his.

THREE

The picture window on the twenty-third floor was huge. Through it one could see most of the Chicago skyline and part of Grant Park and the Outer Drive and beyond the Park and the Drive, the rocky shore line along Lake Michigan.

The furnishings of the office were in keeping with the chaste dignity of the window. Both the ankle deep, wall to wall carpeting and the heavy draw draperies were in excellent taste. So were the big dull green leather chairs and the massive director's desk.

Lew Dix had come a long way, almost to the end of the line. His conservative charcoal gray suit was tailored to his corpulent body almost without a wrinkle. His shirt was crisp, white and expensive. His tie was as conservative as his suit. He liked to think that the gray in his rapidly thinning hair made him look distinguished.

When it was possible, he preferred not to think of the old days. On occasion, when he did, it seemed incredible he had done some of the things he had, taken the chances he had taken. Fortunately, the old days were gone forever, along with Al Capone and Johnny Torrio and the Ghenna boys together with others, including the seven men lined up against the wall of a near-north-side garage to form a macabre valentine.

Dix preferred to forget such things. The Chicago Jungle, as such, was no more. A new order had come into being. A super efficient business organization and a specific allotment of territories had long since superseded the chaos. There were no more diamond belt buckles and very few one-way rides. What had to be done was done quietly by experts. Only a few noisy newcomers tried to keep the old traditions alive. There were times when he almost convinced himself that the wild stories he remembered from first hand participation were merely tales the old men had told between sips of grappa and puffs on their twisted black cigars.

Now it was much better. The money that had once been thrown away on drunken orgies and bullet-proof Cadillacs and hotel suites filled with squealing and willing hustlers now brought substantial dividends when invested in hotels and dry-cleaning plants; in laundries and breweries; in distilleries and wire services and various forms of banking.

Only one thing hadn't changed. That was the law of *omerta*. When the old men from Palermo called you answered. And when you were assigned an assessment you paid.

"Yes, sir," Dix said meekly into the phone. "She didn't show, eh? Yes, sir. I'll take care of it from this end." He started to cradle the phone and gripped the receiver even harder in his moist palms as the rapid stream of Sicilian on the other end of the wire asked a question. Dix's face turned gray as he answered in kind. "No, no, *Signore.* I swear by all the Saints that I dispatched the money."

For some moments after he'd cradled the phone he had to sit very still until he recovered his composure. Then glancing at the onyx clock on his desk he made a calculation. It was thirty-five minutes after four, Chicago time. That made it five thirty-five in New York, the end of the business day. If Linda Lou intended to show, if she intended to deliver the parcel, she should have done so eight hours ago. It seemed incredible that the girl would try to take a powder after all the warnings he'd given her about what would happen to her if she failed him. More likely she'd been hi-jacked. He'd warned her about that, too. No matter how clever a man tried to be, there was always one sonofabitch trying to outsmart him. Who could possibly have guessed that his semi-annual accounting with the elder statesmen of the Mafia was being carried by a nineteen-year-old girl in the form of a gift package wrapped in silver paper? Not even the Internal Revenue people were that clever.

He liked Linda Lou. He had big plans for her. It would pain him deeply if something happened to her or if he was forced to cause something to happen.

Before he acted, he decided to give the girl the benefit of the doubt and pushed the button on his desk. He spoke to his secretary, in a low voice.

"Will you please ring the St. Walter Hotel in New York, Miss Phillips, and ask if a Miss Linda Lou Larson has checked in?"

His secretary repeated the requested information. "Immediately, Mr. Dix."

Dix released the button. He hoped something had delayed Linda or that she was in her hotel room, afraid to complete the delivery, waiting for him to call. After all, she was just a child and from the deep South. And none too bright to begin with.

"Don't open the package," he'd warned her, "and keep your door locked on the train at all times. It's none of your business what you're carrying. But keep in mind at all times that there are a hundred men who would be very happy to kill you for what you're carrying."

That had been to impress her as to the value of the parcel. Now she hadn't even arrived. After all he'd planned for her. And if everything had worked out as he'd hoped, it could have been a very comfortable arrangement. There came a time in a man's life when street cars not only became few and far between, they eventually stopped running.

The corners of Dix's fat, wet lips turned down. His voice was still low and melodious, with only a trace of an accent. It matched the furnishings of the office. Only the words were out of place. "The dirty, chiseling little broad."

After all, he was Lew Dix. Hundreds of thousands of dollars passed through his hands every day and considerable sums of it stayed. He had a home in Lake Forest. He drove a Continental Mark II. It had been twelve years since he'd even been in a police station. He was a big man in Chicago. He was a big man in the organization. It was perfectly proper for him to diddle anyone he wanted to. But if a two bit blonde with a corn-pone drawl thought she could diddle him, she was betting on the wrong horse.

He wouldn't have entrusted the money to her in the first place if the Federal men weren't watching him so closely. Just let the Internal Revenue boys get a sniff at that package and figure what percentage of his income it represented and after he'd done his time in Atlanta or Leavenworth or Alcatraz, another Federal court would send him over to play dominoes with Luciano.

Miss Phillips spoke through the annunciator. "I am sorry, Mr. Dix, but I cannot contact your party. The room clerk at the St. Walter Hotel reports that a Miss Linda Lou Larson has a reservation but she hasn't checked in yet."

"Thank you," Dix said. "Will you kindly ask Mr. Daly and Mr. Morgan to step in?"

He sat back in his chair feeling old and very tired. He disliked matters like this. They smacked too much of the old days. Still, discipline had to be enforced and not even the most reputable businessman could allow himself to be robbed of more money than ten average men made in a year. It was bad for morale. It gave young punks and twists on their way up the erroneous idea that a man was slipping.

Besides, there were the old men from Palermo currently residing on Bleecker Street. And when the Mafia said pay, you paid. Or wished you had.

Dix took a fat cigar from his humidor and eyed the two youths who entered his office with distaste. Even the style in enforcers had changed. There was nothing deadly looking about Daly or Morgan. Their well cut suits were modified Ivy League. They had innocent boyish airs about them. Except for the slight hardness in their eyes and the bulges under their arm pits, they might be college seniors.

"Yes?" Daly asked.

Dix lighted his cigar, "It seems Linda Lou didn't make it."

Morgan rolled his pork pie hat in his hands. "Oh?" he asked with interest.

"So you better go see what detained her. There's a train at six-forty-five."

"If you don't mind," Daly said, "we'll take a plane. It's faster." He breathed on his immaculate nails and buffed them on the palm of his hand. "Any instructions?"

Dix's righteous indignation showed through his painfully acquired veneer. "Just find that goddamn money and turn it over to you know who. It's in a silver paper gift wrapped parcel about so long and so wide."

"We know," Morgan said quietly. "We put her on the train. And—Linda…?"

Dix was silent for a long moment. Not that he'd gotten to first base so far but he was genuinely fond of Linda Lou, as fond as he could be of a broad. He liked her pert young brightness. He liked the way she walked, the way she talked. He liked the way she fended him off, reminding him that he'd employed her to do one certain thing. And that didn't include the use of her body. Most broads started to peel as soon as they learned he was *the* Lew Dix. The little girl from the deep South had promised to be a refreshing relief from the frenzied acrobatics of the usual North Clark Street babes and the stolid placidity of the old country wife to whom he'd been married for over thirty years.

Still, one leak in the dike could be serious. There wasn't always a good *Italiano* boy to put his finger in the hole. And by now Linda knew too much.

"You know what to do."

"We dig," Daly nodded.

Dix disliked the off-beat generation. Their terms confused him. "You dig what?" he puzzled.

"We understand," Daly translated.

Dix opened the door for them. "Then why the hell didn't you say so?"

When they had gone, for some reason he felt cold. He didn't like either Morgan or Daly but they were good men. They knew what they had to do. They had done it before. And, if it were still possible, they would recover the money.

He realized his fingers were trembling and returned his cigar to his mouth. He really felt sorry for Linda Lou. Or was he just mourning his youth? She was too young and pretty, she had too much life still unlived to be forced to face Daly and Morgan. Still, she should have delivered the money.

Depressing the button of the annunciator, he asked Miss Phillips to phone for his car.

"We're leaving a little early, aren't we?" she asked.

"A little," Dix admitted.

As he slipped into his expensive vicuña topcoat he wondered why. He had no special place to go. Most of his old friends were dead, machine gun scars on a cathedral step, closed files in the police hall of records, disintegrating mounds of dirt on lonely country roads. He couldn't even get drunk. Whiskey upset his stomach.

Yes. He'd had great plans for Linda Lou, ever since he'd seen her behind the twenty-six game in one of the taverns he owned. She was to have brightened his old age. She could have had anything she wanted. All she would have had to do was point. It was nice to just look at a young girl. It made a man feel warm and capable again.

He stood a moment looking out the picture window at the deepening dusk. Yes. Linda Lou could have had anything she wanted. Now all she'd have would be Daly and Morgan. Maybe a squib in a New York paper—

The body of an unidentified young woman was found early this morning by....

What difference did it make by whom? Once the bird had flown, who cared about the cage?

Dix drew the heavy curtains. He would go home, he decided, and ask Maria to make some veal parmagiana. While he ate he would drink sour red wine. Then after supper Maria would cover her head with the black shawl and go to church. And he would ask her to burn a candle. He needn't tell her who for.

FOUR

The rental cabins, four in number, were built on a low bluff overlooking a brackish river flowing between silted shallows matted with flowering hyacinth. Closer to the road, hanging over the sagging doorway of an unpainted, cypress-planked building, a weathered sign informed passersby this was DELLA'S PLACE and she had beer and gasoline for sale and cabins and boats for rent.

At the foot of the low bluff a crude pier extended into the shallow water. The only visible signs of life were the nude girl bathing in the river, a high-wheeling flight of vultures and four long-legged white herons spearing fish near the shore. In a few minutes it would be dark but for now the sun still hung over the half-dead cypress trees.

Using one of the row boats tied to the pier as a dressing table, Linda Lou soaped her slight body thoroughly, then waded out thigh deep and splashed water on her face and breasts and shoulders.

This was the hour of the day she liked best. The rented boats were in and the day drunks had gone home to their suppers. Della was taking her nap in preparation for the evening's business. Linda Lou reveled in her solitude. For this one hour there was no slatternly mother to jaw at her, no beery propositions from men old enough to be her father, no amorous male eyes trying to see through her skirt. With night the parking space in front of DELLA'S PLACE would fill with cars, all of the cars filled with men, all of whom would want three things, beer, whiskey and Della. With dark the juke box would compete with the second-hand television set that Della had bought in Fort Myers. There would be laughing and cursing and fighting. Sometime during the night someone would get cut. Then fat Deputy Sheriff Haffey would drive out from Osceola to make an investigation. But Deputy Haffey was as bad as the rest. Della would get him half drunk and honey and sugar him until the fat man would get so excited he'd want to go in the back room. And when he and Della came out again, if the hurt man hadn't been knifed too badly, that would be the end of the matter. It happened every Saturday night.

Linda Lou lifted her head and watched the flight of the vultures. She wished she had wings. "I'd fly so gawddamn far away from here," she thought, "it would take five dollars' postage to send me a penny picture card."

Her mind raced on. She could go to Jacksonville or Memphis or maybe even as far as Chicago. Linda Lou stopped pretending. She and Della had had a big scene the night before and Della had slapped her mouth until it bled. "You're a big girl now," her mother had told her. "I've supported you since you were just a lap baby and it's only right and fittin' you give me a hand in the back room. It ain't that I mind the work. I like it. But it purely pains me to see us missing all the money you could earn. You're young and you're pretty and there is plenty of the boys who only pay me two dollars who would give as much as five to go into the back room with you."

The thought made Linda Lou sick. She was willing to do all the cooking and the cleaning. She was willing to draw beer and wash dishes. She was willing to net bait and sell it, and gut fish for the successful fishermen. But she couldn't go into the back room with just any man. She wouldn't. Someway, somehow, she had to get away from here....

Linda Lou tried to shut out her mother's face and failed. Then opening one eye, she realized she was lying on a hospital bed in New York City with a tired intern examining her.

Seeing she was conscious, the intern asked, "How do you feel, Miss?"

"All right, I guess," she told him.

The nurse assisting the intern covered the lower part of her body with a sheet. "Well?"

The intern washed his hands in a basin, "Nothing serious, I'd say. Just bruised and shaken up a bit. But I think we'd better hold her for a day or two."

The nurse handed him a clean towel. "The officers who brought her in want to know."

The intern nodded, "I'll talk to them. Get her a gown and take her up to Ward B. I'll fill out the report and check her again this afternoon."

The intern walked around and behind the bed and Linda Lou could no longer see him. She could dimly hear his lowered voice and the voices of two other men.

"How is she?" one of them asked.

"I'm Manson," the other man said. "I believe you know Sergeant Hooper."

"Yes," the intern said. "I do. Nice to see you, Hooper. Now as to the girl. I'd say nothing serious. No broken bones. No internal injuries. More shock than anything else. What happened to her?"

"As we get the story," Manson said, "she tried to cross Forty-second Street in the rain and ran into a truck. The driver said he just looked up and there she was."

"It happens every day."

Manson added, "With one exception. What witnesses we could find say she was running when she was hit. You know. Like she was frightened. Or maybe someone was chasing her. She say anything to you?"

"Just that she felt all right," the intern said.

"Is it okay for us to talk to her now?"

"Of course." There was a brief scrape of feet and the intern added, "But before you do I'd appreciate any information you have on her. For my report."

"It's right here," Sergeant Hooper said, "on her Illinois driver's license. The name is Linda Lou Larson. Clark Street Arms Hotel. Occupation model."

"How about money?"

"Four hundred and forty-four dollars and sixty-five cents. Plus the return half of a New York Central round-trip ticket from Chicago."

Linda Lou closed her eyes again. A model. That was a laugh, though God knew she'd tried. But all the agencies said the same thing. Her measurements and proportions were perfect but she was too short. You had to be at least five feet five to work for the better agencies. Some of the smaller agencies didn't care how tall a girl was. All the men who ran them wanted to know was how a girl looked flat on her back. But if she'd intended to go in for that sort of thing she might as well have stayed at Della's. She was trying desperately not to think of Mr. Dix or the parcel but the conversation in the hall made it impossible.

"Chicago, eh?" the intern asked. "What's she doing in New York?"

"That's what we want to ask her," one of the other men said.

Linda Lou pulled the sheet up to her chin and tried to make herself even smaller than she was. When she opened her eyes, two pleasant-faced middle-aged men were standing beside the bed, smiling down on her.

"I'm Sergeant Hooper," one of them introduced himself. "And this is my partner Officer Manson."

Linda Lou acknowledged the introduction with a sweep of her eyelids. "How do you do?"

"We're fine," Hooper assured her. "How about you, Miss Larson?"

Linda Lou tried to smile. "Fine, now. And if it's all right with you gentlemen, as soon as the nurse brings me my clothes, I'll leave."

Officer Manson patted her arm. "Take it easy now, Miss. You had a nasty experience."

You should just know how nasty, the girl thought.

Manson asked, "Do you mind if we ask a few questions?"

Linda Lou tried not to look frightened. "What sort of questions?"

"About how the accident happened."

"Oh. Well, I just tried to cross the street."

"In the middle of the block?"

"I was in a hurry."

"That seems obvious." Sergeant Hooper made a few notes in a small, black leather book. "How long have you been in New York, Miss Larson?"

Linda Lou considered her answer. She didn't know too much about the police, but she did know it was wise to tell them as much of the truth as possible. "Just since this morning," she said. "I came in on the Twentieth Century from Chicago."

Manson smiled, "That drawl doesn't come from Chicago."

"No," Linda Lou admitted. "I was born in Florida. Near a little town on the Tamiami Trail."

Sergeant Hooper wrote the information in his book. "Why didn't you take a cab from the station?"

Linda Lou took a deep breath and lied. "I couldn't get one."

"So you walked toward Fifth Avenue?"

"That's right."

"In the rain?"

"I was wearing a raincoat."

"How about your baggage?"

"I didn't have any."

"You're positive?"

"I'm positive."

Officer Manson took over the questioning. "Look, Miss Larson. Believe me. We're trying to help you. You've had a nasty experience and the doctor says you're supposed to rest, but there are a few questions we have to ask you. Are you in some kind of trouble?"

Linda Lou evaded the question. "I think you'd call it trouble to be knocked down by a truck and have all your clothes taken away and come to in a strange hospital."

"That's not the kind of trouble I mean," Manson said. "According to witnesses, you were running across the street through the rain, as fast as you could run, when you ran into that truck."

"I was hurrying," Linda Lou said.

"Was someone chasing you?"

"No."

"Had someone frightened you?"

Linda Lou liked these men. They were trying to help her and she was tempted to tell them the truth. But if she did, Mr. Dix would kill her or have her killed. She felt as if she was still running, lying in the bed. Mr. Dix would probably have her killed anyway if she didn't recover the parcel. He would never believe she'd been so frightened she'd bolted out of the cab leaving all that money behind.

She wished now she hadn't been so curious, but it was partly Mr. Dix's fault. If he hadn't warned her over and over not to open the parcel and told her a hundred men would be happy to kill her for it, she wouldn't have been so curious to know what she was carrying. So she'd opened the parcel and there was all that money. And from then on she'd been terrified. It had been only natural when the big man had opened the door of the cab and pointed a gun at her through his trench coat pocket that she'd panicked. She hadn't wanted to die. She hadn't run away from Della and waited on tables in Jacksonville and worked in an office in Memphis and become a twenty-six girl in Chicago to die at nineteen.

Manson said, "I asked you a question, Miss Larson. Had someone frightened you?"

"No," Linda Lou lied.

"Then why were you running across the street against traffic?"

The girl said the first thing that came to her mind. "I saw a cab on the other side. Or thought I did."

"In all that rain?"

"Yes, sir."

Manson tried a new line of questioning. "You hadn't had a fight with your boy friend? You weren't trying to get yourself killed?"

"No."

"But you do have a boy friend?"

"No, I don't."

Sergeant Hooper passed the palm of his hand over his mouth, then nodded to Officer Manson. "We're wasting our time here. That will be all for now, Miss."

For a moment Linda Lou was hopeful. "I can leave?"

"In a day or two. The doctor says you seem all right but he wants to hold you for observation."

Linda Lou could feel a fine film of perspiration forming over her entire body. She couldn't stay where she was. She had to get out of the hospital and try to recover the parcel as soon as she could. She protested, "But I have to leave."

"I'm sorry," Sergeant Hooper said. Then he and Officer Manson disappeared again and she could hear them talking to the intern.

"I begged to be sent to Bellevue," the intern said. "But this is earning your shingle the hard way. So a babe gets bumped on her pretty fanny. From the report I have to fill in you'd think she had her uterus taken out."

Both officers laughed.

"You fellows get what you wanted?" the intern asked.

"No," Manson said. "We didn't. The girl is much more scared than hurt. But she's not talking about why she's scared."

"Is that important?"

"It could be. She's both scared and lying. According to the story she tells she was running across the street because she'd seen a cab on the far side. This is Forty-second Street, mind you. At rush hour. With it raining so hard you couldn't see fifteen feet."

"You figure someone was chasing her?"

"Could be. Anyway, I think we'll snoop around a little."

"And the girl?"

"Hold her as long as you can. Just as a precaution. We feel there's something wrong with the set-up. We know she's frightened of something and we'd like to find out what it is before it catches up with her."

"Okay. We'll hold her as long as we can," the intern said.

Linda Lou continued to lie very still after the voices died away. It was the first time she'd ever been in a hospital but she was pretty sure the hospital wouldn't let her go until the police said she could leave.

Meanwhile the parcel of money was getting more and more lost. Anything was possible now. When his New York office phoned Mr. Dix and told him she hadn't arrived, Mr. Dix might even think she'd stolen the money.

She cried silently. She wished she was back in Chicago. She almost wished she was back at Della's. Even if everything had gone right, there was still the other problem to be faced. Mr. Dix wanted her. He'd told her so in his office in so many words while he had tried to put his fat hands where all men wanted to put their hands. Linda Lou lifted the sheet and looked down at her body. But she hadn't let him then and if she did get out of this mess she wouldn't let him when she got back to Chicago. She hadn't gone through all she had only to wind up in bed with a limp old man. If that had been all she'd wanted out of life she might as well have gone into the back room with fat Tom Haffey. At least he hadn't smelled of garlic.

The nurse helped her to sit up and slip into a short hospital gown, then swabbed a spot on the fleshy part of her arm with a piece of cotton soaked in alcohol.

"No. Please," Linda Lou protested, then winced as the hypodermic needle pierced her flesh.

"Doctor's orders," the nurse said crisply. "Just a little something to quiet our nerves."

Linda Lou doubted if her nerves would ever be quiet again. She forced herself to think so she could tell Mr. Dix exactly what had happened. Perhaps, if she told him the truth, he would believe her.

To begin with her train had been fifteen minutes late. Because she was late and frightened she hadn't even stopped to claim her luggage. She'd gone directly to the street from the station and gotten into the first cab she could and told the driver to take her to the St. Walter Hotel.

Two hundred or three hundred feet from the station, the driver had pulled to the curb and mumbled something about his windshield wipers not working and had gotten out to fix them.

Frightened as she was, wondering if it were a possible trick and the driver knew what she was carrying, she had stuffed the parcel between the cushion and the back of the seat. She'd attempted to memorize the driver's license so she could identify him if she had to.

Then what she'd feared might happen, what Mr. Dix had warned her might happen, had happened. A big man, with the brim of his hat turned down and the collar of his coat turned up had yanked the door open and pointed his concealed gun at her.

But had the big man really pointed a gun at her? The more she thought about it the less certain she was.

He hadn't pointed a gun. He'd had his hand in his coat pocket and she, already terrified, had imagined the gun. Her relief was immediate and intense.

For the first time since she'd regained consciousness, Linda Lou allowed herself to hope. Following her line of reasoning, if the man hadn't been a killer, if he hadn't been after the parcel, it could still be where she'd stuffed it, or even waiting for her in the lost and found department of the taxi cab company. To an unknowing eye, it was only a gift-wrapped parcel of no particular value.

She had to remember the name on the cab driver's license. The first name was Mike. She was sure of that. She remembered because she'd thought at the time it was odd to combine an Irish name with an Italian one. She had it now. The last name had been Scaffidi. All she had to do was phone the lost and found department of the cab company and ask them to check Mr. Mike Scaffidi's cab and hold the parcel they found in it for her.

Linda Lou tried to swing her feet and legs off the high bed and partially succeeded before the nurse noticed her and returned her to her former position. "Now, now. We mustn't excite ourselves, must we?" the nurse said. "We wouldn't want to be put in restraints, would we?"

Her body numb and her tongue thick from the sedative she'd been given, Linda Lou attempted to protest. "Cab," she said distinctly. "Must call the cab—" Then the sedative taking hold, her eyelids fluttered shut and her voice trailed off into an unintelligible murmur just as the youthful intern, finished with his paper work, handed the nurse the order transferring her patient from the Emergency Room to a bed in Ward B.

"What gives with her?" he asked the nurse.

"She wanted to call a cab," the nurse told him.

FIVE

Brady didn't know one day could be so long. The click of the keys on the I.B.M. machines and the battery of typewriters around him were so many tiny mallets thudding against the back of his head. The voices of his fellow workers sounded strained and unnaturally loud.

Brady decided to tell no one about his find, especially May. May's sharp tongue was hinged on both edges. Once she learned he'd found the money the news would be all over their neighborhood within an hour. Brady reluctantly admitted something to himself: he'd been a fool to marry May. He'd allowed a few good home-cooked meals and a few hurried dalliances on a divan, after the children had gone to bed, to trap him into a loveless marriage. He'd been a bachelor pigeon, a sitting duck, a fugitive from a lonely hotel room. He didn't love May. May didn't love him. A widow with two children to support, she'd merely traded her body and what homemaking skill she possessed for a steady meal ticket.

And now there was Alice to consider.

At the thought of Alice, Brady forgot the money and considered his fifteen-year-old stepdaughter. Alice had matured early. At fifteen she was as physically developed as she would ever be. Her breasts were larger than May's. She had a pretty derriere and lovely thighs and she insisted on displaying them to him on any occasion when May happened to be out of the house.

"Please," she'd begged him. "Please. I've been with boys but never with a man. Please. Please, Jim. Mother'll never know."

Brady patted the perspiration from his face. There was one word for Alice. Alice was a little bitch. If the situation didn't hold all the potentialities of a family tragedy, it could be very funny. A fifteen-year-old girl who admitted she was no longer a virgin, eager to replace the amateur efforts of the boys with the mature lovemaking of her thirty-four-year-old stepfather. And he didn't dare to tell May. Without question she'd side with her daughter and probably have him arrested for attempting to force his attentions on the child.

"If you don't, I'll tell Mother you did," Alice had said last night. "I'll tell her you've been seducing me since right after you and Mother were married."

Brady put his elbows on his desk and sat with his head in his hands. The mess a man could make of his life, without half trying....

Five o'clock finally came and Brady shrugged into his trench coat and tucked the brief case under his arm. He would count the money in one of the booths in the men's washroom at Grand Central.

Fifth Avenue was gray with dusk. It had stopped raining but the air was raw with promise of winter. As he walked south toward Forty-second Street, he occasionally glanced behind him. No one had been waiting when he left the building. No one was following him. No one knew what he had in his brief case.

He was well pleased with himself until a new worry assailed him. He couldn't take the parcel home. May had sharp eyes. She would immediately spot his bulging brief case and wonder what he was carrying. She might even open it and May was the one person in all the world whom he didn't want to know that he'd come into money. May would have it spent before he could take off his hat and coat.

The little things. The little things that matter.

Brady cut down Forty-third Street to Sixth Avenue and entered a small luggage shop and bought an exact duplicate of his own cheap brief case for four dollars and eight-five cents. During the ride home on the train he could scuff it up and rub a little soot into the leather, May wouldn't be able to tell one case from the other. And after he'd counted the money he could leave his old case with the parcel in it in one of the lockers in Grand Central. It would be perfectly safe there until he figured out some better place to keep it.

When he reached the station he went directly to the lower level washroom. It was crowded with commuters. He had to wait for a stall, then had to get change from the attendant so he could drop a dime in the slot.

Once inside, his anticipation was so great that his hands perspired so badly he had trouble unzipping the case. The parcel was still in it. Sitting on the toilet top he took out one sheaf of bills. They were of three denominations, twenty, fifty and one hundred dollars bills, none of them new, all of them bills that had been in use for a while and would be impossible to trace.

He'd counted to three thousand five hundred dollars and was barely started on a second sheaf when a heavy hand rapped on the door and a man asked: "You going to stay there all night? I got a train to make."

"Just a minute," Brady called.

He went back to fingering the bills but he'd lost track of the total he'd already counted. It was either four thousand five hundred or five thousand four hundred. Either way, he'd barely begun. It would take him at least two hours to count the bills in all the sheaves. And the man outside was rapping again. This wasn't the place or time to count the contents of the parcel.

If possible, so as to give May no cause to wonder, he wanted to catch the 5:35 as usual and he had less than five minutes to get on the train.

He stuffed the parcel back into the brief case and shut it. He left the stall and put the brief case into one of the lockers in the first bank of lockers that he came to. He was starting to close the door when something about the appearance of his brief case stopped him. Then he realized what was different about it.

The plastic tag bearing his name and address and phone number, normally attached to the handle of the case, was missing.

Brady lifted the case and felt under the leather. The tag hadn't fallen off in the locker. He tried to remember when he'd last seen it and was positive it had been on the case when he left Stamford that morning. Otherwise he would have noticed it was missing.

It could have dropped off on the train. It could have fallen off in the drawer. It could have fallen in the stall.

The short hairs on the back of Brady's neck began to tingle.

It could have ripped off in the taxi when he'd had to force the zipper closed after stuffing in the parcel.

There was no use minimizing the matter. A new, potentially dangerous element had been added to a relatively simple experience of finding a parcel of money. If anyone found the tag it could easily be traced to him. The lettering on the tag was specific. It read:

James A. Brady
1134 E. Elm Street
Stamford, Conn.
Stam, 3-4124

SIX

As with the rest of the house the dining room was small. May was telling an endless tale about a wrangle with one of the tradesmen.

"Then I asked him if he thought I was a fool," May droned on. "I told him right to his face that he wasn't running the only meat market in Stamford. A dollar and twenty cents a pound for round steak. And not even a middle cut at that. So I walked right out of the store."

Brady transferred his attention to Alice. It wasn't difficult to do. As usual, she was trying to play footsies under the table. Sitting beside her as he was he couldn't help but see down her loose-necked dress every time she leaned forward to fork a bite off her plate. Intentionally or otherwise, she wasn't wearing a brassiere and every time she leaned forward she made sure he saw the tips of her breasts. They were young and firm and solid. Brady wondered just how much a man was supposed to take.

He was relieved when Jimmy broke in on his mother's conversation. "About that bike," he demanded. "Why can't I have a new bike?"

Brady pointed out that his mother was speaking and it wasn't polite for a boy to interrupt his elders. May immediately defended her son.

"All the boy did was ask you a question. Why *can't* he have a new bike? All the other boys in the neighborhood have new bicycles. And he has to ride that old thing."

Brady started to say that a new bike was out of the question and to preserve the peace changed his answer to, "I'll see."

"And about time," May said. She speared another piece of the steak. "After all, now that we live in Stamford, we have a certain position to maintain."

Oh, for Christ's Sake, Brady thought but was careful to avoid saying it. He didn't want to quarrel with May tonight.

"When?" Jimmy wanted to know. "When will you see?"

To keep the peace, Brady partially committed himself. "Perhaps next payday."

As he spoke, Brady felt Alice reach out under the table and knead his inner thigh, her hot little fingers gradually working higher. The child was getting bolder every day. He wished he knew what to do about it. He was damned if he did and damned if he didn't.

"If you don't, I'll tell Mother you have. That you've been seducing me since right after you and she were married."

And wouldn't that be a pretty mess. With Alice ten years old at the time. Any jury of adults would send him away for twenty years for child molestation, if they didn't order him committed to a hospital for the criminally insane.

"What are you sweating about?" May asked him.

Brady reached under the table cloth and brushed his stepdaughter's hand away. "Nothing. Nothing at all."

He refrained from looking at Alice. In an undeveloped way she reminded him of the girl in the red plastic raincoat. He still wished he knew why she'd been so frightened of him and made a mental note to read the evening paper thoroughly. The accident hadn't been important enough to make the front page but he might find something about her on one of the inside pages.

"Why do I have to wait till next payday?" Jimmy whined. "Why can't I have a new bike right now?"

His whine grated on Brady's ears. Alice's hand had found his thigh again. Brady pushed back his chair and stood up. "All right. For Christ's sake you can have one. I'll give your mother the money in the morning and you can buy one tomorrow."

May was hurt. "Well, you don't need to use profanity in front of the children."

Brady wished he dared tell her what her beloved daughter had been doing to him.

May added, primly, "Just because you had a bad day at the office is no reason for you to come home and take it out on us."

Brady started to tell her he hadn't had a bad day at the office, that it had been the best day he'd had since he had started to work for Harper, Nelson and Ferrel and was afraid he might say too much. Instead, he walked into the living room, picked the evening paper from the table and lighted a cigarette. He felt hemmed in on all sides, as if he were in an elastic trap.

The money he'd found could be the answer. Money could solve a lot of his problems.

Alice followed him in from the dining area and stood beside his chair, running her fingers through his hair. Her voice was a conspiratorial whisper. "You liked what I did at the table, didn't you? I could tell."

Brady whispered back fiercely, "You ought to have your dirty little mind washed out with soap. Don't ever do that again."

"Why not?"

"It isn't right and I don't like it."

Her voice was as hot as her eyes. "Yes, you did. I could tell."

"Stop saying that," Brady said.

The child was sick. She had to be. Normal fifteen-year-old girls didn't act this way. He couldn't think of the name but it was a form of mental disease, coupled with a too rapidly developed body and an over-active thyroid gland. She needed medical care.

May came to the door of the living room and looked at them

suspiciously. "What are you two whispering about?"

"Nothing," Alice said sullenly and left the room.

When May returned to the kitchen, Brady opened his paper but couldn't read the print. It was too blurred. He felt put upon and soiled, as if he'd been rolling in slime. If the child acted that way with him, God only knew what she was doing with boys of her own age. And if she was being promiscuous, it was inevitable she would become pregnant. And probably blame him. Perhaps she was pregnant now and that was why she was determined to be intimate with him. So she would have someone to blame.

"He forced me," the little bitch would tell May with a straight face. "While you were out of the house. I didn't want to but Daddy made me."

And nothing he could say would convince May otherwise.

He wondered if boarding school was a possible solution. If he could think of some way to explain his sudden affluence, there was plenty of money in the parcel to send Alice to a good boarding school. His mind raced on. He could tell May he'd gotten a substantial raise. He would. Just as soon as he had a chance to determine how much money was in the parcel. Ten thousand dollars? Twenty thousand? Thirty?

His paper still unread, Brady forced himself to think.

In the normal course of events no businessman transported so large a sum of money in cash. That was what banks and bank drafts were for. That could mean, it probably did mean, the sheaves of money came from some illegitimate source. He didn't know whether to be pleased or worried by the deduction. It was one thing to deal with an absent-minded businessman. It was something entirely different to become involved with the underworld. The boys on the other side of the fence played rough. They *liked* to kill people and would on the slightest pretext.

Brady turned to the lost and found column in the paper. People had lost watches and rings and purses and cocker spaniels but there was no mention of anything resembling the parcel.

Brady went through the paper thoroughly, scanning each page. He found what he was looking for in the second section.

> Miss Linda Lou Larson, 19, of the Clark Street Arms
> Hotel, Chicago, was admitted to the Bellevue Hospital
> this morning after being struck by a motor vehicle on
> E. 42nd St. Sgt. Joel Hooper of the 52nd St. station says
> no charges were filed against the driver of the vehicle.

He rolled the name on his tongue. Linda Lou. It had a pleasant sound. There was almost magnolia and moonlight in it. Brady glanced back at the filler, wishing there were more details. At least a mention of how badly the girl had been injured.

May finished the dishes and came into the living room. She noticed the tear in his trousers. "And just how did you do that?"

"I fell down," Brady said.

"Your next to your best suit, too."

"I didn't have time to change."

May sighed as she claimed the first section of the paper. "Sometimes I don't understand you, Jim. I should think, having been a bachelor as long as you were, you'd appreciate having a happy family. But no. You want to quarrel all the time." She asked, in sudden suspicion, "You haven't lost your job, have you? Mr. Harper didn't fire you because you were late this morning, did he?"

"No."

"Then why are you acting so strangely tonight?"

"I wasn't aware that I was acting strangely."

May settled herself on the sofa. "Well, you're certainly not yourself."

The evening was as endless as the day had been. Still sullen-eyed, Alice sat on a chair right across from Brady, with her feet on the cushion of the chair and her chin resting on her drawn-up knees, managing, despite her mother's occasional admonition to sit like a lady, to expose herself to Brady more than once. There was nothing unusual about the evening. They listened to Jimmy's favorite television programs until he went to bed at ten o'clock. At ten-thirty, still sullen-eyed, Alice made up her bed in the so-called den and May announced it had been a long day and she, too, was going to bed. Brady wanted to sit up for the late newscast on the chance the newscaster might say something about the parcel of money or the girl in the red plastic raincoat but he hesitated to attract attention to himself and followed May into the bedroom.

He'd taken to showering and shaving at night to save time in the morning and when he did manage to get into the bathroom he had to dodge wet stockings and a pair of May's briefs to get to the sink. This was living? The money could change all this, if he could manage to hold on to it. He meant to.

He deliberately took more time than usual in the bathroom but the bed lamp was still on and May was still awake when he finally returned to their bedroom. As he sat on the edge of the bed and set and wound the alarm clock, she regarded him thoughtfully.

"Are you certain you're all right, Jim?"

"I'm positive," he assured her. "Why?"

"You act funny to me."

"It's your imagination."

As he turned out the light and stretched out beside her, May's voice felt its way through the stuffy darkness. "Are you catching one of your colds?"

"I feel fine," Brady assured her.

He hoped May wasn't in one of her rare amorous moods. After the business with Alice, despite the fact that he was a normal male and the child's fondling had excited him, the very thought of sex at the moment was disgusting. He wanted no part of May or her daughter. May wasn't amorous. Her goodnight kiss was slippery with face cream.

"Well, if you won't tell me, you won't. But *something* is bothering you."

She turned on her side and a few minutes later she fell asleep.

Brady lay staring up into the darkness. A half-hour passed, then an hour. Brady was waiting for the late newscast at midnight. At five minutes of twelve, by the luminous dial of his watch, he eased himself out of bed and tiptoed into the living room. Being careful to keep the volume very low, he turned on the television set. While he waited for the current commercial to finish and the newscast to begin he made himself a stiff highball.

The foreign news came first. Sitting on the edge of one of the straight-backed chairs in the living room, Brady listened without interest to the latest machinations of Nikita S. Khrushchev & Company. Then he realized he wasn't alone in the room.

The girl's hot whisper felt for him through the darkness. "Couldn't you sleep, either?"

Oh, God, Brady thought. Do I have to go through that again? The girl passed in front of the lighted picture tube and he saw that it was even worse than he'd thought. As far as he could tell the child was completely nude and she was no longer a child. She was a small woman complete with jutting breasts, concave stomach and a psychopathic obsession for him.

"I haven't any clothes on," she said proudly.

Brady started to get up and leave the room and couldn't. Alice had plumped herself down on his lap. As her bare flesh touched his, Brady's reaction was normal and immediate. He sat, rigid, ashamed of himself, ashamed of her. "You little fool," he whispered, tersely. "What if your mother should wake up?"

The girl's voice was thick and sick with passion. "She won't. But you know what I told you. You'd better. And right now. Oh, please. Please, Jim."

Why not, Brady thought. If I don't she'll lie anyway. Perhaps this way she'll give me some peace. After all, it's not exactly incest. She's no relation of mine. If she's so hell determined, why not? Then reason asserted itself. Alice was just a child. He couldn't let her do this thing. One hand still holding the highball glass, he tried to push her away with the other.

"Please, Jim. Please help me," she whimpered, then the whimper turned into a moan as she partially accomplished her purpose, only to have Brady turn sideways on the chair and push her away from him so hard she fell sprawled on the sofa.

"You bitch. You filthy little bitch," he cursed her. "Go tell your mother. Go tell her anything you want. But leave me alone. Understand?"

Panting with the effort, he walked down the hall to the bathroom and closed and locked the door. Then he was suddenly and violently sick in the toilet. What kind of a nightmare had he gotten himself into? In another second or two he wouldn't have been able to help himself. Male flesh could only take so much. In another second or two, with her enthusiastic consent and cooperation, he would have taken his own stepdaughter on the chair or the sofa or the floor of the living room.

He ran cold water in the sink and splashed it on his face and body. One thing was certain. Things couldn't go on like this. He had to find some solution.

It was stifling hot in the small bathroom with the window closed. Brady cranked it open to let the cold night air come in and stood motionless, staring down at the street.

A big, dark sedan was cruising slowly between the elm trees. As it passed under the street light in front of the house, Brady could see there were two men in it. One of them was doing the driving while the other studied the numbers on the houses.

Two strangers looking for an address, perhaps the address on a lost plastic tag.

James A. Brady
1134 E. Elm Street

Brady half expected the car to stop. It didn't. It drove on slowly and as the twin red tail lights grew dim and merged with the night, he fought down another desire to be sick. He didn't give a damn whose money it was. He wouldn't give it up. It was his. He'd found it.

After another five minutes he unlocked the bathroom door and looked out. The television was still on but Alice was no longer in the room. He thought he heard her crying in the den.

Still breathing hard, he turned off the television set and went in and lay down beside his wife.

Sleep was out of the question. Brady didn't even try. He was still lying rigid, his muscles tensed and twitching, staring hot-eyed at the ceiling he couldn't see when the first faint tinkle of milk bottles served to herald the brightening dawn.

SEVEN

The big room smelled of medicine and antiseptic and sleeping women. Linda Lou continued to lie with her eyes closed for long minutes after she awakened, listening to the muted and unfamiliar noises, hoping the nurse on duty wouldn't notice she was awake. She hadn't meant to sleep so long. She hadn't meant to sleep at all. It had been the stuff in the needle the nurse in the emergency room had stuck into her.

The sedative had left a film of fur in her mouth. Her head ached in a dull way. As cautiously as she could she opened her eyes part way and studied the ward through her long dark eye lashes.

The only light in the ward was over the night supervisor's desk but judging from the steadily increased tempo of the muted sounds and the way the windows were beginning to brighten, dawn wasn't far away.

She was in a mess, a bad one. There was no talking around that. If Mr. Mike Scaffidi hadn't found the parcel she'd left in his cab and turned it in, there was no telling what Mr. Dix might do or have done to her. As soon as the hospital released her and gave her her clothes and her money, she would take a cab from the hospital right to the office of the taxi company and ask for the lost and found department. If the parcel was there, well and good. If it wasn't she didn't know what she would do.

She began to cry softly. Not even going back to Chicago and saying she'd changed her mind and she was willing to be his girl would save her from Mr. Dix's anger. There had been more money in the parcel than she'd even seen before. She'd counted to sixty thousand dollars before she'd wrapped it up again and even then she hadn't been but a third way through the sheaves.

She cried even harder. Besides, she didn't want to be Mr. Dix's girl. When he had finished with her, she'd wind up a facsimile of her mother. She wanted more out of life than that. Not that taking men into the back room had been any chore for Della. In addition to the nightly bait camp trade, Della had had a succession of "husbands," all big virile men, willing to wink at the way she earned her living as long as there were grits and fried fish and side meat on the table and whiskey in the jug. She remembered Della's last husband well, a red-haired, itinerant sign painter. She had reason to remember him. One day while Della had been sleeping he'd caught her alone on the pier and the man had been hell determined. For all she fought and clawed him, he'd had her shirt up and her levis almost off when Della heard her screaming and broke an oar over his head. Not that her mother cared what happened to her but because she'd been jealous.

Linda Lou wiped her eyes with the sheet. Not that she was still a virgin. Silk and the salesman from Atlanta and the night clerk in Chicago had taken care of that. Silk was the one who'd gotten her away from Della's. Distasteful as it was she deliberately forced herself to think of her last night at Della's to keep from thinking about Mr. Dix and what would happen to her if she couldn't recover the parcel.

It had begun on a Saturday afternoon, just before dusk-dark. She'd been taking her weekly bath in the river and adding gallons of water to the river in tears because Della had burned her one good dress and her shoes because she wouldn't help with the back room trade. All she'd owned to cover herself was a pair of levis and an old blue work shirt, and they were in one of the boats. She had been standing in the river naked as a jay bird when she'd looked up and there he was, squatting on the pier and grinning at her.

"Hi beautiful," he'd grinned. "What are you blubbering about?"

She'd tried to cover her body and couldn't. All she had was two hands. "How long you been squatting there?" she'd asked him and he grinned. "Just. I beeped my horn but I guess no one heard it. You *do* have cabins for rent?"

There'd been nothing else she could do but give up trying to cover herself and wade to the boat where she'd left her levis and shirt and he'd watched her every step of the way. Even now her cheeks burned at the thought. A lot of men had tried to see her but the big youth on the pier had been the first one to succeed.

Nor had she seen anyone quite like him. He was young, not more than twenty-two or three, but he wasn't a boy. Boys didn't wear .45 caliber automatics in shoulder holsters under expensive white suits. Whoever he was, he wasn't local. His suit and broad-brimmed panama hat had cost as much as the new beer coil and second-hand TV set.

"What's your name?" she'd asked him.

"Just call me Silk," he'd told her. "Now if you don't mind, I'd like to see a cabin. One well back from the road, if you have one."

It was as real two years later as if it had just happened. Finished dressing, she'd dried her feet on an old sack and night had crept out of the swamp. In black silence she led the way across the trash-filled yard of which she'd been so ashamed. Time and time again she'd begged Della to do something about the rotting boats and gear and mounds of rusted tin cans left behind by the former owner of the camp.

"Mind your step," she cautioned and Silk had taken her elbow as he'd told her, "I make a practice of that."

Then the neon sign over the door of the bar had come on and Della had come out and stood in the doorway yawning. She hadn't seen them but they saw her and all she'd on was a wrapper and she'd scratched herself where she'd itched as she looked at the cream-colored Cadillac convertible standing in front of the rusted gas pump.

"In the name of God, who's that?" Silk had asked and she'd been too ashamed to tell him it was her mother and instead she'd asked him if that was his car standing in front of the pump and Silk had said it was.

Then they were at the cabin and Silk had held the door open for her and it was the first time a man had ever done that and she'd known right then what she was going to do. She could not hold out against Della forever.

Linda Lou beat softly on the bed with her clenched fists. She could close her eyes and still see the cabin. It matched the trash-littered grounds. The beaver board ceiling was streaked with ugly yellow rain stains. There was no carpet on the floor. The only furnishings were a sway-backed double bed, a chair with a mended leg and a battered dresser that no one used. All the cabins were the same. The only time they were ever occupied were when the Elfers girl came over to help Della with a rush of business, or a fisherman got too drunk to drive home or one of the merchants in Osceola drove out with some high school girl.

Silk had been amused as he'd looked from the naked light bulb dangling on its frayed wire to her. Then he'd taken her in his arms and kissed her. "How much?" he'd asked flatly. "And I'm not talking about the cabin."

She'd liked the way he'd kissed her. She'd liked the feel of his arms around her. If it had to happen sometime, it might as well happen with a man like Silk. At least he was young and clean, sober and smooth-shaven.

"Not for money," she'd told him. "Not for any amount of money. But if you promise to take me out of here, now, tonight, you can have me."

He'd studied her face for a long time. "You mean that, don't you?"

"I never meant anything more," she'd told him.

Then he'd told her he would and she'd let him undress her. And she'd got on the bed with him and he'd made love to her, twice, with the naked bulb shining in her eyes. And when it was all over she'd felt ashamed and she hurt and Della was calling her and she'd had to get dressed again and go tend bar. But Silk had been as good as his word and as soon as the drunks got to milling around that night and Della was busy in the back room, Silk had winked at her and they'd gotten into his big car and driven up to Jacksonville, stopping only in Vero Beach to buy her a dress and some shoes and underthings. And it had been better, much better, the next two nights in the hotel in Jacksonville. No matter what the officers said about him. Silk had been kind and patient with her and she was just beginning to think she was going to like this being almost married when Silk had gone out for cigarettes and she'd heard gunfire in front of the hotel and a few minutes later two detectives had knocked on the door of the room and told her that Silk had been killed trying to hold up a liquor store. And they'd taken her down to the detective bureau and questioned her for hours and then decided she was just a dumb little cracker kid that Silk had picked up. They let her go and advised her to go home. But she hadn't. They didn't know what her home was like. So, after she'd cried herself out and spent the few dollars Silk had given her, she'd gotten a job waiting tables in a Greek restaurant. And the Greek who ran it had been nice and had treated her like a father. Long as the hours had been, it had been like heaven compared to working for Della.

Linda Lou wiped her eyes again. She would probably still be waiting tables for Mr. Pulous if Mr. Mayers from Osceola hadn't come into the restaurant one day and recognized her and she'd been so afraid that when he got home he would tell Della where she was that she'd accepted a ride to Memphis from a middle-aged salesman from Atlanta. But they'd barely got seventy miles out of Jacksonville, not quite all the way to Waycross, before the salesman got so excited from reaching over and feeling her she'd been afraid he would run his car off the road and kill them both and she'd agreed, reluctantly, to check into a motel with him. In broad daylight. And it wasn't even an hour later when they were back in the car and driving toward Memphis. Then he'd taken another motel room in Memphis and he'd hit and tormented her for an hour. He'd finally become so angry at her crying that he'd hit her in the face and walked out and she'd never seen him again.

Of all the places she'd been in since she'd left Della's she'd liked Memphis the best. She liked the office where she worked. It had been big and clean and impersonal. None of the men made passes at her and all the girls had been friendly. They'd taught her what kind of clothes to buy and how to take care of her hair and how to use make-up and advised her to save her money because, with her face and figure, they said she ought to be a model. She'd believed them and when she'd had enough money saved she'd moved to Chicago but all of the larger agencies said she wasn't quite tall enough and while some of the men in the smaller ones had offered to get her jobs, they'd wanted her to go to bed with them first and she'd had enough of that sort of jazz. Silk and the salesman had been the only two men in her life until she'd spent all the money she'd saved and hadn't eaten for two days. She'd been about to be put out of her cheap hotel room. The night clerk said it was a shame for a thing like that to happen to a pretty girl like her and he'd bought her a hamburger and paid the night's rent for her, then spent his night off taking the rent and hamburger out of her body.

Linda Lou closed her eyes tight. Even now, a year later, she didn't like to think of that night. But it had served a purpose. In the morning she'd been so revolted and disgusted and afraid she would wind up a second Della that she'd decided she would take any job she could get. That was when she'd answered an advertisement in the paper for a twenty-six girl, whatever that was. The manager hadn't been going to hire her but Mr. Dix had happened to be in the tavern and he'd told the man to give her the job. And from then on no one had bothered her because they all thought she was Mr. Dix's girl. But she hadn't been. All the old Italian had ever done was breathe sour wine and garlic and give her a few fatherly pats on the fanny until two days before when he'd called her into his office and tried to put his fat hand on her and told her he wanted her to run an errand for him and when she came back from New York she was going to be his girl.

Linda Lou realized a nurse was shaking her shoulder. "Now, now. We mustn't cry like that, honey," the nurse attempted to soothe her. "Nothing can be that bad."

Linda Lou looked at her with wet eyes. What did she know how bad things could be? She'd never had to catch bait and gut fish and tend bar. She'd come from a nice home with a sweet-smelling mother who loved her. She'd never had to give herself to strangers to keep from becoming a bait camp whore. Or let a pot-gutted salesman torment her to get from Jacksonville to Memphis. No fat old Italian wanted her to be his girl or insisted that she carry a parcel of money from Chicago to New York to keep the Internal Revenue Bureau from learning how much he really made. No one was going to kill her.

The nurse shook her even harder. "Now, now. We'll have to stop this. If we don't we'll have to have another sedative. And we don't want that, do we?"

Linda Lou stopped crying as suddenly as she'd started. "No," she said. "We don't."

Miss Hart, Ward B supervisor, answered the ringing phone on her desk, then turned back to the two detectives. "The girl is frightened," she agreed with Sergeant Hooper. "That much of your story I'll buy. In fact, I'll go as far as to say she seems to be terrified of something." She consulted the chart on her desk. "According to the nurse on duty she had a very bad crying spell at five o'clock this morning. But as long as she refuses to talk, I don't see what you can do about it."

"Me either," Manson said.

Sergeant Hooper asked if the psychiatrist had talked to Miss Larson and Miss Hart consulted her chart again. "Yes. He did. For an hour."

"How does she check out with him?"

"He says she seems to be perfectly normal."

Manson shifted his weight from one foot to the other. "I tell you we're wasting the city's time."

"Could be," Hooper admitted. He persisted. "But I still can't get a clear picture of a good-looking girl like Miss Larson being out in a rain like we had yesterday morning. Not with the city swarming with cabs and her with four bills in her purse. And why did she run across the street and get herself run down while looking back over her shoulder?"

"Who told you that?" the nurse asked.

"A news vendor on Forty-second. He was standing under an awning and happened to look up and there she was, cutting through traffic like Boris Karloff was after her."

"He's certain it was Miss Larson he saw?"

"He couldn't miss that red raincoat. And all this, mind you, less than ten minutes after she arrived from Chicago."

"You're positive of that?"

"We checked with the Pullman porters and found one who remembered her. He says she didn't leave her compartment from the time the train left Chicago until it arrived at Grand Central. Also she kept the door locked every mile of the way."

"Then why don't you check with Chicago?"

"We have. That's one reason we're still interested in her. Chicago reports have her listed as a model, temporarily earning her living by running a twenty-six game in a near-north-side tavern."

Miss Hart was interested. "What in the world is a twenty-six game?"

"A game you play with dice."

"What's so strange about that?"

"The tavern is owned by Lew Dix."

"Who's he?"

Sergeant Hooper examined the initials in his hat. "Well, he's a pretty rough boy. One of the few big wheels left of the old Capone mob."

"Then he must be an old man."

"Sweetheart," Manson assured the supervisor, "you could never find a nastier old man. Dix should have been dead for thirty years. The way we have it he not only has a finger in every dirty pie in Chicago but he is also a big cog in the international Mafia. The Chicago police, the F.B.I. and Internal Revenue boys have been panting after him since Edgar Hoover took office. He has a record as long as my arm. The only difference from the old days is now he can afford to hire young men to do all his dirty work."

"And that's why you're interested in Miss Larson."

"Right. We just happened to be on the spot at the right or wrong time, depending how you look at it. We brought the girl here to Bellevue. We went through her purse. We got a little curious. And the girl won't tell us a thing."

Miss Hart was puzzled. "But neither of you are detailed to traffic. Both of you are homicide men."

Sergeant Hopper explained, "That's why we're doing this preliminary snooping. If someone is out to knock off the girl we'd like to know it before she winds up in the morgue and we have to put in overtime. After fourteen years, Vi is getting tired of me eating my supper for breakfast. She says it's almost impossible to keep food warm that long. Then there's the gas bill to consider."

Miss Hart laughed. "You've been on the force too long, Sergeant. You're too suspicious. The chances are the girl's story is true. She saw a cab on the other side of the street and became confused in the rain."

"So confused she bucked Forty-second Street rush hour traffic? Running like she was crazy and screaming, 'No, no, please don't,' and looking over her shoulder instead of where she was going."

"Who told you that?"

"The same news vendor."

It was pleasant talking to the detectives but her work was piling up. Miss Hart asked, "So what are you going to do about her? Outside of a few bumps and contusions, there is nothing the matter with her. She demands to be released and unless you prefer a charge of some sort we're going to have to let her go."

The sergeant returned his hat to his head. "That's the way it seems to stack up. At this late date we can't very well book her for jaywalking. Has anyone inquired for her? Has anybody been interested in that squib we had the papers print?"

"Why, yes, there was," Miss Hart said. "When I came on duty this morning the night supervisor told me that two men inquired for Miss Larson last night."

"They wanted to see her?"

"No. They just wanted to know how she was and when she would be released. You know. The usual."

Sergeant Hooper removed his hat and ran his forefinger unsteadily along the sweatband. "This night supervisor. She didn't by any chance say what these two men looked like?"

"Yes, she did. She said they were young. Pleasantly spoken. Well dressed. You know. Two typical young college men."

EIGHT

The rain the morning before might never have fallen. The smell of wet wool and plastic raincoats was gone. Grand Central Station was merely crowded as commuters elbowed each other aside to walk to their places of business, to catch a shuttle train to Times Square, to pursue the normal routine of living.

Brady felt lost in the familiar crowds. His gulped breakfast was sour in his stomach. His throat was still raw and the inside of his eyelids still burned. He didn't want to go to the office. He couldn't go to the office this morning. He had to decide what he was going to do about the parcel. And before he could make that decision he had to know how much money it contained and if there was any clue to the identity of the loser.

For a change, the train was on time. He had a few minutes to think. He walked up to the street and into the same bar in which he'd had a drink the previous morning. The rye didn't help him think. All it did was increase the sour feeling in his stomach and the acute physical discomfort the carnal contact with Alice had engendered. It had been close, too close. The child was out of her mind. She'd been hell determined to have him and damn near successful. He couldn't go through such a scene again and keep his sanity. He had to do something about her before the situation erupted into tragedy.

Boarding school was a possible solution. That would take money but he had plenty of money. He had a newspaper-wrapped parcel filled with money.

Brady picked up a morning paper that somebody had left on the bar. He looked through it carefully. There was no further mention of the girl in the red raincoat. Bellevue might have released her, or she might still better be lying in traction with a broken back and two broken legs.

He ordered a glass of beer to take the taste of the rye out of his mouth. At least the beer was cold. He sipped it, painfully conscious that whatever decision he came to this morning might be the most important one of his life. The girl in the red raincoat and the Italian cab driver weere the only two people in the world who could possibly connect him with the parcel. The girl, the Italian cab driver and one inanimate object. The lost plastic tag from the handle of his brief case.

Brady studied the brief case he'd bought the night before. Despite his efforts to age it, it looked like a new case. He'd expected May to say something about it. She hadn't. She'd been too interested in helping her brat of a son wheedle a bicycle out of him. When he'd taken on May and Alice and Jimmy he'd really done himself proud. He'd built a nest for a brood of vultures, all three of them determined to feast on him, one way or another.

There was a phone booth in the rear of the bar. On impulse he called the office and Miss Karney answered the phone.

"Good morning. Harper, Nelson and Ferrel."

Brady simulated a husk in his voice. "This is Jim Brady, Miss Karney. Will you please inform Mr. Harper that I won't be in this morning as I seem to have picked up a terrific cold."

Miss Karney was sympathetic. "Of course. You sound terrible, Mr. Brady. You'd better stay in bed all day."

"I intend to," Brady lied and broke the connection.

It was too warm in the phone booth. Or, possibly, he just imagined it. The mild exertion of telling the lie had bathed his body in a cold sweat.

He walked back to the bar and finished his beer. It all had seemed so simple at first. He'd found a parcel in a taxi. Curious, he'd examined it. The parcel contained money. He'd decided to keep it. And now his normally flat and routine world was filled with odd angles.

Mr. Harper might or might not believe his phoned message. Remembering the scene of the morning before, Mr. Harper might think he was just throwing his weight around and decide that one James A. Brady was expendable.

If so, there went his job. Because of one simple phone call. And in a strictly legal sense the money wasn't his. The law was firm on found objects. He should have turned the parcel over to the cab driver. Right now, while he stood in a bar, a thorough police investigation could be under way.

The same was true if the money came from some illegitimate source. Only then he was more involved. The smart money men, the fast buck boys, the hoods from the wrong side of the track made their point with brass knuckles and barrels partly filled with concrete.

Brady used his handkerchief to pat at the perspiration beading his face. And he still didn't know how much money was in the parcel. He still didn't know if the risk he was running was worth while.

The barman picked up his empty beer glass. "Tough night, fellow?"

"Tough," Brady admitted.

For some reason the simple question irritated him. The barman didn't really care how he felt. He was merely making conversation, muttering one of the small amenities with which modern man masks his true emotions. If the barman knew he had a parcel of money in one of the dime lockers outside he would undoubtedly slip him a Mickey and steal the key.

Brady walked out of the bar fingering the key with his change. Fear is a complex emotion. He couldn't force himself to act normally as he walked back to Grand Central. His eyes persisted in looking back over his shoulder like the girl in the red raincoat had looked over her shoulder when she'd run across the street through the rain.

The crowd in the station had thinned. The big rush of commuters was gone. Brady wished he hadn't chosen quite so prominent a block of lockers. He walked past the locker in which he'd left the brief case, then lit a cigarette and tried to look casual as he studied the people around him. None of them looked like detectives. None of them looked like mobsters.

He inserted his key in the slot and exchanged the empty case he was carrying for the bulging one in the locker. Then he closed the locker door and inserted another dime and removed the key and returned it to his pocket.

No hand was laid on his shoulder. No one came up and grabbed him. No one poked a gun in his back. The two men in the slowly moving car that had cruised the street the night before could not have been looking for 1134 East Elm Street.

It felt good to have the case under his arm again. His eyes no longer felt hot. The raw feeling was gone from his throat. Now all he needed was a few hours alone to count the money and ascertain if it contained a clue to the identity of whoever had lost it. The amount of money and possible rightful ownership would determine his next move.

He debated taking the East Side subway and rode the shuttle to Times Square instead. The lower East Side was composed of neighborhood communities. Everyone noticed a stranger. But in Times Square everybody was a stranger.

As he emerged from the kiosk in front of the moving sign around the Times Building, Brady experienced a mild glow and a feeling of importance. It was incredible what having money did to a man. He wasn't out of the woods. He might have a long way to go. Still there had been some subtle change in his physical chemistry. He felt he was an entirely different person from the everyday, sixty-five hundred dollar a year James A. Brady, the translator who rode the New York, New Haven and Hartford five mornings and five evenings a week, every week of the year, legal holidays excepted.

Finding a hotel room was no problem. He could see half a dozen from where he was standing. There was the Sheraton-Astor, the Taft, the Lincoln, the Piccadilly. There was only one trouble with them. They were all too big and important. Important people stayed at them. By chance, he might encounter one of the out-of-the-country clients of Harper, Nelson and Ferrel. While he was supposed to be home in bed with a cold.

He crossed to the east side of Broadway and walked up it, glancing down the side streets as he passed. There were hotels on almost all of them but he decided that one of the theatrical hotels on Forty-seventh

Street would be the most practical.

After passing the foyer of the Palace Theatre he turned east again and continued on down Forty-seventh toward the Avenue of the Americas, better known as Sixth Avenue.

The hotel he finally chose was fairly small with a compact lobby and a ferret-faced, sharply dressed room clerk.

As Brady signed the registration card John A. Smith, the clerk smiled thinly. "Okay, Captain," he said. "You're a little early but Pocohontas will be with you in a few minutes. You pay me. That will be twenty dollars."

Brady started to protest. Twenty dollars was an outrageous price for a room. He could rent a room at the Plaza for that. On the other hand, if he walked out he would call attention to himself and that was the last thing he wanted to do. Besides, what difference did it make? He had lots of money.

He laid a bill on the desk. "Whatever you say."

The exterior of the hotel had obviously been renovated but the modernization hadn't extended to the interior. The elevator was so old the cables creaked. The room was on the fourth floor, shabbily furnished but fairly clean, with a private bath and a good view of a rusted fire escape.

A bellhop with a whiskey breath and wearing a food-stained uniform attempted to take the brief case from him and lay it on the dresser. Brady stopped him.

"If you don't mind, I can manage." He thought a moment and added, "But I tell you what you can do."

The bellhop moved the toothpick he was chewing from one side of his mouth to the other. "What's that, chum?"

Brady peeled a ten dollar bill from his rapidly diminishing roll and gave it to the man. "Get me a bottle of whiskey. Rye."

The bellhop creased the bill lengthwise. "Sure thing, pal. Pitching a little one, eh?"

"You could call it that," Brady said.

Little or no air was coming in the open window. Brady threw his trench coat over a chair and took off his jacket. Then, as an afterthought, he unknotted his tie and took it and his shirt off. God only knew how long it would take him to count the money. He'd paid twenty dollars for the room. He might as well be comfortable.

While he waited for the bellhop to bring the whiskey he washed his hands and face in the bathroom. The small window to the air shaft was painted shut and the small room was stuffy and smelled of cheap perfume and disinfectant. When I pick a hotel I pick a beauty, Brady thought. Still he had the comfort of knowing he was alone. At least Alice couldn't get at him here.

Back in the room, unable to control his impatience, he unzipped the brief case and looked in. The parcel looked just the same as it had the last time he'd seen it. He started to take out one of the sheaves of bills but re-zippered the case hastily as the bellhop knocked on the door.

As the man set the bottle on the dresser and transferred the cracked ice in the silver pitcher he was carrying to a glass one, he glanced at the shirt Brady had hung over the only chair in the room and grinned. "Making yourself comfortable, I see."

"That's right," Brady said.

The bellhop nodded sagely. "It does a man good to cut loose once in a while. Only you're a little early, see? So there may be a slight delay."

Brady didn't have the slightest idea what the man was talking about. He didn't care. Having another glimpse of the money had put him in a generous mood and he told the boy to keep the change from the ten.

The bell man was properly grateful. "Thanks. Thanks a lot, Mister. The desk clerk was a little edgy but I gave him the okay as soon as I seen you. There's a real sport, I says to myself."

As the man closed the door behind him, Brady shook his head to clear it. He'd been away too long. They talked an entirely different language in Manhattan from the one they talked in Stamford.

The bellhop had opened the bottle, probably to help himself to a drink enroute up from the bar. Brady found a glass on the medicine shelf in the bathroom and poured it half full of whiskey. He was too excited to drink it. Instead, after making certain the spring latch on the door had caught, he unzippered the brief case again and dumped the parcel on the bed spread. Then he tore away the silver paper gift wrapping and the newsprint under it.

The sheaves were tightly packed and there were more of them than he'd realized. Nor would it be necessary for him to count each individual bill. He'd counted one sheaf in the stall at Grand Central Station and had come up with either four thousand five hundred or five thousand four hundred dollars. There were forty sheaves of banded bills in the parcel, each manila band initialed L. D. Allowing for the occasional one thousand dollar bill he could see, suppose he roughed in each sheaf at five thousand dollars. Forty times five thousand was—

Brady stared at the money on the bed, incredulous. Unless he was completely crazy, there were two hundred thousand dollars on the bed.

When he could move, he slipped a small piece of white paper out from under one of the bands and read it. Written in Italian, in the same childish scrawl that had penciled the initials, was the cryptic message:

Settlement 1957 account in full.

L. D.

One thing was certain. The money hadn't come from, nor was it intended for deposit in, the Chase National Bank. He had a tiger by the tail and no mistake. The sweat on Brady's body turned cold. Who was L. D.?

He forced himself to think. There had been, he believed, a gangster named Legs Diamond. But that had been years ago, long before his time, back in the prohibition era when New York's Roaring Forties had flown knee deep with bootleg whiskey and needle beer.

He looked at the sheets of newsprint he'd torn from the parcel. The wrapping had come from a three day old Chicago Morning Tribune. Whom did he know who could brief him on the Chicago underworld? Johnny Cass! He hadn't seen Johnny for two years, not since he and May and the children had moved from West 15th Street. But, as far as he knew, Cass was still covering a police beat for the same New York evening newspaper that he'd joined when he'd finished with high school.

There was a phone on the dresser and a phone book under it. Brady found the number he wanted and gave it to the clerk downstairs. He had no trouble getting through to Cass. Johnny was glad to hear from him. They exchanged information about their wives and mutual friends, then Brady inquired, as casually as he could, if Cass happened to know any big shot in either the New York or Chicago underworld whose initials were L. D.

"That would be Lew Dix," the reporter said.

"Is he a big shot?"

"The biggest. He's one of the few big ones left from the old Al Capone mob. The Feds also think he's a spoke in the old international Mafia but no one has ever been able to prove it. Why? What's your interest in Dix?"

"His name came up in connection with a new account we've been offered in Rome," Brady lied. "But from what you've just said about him, I don't know whether we want to do business with him or not."

He ended the conversation as soon as he could without being abrupt. He wasn't at all happy about the information Cass had given him. Seemingly his call had established one thing. If L. D. was Lew Dix, his lucky find was underworld money. But just how hot it was, he had no way of knowing.

On impulse, he pushed the sheaves of bills back in his brief case and stuffed the silver gift wrapper and the newspaper in the basket under the window. Cass had called Dix a big wheel, a spoke in the international Mafia. A hard lump formed in the pit of Brady's stomach. No longer thirsty, he added the bottle of whiskey to the paper in the basket. This was far from being as simple as it had seemed at first. He would need a clear head to think this thing through.

He walked into the bathroom again and ran cold water in the bowl and splashed it on his face and chest and the back of his neck. It helped some but not much. He was still perspiring when he walked out of the bathroom and stopped short, staring incredulously at the girl turning down the spread and top sheet of his bed.

"Hi, honey," she yawned. "Sorry I took so long but I was sound asleep when Joe called me. We didn't expect any customers this time of morning." She took off her dress and lay down.

A lot of things were suddenly clear. Why the room rent had been so high. Why the clerk had called him Captain and said he was a little early but Pocohontas would be with him in a few minutes. Why the bellhop had said he'd known he was a right guy. The racket sprang up periodically among the cheaper hotels. There was no organized vice, as such, in the city. But working together, a room clerk and a bellhop frequently circumvented the law by having the clerk rent a room to a live one for a sum sufficient to cover the amatory services of a girl living in the hotel.

The girl was young and blonde and fairly pretty. She had all of a woman's attributes. After the abortive episode with Alice the night before, Brady was still unnaturally excited. But of all the things he wanted least at the moment, a woman headed the list.

The girl patted the bed beside her and smiled at him vacuously. "Well, now mama's here, let's get on with it, sweetheart." Her smile faded, "Or ain't I good enough for you or something?"

"No," Brady assured her. "It's not that. You're a very pretty girl."

He walked over to the bed to try to explain and then looked up as the room door opened and the ferret-faced clerk and the bellhop came in.

"Did he?" the clerk asked the girl.

The girl was furious with him as she covered herself with the sheet she'd turned back. "You've got a nerve walking in while I'm working. How many times have I told you?"

"Did he?" the clerk repeated.

"No," the girl admitted. "We were just about."

The bell man took Brady's shirt from the chair and handed it to him. "That's what he thought. Get dressed and get out of here, Mister." He explained to the girl. "He's a newspaper man. One of them damn nosy reporters."

Brady paused in the act of putting on his shirt. He didn't want the girl but he didn't want any misunderstanding either. "Now just a minute, fellows. You have this thing all wrong. I—"

While his arms were still caught in the sleeves of his shirt, the bellhop hit him. Then he hit him again, this time so hard the blow knocked him against the dresser, rocking it and causing the fat brief case to slide off and fall on the floor.

"Sure. All wrong," the bellhop sneered. "After Charlie heard you call your paper and ask to talk to the city desk. We'll learn you bastards to nose around."

His arms free, Brady doubled his hands into fists and started for the bellhop but stopped as the other man took a sap from his hip pocket.

The girl on the bed was shocked. "A lousy reporter. And he looks like such a good guy."

The clerk jerked his thumb at the door. "Out. And don't print nothing about this or you'll wish you hadn't. We have a good thing going. And we intend to milk it before the vice squad blows the whistle."

Brady put on his tie without bothering to knot it, slipped on his suit coat, then picked up his brief case and trench coat. He thought he could hold his own with either of the two or even with both of them. But his fists were no match for a blackjack. Besides he couldn't afford any trouble.

"All right," he said. "I'll leave."

He rode down in the creaking elevator between the two men and as he started across the lobby the bell man pushed him unexpectedly and he tripped and fell, the brief case slipping from under his arm and skittering across the tile floor.

"Big shot," the bell man jeered. "Tryin' to con me into thinking you were a right guy by telling me to keep the change from a lousy ten."

Tight-lipped with anger, Brady stooped to pick up his case and the clerk kneed him viciously in the mouth, then picked up the brief case and threw it in his face.

"Out. Get going, Mister."

The brief case under one arm, Brady pushed through the swinging door and out onto Forty-seventh Street. There was the normal amount of pedestrian traffic and his mouth was bleeding so badly that a few of the passersby stared at him but none of them stopped.

Brady wiped his mouth with the back of his hand. This was another new experience. It was the first time he'd ever been beaten up on suspicion of being something he wasn't, then had a fortune thrown in his face.

NINE

Linda Lou studied her reflection in one of the mirrors in the washroom off Ward B. Now that she'd put on her slip, none of the black and blue marks showed. The bump on the back of her head was still tender to the touch but at least they hadn't had to shave her hair.

She sat on a bath stool and started to put on the stockings the nurse had brought her with her clothes. The nylons were ruined. She would have to buy a new pair. Either that or go back to the station for her luggage. But she didn't have time. She didn't have time to do anything before she tried to recover the parcel Mr. Dix had entrusted to her.

Mr. Dix must know by now, he'd known for twenty-four hours that she hadn't delivered the parcel. What action he might have taken would depend on the mood he was in.

She was bitterly resentful as she slipped her dress over her head. She hadn't wanted to accept the assignment in the first place. Just because a girl happened to be young and pretty she could get into the darndest messes.

Her resentment grew. The nerve of the fat old man—he must have grandchildren older than she was. How could he possibly expect her to feel anything for him? She shook her head as she adjusted the straps of her brassiere. Not even for a big car and a clothes closet full of clothes and the Lake Shore apartment he'd mentioned.

Finished dressing except for making up, which would have to wait until she reclaimed her purse, she looked at the list the nurse's attendant had given her.

> Lipstick
> Compact
> Comb
> Gruen watch
> Ring (Costume)
> Driver's license
> I. D. cards
> Wallet
> R. R. ticket
> $444.65

All of it was there. She smoothed her rumpled dress as best she could. Then folding her torn red raincoat over one arm, she walked through the ward to the supervisor's desk.

She would make a sincere effort to get the parcel back. If she did, she would deliver it to the address she'd been given. But if she wasn't successful, there was only one thing she could do and that was to put as much distance as possible between herself and New York and Chicago.

She might even go back to Memphis or Jacksonville. Not even Mr. Dix could find her there. She'd never mentioned either town to anyone in Chicago, not even the girls with whom she worked. True, they'd all kidded her about the way she talked. But a lot of light-haired girls had drawls and the deep South was a big place. And working in the office in Memphis or even waiting tables for Mr. Pulous was preferable to letting Mr. Dix maul her. She'd had enough of that jazz. Not that she didn't think she might learn to like it if she had a fair shake at the business. But she still wanted what she wanted when she'd run away from Della. She wanted a man of her own, a man who would give her a decent home. A young man willing to give her a ring and a marriage license. When he came along he could maul her as much as he pleased. Morning, noon and night. And in between times. She'd even help him. And if babies came, so much the better. That was what the business was supposed to be for in the first place.

As she stopped in front of Miss Hart's desk, the day supervisor gave her a friendly smile. "Are you certain you feel all right, Linda?" she asked. "Are you sure you want to leave us?"

Linda Lou assured her she felt fine and Miss Hart debated telling the girl that the police were interested in her and thought better of the idea. It wasn't really any of her business. She laid the release forms on the desk.

"Then sign here and here. You can pick up your personal things at the custodian's cage just off the main lobby."

Linda Lou signed the releases. "Thank you."

The elevator was crowded. There were more people in the lobby, uniformed policemen and plainclothesmen coming and going, relatives and friends of patients, interns and orderlies and nurses. Linda Lou stood by the bank of elevators studying their faces. If the big man in the rain-sodden trench coat was waiting for her, she couldn't see him. On the other hand, she might not even know him if she saw him again. It had all happened so fast. She'd been so frightened. All of the fear building in her during the long ride from Chicago had popped like a cork in a champagne bottle when she was in the taxi cab.

She found the office Miss Hart had directed her to and having her purse in her possession again bolstered her morale immeasurably. She put on lipstick and powder and immediately felt better.

There were some phone booths in the lobby and Linda Lou looked up the number of the Allied Cab Company. She dropped a dime in the slot and dialed the number.

The man she spoke to was both helpful and courteous but he insisted that no parcel answering the description she gave had been turned in the day before.

"I tell you what, though," he told her. "Nine tenths of our drivers drive their own hacks. And if this should happen to be his day off, the driver of your cab might not have bothered to come back to the garage last night. You don't happen to know his name, do you?"

"Yes," Linda Lou said. "I do. It was Mike Scaffidi."

"Good!" The man had an infectious laugh. "Then you can stop worrying right now, Miss. Mike is one of our most dependable drivers and if you left anything in his cab you'll get it back." He added, "Unless the next fare kept the parcel instead of turning it over to Mike. Just hold on a minute. I think this is Mike's day off but I'll get his address and phone number from one of the girls in the front office."

Linda Lou waited with her fingers crossed until the man came back on the wire.

"I was right," he said. "Mike is off today." He gave her a Bleecker Street address and phone number. "But if it is really important that you get back your parcel today you can probably reach him at home."

"Thank you. Thank you very much." There was no pencil in her purse. She scratched the address and phone number on the back of a card with a bobby pin. Then she called the number the garage man had given her.

She let the phone on the other end ring for a long time but still no one answered. She waited a few minutes and then tried again with the same result.

She hung up the phone but continued to stand in the booth, her slumped shoulders pressed against the wall.

Memphis. That was a laugh. Sure. She could go to Memphis. She could go to Jacksonville. She could even go back to Della's. But why not stop kidding herself? If she couldn't recover the parcel she could never run far or fast enough to hide from Mr. Dix. Sooner or later he'd find her. And, especially if she ran, he would never believe her story about the big man with his hand in the pocket of his trench coat. Following his own twisted line of thinking, Mr. Dix would assume she'd been trying to pull a fast one. He would also assume she'd stolen the money.

She opened the hinged door of the booth. There was only one thing she could do. That was to go to the Bleecker Street address and wait until Mr. Scaffidi came home if she had to wait all afternoon and all night.

She had to get back that parcel.

She walked through the hospital lobby to the street and down the stairs. She stood a moment, hesitant, then walked rapidly down the street to the cab stand on the corner.

In the window of the bar and grill across the street, Daly adjusted the brim of his pork pie hat to suit him.

"There she goes," he said quietly.

Morgan stopped beating time to the record currently playing in the juke box and stood up. "It's about time."

He joined Daly in the doorway and they left without looking back.

The bartender was pleased to see them leave. If he heard *It's a Sin to Tell a Lie* once more he knew he would blow his top. The two men had been waiting outside when he'd opened up that morning but outside of the quarters they'd dropped in the record player they hadn't spent a dollar between them. And that on soft drinks.

At first glance he'd thought they were plainclothesmen on a stake-out. Then he'd decided they were too young. Then he'd realized what they really were.

He'd seen their kind before. For all of their Ivy-League clothes and pork pie hats and well-modulated voices, they were neither from Harvard or Yale.

If they were working their way through college, those two punks were doing it with their guns concealed under the left arm pits of their well-cut coats.

TEN

The weather was nippy but pleasant. Scaffidi couldn't decide if he was pleased that another winter was approaching or not. Bad weather brought more fares. It meant bigger tips. Still, it was more pleasant hacking in warm weather. A man could work in his shirt sleeves. He could listen to the ball games on his radio. What the hell? A man could only earn and spend so much money.

Like working in the rain yesterday. What had it got him? A cold. When he could have been shacked up with Serafina. He was glad he wasn't like some of the boys. Money, money, money. That was all they thought about. As soon as they got their own cabs, they had to hire night drivers. Some of them even hired two men on eight hour shifts and worked their heaps around the clock.

For what? For the privilege of keeping records and paying state unemployment and social security deductions and at the end of the year, a sonofabitch of an income tax, both state and federal. Not forgetting to mention the additional insurance and the wear and tear on their hacks. It wasn't worth it.

Perched on a stool in the corner lunchroom near his furnished room, Scaffidi made plans for the day as he ate a late breakfast of hot cakes and eggs and sausage and tamped it down with a pepperoni-anchovy pizza.

After he'd washed his hack and swept it out he had to do something about his windshield wipers. It might be best to install new ones. Once windshield wipers started to go bad there was little you could do about them. The thought depressed him. He didn't mind spending the money. He liked to do his own work. That way he knew it was done right. But it would take at least an hour out of his day.

He spat on the floor. Always something.

The fry cook leaned his knuckles on the counter. "What gives, Mike? Got troubles?"

Scaffidi considered the question. "No," he said finally. "Everything's good with me. Like in perfectly satisfied."

The more he thought about it, the more positive he was. He'd never had it so good. He owned his hack. It was completely paid for. Having had sense enough not to marry, he didn't have to worry about supporting a wife and a house filled with runny nosed *bambinos.*

He pursued the subject with pleasure. He was free to go and come as he pleased. He could bowl or play cards all night, if that's what he wanted to do. He could drink as much wine and eat as much good food as he could hold. And when he had that other appetite, there were always Maria and Angelina and Serafina or one of the unmarried girls in the neighborhood, happy and willing to accommodate him.

It was a lot of gorgonzola about women not liking to. Women liked it as well as men did. But a man had to know how to make love. Making love to a woman was as exact and exacting a science as designing a ballistic rocket. Everything depended on what you put on a designing board. No man could come home tired from a hard day's work, snarl at his wife because dinner wasn't ready, sit around in his undershirt, unshaven and unbathed, until he was yawning, then push her over on the launching pad, count down from four to zero and expect her to go into orbit. Such things took time and preparation.

"More coffee?" the counterman asked.

Scaffidi shook his head. "No. I gotta go wash the hack and sweep it out."

The counterman winked. "And then—?"

Scaffidi counted out enough money to pay his check and added a half dollar tip. "Then we'll see." He winked back.

He walked up Bleecker Street whistling, nodding now and then to a neighbor or acquaintance. There were so many pleasant things to do. He could spend the afternoon drinking wine and playing cards. He could put on his new blue suit and take the subway uptown to Times Square and take in a movie. He could drop in on Maria or Angelina. He could encore with Serafina.

Scaffidi sucked in his breath at the thought.

Santa mia Madonna! There was a woman for a man to squeeze.

Scaffidi opened the small side door of the abandoned warehouse where he kept his cab when he wasn't using it, or when he didn't leave it in the company garage.

His decision was made. As soon as he'd washed the cab and taken care of the windshield wipers, he'd give Serafina a call. And on his way up to her place he'd stop and shop for supper, bitter green Sicilian olives, whitings pickled in saffron, Genoese salami and moratel. And for the main course, broiled eels garnished with garlic.

The thought made his mouth water. Serafina was as clever at a stove as she was in bed. She cooked with the same passionate abandon. And the wine. He must remember the wine. And a big box of the Turkish pasta she enjoyed. And above everything else, the flowers. Perhaps a dozen yellow roses. Women liked to be made over. He liked to make over them. It was a privilege.

His footsteps sounded hollow in the warehouse as he walked back to his cab. Yesterday's rain had washed the top and sides fairly clean but the front of the hood and the fender skirts were a mess. The white-walled tires were bad, too.

He hosed off the worst of the dirt, then wiped and hosed and wiped the cab again. Then he attacked the white-walled tires with a cleaning agent and a stiff copper brush. The wash monkeys in the company garage never quite cleaned the cab to suit him. Perhaps they didn't have the same pride of ownership that he did.

When he was finally satisfied with the whiteness of the tires he opened all four doors and swept out the cab, front and back with a whisk broom, taking special care to feel between the seat of the rear cushion and the back. People left the damndest things in taxis. Once he'd found a full set of false teeth worth perhaps two or three hundred dollars and turned them into lost and found and the sonofabitch who claimed them hadn't left a buck for him.

Scaffidi was philosophical about it. That was the way the wheel turned. Sometimes it stopped on your number. Sometimes you couldn't win for losing.

He frequently found change. He did this afternoon, a quarter, two nickels, a dime. Scaffidi dropped the change in his coat pocket without a second thought. Change came under the heading of tips. Who could identify a dime?

He swept the dust on the floor in the rear into a small pile and started to scoop it up with a piece of cardboard and picked up a small plastic object that was in the pile. It was a tag off a small piece of luggage or a brief case. Imprinted on the tag was the inscription:

> James A. Brady
> 1134 E. Elm Street
> Stamford. Conn.
> Stam. 3-4124

It was a cheap tag, worth not more than a dime or a quarter in any five and ten or stationery store. Scaffidi started to throw it away and on second thought dropped it into his side coat pocket. It was just possible someone might claim it. A lot of people set a sentimental value on the weirdest things.

He scooped up the dust and discarded it and closed the doors of the cab. The balky windshield wipers could wait. It would take him at least an hour to go buy and install a new set, an hour he could be spending with Serafina working up an appetite. The rain storm had been a freak. There was seldom any really bad weather until after Thanksgiving.

He backed a foot or two to give the cab a last inspection and turned and looked over his shoulder as someone knocked lightly, almost timidly on the small side door.

"Come in. Come in," he called.

A light-haired girl carrying a red raincoat over her arm opened the door and came in and walked quickly toward him. Her voice was as small as she was.

"Thank God I've found you, Mr. Scaffidi."

Scaffidi realized he was holding a wadded polishing cloth and stuffed it in his pocket. The girl looked vaguely familiar but he didn't have the least idea where he'd seen her before or why she should thank God she'd found him.

Linda Lou smiled hopefully. "They told me at the place where you room that you'd gone to the lunchroom on the corner. And the man in the lunchroom said I'd probably find you here."

Scaffidi pushed his cap back on his head. He not only didn't know the girl he could hardly understand her. She didn't talk like a New Yorker. Then he thought he had it. Of course. She had a mouthful of cotton. Like in "Gone With the Wind."

He took off his cap. "So what can I do for you, Miss?"

Linda Lou's hopeful smile wavered. "I'd like my parcel, please."

"Your parcel?"

"The one wrapped in silver paper," Linda Lou continued earnestly. "You must remember me. I rode in your cab yesterday morning. I got in in front of Grand Central Station and you stopped a little way up the street and got out and worked on your windshield wipers."

Scaffidi remembered her in a vague way. "Oh, yeah. I make you, now. You're the babe who stuck me with a meter pull. You said you wanted to go to St. Walter's Hotel. Then while I was working on my wipers you took a powder and ran across the street and got yourself hit by a truck."

Linda Lou forced herself to smile. "That's right. Now may I have my parcel, please?"

"Parcel?"

"The one I left in your cab."

Scaffidi returned his cap to his head. "Not in my hack, Miss. I just finished cleaning it out and I didn't find a thing."

Fighting a wave of panic, Linda Lou asked if he minded if she looked and Scaffidi opened the right rear door of the cab for her. "Go right ahead, Miss."

Linda Lou climbed into the cab and thrust her hand between the leather cushion and the back of the seat. The parcel wasn't where she'd wedged it. Either the cab driver was lying or someone else had found the money, probably the man with the gun in the pocket of his wet trench coat. She turned around and sat on the seat and cried.

Scaffidi hesitated, then got into the seat beside the girl without touching her. "Look, Miss. I don't want to be fresh or anything but nothing can be that bad. What was in this parcel you say you left in my cab?"

There was no handkerchief in her purse. Linda Lou leaned forward and dried her eyes on the hem of her slip. "Money. A lot of money."

Scaffidi whistled softly. Here we go again, he thought. If this was a con game of some kind, he'd never heard of it. He didn't see how the girl could hope to collect from his insurance company by claiming she'd lost a lot of money in his cab without substantial confirmation she'd had a bundle in the first place.

"How much money?" he asked her.

"I can't tell you." Linda Lou recovered some of her composure. She knew it was almost futile to ask. She asked, "I don't suppose you know the name of the man who got into your cab when I got out."

Scaffidi sighed. "I'm sorry, Miss. He was just a fare to me. I don't even remember what he looked like."

Linda Lou promptly told him. "A big man. Dark haired. Wearing a trench coat. Like he'd been walking in the rain. And I think he was carrying a brief case."

Scaffidi remembered the man as vaguely as he'd remembered her. "That's right. Yeah, we talked about you and the accident. I asked him if he'd seen what happened to you and did he want to talk to the cops and he said no."

Linda Lou thought rapidly. If she could identify the man and find out where he'd gone after robbing her of the parcel, Mr. Dix might believe her story. "Do you remember where you took him?"

Scaffidi shook his head. "I'm sorry, Miss. He was just another fare on a rainy day. A short haul, as I recall. But I can't remember where."

"Try. Please."

"This guy is important to you?"

"Very."

Scaffidi tried to remember and couldn't. He wished he could. The girl wasn't his type. He liked his women with more padding. Still, if the matter was as important to the doll as it seemed to be, he wished he could help her. After all, she said she'd left the parcel in his cab and if that was true, he was, in a way responsible for her getting it back if possible. On the other hand, he couldn't stop and frisk his cab after every fare. He took it for granted that most people were honest, and most people were. If they found anything in a cab they usually turned it over to the driver.

"Think. Please," the girl beside him pleaded.

Scaffidi brightened. Of course. His trip book. It would be down in black and white in his trip book. And his trip book was back in his room.

He leaned forward to tell the girl he could help her after all when a man's voice said, "How cozy."

Linda Lou tried to scream and couldn't. Her mouth was dry. Her throat was closed. She knew who Morgan and Daly were and what part they played in Mr. Dix's organization. The other girls had pointed them out to her. So the moment Dix had learned she'd failed to deliver the parcel, he had sent Morgan and Daly to find her.

For his part, Scaffidi was more amused than frightened. He thought he had the picture now. And if this was some form of a badger game shakedown, the little chick with the corn-pone accent and her rah rah boys had gone to a lot of trouble for nothing. Where women were concerned he had no reputation to protect. They couldn't get a dime out of him. On the other hand if it was a heist, he'd been stuck up so many times he'd learned to carry no more than twenty dollars in his wallet. And a double saw buck wouldn't make or break him.

"Okay. Let's get it over with," he said. "What's the caper?"

He started to get out of the cab and one of the men slipped a gun from a shoulder holster and slapped the barrel of it across his face so hard that blood spurted from his nose. "Stay right where you are, grease ball."

Daly slammed the rear door of the cab shut and opened the front door and got in while Morgan opened the door on the other side and sat sideways in the bucket seat, looking at Linda.

His voice completely devoid of expression, he said, "Let's have it, Linda. Where is it?"

Linda Lou cried silently. "I don't know."

"Don't give us that."

"It's the truth."

Morgan reached through the open section of the glass partition and slapped her. "Keep talking. What do you mean you don't know?"

"Just that," Linda Lou told him. She tried to explain. "When my train got into New York yesterday morning, I got in Mr. Scaffidi's cab. And he had to stop a few hundred feet from the station to fix his windshield wipers. While I was waiting a big man in a wet trench coat jerked the door open on the curb side and pointed a gun at me. Anyway I think it was a gun. And when he said he was sorry I thought he meant he was sorry he had to kill me. After all the awful things Mr. Dix warned me might happen, I'd been afraid all the way from Chicago. And I panicked. I opened the door and ran and left the parcel in the cab."

The two men on the front seat looked at each other. "You ever see this man before?"

"No."

"He just materialized out of the rain and pointed a gun at you?"

"I thought it was a gun."

"You expect us to believe that?"

Linda Lou repeated, "It's the truth."

Daly turned his flat eyes on Scaffidi. "Where do you come into this, grease ball?"

Scaffidi took his hand away from his bleeding face. His morning meal was resting uneasily in his stomach. He wished he hadn't eaten the pizza. He'd been wrong about these men. They *were* men, not college boys. He'd seen their type before. And back of whatever names they were using, they were just as much grease balls as he was. They were the type of American born Italians who gave all hard-working, God-fearing, law-abiding American Italians a bad name. The *paesanos* called their kind of men enforcers, men who could get up from a meal and machine gun a fellow being to death, then come back and finish the meal, as if nothing had happened, without even washing their hands.

He spoke slowly, choosing his words with care. "Look, fellows. I don't know what this is all about. Believe me, I don't come in. I'm just here washing my hack when the girl comes in and claims she left a parcel in my cab. Wrapped in silver paper, she tells me. And I never even saw her before, except the one time yesterday morning when she climbed out of my heap on Forty-second Street leaving me with a tripped meter."

"I'll bet. I'll just bet. That's why you were sitting so close. You sold out cheap, Guiseppe. If Miss Larson was going to pay you off for keeping the parcel for her, you should at least have taken her to your room. You'd have been more comfortable that way." Daly got out and opened the back door of the cab. "Get out slowly, Giuseppe. Then turn around and put your hands on the roof of the car."

"He's telling the truth," Linda Lou said shrilly. "You have to believe him, believe me."

Scaffidi got out slowly and put his palms on the roof of his cab and Morgan walked around the rear and covered him with his gun while Daly went through his pockets.

"Find anything?" Morgan asked.

Daly itemized the driver's effects. "Some change. Two ten dollar bills in a wallet. The usual I. D. cards. A set of keys. A rag with polish on it." He held up the plastic tag. "And this."

"What is it?"

"It looks like a tag off a suitcase."

Linda Lou offered, "The man who tried to get into the cab was carrying a brief case under his other arm. Maybe the tag came from that."

Morgan took the plastic tag from his partner and read the name aloud. "James A. Brady." He tossed the tag back on top of the small pile of personal possessions on the polished hood of the cab. "Not bad, Linda. You think fast. You got so scared you panicked and left the money on the seat of the taxi and this guy Brady found it and put it in the brief case he just happened to be carrying. Is that the story? Now what are we supposed to do? Go chasing off to this place Stamford, wherever it is, and scare hell out of some innocent Joe while you and your grease ball stud catch a freighter to South America with the money?"

"No," Linda Lou protested. "Believe me. I don't even know Mr. Scaffidi. He doesn't know me."

Morgan was mildly reproachful. "Shame on you, Linda Lou. The way I heard the story in Chicago you were hard to make. I even heard the boss almost busted his fat guts trying. But of course two hundred thousand dollars is a lot of pry." He took Scaffidi by the shoulder and turned him around. "Now let's have the real story, Giuseppe. *Where is the parcel Miss Larson left with you while she spent the night in Bellevue dreaming up this phony cover that she's trying to sell us?*"

Scaffidi protested. "I don't know. I never even saw the parcel."

Daly lashed out with his gun again, hitting the cab driver even harder this time, digging the front sight of the barrel so deeply into the flesh of his face that blood followed the path of the metal.

Scaffidi screamed with pain and Morgan stuffed the polish cloth into his mouth. "You don't seem to have understood the question. My partner asked what you did with the parcel."

"No," Linda Lou pleaded. "You mustn't hurt him. He didn't have anything to do with me losing the money."

She scrambled out of the cab and attempted to stand in front of Scaffidi and Morgan swept her off her feet with a backhand sweep of his free arm. "We'll come to you later," he said. "Right now we're concerned with your boy friend." He nodded at Daly. "Ask him again."

Daly wiped the blood off his gun barrel on the front of Scaffidi's clean shirt. "In a minute. But I'd better lock the door first. This may take a little time."

ELEVEN

Three little girls were playing hop scotch on the pavement of the short street dead-ending on the East River. As Brady walked past them and stopped at the parapet, leaning his elbows on the stone, he realized that the afternoon shadows were lengthening. He was tired. He had reason to be. Ever since he'd left the hotel he'd walked, not paying any attention to where he was, moving along with the other people on the sidewalks, automatically stopping for red lights and moving on when the lights turned green.

With two hundred thousand dollars under his arm.

He looked at his watch. It was four minutes of five. And he still didn't know what he intended to do. For all he knew it might be too late to do anything. If a couple of punks in the lowest echelon of the underworld were willing to play as rough as the desk clerk and the bell man had been to protect a minor racket, just what would Mr. Dix do to recover his money?

For the hundredth time, Brady considered walking into the nearest police station, laying the brief case on the booking counter and telling the desk sergeant about it.

"Here. I don't want the stuff. I'm frightened."

Two things stopped him. First, the truth was too fantastic. The police would never believe he'd found the money. Such things just didn't happen. He'd be held for investigation and the newspapers would pick up the story. He'd become a one-day sensation.

> Sixty-five hundred dollar a year translator claims he found two hundred thousand dollars on back seat of taxi cab.

After that the reporters would really go to town. They would examine and print every facet of his life, the bad along with the good. He'd never done anything particularly bad but there were some episodes he would prefer to keep private. Then there was May. Angry because he'd failed to tell her about finding the money, thinking that he'd intended to hold out on her, there was no telling what May might say to the reporters. Then there was May's daughter, Alice. If Alice was old enough at fifteen to want to be treated as a woman, she was old enough to feel scorned. And there's an old and very true adage concerning that one.

All in all, the thing would be a mess. When the newspapers had finished with him he might not have a wife. He might not even have a job. The firm of Harper, Nelson and Ferrel would consider the whole affair undignified.

Brady pushed himself away from the parapet and walked back the way he had come. If the money really belonged to a big time Chicago mobster, the no longer mysterious Mr. Dix would be equally unappreciative. He would want his money, not a series of newspaper clippings and a police receipt. And if Brady turned the money over to the police there was a very good chance that they would impound it.

For whatever purpose the money was to have been used, whoever was to have received it as settlement in full for 1957, there was only one logical reason for transferring such a large sum in cash. Mr. Dix hadn't wanted it to show on his books. He had been willing to chance its being stolen as long as it couldn't be traced to him. And if he, Jim Brady, were to call attention to the fact that Mr. Dix had so much money in cash, he might bring the Internal Revenue boys into the affair and Brady doubted very much if Mr. Dix would want to go to jail on a charge of income tax evasion.

Brady's mind continued to race along. If the girl in the red plastic raincoat had been acting as an agent in the matter, if she'd been carrying the money, she'd had reason to be frightened.

He mentally reconstructed the scene. After falling in front of the station, to keep his barked knuckles from bleeding all over his coat, he'd thrust his hand into his pocket. His hand had still been in his pocket when he'd yanked open the door of the cab. And thinking he was from some rival mob and had come to hi-jack the money, the frightened girl had naturally assumed his hidden hand had been holding a gun.

And just how to explain that to Mr. Dix?

Brady walked on wearily. He couldn't go to the police. Even if he knew how, it seemed unwise to contact Dix. All he had to offer was his unsubstantiated word against whatever story the girl might choose to tell. Even if he returned the money, the odds were ten to one the matter would finally be settled by the harbor police pulling another floater out of the river.

Brady was honest with himself. There was a third reason for keeping the money. It was his one big chance to get out of the mess he was in. The money was his. He'd found it. If he could sit tight for six months or a year, go right on as if nothing had happened, he could leave May five or ten thousand dollars to tide her over until she sold her bill of goods to some other home-hungry male.

Brady walked down the steps of the next subway entrance he came to. For the present, however, if he wanted to avoid a family quarrel, it would be better for all concerned if he was on the 5:35 when it arrived in Stamford.

When he reached Grand Central Station Brady opened the locker to exchange the case he was carrying for the empty one inside. Then it occurred to him that for some reason or another he might not be able to get to the locker each day and if he remembered correctly, they were checked and cleaned out every twenty four hours. You had to identify your property to recover it, plus pay an additional charge. But a baggage check was good for thirty days.

He stood in line at the check room counter wondering what the bored attendant would do if he knew what was in the fat brief case.

After checking the brief case containing the money he barely had time to buy a paper and still catch the 5:35. He was already settled in his seat when he realized he'd forgotten to take the new brief case out of the locker. He hoped May wouldn't notice he was arriving home empty-handed. If she did, all he could do was say he'd left the case at the office.

May didn't say anything when she picked him up at the station. For some reason she was unnaturally silent and tight-lipped.

Supper was never a pleasant meal. Tonight it was really dreary. Over-excited by the purchase of his new bicycle, Jimmy monopolized the conversation. The only time May spoke was to ask for something to be passed. Alice's eyes were puffed and red as if she'd been crying all day. Tonight there was no footsy and no kneesy. The fifteen-year-old ate silently, glowering at Brady between bites.

When supper was over, instead of helping her mother with the dishes, Alice asked to leave the house on the pretext of doing her homework with the girl across the street. Brady expected May to protest. She didn't. Instead, she asked Brady to give Jimmy a dollar so he could go to the movies.

Brady gave his stepson the money and walked into the living room and re-read his paper to make certain he hadn't missed a follow-up on the girl in the red raincoat. Also, there was no advertisement in the lost and found column that could even remotely be construed to concern the money he'd found.

He lit a cigarette from the one he was smoking and saw that instead of washing the dishes, May had come into the living room and was sitting on the same straight-backed chair on which he'd gone through the nightmare with Alice. Her hands were folded tightly in her lap. The corners of her thin lips were turned down in the 'you-sonofabitch' expression that always preceded a scene.

"What did I do now?" he asked.

"You don't know?"

Brady forced himself to speak casually. "No. I haven't the least idea."

"Hah."

"Just what does that mean?"

May told him. "Mr. Harper phoned this afternoon."

His cigarette no longer tasted good. Brady put it out. "Oh?"

"You didn't go to the office today, did you?"

"No," Brady admitted. "I didn't. What did you tell him?"

"What could I tell him? I told him your cold was much better and you would be in in the morning."

"Thanks."

May felt sorry for herself. "All right. I lied for you. I may even have saved your job. I think I have a right to know. Why didn't you go to the office?"

Brady couldn't think of any reason, at least any that he could tell May. He told her the partial truth. "I just did not feel like it."

"When you know what losing your job could mean to all of us?"

"I'm not going to lose my job."

"How do you know? Mr. Harper is very nice. But he certainly wasn't pleased. And us with the house and car payments to make. And fuel to buy. And school clothing for the children. Don't you care what happens to us?"

Brady was tempted to tell her he didn't give a damn what happened to either her or her juvenile monsters. For the sake of peace, he temporized. "It was just one of those things. I had to have a break of some kind, do something different."

May sniffed. "Hmm. Housework gets monotonous, too. Are you in some kind of trouble, Jim?"

Brady lighted another cigarette. "Don't be absurd."

May persisted. "I don't think I'm being absurd. Something is worrying you. You didn't sleep half an hour last night."

"How do you know?"

"I heard you prowling around."

"I wanted a drink of milk."

"In the living room?"

"All right. So I had a highball."

"Then kept right on drinking all day."

"What makes you think that?"

"I can tell by looking at you. Your breath almost knocked me over when I met you at the station. You've been in a fight. And you left your brief case somewhere."

Brady touched his slightly puffed lip that the bellhop and clerk had given him. "All right. I didn't go to work. I spent the day in a bar."

"Why?"

"No particular reason."

May's voice was shriller than Brady had ever heard it. "I think you're lying, Jim Brady. And if what I think is worrying you is so, God help you, that's all."

Brady was angry with himself and impatient with her. "I don't know what you're talking about."

May stood up. "I think you do. What were you and Alice doing in here last night?"

Brady answered her. "I wasn't doing a thing. She just happened to come in while I was making a highball. And I told her to go back to bed."

"I don't believe you." May pounded her clenched fist on the television cabinet. "I think you're having an affair with the child. I think you're having illicit relations with her. And if I find out I'm right, God help you, Jim Brady. I'll see that you go to prison for the maximum time the law provides."

Once started talking, she couldn't seem to stop. "You might as well know right now I wouldn't lift a finger to help you. I don't care *that* for you. I just married you for a home for myself and Jimmy and Alice. I've tried to be a good wife. But that doesn't include letting you play fast and loose with my daughter."

Brady tried to stem the torrent of words by pointing out that Alice was just a child and May laughed, thinly.

"She's as mature as I was when I married her father. And about the same age. Besides, what difference does that make? I know how men are. All of you. The younger a girl is the better. And after all, Alice is no relation to you. No real relation."

"I'm her stepfather."

"Also her lover."

"I swear not."

"Then why is the child always touching you and mooning around you? Why are the two of you always whispering in corners? I should have known when I came in here last night. Your faces were the picture of guilt. What were you planning? Last night's rendezvous? After you were sure I was asleep. Where did you do it? On the sofa or on the floor?" In her hysterical anger the blonde woman stopped pounding on the television cabinet and beat on Brady's chest. "Tell me. How long has this been going on? How many times have you been intimate with Alice?"

The whole scene was ridiculous. If it hadn't been so serious, Brady would have laughed.

May continued to pound his chest. "Confess. Tell me the truth."

Brady caught both her wrists in one of his hands and pushed her away from him. "You'd better lower your voice or the neighbors will hear you."

"I don't care if they do."

"How about our 'position' in Stamford?"

"If I find out I'm right you won't have to worry about position, only about how many years you're going to get for contributing to the delinquency of a minor."

Brady was tempted to ask how anyone could possibly contribute to Alice's delinquency. At fifteen the child was mentally and morally corrupt. He refrained. It was all so sordid, so futile.

On impulse, he walked into the bedroom and got his good suit from the closet and picked out a fresh shirt. He had to get out of the house, if only for a few hours.

May followed him into the bedroom and watched, her eyes sullen, as he dressed. "Where do you think you're going?" she asked.

Brady said, "Out."

"Out where?"

Brady told her the truth. "I haven't the least idea. Possibly one of the bars near the station."

"I think you've had enough to drink."

"All right. So I'll just talk to the bartender."

Brady transferred his change and wallet and keys to the pockets of his good trousers, then transferred the claim check for the brief case from one watch pocket to the other.

"What's that for?" May asked.

"Just some company correspondence," Brady lied. "I didn't want to carry it around."

He glanced sideways at his wife. The first of her anger over, May seemed to realize she'd gone too far. The next act in the tragic comedy would be self-pity. She took a soiled handkerchief from the pocket of her house dress and dabbed at her eyes. "You have to admit I have a right to be suspicious."

Brady shrugged into his coat. "Especially since you just married me for a home for you and the children."

May searched for something to say, and could only ask, "Will you be late?"

"I haven't the slightest idea."

"But you are going to work tomorrow?"

"I imagine so."

Leaving her sitting on the bed, Brady walked out into the other room and got his trench coat from the hall closet and let himself into the garage through the kitchen door. He was still so angry he was trembling.

Brady backed out of the driveway too fast and almost collided with a smart convertible cruising slowly up the street. He braked just in time and rolled down his window and thrust out his head and said, "Sorry."

There were two people in the other car, a man and a girl. With the top up it was too dark for him to see the girl's face but the driver was young and clean-cut looking, wearing a pork pie hat.

"Sorry," Brady repeated.

"Think nothing of it," Daly smiled. "They tell me these things happen."

TWELVE

As the big Viscount II circled over Manhattan, Lew Dix looked down without interest at the multi-colored lights.

He felt old and tired and put upon. When a man had climbed as high in the rackets as he had he should be able to rest. He shouldn't be bothered with minor details. He should be able to transfer some of the organizational responsibilities to his underlings.

Dix tried to be fair. On the other hand two hundred thousand dollars wasn't minor. Morgan and Daly were good men. They'd handled a dozen affairs like this without giving him any reason for complaint. If, as Morgan had said over the phone, his presence in New York was imperative, Morgan knew what he was talking about.

Then there were the old men from Palermo. It was cool in the air-conditioned jet-powered plane but Dix could feel a thin film of oily perspiration on his forehead and cheeks. No matter how high a man climbed he was still subject to the law of *omerta*.

The money had to be recovered. It had taken considerable time and sacrifice to get it together. And, at the moment, with the market as it was and nosy Senate investigating committees probing the links between certain business operations and the gangs, he wouldn't be able to replace it without considerable financial loss and expenditure of time. And if the old men from Palermo should get the erroneous idea he was stalling, or trying to evade paying his just tribute....

Dix preferred not to think of it. No matter how big a man got he was just a small cog in the over-all picture. And while Daly and Morgan might, on occasion, fail to complete an assignment, the enforcers for the Mafia never failed. And no one knew who they were. One might be the barber who had shaved you for years. Or the man who ran the fruit store on the corner. Or talent imported from some far corner of the spidery empire. Or your best friend.

The thought made the short hairs on the back of Dix's neck tingle. Once, long years ago, when he'd been a young man, he'd had such an assignment. He could still see the shocked surprise on Luigi's face when he'd shot him.

He said a hurried Hail Mary and crossed himself. It was not good to think of things like that.

The 'Fasten Your Seat Belt' panel winked on and Dix allowed the pert stewardess to help him with the web belt. She smelled sweet and young and reminded him of Linda Lou. Then he became infuriated. Over the years dozens of girls had carried money for him without ever losing a penny. If he remembered correctly, when the method of transference of funds had first been put into practice, back in the days of Johnny Torrio, a sweet young thing by the name of Virginia something had been the first courier. And if a reluctant little baby-faced fugitive from the South thought she could pull a fast one on Lew Dix, she'd whistled her last chorus of Dixie.

Dix snorted his disbelief. A big man in a trench coat had climbed into her cab and pointed a gun at her, had he? He would take care of Miss Linda Lou personally. But not until after he'd recovered his money.

The landing at La Guardia was without event. Dix didn't want to stay in New York too long. He had to get back to Chicago as soon as he possibly could. When the cat was away the mice not only played, they nibbled at the cheese. The week he'd had to spend in upper New York State for the meet the year before had cost him a small fortune. His receipts had fallen off thirty per cent. It was incredible what dishonest employees could do to a respectable businessman. If they were not watched every minute, crooked tavern and gambling house managers, fast-talking hotel and laundry and brewery superintendents would steal a man blind. Even the two dozen or so whores in the three small houses he still operated, more as a sentimental link with the old days than as a money-making proposition, had reported that they hadn't turned a dime's worth of tricks while he'd been gone. And he knew better than that. That was one commodity in which the demand always exceeded the supply.

Morgan was waiting for him by the gate.

"You find it yet?" Dix asked.

The younger man shook his head. "No. But we think we have a good lead."

Neither man spoke again until they were in the big black limousine that Morgan had rented. Then, popping one of his dyspepsia pills in his mouth, Dix said, sourly, "All right. Let's have it."

Morgan drove deftly through traffic, not turning his head as he talked. "Well, as I told you over the phone, the girl claims she got into this cab and when a big guy got in and pointed a gun at her, she panicked and took off, leaving the parcel on the seat."

Dix snorted.

Morgan continued. "We felt the same way. We thought the girl was pulling a fast one. We thought she had it rigged with the cabby to hang on to the money while she made her story good by letting a truck hit her and having to spend a night in Bellevue."

"Go on."

"So we made certain the parcel wasn't on the hospital list of her personal possessions and waited until they released her when we trailed her down to Bleecker Street and into an abandoned warehouse where a *paesano* named Mike Scaffidi garaged his hack. When Daly and I walked in they were sitting cozy in the back of the hack and we figure she is just about to pay him off for holding the money for her. But when we haul him out of the cab and ask him where the money is he protests he doesn't know anything about it. He claims he doesn't even know Linda and his only connection with the affair is her getting into his cab in front of Grand Central and then coming down to the warehouse and asking for the parcel she says she left in his cab. And the girl backed his story. It was then that she gave us the bit about the big joker in the trench coat who pointed a gun at her."

"You talked to the cab driver?"

Morgan was annoyed. "A little too hard, I'm afraid."

"Did anyone see you?"

"No. We're clear on that score."

"Then why have me make this trip?"

Morgan explained. "It's a little complicated. While we were talking to Scaffidi we found this." He took the plastic tag from his pocket and handed it to Dix. "It isn't much. But it was all we had to go on. The girl wouldn't talk. Scaffidi couldn't. But the tag was in his pocket and before Linda clammed up she swore that the man who pointed a gun at her had been carrying a brief case under his other arm."

Dix looked at the tag on his palm. "I see. So you figured if there had been a man with a gun this might have come from his brief case."

Morgan nodded. "That's it."

"Assuming Linda's story is true."

"We didn't think so at first. But now we do. Anyway, as I said, it wasn't much to go on but it was all we had. So we drove up to this place Stamford and did a little discreet talking around and found out all we could about this guy Brady."

Dix read the name on the tag. "James A. Brady."

"Is the name familiar to you?"

"No. Should it be?"

"That's what Daly and I would like to know. He's about thirty-four or five, with a good war record. He lives in a so-so house with a faded blonde who has two children by a former marriage, one of them a hot-pantsed little bitch who almost raped Daly before he could get out of the house after he rang the bell, pretending he was selling magazines to work his way through college. She'd just come home from school and her mother was out shopping, see. Anyway from what the girl told Daly, on the surface at least, Brady is a sixty-five hundred dollar a year translator for a firm called Harper, Nelson and Ferrel. And he comes into Manhattan every morning on the train that would put him in Grand Central about the time the Twentieth Century gets in."

"Go on."

"And he left for town on schedule yesterday morning. When he left the house he was wearing a trench coat and carrying a brief case."

"With a name tag on it?"

"That's right. Daly didn't show the girl the tag but he got the question in without her becoming suspicious."

"And this is the tag?"

"We don't know. We think so. Anyway, it connects him with Scaffidi and he answers the description of the man Linda says climbed into the cab and pointed a gun at her. And we think he has the money."

Dix lit one of his twisted black cigars. "Then why don't you and Daly work on him and get it back? Why make me fly eight hundred miles?"

Morgan told him. "Because after we talked it over, we decided the whole affair was a little too pat, a little too coincidental. Stop and figure it out. The guy comes into Manhattan at just exactly the right time. Out of thousands of cabs in the city he picks just exactly the right one. And since when do white-collared office workers carry guns?"

Dix smoked in silence for a moment. "I'm beginning to see what you mean. You figure someone tipped him. You figure there's a leak in the organization."

"Either that," Morgan said flatly, "or it is even worse. Try this one on for size. What if one of the New York mobs has planted someone on us? Maybe Miss Phillips in your office. As I get the picture, under the present city administration and what with all those Senate investigations, things here are not only very disorganized but some of the boys are actually going hungry. They don't know where their next Cadillac is coming from." He continued. "Now you and I and Daly know where that two hundred grand was going. And if it doesn't get where it's supposed to we know what might happen. And with the three of us out of the picture the whole setup in Chicago will be thrown up for grabs. And what would be more logical than for the boys who caused it to happen to take over? And that's why we phoned you."

"I'm glad you did," Dix said. His cigar no longer tasted good. His heartburn was worse. The old days never really died. Not in his line of business. There was always some young wolf or pack of wolves hopeful of pulling down an old one.

He didn't like what he was thinking. The theft of the money might well have been planned. For the sake of the money itself and also because the men who planned it knew that at the moment he was financially overextended and would have difficulty raising another such sum. By stealing a lousy two hundred thousand dollars and discrediting him with the Mafia, it was possible whoever had stolen the money was hoping to tear down the multi-million dollar organization he'd spent his life in building. And once they'd torn it down they would step in, rebuild it and open up again under new management.

Morgan drove through the heart of the city to the Skyway and north on the Skyway to the beginning of Merritt Parkway.

Dix asked, "Have you been able to get a make on this Brady? Have you traced any connection?"

Morgan shook his head. "No. Like I said. On the surface he's a sixty-five hundred dollar a year translator. But here's something you might think over. Both Daly and I have. A job like that is a perfect cover. He's in a perfect position to be wired in on the rackets in half a dozen countries." He added, sourly, "And here's something else you might think over. We might just be up against the big boys themselves. This Brady's father was the assistant American consul in Napoli for three years. And this Brady spent all of his summers in Palermo. He speaks Italian like he'd been born with a mouthful of ripe olives."

"Daly got all this from his daughter?"

"Stepdaughter. Daly couldn't make up his mind whether the girl was nuts about the guy or hated his guts. Either way she was willing to talk about him. But before he could get any more out of her, Mrs. Brady came home with the groceries and said they couldn't afford any magazines and he left."

Dix rode in grim silence. This thing could be big, as big as anything he'd ever faced. It could mean much more than the loss of the money. Had the powers that be discovered he kept three sets of books? One for the Internal Revenue Department. One to show the Mafia accountants. One to keep track of how much money he'd really made. For while a man could cheat on God, while he could chinsey on his tithes, he couldn't chisel on the old men from Palermo. Not for long.

Dix sweated as he hadn't sweated for years. As he now saw the situation it could be one of three things.

Brady was a sharp independent operator with a wire into his own organization who had made a lucky strike.

He was a member of a New York mob who'd heisted the money in an attempt to discredit him and take over his organization.

He was one of the inner council, using his job as a translator as a cover and he, Lew Dix, had been found out and marked for death by the inflexible law of *omerta* and the theft of the money was merely the first pointing finger of the black hand that was slowly closing around his throat. Dix beat his flabby fist on the padded dashboard of the car. One way or another, he had to know.

He flicked his cigar out the rolled down window and watched it die in a shower of sparks as it bounced off the pavement. "Where is Daly now?"

"With Linda Lou," Morgan told him. "She didn't want to do it. In fact, she was downright reluctant." He added, wryly, "But we managed to convince her it was to her best interest to ride out to Stamford with Daly and make a positive identification."

"And did she?"

"So Daly said on the phone just before your plane landed."

"Where was he calling from?"

"A drugstore in Stamford, a few doors from the tavern where Brady is drinking."

"And that's where we're headed now?"

"It is."

"Then why don't you drive faster?"

Morgan told him. "Because I don't want to be picked up for speeding. After that business in the warehouse I would just as soon not have *any* contact with the local police."

THIRTEEN

Brady was careful not to drink beyond his capacity. He couldn't afford to get drunk. All he wanted to do was blot out the scene with May.

He finished his highball and ordered another, sipping it slowly to make it last at least an hour. Then he ordered a third highball. He would watch the eleven o'clock newscast and then go home. There was nothing else he could do tonight. Despite the unpleasant scene with May and the Damocles-like sword of Alice hanging over his head, if he wanted to keep the money, and he did, his life on the surface had to continue on its normal, dull, level plane. He couldn't risk any suspicion. He had to be plain James A. Brady, commuter. In the morning he would figure out something.

The barman paused in front of him. "Sort of quiet in here tonight, eh?"

"Quiet," Brady agreed with him. At that moment the newscast came on. There'd been a big fire in St. Louis. Gamel Abdel Nasser and his Arab Nationalists were still raising hob in the Middle East. A Broadway showgirl was marrying a wealthy Texas oil man. The longshoremen were threatening to strike again. A cab driver had been beaten to death in an abandoned warehouse on Bleecker Street.

Brady started to get off his stool. He froze half on and half off as a picture of the murder scene was flashed on the picture tube and the telecaster's words imprinted themselves on his consciousness:

"The dead driver, Mike Scaffidi, had driven for Allied Cab Company for the past ten years and was considered by officials to be one of their most valuable ownerdrivers. Police from the Charles Street Station who first answered the call believe Scaffidi, known as a ladies' man, may have been beaten to death by the boy friend or husband of one of his neighborhood conquests...."

The lump in Brady's throat grew larger as he studied the picture on the screen. The dead man sprawled on the cement floor of the garage was definitely Mike Scaffidi. And the dead man had taken a terrific beating before he died. His bloody face was criss-crossed with wounds that looked like they'd been made with a knife or possibly the sight on the end of a gun barrel.

The newscaster went on:

"However, Detective Sergeant Joel Hooper and First Grade Detective Sam Manson, attached to Center Street Homicide, are investigating a theory that Scaffidi's murder may be connected with a blonde girl carrying a red plastic raincoat and recently released from Bellevue Hospital who is known to have made inquiries about the dead man's whereabouts shortly before the time of death as established by the medical examiner's office...."

Brady held his breath as he waited for the newscaster to continue, but the picture changed and tomorrow's weather was being discussed.

Noticing Brady's half-extended glass, the barman asked, "A nightcap, Mr. Brady?"

Brady shook his head. "No, thanks. I've had my quota."

He picked up his change and stood, undecided. This could not be coincidence. No matter how far you stretched it, coincidence wouldn't stretch that far. A blonde carrying a red plastic raincoat. A dead cab driver beaten to death in an abandoned warehouse. Whoever had killed Scaffidi *had* to be looking for Brady.

On impulse, Brady entered the phone booth in the tavern and dropped a coin in the slot and dialed his own phone number.

May answered the phone. "The Brady residence."

"This is Jim," Brady told her. "Don't ask me why. Don't ask me any questions. But this could be very important. I have to know. Did anyone but Mr. Harper phone the house and ask for me today?"

May sounded puzzled. "Not while I was home. Why?"

Brady ignored the question he'd asked her not to ask. "Are Jimmy and Alice home? Ask them."

There was silence at the other end of the wire. Then May said, "They say no. But Alice says that the young man who was here this afternoon selling magazines to put himself through college asked her a lot of questions about you. Why? What's this all about, James?"

"Put Alice on," Brady said.

The fifteen-year-old girl's voice was as sullen as her eyes had been during supper. "Yes?"

"This magazine salesman," Brady said. "What kind of questions did he ask about me?"

"Where you worked. How much you made. And what you did for a living. And how long we'd lived here and where we lived before. Just questions."

"And you told him?"

"Yes."

"What did he look like?"

"Young. Good looking. Typical Ivy League." The girl went on, spitefully. "And what's more, *he* liked me."

Brady cradled the phone and supported his weight by his shoulders as he slumped against the wall next to the phone. Whoever had killed Scaffidi was looking for him. The lost tag *had* been found. They knew where he lived.

He was reluctant to leave the phone booth and he hated leaving the tavern. Outside, the street was semi-deserted. There were the usual lights in the railway station but most of the stores were closed. There were few people on the walk and little vehicular traffic. No one seemed to be interested in him. He walked past an expensive black limousine parked at the curb to reach his own car, glancing sharply at its occupant as he did so. At least he had nothing to fear from him. He was merely a flabby-faced elderly Italian chewing on a black cigar. Brady couldn't see the driver but the limousine was undoubtedly chauffeur driven and the elderly Italian a big shot from one of the mansions rimming the golf course. He was probably waiting for his wife and family to arrive on the theatre train from Manhattan.

His whole body was trembling so badly Brady flooded his engine trying to start his car and had to grind on the starter again. When he did pull away from the curb he pressed too hard on the accelerator and the car jack-rabbited down the street before he could get it under control. When he did, he paid more attention to his rear vision mirror than to the street in front of him. Now he was out in traffic and there were several cars behind him but he had no way of knowing if any of them was following his car. All he could see was headlights, one pair identical with another.

He circled the business section, then instinctively turned down the street where he habitually turned and drove to his own street.

As he neared his own house he could see there was a light in the living room. There were also lights in the bedroom he shared with May and the den. Both May and Alice must be up waiting for him. He started to turn into the driveway and didn't. Instead he drove on slowly. He couldn't stand another scene with May tonight. Judging from the tone of Alice's voice over the phone she was in a mood to exact her revenge because he'd scorned her somewhat immature charms.

He angled up the next side street and circled back the way he had come, then down an arterial highway to its juncture with the Merritt Parkway and turned south on the Parkway to Manhattan.

It should be a good proving ground. The night traffic on the Parkway was light. If he was being followed, if someone wanted to kill him, there wasn't a better place to crowd his car off the road. He *had* to know. He couldn't spend the rest of his life looking back over his shoulder and shying away from shadows. On the other hand, if Lew Dix or his boys should stop and question him, what could they prove? That he'd lost the tag off his brief case in Scaffidi's cab.

Brady made certain the baggage claim check for the brief case with the money in it was in his pocket. Then struck by a sudden thought he fumbled through his change until his fingers found the key to the Grand Central Station locker where he'd left the new brief case. And if they insisted he had the money he could give them the key and they could open the door themselves and find the empty brief case, *minus a name tag.*

He stopped to pay a toll and drove on. So far no one had tried to stop him. No one had tried to crowd him off the road. It could be he was running away from the men who had tortured and killed the cab driver. It could be he was running away from a shadow, that the young man who'd questioned Alice had really been just what he'd said he was, a young man working his way through college.

Brady wiped his face with the sleeve of his trench coat. Either way he was gambling for a fortune, a chance to get off the treadmill. With a bank roll of two hundred thousand dollars he could live like a king in Paris or Madrid or Rome. He could even open his own import-export company.

He passed through a second, then a third toll stop. There was more traffic now. If the driver of any of the cars in the stream of headlights behind him was concerned with him there was no evidence of it.

When he reached Manhattan most of Brady's fear left him. He no longer felt so alone. There was something eminently comforting about the tall buildings and normally heavy flow of traffic. Manhattan never went to bed. Manhattan was always awake and alive.

His self-confidence and belief in his own ability to take care of any situation that should arise returned as he drove down one of the off ramps of the Skyway and east to Eighth Avenue and parked in front of a brightly lighted bar and grill.

Brady felt slightly sheepish. He'd spooked. He'd seen the picture of a dead man on a television screen. He'd heard a routine newscast and had taken off like the devil had been after him. So Mike Scaffidi had been murdered. Metropolitan Homicide was on the job. And the Center Street boys were smart operators. The chances were that whoever had beaten Scaffidi to death was already in custody.

He locked his car and entered the grill and as he sat at the counter he realized after ordering coffee, that he was hungry. So he ordered a steak, french fries, a side order of onion rings and rolls.

When the counterman brought him his coffee, a passing thought amused Brady. He could afford six steaks if he wanted them. He had a lot of money. He had all the money in the world.

He had two hundred thousand dollars.

FOURTEEN

Linda Lou sat very small and still between Mr. Dix and Morgan as Morgan braked the big, black car to a stop across the street and three or four buildings down from where the car they'd been following had parked.

She could barely see through the slit in her puffed right eye. Her arms still ached from the twisting Morgan had given them. Her stomach hurt where Daly had kicked her. She wished now that instead of trying to recover the money she'd told the whole story to the two detectives who had questioned her in the hospital and asked them to protect her. Now that it was too late she knew that all the pretending in the world wouldn't get her out of the mess she was in. She'd seen Morgan and Daly kill a man. They'd forced her to identify the big man who'd gotten into the cab. They intended to kill him as soon as they recovered the money. Once they had the money, they'd kill her. She was a witness against them.

Hardly daring to breathe for fear of calling attention to herself and being punched again, she clung to her one small consolation. At least neither Daly nor Morgan had abused her as a woman. They boasted they didn't like women that way. Nor did Mr. Dix have any further interest in her. On the long ride in from Stamford he hadn't felt her once. The flabby old man was frightened. All he could think of was the money.

Glancing in the rear vision mirror she saw Daly park his rented automobile and hurry down the walk. When he reached the car he opened the door and got in.

"What do you think?" he asked Mr. Dix.

Dix thought for a moment. "Frankly, I don't know. I thought when the guy first took off he was scared. Now I just don't know. He could be leading us into a trap. We could walk in there and try to waltz him out and find ourselves in the middle of a lot of heat."

"That's the way I feel," Daly said.

Morgan lighted a cigarette. "Well, we can't just sit here. On the other hand, we can't just go in and blast him. There are too many witnesses for one thing. For another, if we do that we might as well kiss the money goodbye. We've got to get him out of there so we can talk to him."

Linda Lou tried to repress a shudder and failed. She had seen Morgan and Daly "talk" to Mr. Scaffidi.

Sensing the movement beside him, Morgan looked sideways at her. "How about the girl?" he asked. "Why don't we send her in? She could tell him she wants to make a bargain with him and she's willing to go to a hotel with him to bind the deal. Anything, to get him out of there."

From the back seat, Daly said, "It's an idea. But I still think we should have stopped the guy on the Parkway."

Dix took the cigar from his mouth. "With you boys as hot as you are and the whole highway crawling with cops? They'd have been all over us so fast we wouldn't know what was happening to us. I counted five patrol cars on my way in, not including two parked at toll stations. You have to think these things through. That's why I'm still alive and top dog while most of the other boys are dead." He returned his cigar to his mouth. "Yeah. Sending Linda Lou in may work. Judging from the way he's operated so far, Brady is much too smart to fall for the hotel bit. But he will be curious to find out what her gizmo is."

Daly protested, "But can we trust her?"

Morgan lifted his hand from the wheel and slapped Linda Lou so hard that fresh tears spurted to her eyes, then he doubled his hand into a fist and drove it into her unprotected abdomen. "Yeah. I think we can trust her," he said. "She should know by now what will happen to her if she gets out of line again. How about it, Linda? Do you want to go in the restaurant and try to waltz the guy out for us? Or do you want Daly and I to work you over again right here in the car?"

"No, please," Linda Lou begged. "Please don't hit me again."

Morgan handed her a clean handkerchief. "Then stop bawling and put on fresh make-up and go see what you can do with Brady. Tell him how clever you think he's been and that you want to throw in with him. The guy acts to me as if he's fed up with the bag he's shacked up with and the prospect of a quivering little piece of juicy quail should interest him, even if he knows there's a gimmick. Tell him you want to play on his side. Tell him anything. But get him out on the street."

Her slight body numb with pain, still gasping for breath, Linda Lou opened her purse and after wiping away her tears, she did what she could with lipstick and compact. It wasn't much. There wasn't anything she could do about her swollen eye or puffed lips. Not that she cared. She didn't want to be pretty. All she wanted right now was to get out of the car. And once she was out she knew what she was going to do. No gawd-damn big sonofabitch, no three gawd-damn sonsofbitches, could treat her this way. Some people claimed that crackers could be mean. She'd show these three spaghetti-eating bastards just how mean one cracker could be. She'd talk to Brady all right. She'd warn him who was waiting outside and tell him to call his own gang and blast Mr. Dix and Daly and Morgan right off the street. And after she'd warned Mr. Brady she'd go to the police—and tell them the whole story, including who'd killed Mr. Scaffidi.

Daly was still dubious. Leaning his arms on the back of the front seat, he said, "I still don't like it. What if she tips the guy? What if she blows the whistle?"

Dix slipped Morgan's spare gun from his coat pocket and pressed the muzzle of it firmly against the girl's temple. It felt good to be holding a gun again after so many years, to know the surge of power it gave a man. "Linda isn't going to tip anyone or blow any whistle, are you, Linda?" he asked quietly. "Because Linda knows what will happen to her if she does. Don't you, Linda?"

Linda Lou returned her compact and lipstick to her purse. "Yes, Mr. Dix."

The old man opened the door of the car on his side and got out and helped her onto the walk. "We'll give you five minutes," he told her. "Then, trap or not, witnesses or no, we're coming in and blow Brady out if we have to."

Linda Lou straightened the seam of her stocking. "Yes, sir. Whatever you say, Mr. Dix."

She walked to the rear of the car and waited on the curb until a short stream of taxicabs and private cars passed. As she stood there, a drop of rain fell on her face. It was going to rain hard again and soon. When the street was clear she crossed to the opposite curb and opened the door of the bar and grill and sat on a stool at the counter beside Brady.

Seen close up, he didn't look like a killer. He was merely a tired man in his early thirties with an attractive swatch of gray in his black hair.

Busy with his thoughts and a cup of steaming coffee, he didn't notice her at first. The counterman did and was shocked.

"Holy smoke, Miss," he gasped as he studied her swollen face. "Who hung one like that on a pretty doll like you?"

Brady turned on his stool to glance at the girl and almost spilled his coffee. Even with one of her eyes swollen almost shut he recognized her immediately. There was no doubt about it. She was the girl in the red plastic raincoat, the girl who had been in Mike Scaffidi's cab.

"I'll have a cup of coffee, please," Linda Lou told the counterman.

"Yes, Miss. Right away," he smiled.

Brady lowered his own cup to his saucer. He felt as if someone had opened an artery and all of his newly regained self-confidence had drained out. He'd been followed from Stamford after all and he was back in flight again, even sitting on the stool. Not knowing what else to do, he waited for the girl to speak. She was silent until the counterman moved away to serve another couple. Then she spoke in a very low voice.

"There are three of them in a car outside. Mr. Dix and Morgan and Daly."

Brady thought if she was trying to impress him she'd succeeded. After what Johnny Cass had told him even the name Dix terrified him.

Linda Lou added, "Morgan and Daly are the ones who killed the cab driver. They beat him to death with their guns because he couldn't tell them where the money was." She spooned sugar into her coffee. "And I had to stand there and watch it. After they finished with him they did this to me."

Brady wondered what the girl expected him to say. He said, "I'm sorry. Believe me, Miss Larson. I'm sorry."

Linda Lou sipped her coffee and returned the cup to its saucer. "And they're waiting outside to kill you," she went on, "just as soon as they make you tell them what you did with the parcel. I'm supposed to get you out there by telling you how smart I think you were and that I want to throw in with you and you can take me to a hotel if you want to. But we wouldn't get twenty feet before they jumped you. So if you want to get out of this alive, you'd better call you own gang, fast."

Brady protested, "But believe me, I haven't got a gang."

Linda Lou studied his face. "Don't try to lie to me, Mr. Brady. Please. This is too important. I know you're the man who opened the cab door and frightened me."

"Yes," Brady admitted. "I am." He thought a moment. If the situation was as serious as it seemed to be, there was no use mincing words. All he could do was tell the truth. "But all I did was open the door. I didn't even know there was anybody in the cab."

Linda Lou was skeptical. "You didn't point a gun at me and start to say you were sorry you had to kill me?"

Brady held up his right hand. "I swear."

"Then why did you have your hand in your pocket?"

Brady showed her the scabs on his recently barked knuckles. "Because I fell down in front of the station and I was trying to keep from getting blood all over everything."

Linda Lou looked into his face for a long moment and believed him. She'd never been too certain there'd been a gun. She asked, "But you did find the money?"

Brady considered his answer. It had been all right for him to have taken chances but now it looked like certain death. And a dead man couldn't spend money. As he saw it now the only thing he could do was get off the hook with a whole skin if he could. The girl seemed to believe him. Perhaps she would intercede with Mr. Dix for him. He didn't like to let go of the money. But if he had to, he had to. He would have to find some other solution to his marital problems.

"Yes," he admitted. "I found the money. And I stuffed it into my brief case. That's when I must have lost the damn tag."

"But someone in Mr. Dix's organization in Chicago did tip you I was carrying the money and what time I would get into New York?"

"No. I just happened to get into your cab."

"You expect me to believe that?"

"It's true."

"You haven't got a gang?"

"No."

"And you don't belong to a New York mob that's trying to move in on Mr. Dix?"

"No."

If the situation wasn't so dangerous, if he wasn't so stinking with fear, Brady could have laughed. This could not be real. He couldn't be sitting here at two o'clock in the morning listening to a nineteen-year-old girl talking in a magnolia blossom and honey-suckle accent about gangs and mobs moving in on one another. Only the girl's badly punched face and his knowledge that Scaffidi was dead gave any credence to the scene.

Linda Lou persisted. "But you are a member of the Rafia?"

"I beg your pardon?"

Linda Lou was impatient. "The Rafia. As I get it from listening to Mr. Dix and Morgan and Daly talk, it's a sort of high-class club for bad Italians."

Brady perspired even harder, "You mean the Mafia."

"That's it."

Brady shook his head. "I'm sorry." He tried to make his position clear so the girl could make it clear to Mr. Dix. "Look. I don't have a gang. I'm not a member of one. I don't belong to the Mafia. As far as I'm concerned it's just a name I read once in a while in the newspapers."

"Then what *do* you do for a living?"

"I'm a translator. I work for an import-export firm on Fifth Avenue."

"But you do have a gun?"

"No," Brady said. "I'm sorry."

Linda Lou put her small hands on the counter and her mouth worked as she silently cried. It seemed that for the fourth and most important time in her life she'd bet on the wrong horse again. She'd picked another loser.

"Why?" Brady asked.

She told him. "Because if what you say is so, we're dead." She glanced at the door of the grill. "In just a few more minutes Mr. Dix and Morgan and Daly are going to come in that door and take us away from here and beat where the money is out of you. Then they're going to kill you and me along with you because I didn't do like they said. They'll kill us just like they killed Mr. Scaffidi."

Brady felt a drop of sweat tickle all the way down his side. The game was up. He'd lost. But he couldn't let anything more happen to this girl because of him. He'd caused her enough suffering.

It was futile to try to make a deal with Dix. Dix would take the money and kill them anyway, if only to protect himself in the Scaffidi matter. But there was one thing he could do. If he could get the girl out of the restaurant he could go to the nearest precinct station and tell the police the whole story. He could give them the claim check for the money and take whatever lumps he had to take. But meanwhile the girl would be safe.

He took a ten dollar bill from his pocket and laid it on the counter. "For the steak and the coffee," he told the counterman. "Is there a back way out of here?"

"Yes," the counterman said, "there is. The kitchen backs on an areaway that comes out between two buildings on Forty-ninth Street."

Brady helped Linda Lou to her feet.

"Where are we going?" she asked him.

He told her, "Out the back way and run for it. There's a police station not far from here and it may just be we can make it."

The areaway outside the kitchen door was narrow and not lighted and smelled of the garbage containers that lined it. Gripping the girl's elbow, Brady hurried her toward the not distant street lamp he could see. Just as they reached the mouth of the areaway a man stepped out of the night and blocked their way.

"I warned the old man," Daly said. "I told him something like this might happen." He jammed the barrel of his gun into Brady's side. "All right, now, you smart bastard, you've had it. Walk out of here and down to the corner and across Eighth Avenue slowly. Then turn right on Eighth and keep going until you come to a big, black car."

Gambling that the other man wouldn't want a shot to be heard, Brady ignored the command and hit Daly as hard as he could. Daly's head hit the wall and the gun clattered to the cement walk.

"Run," Brady shouted to Linda Lou.

She tried to run and slipped on the wet sidewalk and fell just as Daly regained both his feet and his gun. In the clear, all Brady had to do was run. The man didn't dare to shoot him until he learned where the money was hidden. But he couldn't leave the girl. Retracing his steps, he gripped Daly in a bear hug and tried to wrestle him off his feet and the gun exploded between them.

Even muffled as it was by their bodies, the gun shot sounded unnaturally loud. Daly stood a moment, then went limp in Brady's arms and slumped to the walk.

His breathing labored from the struggle, sweat almost blinding him, Brady took a step toward the girl, then stopped and looked from the gun in his hand to the motionless figure of the man lying face down on the pavement.

In killing him he'd plugged up his last avenue of escape. Now he couldn't go to the police. Now no sane jury of men and women would believe his fantastic story that he'd just opened the door of a cab and found two hundred thousand dollars on the seat. They would assume that this was an internecine affair between gangs and he'd killed the man on the pavement for possession of the money.

The shot had been heard. A police whistle was blowing. The implacable wheels of the law were beginning to turn. As Brady stuffed the gun in the pocket of his trench coat, the sharp nails of Linda Lou's fingers bit into his arm.

"What are we going to do now?" she asked him.

"I don't know," Brady admitted. "But we can't wait for the police. If we do they'll charge me with murder and probably book you as my accomplice." He added, bitterly, "For all I know, seeing that I still have the money, they may charge us with Scaffidi's murder and make it stick. We have to get out of here."

"Whatever you say," she said.

In falling she'd twisted her ankle and limped badly. Brady half carried her toward Times Square. He was completely exhausted but he forced himself to move. This, then, was the end of the tragic comedy of errors that had begun one rainy morning in Manhattan.

FIFTEEN

The rain was no longer just a shower. It was falling in great drops that bounced noisily on the pavement. The dimly lighted side street was beginning to fill up with people, morbidly curious about the police sirens and whistles. A black rain-coated figure was running up the middle of the street.

On the theory that a couple was less likely to be suspect if they were hurrying toward the scene of a crime rather than away from it, Brady reversed his direction and helped the girl beside him limp back to the mouth of the areaway seconds before the running policeman went past them. A squad car followed the policeman and by the time he and the limping girl had walked half way back, a second police car turned east off Eighth Avenue and disgorged two uniformed officers intent on keeping the onlookers away from the motionless figure on the walk.

"Keep back. Stand away from him," one of the officers ordered. He spoke crisply to the recently arrived patrolman. "Help Jim keep them moving, Murphy. The homicide boys raised hob the last time there was one of these little affairs. The damn ghouls not only tracked up all the evidence, they picked up everything but the body."

"Yes, sir," the patrolman said. He turned and faced the crowd. "You heard the lieutenant. Keep moving."

As Brady and Linda Lou approached the scene, he pointed the end of his night stick in their general direction, "That includes you, Mister. Don't just stand there gaping. Walk your girl out in the street and around him."

Brady was pleased to. He walked Linda Lou out onto the pavement and up to the corner and across Eighth Avenue. On the far corner he hesitated, briefly. "Where were Mr. Dix and this other hood you spoke of waiting?"

Linda Lou shielded her eyes against the rain as she looked up the street. "In a big, black car. But it isn't there now. They probably drove away as soon as they heard the rumpus."

"Probably," Brady agreed.

He helped her north on Eighth Avenue. A third police car was parked in front of the bar and grill. As he looked across the street, the counterman who had served them came out on the walk accompanied by a plainclothesman. The detective went over to Brady's car and tried a door and then said something to the counterman. Trying to shield his head from the rain with his apron, the counterman shrugged and returned to the lunchroom, while the detective continued to try the car doors, then cupped his hands to the wet glass of the front window as if hopeful of reading the name on the registration slip on the steering wheel.

"That takes care of my car," Brady thought.

He felt trapped. Even now a police cordon was being thrown around the district. He and the girl couldn't stay where they were. Nor, if her twisted ankle hurt her as much as it seemed to, could he expect her to walk much farther.

"Now what?" Linda Lou asked,

"I don't know," Brady admitted. "But we've got to get away from here."

"Why don't we take a cab?"

Brady considered the suggestion. Taking a cab would merely prolong the inevitable. By law all cab drivers kept trip books. And no matter how many times they changed cabs, it would be simple police procedure to trail them from where they were now to wherever they asked to be taken. More, a cab driver would be another witness against them. If and when they were charged with the murder of the dead hoodlum, the cab driver would testify he'd picked them up across the street from the restaurant a few minutes after the shot had been fired.

"We can't," he said crisply and explained why.

Linda Lou rested her hand on the door of the convertible beside which they were standing. "Then why don't we use Daly's car?"

"Daly's car?"

"Yes. This one. He rented it to drive me up to where you live so I could identify you."

Brady looked at the convertible. It would take the police hours, even days to trace the rented car. Then they might not connect it with him.

He opened the door of the convertible and looked in. The key was in the ignition. He helped Linda Lou in, then walked around the car and slipped behind the wheel.

"What hotel are you staying at?" he asked her.

Linda Lou told him. "None. I had that accident right after I got into town and they took me to the hospital. Then a couple of hours after they released me, there was the business with Scaffidi."

Brady started the car and drove south on Eighth Avenue. "Of course."

If there was a cordon around the district it wasn't complete as yet. No whistles blew. No sirens screamed. No one tried to stop them. Even if the girl had checked into a hotel, going there wouldn't have been a very good idea. It was the first place that Dix and his remaining killer would look for them.

Brady drove aimlessly for a few minutes, trying to think. Any hotel in Manhattan was out. Once the police dragnet had been put into effect plainclothes detectives and uniformed officers would comb every hotel on the island. Nor could he take the girl home for several reasons. One, once the police had broken open the locked doors of his car and gotten at the registration slip on the steering post they would know his name and address. Two, he could imagine May's face if he was to walk in with a pretty nineteen-year-old girl and say, "I've just killed a man and the police are looking for us. We'll have to hole up here for a few days until I figure out the best thing to do. Miss So and So, this is my wife, May. May, I want you to meet Miss—"

"What is your name?" he asked the girl beside him. "Your *real* name?"

"Larson. Linda Lou Larson," Linda Lou told him. "Most of the girls I worked with called me Linda. But my full name is Linda Lou."

"Of course," Brady admitted. "I read it in that squib in the paper."

He'd not only read the name, he'd liked it. It just went to show how disorderly his thinking was. He wasn't in any mental condition to make a serious decision, not one as serious as this, one on which his life might depend. So much had happened so fast he had to have time to allow his head to clear.

He asked, "Do you know anyone in New York who might agree to hide you?"

Linda Lou shook her head. "No."

"How about back there where you came from? And I don't mean Chicago."

Linda Lou shook her head more emphatically. No matter what happened to her she wouldn't go back to Della's. "No. I don't have any place to go back to."

"That makes two of us," Brady said.

It was incredible how fast his life had changed. Two mornings before he'd been a complete nonentity, a pliant if dissatisfied commuter, enroute to a job he despised. Now, in the morning, the newspapers would be filled with his name. His picture would be on the front page. He'd killed a man. Other men wanted to kill him. He was being hunted by the police. He had two hundred thousand dollars he didn't even dare to claim, let alone try to spend. All because he'd opened a cab door.

The thought grimly amused him. He laughed.

Linda Lou's twisted ankle was sore and she could feel it beginning to swell. As far as she was concerned there wasn't anything amusing about the situation. "What's so funny?" she asked.

"The whole damn thing," Brady said. "I don't know if you quite realize it yet, Miss Larson. But you and I are in a mess."

"I realize it," Linda Lou said. She touched her swollen eye. "Remember they pounded me for two hours. They thought I was lying about the money."

All Brady could do was to say he was sorry.

Trying to keep away from the brightly lighted section he turned right at the next corner and several blocks later he found they were at the approach to one of the northbound ramps of the Skyway. He drove up the ramp for lack of any reason not to. It didn't matter much where they went. It was only a matter of time before either the police or Lew Dix caught up with them.

Then he thought of the cottage at Lake Popolo. During the summer just past, not content with moving from Fifteenth Street to Stamford, May had insisted on renting a cottage on a lake for two weeks so Alice and Jimmy could get even closer to nature.

The two week-ends he'd spent at the cottage had been the most miserable four days of his life. The sleeping facilities had been, to say the least, inadequate. The meals cooked over a kerosene stove had been worse than usual. Alice had used the pretext of changing from her play clothes to a bathing suit to expose herself to him on every occasion that May was out of the cabin. The only sanitary provisions had been a small building at the end of a weed-grown path. And during his two week-ends at the cottage not only had hordes of mosquitoes found their way through rusted screens but something Jimmy claimed was a hoot owl kept him awake all night.

Brady thought on. On the other hand, the cottage was in the loneliest and most secluded spot he'd ever seen. It was less than a hundred miles from New York but once you reached the cove of the lake on which it stood, you might have dropped back in time a hundred years.

There was no resort area, no store. It couldn't be reached by bus or train. The only access to the cottage was a rutted county road. True there were two dozen or more other cottages on the lake but none of the owners lived in them after Labor Day. In fact, the day he and May and the children left, the farmer who owned the cottages had driven up in a truck to take in the swimming float and board up the doors and windows for the winter. He'd never thought of it before. He'd had no reason to. But the cottage would make an ideal hideout. Perhaps he and Miss Larson could hole up in it for a couple of days, until he could figure out what to do. It should be a fairly easy job to pry a few boards off the windows.

He glanced sideways at the girl beside him. "Do you trust me?"

Linda Lou was practical. "I don't seem to have much choice. Why?"

Brady told her. "I've just thought of a place where neither Dix nor—what did you say that other hood's name is?"

"Morgan."

"Where neither Dix nor Morgan nor the police can find us. A cottage on a lake."

"How do you know it will be safe?"

"Because no one lives there after Labor Day. The lake is deserted. This summer, I rented it for the last two weeks in August."

"You lived there alone?"

"No. With my wife and two children."

"Then there is a Mrs. Brady."

"Unfortunately."

"Why unfortunately?"

"Let's just say we don't get along." Brady glanced in his rear vision mirror at the headlights of the cars behind them. "Well—?"

Linda Lou folded her hands in her lap. She knew what would probably happen in the cottage. Still, even that was preferable to taking another beating and then winding up being killed. "It's all right, I guess," she said. "At least it will be better than just riding around in the rain."

"Good," Brady said. "Good."

He crossed the George Washington Bridge and turned north on U.S. Highway 9W. He wasn't too familiar with 110 this side of the river. He'd only driven the highway the two times he'd stayed at the cottage.

Brady glanced sideways at the girl again. Even with her face punched out of shape by a pair of sadistic killers, she was very attractive. She had a certain youthful freshness and an aura of vitality.

"If I haven't said it before," he said, "thank you for saving my life."

Linda Lou clasped and unclasped her hands. "It was the only thing I could do. After watching them do what they did to Mr. Scaffidi."

Brady wondered how a girl like her had ever become tied in with a man like Dix. He asked her.

"I came a far piece for that," the girl said wryly. Her pride forced her to add, "But if you mean am I his girl, the answer is no. He wanted me to be but I wouldn't. All I was doing was carrying the money. And I didn't want to do that."

The highway was slick with rain and unfamiliar. Brady let the matter drop for the time and paid attention to his driving. They rode in silence for miles without a stop. Fortunately the gas tank had been almost full when they'd left the city. If possible, Brady wanted to reach the cabin without stopping for gasoline. To stop would mean leaving a trail. And whatever Dix was, he was big time. A man didn't rise into the upper echelons of any organization by being dumb.

When he finally reached the turn-off he drove past it and had to make a U turn and drive back.

"How far now?" Linda Lou asked him.

Brady estimated the distance. "Perhaps eight or nine miles."

The state road he'd turned off on was surfaced. The road leading back through the hills wasn't. When he reached it it was more of a small river than a road, the water running tire deep. Only the fact that a good share of it ran across surface shale made it passable. Twice he had to back up and make a run for it to pass low spots. Then just when he could see the rain dimpling the surface of the lake, on the far side of the lake from the cottage, the car bogged down completely.

It was senseless to spend the night in the car with the cottage so near. "It looks like we'll have to walk the rest of the way," Brady said. "Then I'll come back in the morning and see what I can do about getting the car unstuck."

"Whatever you say," Linda Lou said.

She tried to limp through the uneven muck and couldn't. Her twisted ankle had swollen to twice its normal size. Brady solved the problem by carrying her and by the time they reached the cottage both of them were as wet as if they'd swum the lake.

One thing was in their favor. It was as easy to pry off the boards from the door as Brady had thought it would be. Once he'd pried off the boards he carried Linda Lou inside and sat her on one of the built-in bunks and looked for and found a coal oil lamp.

The cabin was cold and smelled musty. Its one good feature was a small fireplace. There was some dry wood in the shed. Brady found an old newspaper and started a fire. As soon as the fire was burning well and beginning to throw out some heat he took two blankets from a shelf in the closet and gave one of them to Linda Lou.

"You'd better get those wet things off and wrap up in this. We might as well have stayed in New York and let Mr. Dix kill us as to die of pneumonia. Meanwhile I'll light the stove and put some water on to heat. And when it's hot, I'll work on your ankle."

Linda Lou undressed as modestly as she could and sat on a straight-backed chair facing the fire with the blanket draped around her bare shoulders. As the cottage began to warm an almost feral smell replaced the mustiness. From the corner of her eyes she could see Mr. Brady undressing in front of the meager heat from the yellow-blue rings of the kerosene stove. He was a big man, powerfully built, with good muscles. If she had to spend the night with a man she was glad it wasn't someone like the middle-aged salesman from Atlanta or the nasty little hotel clerk. At least Mr. Brady wouldn't expect "extras."

The aroma of boiling coffee drowned out the feral smell and a few minutes later Brady crossed the room to her with a steaming tin cup in his hand. "I found half a can of coffee on the shelf over the stove. Also a small stock of canned goods. At least enough to last us for three days."

Linda Lou was grateful. "Thank you." She'd never tasted better coffee. Mr. Brady was a thoughtful man. He'd given her a cup of coffee before he started to wallow her. If he was any of the other three men she'd known, she'd be flat on her back by now.

She watched Mr. Brady walk back to the stove, having trouble with his blanket. From time to time it slipped and gaped open and she could tell he was as embarrassed as she was about it. When he returned he was bringing a large kettle of warm water.

Brady put the kettle on the floor and knelt in front of Linda Lou and examined her swollen ankle. When he'd finished, he said frankly, "I could feel around for an hour and not be able to tell a thing. But if anything's broken, it's one of the very small bones." He put the girl's ankle in the water. "If it's just a strain the hot water should help. And in the morning when I go back to the car I'll look in the glove compartment. I think binding it would help and sometimes rented cars have first-aid kits."

Linda Lou thanked him. She liked sitting in front of the fire with him. She liked Mr. Brady. She knew she could grow to like him very much. She wished just once before she died it wouldn't have to be like this. She hoped just once a man would want her because he liked her and not just because she was a woman.

From time to time Brady added wood to the fire but they didn't speak again until he decided the water had cooled to a point where it wouldn't help her ankle any further. Then he lifted Linda Lou from the chair and carried her to one of the bunks. He sat down and looked at her bruised face.

"They gave you a rough time, didn't they?"

Linda Lou's indignation overcame her embarrassment at what she was sure was about to happen. "They damn near killed me."

Her slim body tensed as she waited for him to slide his hand under the blanket and begin the preliminary squeezing and feeling she'd learned to expect from men. Her head ached. Her ankle still hurt. She'd never been so tired nor so frightened. She wanted to get it over with so she could go to sleep and pretend for a few hours that everything was all right.

To hurry him along she threw back the blanket. "All right. Let's get it over with. If I have to, I have to."

"A real rough time," Brady repeated.

He sat studying the girl's body in the yellow light of the oil lamp. It was a beautiful body, well-proportioned and exquisitely joined. But there was a nasty bruise on her stomach, another on her inner thigh and half a dozen smaller ones, all beginning to color. He touched the bruise on her stomach. "Who did that?"

"Daly."

"He's the one I killed?"

"Yes."

"I'm glad."

Linda Lou waited for him to take her. When he didn't, she said, impatiently, "Well—?"

Brady fingered the bruise on her thigh. "You want me to make love to you?"

"I can't stop you."

"But you'd rather I wouldn't?"

"Yes."

"As you said, if you have to, you have to. And you just want to get done with it?"

"Yes."

Brady covered her with the blanket. "In that case, let's skip it."

Linda Lou couldn't believe it. "You mean you don't want me?"

Brady was as honest with her as he was trying to be with himself. This had nothing to do with morals. It simply wasn't the time or place. Because of him the girl had been beaten half to death. She still might die because of him. She'd seen enough of the worst side of men. It was time someone gave her a break.

"No," he said. "It isn't that. Of course I want you. After what's been happening during these last few days and nights and now after looking at you, I can't think of anything nicer. But I can do without. I intend to." He continued to be honest with her. "But if by any chance we should happen to get out of this mess, I'd like a rain check."

"What does that mean?"

"Some other time."

"Just because I'm pretty and I'm a girl?"

Brady considered his answer. "No." He meant it. He liked Linda Lou. He liked her very much. She was different. She was naive and knowledgeable at the same time. More important, she was basically honest. If she loved a man there would be no meal ticket business about it. "No," he repeated. "Because I like you and I'd like to know you better." He smiled to relieve the tension. "You can believe this or not, Miss Larson, but the first time I saw you you were walking past a bar on Forty-second Street where I was having a drink. You were wearing your red plastic raincoat and probably looking for the cab that started this whole darn thing. And the moment I saw you, without even knowing your name or who you were, I said to myself, 'Now there's the kind of a girl I should have married.'"

Linda Lou was pleased. "You didn't."

Still smiling, Brady raised his right palm shoulder high. "Scout's honor."

Linda Lou studied his face. He meant it. For as far back as she could remember, this was the only man she'd ever met who'd really been kind to her. Other men had given her rides and presents and sweet-talked her, but they all had had one thing on their minds. None of them had thought of her in terms of marriage.

Quick tears formed in her eyes and Brady said, "Here, now. None of that. It's wet enough outside. I didn't mean to make you cry."

"It's all right," Linda Lou assured him. She tried to explain why she felt the way she did and once she'd started to talk she couldn't stop. It had been bottled up in her so long. She had to tell someone. She told him the whole sordid mess from the night she'd driven away from Della's with Silk to the afternoon when Mr. Dix had sent word he wanted to see her in his office.

It was warm and still in the cabin when she finished. The only sounds were the drum of the rain on the roof and the scrape of a wind-blown tree branch on the shingles.

Brady wished he knew what to say to the girl. He wished he could tell her that now she'd met him everything was going to be all right. He couldn't. For all he knew, somewhere out there in the night, in spite of all the care he'd taken, now, right this minute, Mr. Dix and Morgan might be trailing them to the cottage And if they were, he and Linda Lou were dead. Not even giving the money back would save them now. He had killed one of Dix's men. Linda Lou was a witness to Mike Scaffidi's murder. And even if Dix wasn't successful in trailing them here, where could they go? On what?

He made certain the door was bolted and put more wood on the fire. Then, in an attempt to keep Linda Lou from thinking about what she'd just confided in him, he sat back on the edge of the bunk and told her about May and Alice and his dreams and aspirations and of the places he'd lived in as a boy and had once hoped to revisit. The fire had burned low when he was done and dawn wasn't far away.

Brady kissed Linda Lou's cheek. "Now we'd better get some sleep." He stood up and blew out the lamp and crossed the room and lay down on the other bunk. "Good night."

The ache in her ankle had moved to her breasts. Her flesh felt hot. Her thighs felt heavy. She didn't want to be alone. Now that Mr. Brady hadn't, she wished he had. With Mr. Brady it might be different. With Mr. Brady the heretofore violation of her privacy might take on meaning and purpose. She suddenly wanted him to enjoy her. She wanted to know him. She wanted him to like her. She waited a long moment, then called softly, "Jim—"

"Yes—?" Brady asked.

"Please come back."

"You know what will happen if I do."

"I know."

Brady's preliminary love play was brief and actively intimate but gentle. Neither of them spoke again but for the first time since she'd given herself to a man, Linda Lou gasped with pleasure. For the first time she didn't feel ashamed or dirty. This, after all, was woman's major function. She enjoyed feeling complete, knowing she was giving pleasure.

She felt as if she was floating in space and the concerned voice speaking to her seemed faint and far away.

"Are you all right?" Brady asked her.

Linda Lou was too embarrassed to tell him the truth. No man would believe a nineteen-year-old girl could be so completely ignorant of the normal functions of her body, especially a girl who'd admitted she'd permitted three other men to know her.

"Oh, yes," she told him. "Oh, yes."

She was glad it had happened with him. She was glad she hadn't known what the relation between a man and a woman could mean. If she had, she might not be here. She might not have been so reluctant to help Della in the back room.

SIXTEEN

An early rising squirrel, or so he thought at the time, awakened Brady by scampering over the wooden shingles of the cottage in pursuit of a rolling acorn.

He opened his eyes. The rain had stopped. Bright sunlight was feeling its way into the room through the crack around the door and in through the cracks between the boards of the boarded-up windows. Even with the fire in the fireplace dead, it was over-warm in the cottage.

He lifted his left wrist gently so as not to disturb the sleeping girl whose head was pillowed on his chest. His watch said it was almost noon.

He looked at Linda Lou, then brushed her cheek with his lips. It was small wonder he'd slept so late. It had been long after dawn when they'd finally called it a night. The girl was an enigma. She'd been like a child with a new toy, insatiable. Child and woman in one, she was completely delightful. If he could get them out of this mess they were in he intended to do what he could to make their new-found relationship permanent. For the first time in his life, after spending a night with a demanding woman, instead of feeling emotionally and physically depleted, he felt strengthened. Instead of meekly riding the 8:01 or 8:25 he wanted to go out and slay dragons and bring them back and lay them at her feet.

Moving an inch at a time so he wouldn't awaken her, he slipped his arm from under her shoulders and stood up. Quietly he lighted the kerosene stove and made coffee. Then while he waited for it to boil he unbolted the door and stood in the doorway looking at the lake. Its surface was blue and placid. There was a smell of pine and wet, fertile earth. The sun, directly overhead, was hot enough for it to be July. From where he stood he could see the roofs of three cottages on the other side of the lake. No smoke was issuing from their chimneys. There was no sound but the twittering of the birds in the trees and the scolding and scampering of the squirrels.

Living in the country, he decided, could be wonderful. It all depended on the person with whom you were living.

He'd been right about one thing. None of the summer people lived on the lake after Labor Day. It was as if he and Linda Lou were in a world of their own. He turned and looked at her. If there was anything more beautiful than the unclothed form of a sleeping woman he'd never seen it. Narrow as the bunk had been it had been wide enough for two. He meant to keep it that way. True, he and Linda Lou had started at the wrong end of courtship. They'd started with the end result instead of the preliminary overtures. A man was supposed to woo a woman, bring her flowers and candy and put a ring on her finger before they went to bed.

But he'd traveled that route with May. And in the night just past he'd known more pure pleasure than he had in all his five years of marriage.

He wished he knew what to do about Dix and knew even as he wondered. There was only one thing he could do. He was glad now that he had, but he'd really spooked after leaving the restaurant. Even after he'd killed Daly he should have carried out his original intention to go to the police. Without outside help he and Linda Lou couldn't run far or fast enough to keep ahead of the Chicago mobster. Sooner or later Dix would find them and when he did find them he'd kill them. He had to maintain face in the circles where he moved.

Brady found his cigarettes and lit one. He would get nowhere by running away. He couldn't keep the money. He knew now that he'd realized it almost from the start. The money had merely been a symbol of his unfulfilled dreams and his keeping it as long as he had was a gesture of defiance.

The only thing he could do now was jack up the bogged down car and take Linda Lou back to Manhattan and reclaim it. With the money in their hands they would go on down to Center Street, tell the police the whole story and ask for protection.

He tried to remember the names in the television newscast about the Scaffidi murder and did. Sergeant Hooper and Detective Manson. They were the officers in charge of the investigation. When he reached Center Street he'd ask for them, lay everything on the line, holding nothing back.

It would mean losing his job. But it wasn't much of a job and the loss of it would solve two major problems, May and Alice. Without a job, he wouldn't be a good meal ticket and May would have to dig out her bottle of peroxide and a new lipstick and bait a trap for another sucker. One thing was certain, he would never go back to 1134 E. Elm Street, no matter what happened.

The legal aspects concerning him personally were more intangible. He'd killed a man but the man had been an armed gangster trying to kill him. Surely a judge trying the case would take that into consideration. The most he could be charged with was manslaughter or it might even be considered justifiable homicide. The judge would give him a few years sentence if any. Maybe he'd even go free when it was pointed out that he'd returned the money voluntarily.

Linda Lou had nothing to fear. She wasn't guilty of anything. The State would be grateful to her if she gave evidence against Morgan and Dix in the Scaffidi affair. And when he'd done his time, if he was given a prison sentence, he and she could go away together. They could get the hell out of New York, perhaps even go to France or Spain and start all over. He could always get a job abroad and they could marry and settle down and have babies and live the way a couple should live. Their attraction for each other wasn't entirely sexual. The last thing she'd told him before they'd gone to sleep had been:

"I don't care what we do, Jim. You figure this out however seems best to you, as long as we can be together. I've been looking for you a long time and I'm not about to give you up. If you can forget what I've told you, as far as I am concerned, you're the first man I ever really knew. I intend for you to be the last. And you can whop me or beat me or put babies in me, whatever you've a mind to do, just as long as you never send me away, just as long as you want me to be your woman."

Your woman. The words had a pleasant sound. And Linda Lou had more womanhood in her little finger than most women had in their entire bodies.

He realized the coffee was boiling and drank a cup. Then turning the flame low to keep it hot until Linda Lou woke up he wrote her a short note and put it under a clean cup on the chair next to the bunk. The note was brief and to the point:

> Sweetheart:
>   Back in a few minutes. Have gone to see about
> getting the car unstuck. Don't worry about a thing. I
> think we can work this out. I love you very much.
>   Jim

Then whistling softly to himself he dressed and walked down the steps of the cottage and around the lake to where Daly's rented car bad bogged down…

Seconds after Brady left, Linda Lou stretched and yawned, then opened her eyes a little and was disappointed to find herself alone. She closed her eyes again and lay for a long moment, sleepily content and filled with grateful wonder. After her previous experiences of this kind, even with Silk, she'd awakened feeling tired and soiled, disgusted with herself to think she'd allowed such a thing to happen. This morning it was different. She felt clean and refreshed and glad that it had happened. It had all been so natural, so right, as if it was meant to be. She opened her eyes and smiled at the ceiling. God had been looking after her, after all. He hadn't allowed it to happen until she'd met the right man. She didn't feel guilty about Jim being a married man. Not after the things he'd told her about his wife. They could wade that creek when they reached it. It would be nice if Jim would marry her. It was always so much better for the children. No one could call them little bastards, like they called her. Still she'd managed to survive. And no piece of paper or gold ring could make a woman love a man. It was something that happened inside you. All of a sudden. You suddenly were not alone any more.

She swung her bare feet to the floor and saw the note under the cup. Jim called her his sweetheart. She wasn't to worry about a thing. He loved her very much.

Without conscious volition she pressed the note to her breasts. Jim didn't just like her, he loved her. When he came back she'd prove how much she loved him. Still they couldn't make love all the time and men were seldom amorous in the morning. She'd learned that much from Della. She had to be practical about this thing. She began by putting on her bra and sheer panties she'd hung over the back of the chair to dry. Then she made up the bunk bed and drank a cup of hot coffee.

When she'd finished with the coffee she washed her bruised face in cold water, put on powder and lipstick and combed her hair. Starting to put on her dress, she felt sticky. After the rain and all that had happened she needed a bath. Your best friends might not tell you but the man you loved might. And she wanted to be clean and fresh for Jim when he came back.

Carrying her dress and shoes and a bar of soap, she walked to the open door and looked at the lake. It looked a lot like the river back home except that it was bigger and probably deeper and there were no mangrove or palm trees or white herons.

She was halfway down the path to the lake before she realized she wasn't limping and her ankle no longer hurt. She stopped and looked down at her ankle, then felt it. It was no longer tender to the touch. The swelling had almost disappeared. And that was one for the book. Now that she had a man of her own she knew how to cure a sprained ankle.

She continued down the walk covered with fallen pine needles and reached the edge of the lake. She felt the water with her toes. It was cold but not too cold. Linda Lou put her shoes on a fallen log and laid her dress on top of them. Then after removing her underthings, she took the bar of soap and waded into the water.

It was much colder than her river had been but even this late in the year the sun here was almost as hot as Florida sun. Compressing her lips she waded on doggedly until the water was thigh deep. Then holding her breath, she dashed the icy water on her upper body and soaped it thoroughly and sank to her shoulders to rinse the soap away.

After the initial shock the water didn't feel so cold. So she swam for a few minutes, being careful not to wet her face or hair. In a few minutes, Jim had said. And she wanted to look pretty for him. She got to her feet and looked at the bruises on her body. As pretty, she thought, as she could look after Morgan and Daly had finished with her.

"Talk, you little bitch," Daly had grunted as he'd punched her in the stomach. *"Where's the money?"*

As if she'd known. She still didn't know. All she knew was that Jim had it. And what he did with it was up to him. He was the man. She was glad he'd killed Daly. It was going to take days, perhaps weeks, for the discoloration to fade. Now, when she wanted, for the first time in her life, a man to like the way she looked.

She studied her body. Bruised and discolored as it was it seemed incredible to her that Jim could have been attracted to her. But he had been.

In between times they'd talked and he'd told her more about the fascinating places in which he'd lived as a boy. She decided she liked Paris best. Even the names of the streets and districts had a romantic sound. Rue de Longchamps. Place de la Bastille. The Bois de Boulogne. The Left Bank. Montmartre. The Champs Elysées. She pretended she was living in Paris and she was Mrs. James A. Brady and she and Jim had six children. She named each child as she pointed to imaginary little beads in the water. There was Jim Junior and Honore, Henri and Gigi, Yvette and Paul.

Linda Lou stopped pretending and ran her hands over her flat body. She could be carrying the first of them now. The thought made her blush. After the way she'd acted, if it was possible for a woman to conceive more than once in one night, she probably had a whole family inside her.

A drifting cloud covered the sun and both air and water were suddenly cold. She waded ashore wishing she'd remembered to bring a towel. Now she'd have to run for the cottage and dry herself there before she dressed.

Snatching her clothing from the log she ran up the path to the cottage and stopped just inside the doorway, her lips working but the screams welling up inside her unable to get past the constriction in her throat.

As big and fat and flabby as ever, Mr. Dix was eyeing her with approval. "Come in. Come in, Linda," he invited. "You look very pretty this morning. The night must have agreed with you."

Linda Lou covered herself with her dress as she looked past him at the bunk. His eyes agonized over the wide strip of tape plastered over his lower face and mouth, blood streaming from a cut on his forehead, Jim Brady was sitting on the bunk with the muzzle of Morgan's pistol pointed at his head.

"Very pretty," Dix continued sourly. "I offered you everything a girl could want. But no. You couldn't see me. You had to go for a lousy lone-wolf hi-jacker." He nodded at Morgan. "Hit him again. The chump likes to be hurt."

Morgan slapped Brady with the barrel of his gun. "A pleasure."

Linda Lou crossed the room and tried to protect Brady with her body. "No, please," she begged. "Don't hurt him. You can do anything you want to me. But please don't hurt him."

Morgan paid Brady grudged admiration. "You must be good, fellow."

"Take off his gag," Dix said. "Now that we don't have to worry about him warning Linda, I want to hear the bastard yell when you hit him. So who's to hear? You picked quite a hideout, Brady. If we hadn't been smart, also a little lucky, we could have looked for you for ten years."

Linda Lou sat on the bunk beside Brady. "How did they find us?"

Brady wiped blood out of his eyes with the back of his hand. "They haven't said. I just blundered up to the car like a fool and there they were, waiting for me."

Linda Lou tried to stanch the flow of blood from the cut on Brady's forehead with her underwear and Brady stopped her.

"No. Put them on," he said curtly. "They'll hurt me worse before they're through. And just because they're going to kill me is no reason for you to give them a free show."

Morgan hit him again. "How noble. That one's for Daly, you bastard. And just wait until I get around to myself and all the trouble you've caused us."

Linda Lou turned her back and dressed as hurriedly as her fear-numbed fingers would permit.

Dix continued to admire her. "Broads. When I was twenty I thought I understood them. Now I'm sixty-five I'm beginning to wonder." He used the barrel of the gun he was holding to wave the subject aside. "All right, Brady. You can make it as easy or as tough on yourself as you want, before you get what that cab driver got. What's the set-up? Were the three of you in on this?"

Brady shook his head, "No. No one was in it with me."

"You just opened the door of a cab and there was two hundred thousand dollars."

"That's right."

"You're lying. You and the girl and the driver were in this together. Then you left him to take his lumps and you and the girl were going to take a powder with the money. But Daly and Morgan got to the warehouse too soon."

"That isn't so," Linda Lou cried. "If it's anyone's fault, it's mine. You talked so much about what could happen to me I got frightened and left the money in the cab. Then last night in the restaurant, even if he was a stranger to me, I couldn't let you kill Jim. That's why I warned him and we tried to get out the back way."

Morgan smiled thinly. "You never met the guy before last night?"

"No."

Morgan glanced at the rumpled bunk on the far side of the room, then looked at the girl. "Well, you sure got acquainted in a hurry."

Dix motioned him to be silent. "What the broad did or did not do is immaterial now. The only thing that matters now is the money." Perspiration beaded on his flabby jowls. "I'm going to level with you, Brady. Just so you understand how far I'll go to get it back. The money is a Mafia pay-off, what I owe the boys from my last year's take. And if I don't get it back and deliver it to where it's supposed to go within the next few hours what happened to Scaffidi and what is going to happen to you could happen to me. Do I make myself clear?"

A piece of adhesive was clinging to Brady's upper lip. He picked it off. "Very clear." He'd never wanted anything so badly as he wanted to turn over the claim check in his watch pocket. The two men had overlooked it when they were searching him. But he knew the moment he did, he and Linda Lou would be killed. His knowledge of where the money was was their only insurance. "So—?"

Morgan suggested, "Maybe I'd better belt him a few more times."

Dix shook his head. "No. You'd probably hit him too hard, like you did that dumb cab driver. And he has to stay alive long enough to tell us where the money is."

Brady tried to think. He didn't have the least idea how the two men had found him. Coming to the cottage had been a mistake. They could beat him to death in here without anyone being the wiser. He should have holed up somewhere in the city where there would have been people and potential witnesses. The thought gave him an idea. It was a slim chance at best but seemingly the only one they had.

"How about making a deal?" he asked.

"What sort of a deal?" Dix asked.

Brady put his arm around Linda Lou's waist. "Our lives for the money."

"The money is intact?"

"It is."

"Where is it?"

Brady shook his head. "Oh, no. That's part of the deal. You take us back to town and agree to turn us loose and I'll tell you."

"Where back to town? What part?"

Brady thought quickly. This thing had begun on a Monday morning. That made today Wednesday. After school on Wednesdays, Jimmy went to his gym class at the Y. Alice took her dancing lesson. And May played bridge with a neighborhood club that met at one of the members' houses. None of them would be home until after six o'clock. He knew.

Unless May stopped on her way home for a container of chop suey or a couple of pizza pies, he had cold cuts and potato salad for Wednesday night supper.

So there would be no one at the house all afternoon. If he could trick Dix into taking him and Linda Lou to the house he might possibly be able to get hold of the loaded service revolver he'd brought home from Korea and kept in the top right hand drawer of the dresser he and May shared. Even if Morgan and Dix gunned him down in the bedroom before he could kill them, at least he had a ghost of a chance and someone was almost certain to hear the shots. Anything was better than being beaten to death and watching Linda Lou be beaten and then wind up at the bottom of the lake.

"Don't listen to him," Morgan said. "I can beat the truth out of him."

Brady didn't feel brave. He was merely stating a fact. "I doubt it. Because as soon as I talked, you'd kill me. And my only chance of staying alive would be to keep my mouth shut."

Dix seemed undecided. "Where in town would you want us to take you?"

Brady told him. "My house in Stamford."

Dix and Morgan exchanged quick looks and Morgan asked, "Who do you think you're kidding? We—"

"No," Dix stopped him. "Let him talk." He looked back at Brady. "The money is in your house?"

Brady shook his head. "No, it isn't. But the key to a certain locker in Grand Central is."

"A locker in Grand Central, eh?" Dix mused. "And just where in your house is this key?"

"Oh, no," Brady countered. "No deal. If I told you you'd kill us here. And the deal I offered is the money in exchange for our lives."

Linda Lou protested, "But you can't trust them."

"He has no choice," Dix said. "A locker in Grand Central, eh? That sounds correct. From what we've learned of your movements you had to pass through the station several times. And what better place to hide the parcel than a locker. I've used that dodge myself." He made his decision. "Okay. We'll take you back to Stamford. You give us the key. Then while one of us stays to keep you company, either Morgan or I will ride in and see if the money's where you say it is."

"And if it is?" Brady asked.

"We'll see," Dix said. "We'll see."

SEVENTEEN

The traffic was normal for a week day. Instead of driving back to Manhattan on U.S. 9W, Morgan crossed the river on the Bear Mountain Bridge and drove through Peekskill and down an interlinking system of secondary roads to Stamford.

No one, not even the toll taker on the bridge, paid any attention to the big black car carrying three men and a girl. Before leaving the cottage, Dix had allowed Brady to clean up as best he could and there was nothing about the wide strip of adhesive tape on his injured forehead to cause any undue curiosity. No one who saw him would have the slightest inkling that he and the slight light-haired girl beside him were on their way to die.

Brady rode in the back seat with Linda Lou, his right hand holding her hand, his left arm around her shoulders, grateful that no matter what happened when they reached Stamford they'd had the one night together. From time to time, when the opportunity presented itself, as in the two instances when they'd stopped to pay toll and when they had the tank of the car filled with gasoline, he had been tempted to call out or try to make a break but the gun he knew was resting in Dix's lap restrained him. After all, he'd started this thing by not turning the money in when he found it. He didn't want an innocent person's death on his conscience. Turned sideways on the front seat so he could watch them at all times, his left arm resting on the back of the seat, Dix had warned him what would happen if he even tried to attract attention.

"Believe me, Brady," the other man continued to warn him. "I've got nothing to lose if I don't get that money back. So one peep out of you and Linda gets it. Right through her pretty little belly. Also you and anyone you try to tip."

Between warnings, the old man spoke foulmouthed obscenities concerning the night just past and Brady's relations with Linda Lou, phrasing his comments in lewd four-letter words, almost as if he was experiencing a vicarious satisfaction by commenting on the intimate pleasures the frightened girl in the back seat had refused him.

"Everything. I could have given you everything," he reminded her.

Brady stopped the flow of lewd comments momentarily by remarking, "Except for one thing."

"What's that?" Dix asked.

"You figure that out," Brady said.

For a moment, money or not, he thought Dix was going to shoot him. He didn't. The old man merely scowled and continued to mouth obscenities.

Seemingly, Morgan was moderately familiar with Stamford. When he reached the outskirts of the village he turned corners and angled down side streets without having to ask how to get to 1134 E. Elm Street. Then when he reached the house, instead of parking at the curb in front he drove up the drive and into the attached garage.

They were barely inside when May opened the door leading from the garage to the kitchen. Instead of being dressed for her weekly bridge club her hair was still metallic with curlers and she was wearing an old cotton wrapper she frequently wore when she was working around the house.

"I see you found them," she said dryly.

Morgan touched the brim of his hat, then got out of the car and closed the overhead door of the garage. "Thanks to you, Mrs. Brady. He was right where you told us he might be. Both him and Miss Larson."

Brady fought down a desire to be sick on the floor of the car. He had no idea May hated him this much.

"Thanks. Thanks a lot," he said bitterly.

"I don't owe you a thing," her voice was thin. "Not after what you did to my daughter. And when Officer Morgan and Captain Dix told me there was still another young girl involved, one of the secretaries at your office, I couldn't imagine a better place for you to carry on your cheap assignation than the cottage we rented last summer. And I told them so. No wonder you've been acting so strangely lately."

It took a moment for what she had said to penetrate Brady's mind. May had called the two gangsters officer and captain and had implied that Linda Lou was one of the girls in the office. "Now wait just a minute," he said. "There's something very wrong here. Just what did these men tell you?"

Dix motioned him out of the car. "Stop yakking and get into the house. And don't open your mouth again until I tell you to. If you do the girl is going to get it right here in the garage."

Brady got out of the car and helped Linda Lou out. Her voice very small, she told him, "Don't worry about me. You do what you think is best."

May smiled a thin smile. "How touching. You must be more of a man than I realized. First Alice. Now this cheap little bitch." She looked back at Dix. "Now you've found them, do I get the rest of the reward right away or do I have to wait until he's indicted?"

"Right away," Dix assured her. He cleared his throat. "Just as soon as Mr. Brady gives us a little additional information about the money he stole."

"Reward? The money I stole?" Brady shouted. "What kind of a line did you hand my wife? Just what did you tell her?"

Morgan swung the barrel of his gun in a vicious arc that exploded against Brady's cheek and knocked him to his knees on the kitchen floor. "Naughty, naughty," he reproved him. "Captain Dix warned you to keep your mouth shut until you were told to talk."

Brady tried to get to his feet and couldn't until Linda Lou helped him, "You bastard," she cursed Morgan. "You pain-loving bastard. Just how *do* you get your kicks? When you are beating on someone or when someone is beating on you?"

His face livid with anger, Morgan slapped her. "Shut up."

The house, as usual when he was away, was over-warm. All the windows were tightly closed and May must have pushed the thermostat up as high as it would go. Still partially supported by Linda Lou, Brady stood gasping for air and shaking his head in an attempt to clear it.

Dix increased the pressure of the gun muzzle nudging his ribs. "The key to the locker, remember?"

Stalling to give his head time to clear and with Linda Lou still helping him, Brady walked down the short hall into the living room.

Her bare feet showing under her bath robe, her eyes red and puffed from crying, Alice was sitting hunched on the sofa hugging her knees. She gave Brady a quick glance, then looked away.

At least part of the picture was clear. "So you finally did, eh?" Brady asked the fifteen-year-old girl. "You finally told the nasty lie you said you'd tell. Well, I hope you're satisfied."

May explained to Dix. "I thought after what she told me and all that the child has been through it would be best if I kept her home from school today."

"Sure. Sure," Dix said impatiently. "That's your business. Now we have a little business with your husband. Okay, Brady. Stop stalling. Where's the key?"

Brady took a deep breath and held it a moment. This was it, one way or another. He'd stalled as long as he could. "In my bedroom," he said. "I'll go get it."

"I'll go with you," Morgan said.

"Yeah," Dix said. "And so will I. Get moving, Brady."

With Dix close behind them, the hard muzzle of his gun prodding the small of Brady's back, he and Linda Lou went into the bedroom. Brady walked across the room to the dresser. Everything would depend on the next few seconds. If he could get the drawer open and the gun out he might possibly be able to turn and kill at least one of them before they killed him. If he was lucky he might not even be killed. It was one thing to shoot an unarmed man. It was something else when the man was armed and able and willing to shoot back.

He was reaching for the drawer pull when May who had followed them into the room said, "If it's a key you're looking for, Captain Dix, he won't find it in there. There's nothing in that drawer but handkerchiefs and the automatic pistol he brought back from Korea."

Brady made a desperate attempt to open the drawer all the way and succeeded in opening it about an inch when Morgan slammed it shut and Dix took the gun from the small of his back and used the barrel in a series of vicious blows that chopped him to his knees for a second time.

Kneeling on both knees, clinging to Linda Lou's legs, resting his bleeding head against her thighs, Brady heard the drawer open and Morgan say, "There's a gun in there, all right. A .45 Colt automatic."

"Don't touch it," Dix warned him. "Leave it right where it is. And wipe off that drawer pull. We don't want to leave any prints."

Brady heard the drawer close again. Then May was speaking. Her voice sounded as though she was shaking her head.

"I just can't understand what got into him. He was always such a steady man. But I suppose he realized that what he'd done to poor Alice was bound to come out sooner or later, because the poor child wouldn't protect him forever, so he figured he'd take the money you say he stole and clear out and take another girl with him for good measure." May sniffed. "I don't know what it is about men, all of you. But if it's young and still a virgin you've just got to have it."

Morgan touched the brim of his hat again. "Yes, ma'am."

Dix's face was pale with anger as he pulled Brady to his feet. "That's just a taste of what you're going to get. The key. Give me the key."

Linda Lou wiped the blood from Brady's eyes with her fingers. Her voice was low and intense. "Please, Jim," she begged. "Don't let them hurt you any more. Give him the key. I'm not afraid to die."

May was amused. "Listen to her. She's not afraid to die. Aren't you being rather melodramatic, young lady? You may be in the family way. I hope you are. But I doubt very much if you'll die from what happened to you last night."

Brady fumbled the change in his pocket and separated the locker key from his silver. As with the claim check, Morgan had overlooked it when he'd searched him. It might work. It might not. But if what he had in mind did work, it would give him a few more hours, a few more hours alone with one of them while the other drove into town and opened the locker and found only the new, empty brief case.

"Okay," he said quietly. "I'm whipped." He tossed the key on the dresser. "There."

Morgan swore softly. "He had it on him." He picked up the key and examined it. "He had it on him all the time."

"I thought you searched him," Dix said.

"I did," Morgan defended himself. "But you were so anxious for me to tape his mouth so he couldn't warn Linda before you got down to the shore of the lake to watch her standing naked in the water, I must have overlooked it." He tossed the key on his palm. "Not that it matters now. Do you want me to drive in and get it?"

Dix dropped his gun into his pocket. "No. You stay here and keep an eye on things. I'll drive in. And before I come back I'll drop it off where it was supposed to be two days ago."

"Whatever you say," Morgan said. "You don't even have to come if you don't want to. Just give me a call and say everything is all right. I'll be glad to take care of things out here."

"I may do that," Dix said.

He started for the door and stopped as May said, "Just a minute, Captain Dix."

Dix turned and looked at her. "Yes—?"

"Am I to understand you think my husband hid the money he stole in a locker in Grand Central Station?"

"That's right."

"And if it's there I'll get the rest of the reward?"

Dix was amused. "Yeah. Sure. You'll get everything that's coming to you. That's why I'm leaving Officer Morgan here."

Brady said angrily, "What's this Officer Morgan and Captain Dix bit?"

"You stay out of this, Jim," May said. "You made your bed and you can damn well lie on it. I have to look after myself and Alice and Jimmy." She looked back at Dix. "Then, while you are down at the station, if the money does not happen to be in the locker, if I were you, I'd check the parcel room. Because the other night when he was dressing to walk out on me, walk out on Alice, for this little piece of southern fluff, I saw him transfer—"

Brady tried to stop her, "No. Please, May. For God's sake, you don't know what you're doing."

"Go on, Mrs. Brady," Dix said. "When you saw him dressing to walk out on you, you saw him transfer what?"

May told him. "A baggage claim check. From the watch pocket of the pants he'd worn to work to the watch pocket of the pants he's wearing now. And when I asked him what it was for he said it was for his brief case, that it was filled with office correspondence and that rather than carry it around he'd checked it at the baggage counter."

Morgan slapped Brady with his gun, then muscled him up against the wall beside the dresser and hooked his fingers in his watch pocket and pulled so hard the cloth tore and the paper claim check fluttered to the floor.

Dix picked up the piece of cardboard and said, "Not bad. Not bad at all, Brady." He smiled at the claim check as if it were a last minute reprieve from the governor. "Sure. This is it. It can't be for anything else." He glanced at Morgan. "Now we can do what has to be done and both of us can go back to town."

Brady almost felt sorry for May. She looked older than he'd ever seen her look. The crows feet around her mouth were more pronounced. Her neck muscles sagged. She looked much closer to forty than the thirty-four she claimed to be.

No longer as certain of herself as she'd been, she said, "You do that. And take Jim and his girl friend with you. I'll swear out the warrant for statutory rape and contributing to the delinquency of a minor at the local station." She held out her hand. "But if you are certain the claim check will enable you to recover the money Jim stole from Harper, Nelson and Ferrel, before you go, I want the rest of the reward."

"Lady," Dix laughed at her. "You slay me."

"Who did they tell you they were, May?" Brady persisted.

"Captain Dix and Officer Morgan of the Manhattan Bunko Detail."

Brady shook his head. "Uh-uh. Dix is a big-shot Chicago hoodlum. And Morgan is his paid killer. And I didn't steal any money. I found it. And because I did they've already killed one man, the taxi driver who was beaten to death. And now that you've gotten them off the hook, they're going to kill us, too."

May pressed her hand to her throat. "Oh, no."

"Oh, yes," Morgan said pleasantly. "But thanks very much for your co-operation, Mrs. Brady."

Brady turned his back to the dresser and looked past the woman he'd married at the fifteen-year-old girl standing just inside the bedroom door. He didn't care what May thought. He did value Linda Lou's opinion. "Tell your mother the truth, Alice," he said quietly.

Still sullen-eyed, the girl looked down at her bare feet. "I did," she whispered.

"The truth," Brady persisted. "Start with what happened the other night when you came into the living room without a stitch of clothes on. Tell her how you sat on my lap and tried to get me to be intimate with you. Tell her how close you came to being successful. Then tell her what you told me you would tell her if I continued to refuse to be intimate with you. Go ahead. Tell her, Alice. Then admit any wrongdoing between us has all been in your own sick mind."

The girl raised her eyes to his, then turned and pressed her face to the wall and sobbed.

May broke the deep silence that followed. "You fool. You little fool. And I believed you."

Dix kissed the claim check he was holding and put it carefully into the small change compartment of the same side coat pocket into which he'd dropped his gun. His good nature completely restored, he smiled, "Very interesting. But absolutely nothing to do with us."

"What if the shots are heard?" Morgan asked him.

The old man shrugged. "They won't be. Not with all the windows closed. No one will know a thing about it until the boy comes home from school."

All the time he'd been directing attention to Alice, Brady, hands behind his back, ostensibly supporting his weight by gripping the flange of the dresser, had been frantically working at the drawer pull. He had the drawer open now and the feel of metal was good in his hands.

What followed was confused. Morgan was the first to see the gun. "You tricky bastard," he gasped and fired, then dropped his gun and pressed both hands to his stomach and screamed, "Shoot. Shoot him, you old fool."

Dix tried but the metal sight of his gun caught in the lining of his pocket and there was a rip of cloth as he pulled hard without getting the gun completely free.

May and Alice were screaming now and Linda Lou was scrambling on the floor for the revolver that Morgan had dropped. His right shoulder numb from the one shot Morgan had managed, Brady transferred his gun to his left hand and the bullet he fired at Dix gouged a hole in the plastered wall.

Dix tried one last time to free his gun, then ran bleating out the bedroom door as Brady fired for a third time and missed him again. Before he could fire a fourth time, the old man was through the kitchen and into the garage.

Blood from the pistol whippings he'd taken dripped into Brady's eyes and partially blinded him. He was sick from the pain in his shoulder. But when he heard the overhead door in the garage screech open he tried to stagger after Dix, only to trip over the now motionless Morgan.

Linda Lou helped him to his feet. "No," she said. "Not wounded like you are. Let him go. Besides, he won't get very far. And he won't get what he's after." She held up the cardboard claim check. "This ripped out of his pocket when he tried to get his gun to kill you."

A long silence followed. Alice continued to sob. Then, her thin lips working wetly, May said, "I don't suppose there is anything I can say."

"No," Brady said. "There isn't."

EIGHTEEN

The seat of the straight-backed chair was hard. The large outer office smelled of stale tobacco and fresh sweeping compound. Despite the lateness of the hour, while most of the city slept, here there was sound and color and motion. Telephones rang incessantly. There was a constant procession of plainclothesmen and uniformed officers entering and leaving the inner office. Brady glanced at the two detectives who'd brought him down from the detention cell. They looked like pretty good Joes. Most policemen were. They did a big job for small pay and smaller glory.

In spite of the handcuffs on his wrists and the dull pain in his bandaged shoulder and head, he didn't feel too badly. No matter what the law did to him for killing Morgan and Daly, he felt free, really free, for the first time in years. No matter what the big brass decided, he was finished with riding the 8:01 and 1134 E. Elm Street. That phase of his life was over.

He looked up, mildly puzzled, as Bill Gleason entered the office and spoke to the lieutenant in charge, then came over to where he was sitting. His fellow translator seemed embarrassed. "Hi."

"Hi," Brady countered. "You're out a little late, aren't you, Bill?"

Gleason was more embarrassed. "Well, there was a big pow-wow at the office and Mr. Harper asked me to wait. As you can imagine, when this thing broke in the evening papers, with reporters and cameramen swarming all over the place, he blew his stack."

"I can imagine," Brady said. "And after he and Mr. Nelson and Mr. Ferrel talked it over, he sent you over here to tell me I was fired."

"You know how the old man is."

"I know."

Gleason took a slim packet of papers from his pocket. "For you, the usual. Official notification of termination of employment. Your pension plan refund. A check for two weeks' severance pay. And some personal correspondence that came in today."

Brady accepted the papers. "Thanks."

Gleason made certain he understood. "Nothing personal, understand, Jim. If there's anything I can do—lend you a few hundred dollars, get you some cigarettes—"

Brady was deeply appreciative. "Thanks a lot, Bill, I'll make out. But thanks."

"Well. Good luck." Gleason started to turn away and turned back. "Look, Jim. Just so I can tell the other boys in the office when they ask me. Is it really true you found two hundred thousand dollars on the seat of a taxi cab and spent last night shacked up in a lake cottage with that pretty little nineteen-year-old Southern doll whose picture is all over the front pages?"

Brady considered the question. It was useless for him to try to protect Linda Lou's reputation. Sergeant Hooper of Manhattan Homicide was a very thorough man and his and Linda Lou's signed statements covering every phase of the case, even to the estimated times they'd been intimate, were a matter of public record. Looking back, it seemed more like a lovely dream than something that had actually happened. He hoped he could make it real. He meant to try. "Well, yes," he said. "That's what happened."

Gleason sighed. "It should have happened to me. I get so fed up with riding the subway to the office every morning, then riding the subway back home every night, then getting up the next morning and—"

"I know," Brady sympathized. "Believe me. That's how this whole thing started."

When Gleason had gone he looked through the papers he'd brought him. Two week's severance pay after working for a firm ten years wasn't very much compensation. However, the ten year pension refund came to a tidy sum. At least it would pay for the divorce. There was nothing else of importance, notice of a special meeting of the Veterans of Foreign Wars, two small bills he'd had sent to the office and what appeared to be a personal letter from the French perfume firm of Honore Lachaille and Bergerac. No longer interested in anything remotely connected with Harper, Nelson & Ferrel, he slipped the letter in his pocket unopened.

More officers entered and left the inner office. One of them, who introduced himself as a Federal agent, stopped to squat beside Brady's chair to verify a point in the lengthy statement he'd dictated to a police stenographer.

"This white slip of paper pertaining to settlement in full of his 1957 account and signed L. Dix. You're sure it was in the parcel when you opened it?"

"Positive," Brady said. "It was tucked under the band around one of the sheaves of bills."

The agent seemed pleased. "Thanks, fellow. It may be just what we've been looking for. We've been trying to establish a Mafia connection with the gangs in this country for a long time. Now, with that little slip of paper and your and Miss Larson's testimony that Dix admitted it was a Mafia pay-off, maybe we can get somewhere."

The wait dragged on. To kill time, Brady opened the letter from Honore Lachaille and Bergerac.

Written in precise French, Monsieur Lachaille, as senior partner of the firm bearing his name, wished to assure Monsieur Brady he was deeply appreciative of the personal and efficient attention he had given to their account. Further, while Monsieur Lachaille had no wish to be unethical, as Honore Lachaille and Bergerac were expanding sales to include a complete new line of exports, if at any time M. Brady should terminate his present affiliation with Harper, Nelson and Ferrel, Monsieur Lachaille would be happy to discuss the possibility of his becoming the English speaking Paris representative of Honore Lachaille and Bergerac at a *salaire* commensurate with his proven ability.

One of the detectives guarding Brady was interested. "You can read that stuff, eh?"

"Yes."

"From the look on your face it must be good news."

Brady folded the letter carefully and returned it to his pocket. "It is."

It was. It didn't matter where he lived. It wasn't riding the 8:01 or the subway or the bus to work that made life dull. Under the right circumstances, riding to work every morning was merely modern man's way of slaying dragons. And he couldn't think of anything more pleasant than riding the Paris underground or a commuter train into the Gare St. Lazare to slay dragons for Linda Lou.

Sergeant Hooper brought him back to reality by beckoning his guards to escort him into the inner office. In the doorway Hooper removed the handcuffs and said, "I'm going to level with you, Brady. You were foolish in trying to hold on to the money. But I don't think we can convict you of a thing but doing us a favor. Whether the District Attorney asks the Grand jury to indict you or not is up to him. So just tell him the truth, the whole truth and nothing but the truth."

"I intend to," Brady said.

Inside the office, Sergeant Hooper motioned for him to sit on a straight-backed chair identical with the one on which he had been sitting, with one major difference. Linda Lou was sitting in the next chair. With her face washed clean of make-up she looked even younger and more wholesome and very concerned.

As Brady sat down she squeezed his hand and whispered, "They told me you were all right but I worried. How do you feel, Jim?"

"Fine. I feel fine," he assured her. "And you?"

Before she could answer, an older, white-haired man fingered through the now familiar sheaves of bills on his desk and said emphatically, "I agree with you Federal men. The only thing the money can be is a Mafia pay-off, a percentage tribute levied against Dix's profits." He glanced at the night-filled window of the office. "And if that's the case the poor devil would have been better off to have turned himself in to us. The Mafia plays rough and it isn't going to appreciate all the attention that's been turned on it. Right now the guy is probably slinking around out there some place, not knowing just when a knife or a bullet is going to catch up with him."

"That's what we think," Sergeant Hooper said. "Now, about Miss Larson and Brady."

The white-haired man swiveled in his chair. "Yes—?"

Hooper continued, "We aren't charging the girl with a thing. But we would like to hold her in protective custody for a few days as a material witness, at least until we pick up Dix."

"That seems to be a reasonable request."

"Now on to Brady," Hooper said. "True, he has killed two men. But both of them were known killers, both of them were trying to kill him and I doubt that if we do take him before the Grand jury they'll find him guilty of anything but justifiable homicide."

The older man nodded. "You have a point. From where I'm sitting I'd say it all depends on his previous civil record and the depth of his gang involvement." He broke off to answer the ringing phone on his desk. "I see," he said into the mouthpiece. He listened a moment longer, then handed the phone to Sergeant Hooper. "Your office. Two of your prowl car men think they spotted Dix down on the lower East Side but before they could pick him up he disappeared into the mouth of an alley and they heard a burst of sub-machine gun fire. When they reached the spot and turned their lights on the spot all they could find was a lot of blood. And of course, none of the *paesani* in the neighborhood knew anything about it."

"That's about the way they do it," Hooper said, then spoke tersely into the phone.

Brady whispered to Linda Lou. "I asked you how you felt?"

She folded her hands in her lap. "That all depends."

"On what?"

She whispered, "On whether you still like me."

"Why shouldn't I like you?"

Color crept into her cheeks. "Because of the way I acted last night."

Brady simulated surprise. "I thought," he whispered back, "that all young wives in love with their husbands acted that way."

"I'm not your wife."

"No," Brady admitted. "But you're going to be. As soon as I get out of this mess and can get a divorce."

Linda Lou forgot to whisper. "You mean that?"

"I never meant anything more. I just got a letter from a French firm offering me a job in Paris. How about it?"

"You mean go to Paris with you?"

"That's what I mean."

"As Mrs. Brady?"

"Yes. How about it? Will you?"

Ignoring the men watching them, Linda Lou cupped his face between her hands and kissed him. "Oh yes," she said.

The white-haired man behind the desk cleared his throat and Linda Lou sat back on her chair.

The District Attorney was more amused than annoyed. He was also a little sad. It had been a good many years since any woman had kissed him the way the light-haired girl had just kissed Brady. "And now," he said, dryly, "if Miss Larson and Mr. Brady have concluded their pledge of mutual affection and discussion of future plans, suppose we get on with our talk of what we're going to do about Brady and call this a night and go home."

Sergeant Hooper returned the phone to the desk and wiped his face with the sleeve of his coat. "At least I know what we can do about her. We might as well let her go. There's no use holding her as a witness. It was Dix. And he's dead. Two men working in from the other end of the alley just found his body stuffed into a trash can."

A long moment of silence followed. Then the District Attorney said, "Good. Now let's get on with it, Sergeant."

"Yes, sir."

"You pulled a package on Brady?"

"No, sir."

"Why not?"

"He doesn't have one."

"You meant he has no previous record of gang affiliation?"

"He has no record, sir. Not even a traffic violation. And both his work and war records are excellent."

"I see," the District Attorney said. He leaned forward. "Then suppose you tell me this, Mr. Brady. Just how in hell did you become involved in this thing?"

"Well," Brady said. "My train was late. It was raining. I couldn't get a cab at the station. So I walked up Forty-second Street toward Fifth Avenue. Then I saw what I thought was an empty taxi, with the driver fixing his windshield wipers."

"And all you did was open the door of the cab."

"Yes, sir. All I did was open the door of the cab."

THE END